BELLE & BEAST

*A RETELLING OF BEAUTY
AND THE BEAST*

Rebecca Fittery

Copyright © 2020 Rebecca Fittery

All rights reserved

The characters, places, and events portrayed in this book are fictitious. Any similarity to real persons, living or dead, is coincidental and not intended by the author.

No part of this book may be reproduced, or stored in a retrieval system, or transmitted in any form or by any means, electronic, mechanical, photocopying, recording, or otherwise, without express written permission of the publisher.

ISBN: 9781736112205

Cover design through Canva.
Map design through Inkarnate.

*To my husband, Steve. You believed the worlds in
my head could exist on a page before I did. Then you
put up with me pouring them out. Thank you.*

CONTENTS

Title Page

Copyright

Dedication

Map of Istoire

Map of Asileboix and Croiseux

Prologue

PART I – The Rose   1

Chapter One   2

Chapter Two   14

Chapter Three   40

Chapter Four   56

Chapter Five   71

Chapter Six   96

Chapter Seven   118

Chapter Eight   126

Chapter Nine   137

PART II – The Prince   155

Chapter Ten   156

Chapter Eleven   176

Chapter Twelve   191

Chapter Thirteen	208
Chapter Fourteen	227
Chapter Fifteen	245
Chapter Sixteen	284
Chapter Seventeen	312
Chapter Eighteen	323
Chapter Nineteen	332
Chapter Twenty	352
PART III – The War	359
Chapter Twenty-One	360
Chapter Twenty-Two	370
Chapter Twenty-Three	393
Chapter Twenty-Four	396
Chapter Twenty-Five	400
Chapter Twenty-Six	410
Chapter Twenty-Seven	415
Chapter Twenty-Eight	423
Chapter Twenty-Nine	428
Chapter Thirty	440
Chapter Thirty-One	443
Chapter Thirty-Two	449
Epilogue	455
Afterword	465
Acknowledgements	467
About The Author	469
Books In This Series	471

MAP OF ISTOIRE

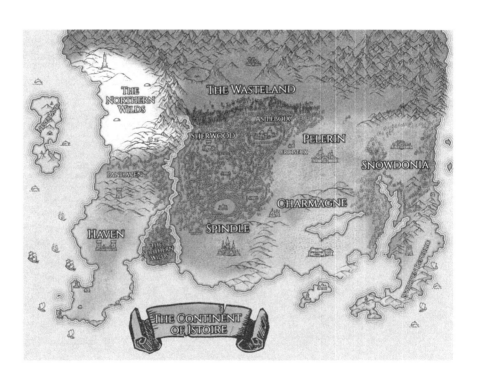

MAP OF ASILEBOIX AND CROISEUX

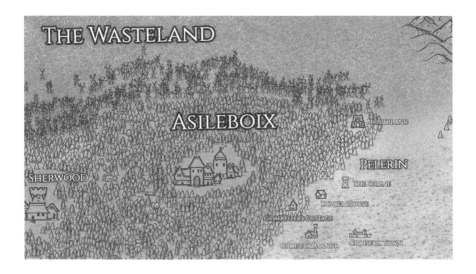

PROLOGUE

Cicadas buzzed from the nearby woods. A hot summer sun was beginning to lower itself behind darkening trees, streaks of orange and red reaching up into an almost cloudless sky. Although the forest was surrendering to shadows, the meadow was filled with dusky light. A warm, dry summer breeze stirred the air. Eddie ran his hands along the tops of long grass as he ambled towards a colony of sleepy beehives. The hives radiated a low pitched hum that was soothing; just barely audible above the cicadas from the forest.

The grass looked ready for hay-making. Eddie hoped his father would allow him to throw bundles up to the wagon again this year. Belle told him that it was a common laborer's job, but he enjoyed the feeling of hard work, of testing his strength and being part of something bigger than himself. His father always said that they *were* common folk, even if they lived in a big house now. Besides, common or not, the laborers who helped with hay-making had the best stories around the dinner fire at night.

A light blinked on to his left. He could just make out the path leading to the gamekeeper's cottage from where he stood and considered running over to see what Monsieur Veneur had killed that day. Quickly dismissing the notion, he trudged toward the beehives instead. Belle was expecting him. The distance from her house to Croiseux Manor wasn't far, but he would still need to run to make it back for dinner.

A door slammed in the direction of the Dower House. He watched a small figure run across the lawn. Belle must have seen him from a window. He stopped to wait for her, breaking off a stalk of grass and swishing the air with it as he did so. She wouldn't be happy with him. She would probably refuse to be the fair maiden in their games of Beast Hunters, or worse, refuse to play with him at all. *Having a girl as a best friend is a tricky thing*, he thought morosely, *especially a girl like Belle. Lady Belle*, he corrected himself. With the news he brought, she would surely be insisting on her title tonight.

"Eddie!" she called out when she was close enough. "I mean, Edouard," she corrected herself, panting slightly as she came to a stop before him. "What did your father say?" Her face was excited and full of hope, if a little sweaty. One of her sky blue hair ribbons was starting to slide free of her light brown hair, dangling loosely from the end of her pigtail. "You did ask him, didn't you?" she pressed.

"Yes, I asked."

"Well, then, when can we move back?"

"You can't," Eddie admitted, miserably. "My Da said he can't give your house back, and that your Father wouldn't like to hear talk of it."

The sudden shock on Belle's face was quickly replaced with rage. "Liar!" she yelled. "Your father just wants it for himself!" Fists balled at her side, her mouth screwed up as if she had tasted something sour. "You're all thieves! Just wait until I tell my father. You better look for a new house right now, Edouard Marchand, because he'll toss you out on your ear! And if your sister changed anything in my room I shall pull her hair. And hide her dolls. And have her banished!" Sobs punctuated her words, and with each sentence, she pushed him back a step.

Eddie let her. He let her down. Guilt and shame gnawed at him. He hated upsetting his friend. But he didn't like her accusation about his father. His sense of justice pushed him to speak.

"Look here. My Da said that your father *asked* us to buy it because he couldn't take care of it anymore. Something to do with the Beast War. He was just trying to help!"

"Oh, is that what your *Da* said?" Belle sneered. "My father would never let go of beautiful Croiseux to anyone, much less a little merchant family that called their father and mother *Da* and *Ma*. How ridiculous. I will talk to Papa tonight and you will see how much your *Da* knows! I hate you!" With one final push that sent Eddie to the ground, Belle turned and ran back toward the dower house, her loose hair ribbon fluttering down to join Eddie in the dirt. After a few steps she turned her splotchy, tear stained face toward him. "Go and pack your things Eddie, we shall come to take our house back tonight, you'll see. I'll throw away anything you leave!"

He watched her run into the Dower House. A few stars twinkled in the rapidly darkening sky, and the quiet buzzing of the bees was audible again in the wake of sudden silence. The cicadas were quieter, shocked, undoubtedly, by the unladylike outburst from Lady Belle.

Eddie felt wretched. His best friend in the world hated him. And although his Da had told him in no uncertain terms that the house was theirs, Belle always got her way. No doubt they would be out of Croiseux Manor and back to town by tomorrow. Now he had to go home and explain things to his Da, which would mean trouble, since his father had told him not to go upsetting Belle about it. Besides which, his mother and sister had completely changed Belle's old room which would just set Belle off even more. Eddie sniffled as he stood up and dusted off his breeches.

A patch of blue among the green grass caught his eye, and he stooped to pick up Belle's lost hair ribbon. He rubbed the silk with his thumb, then dropped it into his pocket. Maybe if he returned it to her with a present they could be friends again. *I'll have to ask Ma what sort of present Belle would like.* She hadn't seemed to like the salamander he had presented to her last week. He and LeFeu had spent the whole morning tracking one down and catching it for her.

A rustling from the woods pulled him from his thoughts and reminded him of his Da and Veneur's warnings about the forest. He would be late for dinner if he wasn't quick, which would make Ma angry. With one more glance at the dark trees beyond the beehives, he turned and ran towards the kitchen garden, winding his way nimbly through the fruit trees, to face another round of angry people.

*　*　*

Belle slammed the door to the Dower house and continued running toward Papa's study. Bursting through the door, she ran over to his large desk, and threw herself onto his lap.

"My dear girl!" her father exclaimed, kissing the top of her head as he hugged her. "What's the matter?" He chuckled quietly. "Did you lose another hair ribbon? That happens often enough that it doesn't warrant tears."

Belle wiped her face on her shawl as primly as a sweaty, red-faced, almost ten-year-old could, and looked up at her Papa.

"Eddie says that *his* father says we cannot have our house back!" She cried. "He said that you *gave* it to them because we couldn't look after it! How *stupid* he is! As if the Beasts have anything to do with Croiseux. I know his father is lying just to keep our beautiful house for his very own."

"Ah, I see," her father murmured "Is that what this is about?"

"Yes Papa," Belle slid off his lap and stamped her foot. "His father said that you wouldn't want us talking of it since it's all been settled, so I told him that you would never sell our beautiful house to someone else, let alone a trade family from our own town! Eddie is *such* a liar and I set him straight."

"Rosebelle Montanarte, I have heard enough." Belle's father drew himself up in his chair, a frown on his face. "Young Master Marchand was quite right in what he said."

Belle looked at her father in shock.

"All that Master Eddie said is true. I didn't think you were old enough to care or understand, so I kept our situation from you. Perhaps that was wrong." Lord Montanarte sighed, taking off his spectacles and rubbing his eyes before continuing.

"Rosebelle, you know that the Beast Wars have begun again. We lost Montanarte Castle in the first attack. I knew we couldn't sustain Croiseux for long without its income and begged, yes begged, Monsieur Marchand to buy it from me. The sale has allowed us to retain ownership of the little Dower House and its lands, as well as provide us with a small income."

"Live here?! In Grandmere's old house? For the rest of our lives?! I would be ashamed to live here while someone else lives in Croiseux!" Belle looked into her father's face incredulously, but he was unmoved.

"Belle, our course is set. We may have lost much, but we have each other."

Belle stilled as her father sat up straight in his chair. He adopted his "Lord" face, the one he used when going to parliament. "As such, I expect you to act with the dignity befitting a Lady Montanarte. You must learn to take the trials of life gracefully and make the best of them. You may take your mother as an example." He smiled toward the doorway, and Belle turned as her Mama stepped into the room, holding Belle's sleepy younger sister, Rochelle, on her hip. "You married me to escape life with an old scholar, and I'm afraid you've landed in exactly the same place, my dear." He gestured toward the stacks of books and paper on his desk.

"Hush, Maurice, I'm exactly where I want to be. You know I didn't marry you for any of that." They shared a tired smile.

"Belle," Lord Montanarte addressed his older daughter once again, "you acted in a manner ill befitting one of our station toward someone of a lesser social rank. I'm disappointed. You'll give an apology to Master Eddie when we see him at Chapel."

Belle opened her mouth to protest, but a glance at her father's forbidding expression told her that to argue would be in vain. "Yes, Papa," she replied, balling her fists in her shawl and dipping a curtsy. Then she ran from the room and up the stairs to her own small chamber, throwing herself on the bed and crying bitterly.

Some time later her mother came in, placing a tray with food on her nightstand, and stepping softly over to the bedside to rub her back. "I know it will be hard, my darling, but all hope is not lost." Belle turned her face away, but didn't pull back from her mother's soothing touch. "We can talk in the morning—but don't forget to eat. Mrs. Comfry made your favorite sandwiches. Goodnight, my dear."

After another good cry and several kicks to her bed, as well as a few of her softer toys, Belle dried her eyes and started nibbling her food. Soon she had devoured both sandwiches and the cooled tea, and got ready for bed. Wandering over to her window, she looked out into the night. The lights of Croiseux Manor were just barely visible in the distance. Bitterness rose up at the sight and she turned away, looking toward the woods. After watching the sway of trees in the warm night breeze for some time, she mumbled, either to herself or the trees, "If I can't have Croixeux, then I want something even better." She turned back toward her bed, blew out the candle, and quickly fell asleep.

* * *

Andrus stood wearily, stroking his horse's neck, eyes scanning their surroundings. After Clement returned from his discussion with the neighboring estate's gamekeeper, they would be able to head back to the castle. A hot meal would have to wait until after their report. *Being the son of the Prince of Asileboix means more missed meals than one might think*, Andrus ruminated. His stomach growled in protest. At sixteen, Andrus was nearly always hungry, and the swift pace they had set over the last few days hadn't left much time for food. *Ah, the cozy life as an heir to the crown.* Still, completing his Forest Guard training would make him a good ruler in the future. It was also a perfect way to gain the respect of his soldiers and woodsmen.

His current patrol was part of an extra sweep in preparation for his older sister's wedding. Rumors of beast sightings had increased in the last few days. His father feared that they would soon be swept into the conflict already overwhelming nearby Pelerin. Since their woodland principality bordered the Wasteland, the land of the Beasts to the north; his father had ordered an immediate review of their defenses.

Shouts reached Andrus' ears over the deafening racket of the cicadas. His heart pumped faster. This far from the Wasteland, a Beast sighting was highly unlikely, but they had come across the remains of partially eaten woodland animals, and inexplicable areas of dead or dying woodland over the last two weeks, signaling something unnatural lurked in the woods.

The shouting intensified and the cicadas fell silent. Andrus decided to investigate. Pulling an arrow from his quiver, he nocked it gently. Dusk was the perfect time for a Beast attack. Laborers would be on their way home, tired from a day's work and less alert to danger. As he slipped carefully between the trees, the forest thinned and a hay meadow appeared. Through a gap in the trees, he quickly spied the source of the shouting. Two children were standing near what looked like an apiary. A girl was pushing the other, a boy roughly her own height, and finally knocked him backwards. She took off running, turning to fling one more diatribe at him before continuing on toward a small house, the lights of which were visible in the distance. It had to be the Dower House. Andrus had seen it marked on the huge map in his father's cabinet room, just over the border in Pelerin. He looked around to confirm there was nothing else lurking along the tree line. He must have missed the boundary stone marking the start of the Dower House woodland while he was following the sound of the little girl's yells.

After a moment, the boy stood and dusted himself off. He

picked something up from the grass and examined it closely. Andrus relaxed. The shouting had been nothing more than a spat between children, and much less violent than the fights he and his sister Marguerite had gotten into at that age. He stood up to return to the horses. An errant twig snapped under his foot as he took his first step, and he bit back a curse. Dropping back into a crouch, he glanced toward the boy.

Keeping his presence in Pelerine land secret was essential. As an heir to the Principality of Asileboix, any move he made in the outside world would be scrutinized. He didn't need to add a trumped up political incident to his father's list of problems. The boy glanced toward the trees concealing Andrus, then up at the sky. After a moment, he turned and headed south, in the direction of a small orchard.

Breathing a sigh of relief, Andrus slipped his arrow back into its quiver. He watched the boy go, then turned and went back to the horses. Clement arrived a few minutes later.

"Matthieu Veneur sends regards to your family, Sire," Clement said as he rubbed his horse's nose. "He's spotted two killings in the last month like the ones we saw by the northern outpost. We'll have to add that to our report tonight. Your father won't like having his suspicions confirmed, eh?"

Andrus shook his head. "He has a knack for seeing the truth of things. We can hunt the Beasts down after the wedding and restock the outposts. We'll be prepared."

Clement nodded and hoisted himself up onto his horse. Andrus followed suit and they turned their mounts back up the game path, toward home. Twilight was falling fast among the trees, but the game path was still visible.

Once they made it to the main road, Andrus pulled alongside Clement and described the scene he witnessed with a small chuckle. "We should have Monsieur Veneur warn the children off from the woods next time you go see him. We don't need an international incident to worry about on top of everything else."

"Aye," Clement answered, "I'll talk to him on our next

round. Once your father approves the new guard patterns I'll need to give him notice anyway. He'll revive the old tales of the *beastly* Asileans again, in case those villagers have gotten curious during peacetime."

Andrus laughed softly, "Those old tales hit closer to the mark than Veneur would guess—I gave you a few scars when I was younger, didn't I, Clement?" Andrus caught a flash of white teeth as Clement grinned at the memories. "Either way, we can't have anything upsetting Marguerite's wedding, or my mother will be on the warpath against beast and men."

"Too true." Clement laughed, then raised his eyebrows at the prince. "Is that your stomach growling? Come on, let's get home." Cicadas trumpeted their movement as they sped toward the safety of ancient castle walls, oblivious to the pair of yellowed eyes watching their progress.

PART I – THE ROSE

CHAPTER ONE

Eddie - 15 Years Later

"Captain Marchand!"

My ears twitched at the sound of Private Oger's anxious voice. "Think he found them?" I muttered to my best friend and first sergeant, Henri LeFeu. We stooped over a rough map, scratching notes for my battlefield report.

Henri shrugged, turning to look at the soldier hustling toward us. I shielded my eyes from the late autumn sun as I followed suit. Its rays stabbed my vision but did nothing to warm the frosty air.

Oger staggered into view, dirty but unscathed. Two men jogged more slowly behind him, bearing an occupied stretcher. *They obviously found someone.* I steeled myself for more bad news. Oger pulled up short, throwing a quick salute.

"Sir, I found Third Squadron holed up in a stand of trees over that ridge." He gestured across the now defunct battlefield, hazy pockets of smoke obscuring the distant trees.

"All alive but sustaining heavy wounds." His words were almost incoherent as he struggled to catch his breath. "We brought the worst off with us, but the rest need help too. Is Doc Martine nearby?"

"No, he set up down the valley." I jerked my chin toward a nearby creek. "Sergeant Hevre's squad is pulling water for the mess tent. Tell him to get up here with his men. I have some stretchers we can use."

Oger doggedly started into a run. I turned back to LeFeu.

His voice rasped out as he scratched a note on our map. "So there's our missing squad. They must have fallen back in that last wave of Beasts.

"Creator knows I thought they were dead. That's one time I'm happy to be wrong," I joked, wryly. "Besides, now I can submit a complete report. Lieutenant Colonel Hevre always gets on my case about loose ends."

LeFeu glanced up at the mention of our Lieutenant Colonel. "You'll have to give it to the general's office. Lieutenant Colonel Hevre's gone. Lost in the last push. Beasts broke through the line near the river. I thought you knew."

I cleared my throat, my voice suddenly thick. "He's really gone?"

LeFeu nodded as he gathered up our papers.

Not the time to grieve, Eddie. I gave myself a small shake. Wordlessly, I turned and stalked into my makeshift command tent, LeFeu on my heels. My stomach growled as I shoveled a week old biscuit into my mouth, washing it down with a flask of water. *I could use something stronger right now.*

LeFeu cursed as he untangled a few stretchers from the disheveled heap on the other side of my tent. They were little more than scraps of old tent fabric, or in some cases, threadbare overcoats, tied haphazardly across broken tent poles. Most were filthy, and several had bloodstains, but they were sturdy enough.

Sergeant Hevre and Private Oger swept into my tent as I stepped over to help LeFeu. I glanced between the two of them. From the tired but cheerful look on Sergeant Hevre's face, he hadn't heard about his father. Lieutenant Colonel Hevre had been universally loved and respected. News of his death would spread quickly. I didn't want his son hearing about it by happenstance.

My hand strayed toward the lucky charm in my waistcoat

pocket, but I caught myself before I could actually pull it out, pointing toward LeFeu instead.

"Private Oger, assist Sergeant LeFeu with those and wait outside. I'll be with you shortly."

Sergeant Hevre moved toward the pile of stretchers as well, looking back questioningly as I grabbed his shoulder.

"Not you. Wait here a moment."

He held open the tent flap for LeFeu and Oger as they lugged their bundles outside. I sunk heavily into a stool at my desk, indicating the empty one across from me when he turned back.

"Have a seat. I assume you haven't heard about your father."

He complied quickly, a question on his face as I marshaled my words. I shifted in my chair, uncomfortable with my own pushed-aside grief, hating to be the one to deliver the worst possible news to my old mentor's son. The Lieutenant Colonel had been stationed well away from the action. Of all the men we lost today, he shouldn't have been one of them.

But even though we had just won a decisive victory, our position wasn't secure yet. I needed Hevre out in the field again as soon as possible. I clenched my fists. There was no way to soften the blow, so I dealt it quickly.

"He's gone, Hevre. Killed in the last push. Beasts broke through the line. There were heavy casualties. I'm sorry."

Sergeant Hevre looked at me blankly, then surged to his feet, taking a few faltering steps toward the exit. Halting mid-stride, he stood suspended between his desire to find his father, and his duty to me. All at once he collapsed back onto his seat, head in hands. A pulse of sorrow clenched my heart as I caught the anguished look on his face.

"You know I served under him when I first joined up. He was an exceptional man." I cleared my throat, putting my hand on his shoulder briefly.

"I know you need to grieve, but your unit needs you." He nodded, head still in his hands. I pulled back to give him space.

"I'll take your men to retrieve Third Squadron. Pull yourself together while I'm gone." I clapped his shoulder one more time, then stood, edging around him and ducking out of my tent. LeFeu stood just outside.

Angling my head away from the men, I muttered a stream of instructions to him. "Give him a few minutes, then keep him busy until I return. Stay here in case Captain Robert arrives to relieve us—should be any minute."

LeFeu cast a dark look at me. The voluble Captain Robert wasn't his favorite person.

"Why don't you stay here? I'll lead the retrieval of Third Squadron," he asked, with studied nonchalance.

"Sorry old friend. This is my last chance to stretch my legs before sitting in meetings all night. Besides, I want to see their condition for myself."

He frowned. "Hurry back, will you?"

I flicked an eyebrow at him and turned toward the others. Oger stood with what was left of Hevre's first squad, empty stretchers in their arms.

"First Squad," I barked out, noting their torn and bloodied appearance. Some shivered, soaked and dripping from their work at the nearby stream. They should be warming up by a fire, but we needed every able-bodied man right now.

"Sergeant Hevre is preoccupied right now. You'll be assisting me and Private Oger with retrieving some of the heavily wounded and getting them to the Doc." I turned to Oger. "Lead on."

Feet pounded on frostbitten earth as we quickly settled into a light run. I fell in at the back. My muscles ached from the battle we fought over the last two days, my limbs heavy from lack of sleep. They were all just as exhausted, but none of us would leave our brothers behind.

We split into pairs as we reached our destination, Oger helping me triage team members. It took two trips, but we got everyone to the crowded hospital tent in no worse condition than before.

I stole a few minutes to check in on the others awaiting

treatment. Despite my best efforts, the atmosphere was grim. We lost too many friends to delight in victory just yet.

As I pulled back the rough canvas of my tent again, my eyes passed over LeFeu, digging through paperwork, and landed on Captain Robert. He paused as he shoveled spoonfuls of unidentifiable grub into his mouth, indicating a bowl on the other side of my desk. Stepping over to it quickly, a groan escaped as I took my first bite of real food after a week of field rations.

Wolfing down our hasty dinners, I briefed Robert on our position in between bites. When we finally finished, I leaned my forearms against my desk, bone tired.

"I'll take these over to the general's office for you," LeFeu offered, stuffing my final reports into his knapsack. I nodded my thanks.

Robert stood up, grabbing his empty bowl and falling in next to LeFeu with a cheery grin. "I'll walk you there. The mess tent is on the way." They walked out together, Robert chattering away, as LeFeu politely pretended to listen, his face as stoic as ever.

As they exited, I caught a glimpse of a few officers huddled around a fire pit. They hunched over their food, weatherbeaten faces pulled down in sorrow. Each lost more men today than we had in the previous twelve months. The last few days of savage fighting had clearly taken their toll. I felt the same emotions weighing my shoulders down. I shrugged reflexively, stretching my arms to try and clear them. *Time for your meeting with General Des Concordes*. Grief would have to wait again.

Getting to my feet, I paused to scrub some of the blood and dirt from my face and uniform before heading to the General's tent.

My reflection wavered in the dirty water. I had been lucky, sustaining only minor wounds in the worst of the fighting.

Two Beasts snapped up at me in my memory. They had broken through our section of the line, their over-sized canine teeth tearing at my side and leg, the desire to rip my flesh burning in their eyes.

The one at my thigh almost missed me in its eagerness, inflicting only a glancing bite. The other's attempt at opening up my abdomen had been prevented by my leather jerkin. They weren't given another chance.

I had been able to patch myself up quickly once the fighting stopped, having picked up sawbones training in my years of service. It was lucky that most of the blood on my clothes wasn't my own.

I don't know if that is luck, actually, I thought to myself. Guilt flitted around the corner of my mind. I was alive, it was true, but some of my best men weren't. Their lives were given in one great push to decimate the beast hoard. I shook my head at my reflection. It had worked, so maybe it was worth it. Maybe we would have peace.

I placed my hand over the pocket holding my lucky charm. Peace. *Could it really be within our grasp?*

* * *

I glanced down at the shining silver medal pinned to my chest. It seemed to mock me as it scattered sunlight onto the dead grass; ground where the blood of those who deserved it more cried out. What General Des Concordes had called valor seemed more like bullheadedness to me. My men were the ones that had held the line at the most desperate hour, enabling fresh cannons to be re-positioned in response to the hoard's changing tactics, slowly gaining ground inch by inch.

Hold the line. Put your next foot forward. Defend the man beside you. Defend yourself. Fight with sword, or flintlock, or knives, or fists until every enemy had been hunted down, or you were dead.

Cold air knifed through my lungs as I drew a long breath. Winter had arrived in the month since our final battle. The days were growing short. My men were due to meet me in our current headquarters: an assembly room in a nearby tavern. Word had almost certainly spread that we were being released—the chance of being home before Winter Solstice celebrations was on everyone's mind. I lengthened my stride as the tavern came into sight. No need to keep them waiting.

Warmth rolled across my face and raucous noise hit my ears as I pushed through the door. Securing it behind me and greeting the barkeep, I proceeded to my temporary command center. After returning the men's salute and putting them at ease, I stood before them, my hands clasped behind my back.

"As at least half of you have no doubt heard, we're being disbanded and released at morning mess tomorrow."

A chorus of cheers and whoops sounded out, quickly silenced by LeFeu's loud whistle. I couldn't help but grin. "As I said, you're free to be undisciplined, lazy slobs after morning mess tomorrow. But until then, I expect each of you to act like the disciplined war heroes you've proved to be."

"Even me sir?" Private Oger shouted from the back. LeFeu sent him a trademark glower at his lack of decorum, but the soldier pretended not to see.

"Even you, Oger. Your uncanny ability to be first to the mess hall every day is definitely heroic."

The men roared in laughter, those closest to Oger smacking the back of his head while he grinned sheepishly.

"In truth, each one of you deserves a piece of the medal they pinned to my chest this morning. I'm proud of you, proud to have served alongside the best Pelerin has to offer. My only regret is that so many aren't here with us tonight, tasting victory and planning a return home. That was the least they deserved." I paused to take a breath and compose the emotion welling in my eyes. The atmosphere had turned somber, feet shuffled uncomfortably and throats cleared surreptitiously.

"But tonight we celebrate! I've arranged with the barkeep to supply you with three rounds—one to the memory of those not with us, one to the valor of the those beside us, and one to a long life with those we love ahead of us. Dismissed! Get out of my sight!"

An ear-shattering roar broke out, everyone scrambling to claim their rounds from the barkeep in the main tavern. Many stopped as they filed out to shake hands with LeFeu and myself. I didn't worry about them becoming too rowdy. Most of them were older and would want a good night's sleep before journeying home. Even the younger ones like Oger were unlikely to overindulge. There were preparations to be made before gaining freedom tomorrow. Besides, the war had aged all of us, even if we were young in years.

I followed the last of the men into the barroom, LeFeu shuffling over to the bar to gather our pints. Settling in to a corner table near the fireplace, I couldn't help but laugh at the drinking song some of them had started, complete with a dancing game similar to one played in my own hometown.

I caught LeFeu's eye as he muscled his way over, nodding my head toward the entertainment. He just grunted, settling in across from me and taking a swig of his pint.

LeFeu was never one for frivolity. He had few words at the best of times, becoming more like his reticent father every day. Monsieur LeFeu was our town's blacksmith. Before we signed up for the war, Henri had been his apprentice.

I suppose he'll slip right back into it once we get back. I can't imagine him as anything else. Even with all of his regular duties, he found time to help at our battalion's forge, assisting in the endless needed repairs.

He'll go back to the forge, and I'll go back to Croiseux Manor. It would be a far cry from the constant fighting of the last five years.

And of course, I would finally marry Belle. A consolation prize if ever there was one.

Absently, I pulled out the hair ribbon she had lost so long ago. Trinkets from the war dangled from it, knotted along its length, including a broken Beast tooth Doc Martine dug out of my arm two years ago. I remembered that battle fondly. A nasty injury for me, but otherwise a huge success for my squad, earning me a promotion to Captain.

Rubbing my thumb along the length of blue silk, as I had done an hundred times before, I thought of the letter even now on its way to my parents. I had announced my traveling plans, and included a shorter note to be passed on to Belle. Just a few weeks and I would see them all.

The memory of the day I officially proposed surfaced before my eyes as I stared into the fire. She had been beauty personified, surrounded by flowers on the back garden of Croiseux Manor, exactly where she was born to be. Bits of gold glimmered in her light brown hair, threatening to outshine the sun's warm rays. Her normally steady amber eyes had lowered while I made my speech. She was generally in complete command of herself, but in that moment she had been speechless, lost in emotion, no doubt, as I had been. I could hardly remember what I had said to her, other than to assure her of my devotion and ask that she would become my wife upon my return from war.

She had stood up suddenly, pressing a hand to her heart and turning toward the forest. The proposal itself couldn't have been a surprise. Our families had expected us to marry for years, and I had loved her since we were children. But for a moment I had thought she was going to make a run for the woods.

I chuckled at my nonsensical younger self. She had turned back, accepting my offer of course, her normally reserved expression broken by a tiny smile and tears. The tears had been proof to my nervous young heart that she really did love me as deeply as I had always loved her.

My smile grew as I perused the memory of that golden afternoon. The celebration and planning, our innocence and trust in the future—the warmth of it competed with the fire in front of me. I had rationed that memory to myself carefully over the darkest nights of the war.

"Ready to marry her?" LeFeu inquired, nodding toward the old hair ribbon. He tore off a bite of bread and cheese, delivered alongside fresh drinks by the barmaid.

"Of course," I replied, folding my lucky charm carefully before dropping it into my pocket. Grabbing a bite of my own food, I chewed for a minute, watching Oger give a raucus toast on the other side of the room. "It will be like a waking to a glorious sunrise after a long nightmare."

LeFeu gave me a thoughtful look.

"What?" I demanded between mouthfuls of bread.

"Should have married her before we left."

I frowned. I hadn't wanted to leave her a widow, or not free to make her own choices if I came back maimed or changed. That had been the whole reason I agreed with her request to forgo formal betrothal documents. She had her family to look after, and if anything happened, I didn't want to put her in a difficult situation. Da would have settled a dower portion on her if I had died, so there was no need to push the issue. LeFeu knew all of that too.

"You know why I didn't," I reminded him, unable to keep the exasperation out of my voice. "Why do you say that?"

"You've loved her for a long time, but you don't know her anymore. She was always hard to read. What if things have changed? What if *she's* changed?" He shook his head. "Would've been better to go home knowing everything was secure, instead of trying to marry a stranger."

Typical LeFeu. He hated leaving things to chance. It made him a very effective officer, but didn't recommend him as a counselor for love. He had botched things with his own girl before we left. I wasn't about to take his advice.

"You're one to talk. What about Hazel?"

He grunted. "That's different."

"No it isn't. She was practically throwing herself at you before we left, and you did nothing!"

His neck flushed bright red. A rare occurrence for the normally calm and taciturn Henri LeFeu.

"She wasn't throwing herself at me. She was just as attentive to you. Just friends, as we've always been."

"Well, she didn't give this friend her Prayer Book copy to take with him," I needled, amused at his growing frustration.

"She only had one, so that's not surprising. She'd hardly tear it apart to split between us." He tore into his bread again savagely.

"Relax Henri, I'm only teasing. But I did think she was trying to get your attention before you left. Will you court her when we get back?"

He took a long drink before meeting my eyes. "I don't know. Like I said, she may have changed, or may not like how I've changed. Maybe she's married."

"Come on, you're not so different," I shot back, pulling in the new pint the barkeep had sent over. "We would have heard if she married."

"Says you. The village lads would be daft to have left her alone all these years."

"I'll pass no judgment on the brains of our village lads, but if Hazel cares for you as much as I think she does, she'll have sent any number of them off with fleas in their ears waiting for you, just like my Belle."

He looked at me skeptically as we turned to shake hands with a slightly tipsy soldier who had wandered up to our table. After listening to his thanks and wishing him well, we finished our food and wrapped ourselves up against the cold, shepherding the most unbalanced of our men back to their tents.

Before entering his own tent, LeFeu hesitated and turned back to me. I stood waiting to hear what he would say, stamping my feet in an effort to knock feeling back into them.

"If she ever *was* in love with me, I don't think I have much chance now. Everything will have changed in Croiseux." He grimaced, then bid me a quiet good night. I shook my head as I entered my own tent.

Things change in Croiseux? We had been fighting a war to make sure nothing needed to change there. Nothing ever happened in our little corner of the world, and nothing ever would. It would be exactly as we left it: placid, peaceful, and everything proceeding according to plan.

CHAPTER TWO

Belle

L eaning back in my father's desk chair, I stretched my arms in front of me, shaking out cramped hands. Re-writing Papa's crabbed notes took considerable concentration. My current project described an arcane magical blood ritual he had been intent on researching a few months ago. He had stumbled upon it in a book dedicated to the cult of the Lady of the Woods, his life's unflagging interest. For a time, he had been intent on understanding the spell and how it related to the Lady. He had even gathered a few of the objects needed to perform it, completely disregarding the newest royal ban on magic.

"But it's just as an academic exercise!" he had insisted when I pointed the potential consequences. "Why, Monsieur Marchand is the one who found the ground orb root for me, and he's the district magistrate. He'd know if there might be any difficulties!" That was enough to put an end to the matter in his mind, while I was left wondering what sort of difficulties those who broke the law *did* find themselves in.

I hadn't been left to worry long. A few days later, Papa noticed a comment in the margin of the spell book referencing a link between the rulers of the neighboring Princedom of Asileboix and the ancient Lady of the Woods. It overtook his interest immediately, much to my relief.

As glad as I was to have this particular project behind us, the subject was too interesting to allow it to vanish into oblivion. After rewriting everything legibly, I planned to bundle it all into one of the secret niches hidden around our our ancient house. Safe and sound, waiting to be found by some future Montanarte scholar, after the fear of magic abates and interest in the old ways rekindle.

Assuming that day would come. More probably, the pragmatic future Montanarte would discover it and shake his head at such heathen ancestors, before burning hours worth of work completed by Papa and myself. I chuckled and gave a mock frown to my hypothetical descendant.

Stacking the papers neatly on top of Papa's original notes, I slid the bundle into an oilskin envelope. They were destined to hide in a small cavity behind one of the decorative panels outside the sitting room I recently found while helping Hazel clean. I liked to think it would lurk there, mocking any royal visitors we receive as they sweep into our sitting room.

Not that we would receive any. I scowled. My parents were graced with the titles of Marquess and Marchioness of Montanarte, as well as Earl and Countess of Croiseux. They should receive regular visits from the most glittering families in our country, but that had ceased years ago. Papa had lost the wealthy Montanarte estate at the beginning of the Beast Wars when I was a child, selling our smaller estate, Croiseux Manor, shortly afterward. Although our titles remained, all that engendered the prestige to go with them did not.

The study door creaked opened. Rochelle entered, balancing a tray against her hip as she pushed the door shut behind her, somehow managing not to spill tea and toast on her faded wool gown. Her cheerful voice floated over as she navigated furniture and stacks of books.

"I've been charged with bringing you a restorative. Mrs. Comfry said you didn't eat much breakfast this morning and would need something to spur you on."

I smiled as she set the tray down. "I don't believe I've ever needed anything to 'spur me on', exactly, but I wouldn't say no to a cup of tea. Actually, I've just finished up with Papa's last project, so your timing is perfect."

My sister poured out two cups as I nibbled on a slice of buttered toast.

"How do you think Papa's new research is going?" Chelle asked around a sip of tea. "Mama's wondering if she's been abandoned for the Lady again."

We shared a smirk at our mother's running joke. I didn't think I would be as lighthearted about my husband's obsession with another woman, mythical or not, but I was glad Mama could see the humor in it. After finding the reference between the Lady of the Woods and the Asilean royal family, Papa had made it his mission to gain access to their library at Asileboix Castle. Few Pelerines had been granted admittance to the princedom in generations, but that hadn't stopped Papa.

Through a connection he maintained with someone in the Department of Alliances, Papa discovered that the current prince had made several overtures a few years ago to establish a diplomatic relations with Pelerin. At the time the prince had been adamant about cementing such an alliance by marriage. Not surprisingly, those attempts failed. Tales of the Beast Men of Asileboix were favorites among children across the entire kingdom. Our countries had never been allies, and the disaster of the former Asilean princess' wedding, over fifteen years ago, hadn't been forgotten. Even a royal title wouldn't be much of an attraction for young ladies at court. There was a dearth of unmarried princes in our own royal family.

I wouldn't have minded being offered a royal title and a chance at adventure. Those kind of offers don't get extended to impoverished nobles living in obscurity; no matter how close that obscurity was to the Princedom in question. Somehow, Papa had used all of that information to facilitate an invitation to the Asilean court and was even now immersed in their library.

My sister's cup clinked as she set it down. "Do you have *any* idea when he might be home?"

"I can't imagine it would be much longer," I replied. "He's bound to be wearing out his welcome through persistent questioning. Papa's tact isn't his strongest quality."

Rochelle snorted, pushing a lock of brown hair out of her face. "Do you remember when he told the Baron of Comfrois that his nose looked like an etching of a plague victim? I could have died from laughter."

"You almost did! You choked on your biscuit!"

"The thing is, I knew which etching he was talking about—it really did look like the Baron!" She laughed even harder. "Oh Belle, don't shake your head at me. He wasn't worth the effort if he couldn't take a joke. Besides, he was always trying to talk Papa into some scheme or another."

I grimaced, setting down my tea and toast. "That's true. But he was one of the few of our rank who would still receive us. Any connection like that was worth saving. Maybe he and his wife would have sponsored us at court events, and we would be settled happily by now."

My sister eyed me quizzically. "Now that the Beast Wars have ended, you *will* be settled happily—with Eddie."

"Master Edouard," I corrected her. "And yes, to be mistress of Croiseux will be a happy thing. But my title will die with me, and Croiseux will never be what it once was." I shifted in my seat. "Enough of that. I'm content. I only worry about *your* future. I'd like you to be settled with a noble family as you deserve. After all, Mama managed a Marquess even though she had no title. You're just as beautiful as she is."

Rochelle frowned and set her cup down. "I don't have the same ambitions as you do Belle. As long as my husband loves me and we have a roof over our heads, I think I can be happy."

I rolled my eyes at her. Chelle had always had a romantic streak, but at eighteen, she should have lost it by now.

The door pushed open, revealing our mother, spectacles on her head and sewing apron askew.

"There you two are! I've just spotted your father at the stable. He'll be here any second!"

Rochelle squealed and rushed out of the room, tea and toast forgotten. I stood up to follow, picking up the oilskin envelope filled with research as I did so.

"Wait, Mama!" I called before she could escape the room. Plucking her spectacles from her head, I reached around to untie her apron.

She laughed, patting her hair. "I completely forgot I was wearing those."

"You look perfect, Mama. Off you go to your knight in shining armor. I'll put these with your basket." She flashed me a smile, tracing Rochelle's steps to the front door. Folding her apron carefully, I tucked it along with her glasses and the research into the crook of my arm and picked up the small tea tray. As I left the room, I bumped into Hazel, my best friend and our maidservant.

"Hazel—thank the Lady! I need some help." I handed her the tea tray with a grin. "Please take this back to Mrs. Comfry. Ask her to send another to the sitting room with whatever leftovers are available. Papa just arrived and will need 'fortifying' as she calls it."

"Yes milady," Hazel replied, dipping a demure curtsy as she took the tray from me. I laughed and she winked at me. Although I'm usually a stickler for observing rank, Hazel is one of my only real friends. Even when she's serving at the house, we address each other as we always have. She has the sort of friendly personality that charms everyone, regardless of station. I find it difficult to form connections, even with those few that would be socially appropriate to my rank, but not so haughty as to ignore me because of our poverty. In spite of our differences, we've been best friends since we learned to walk.

"Can you put these in my mother's sewing basket? She'll probably want them again before lunch." I balanced the folded apron and glasses on the tray, and Hazel maneuvered gingerly before turning back to the kitchen.

The front door opened and shut, followed by a low murmur of exclamations. Hurrying my steps, I rounded the corner just in time to see Mama disappear into the sitting room. I smiled, rushing to the hidden panel and stuffing the research packet inside, before walking the remaining few feet to the sitting room door.

"Oh Papa! What did you bring me, a rose or a bell?" I sang out as I entered the room. I knew very well that he wouldn't have either. It was a longstanding joke when he left for long trips, he would return with seashells for Rochelle and either a rose or a bell for me. Since he had missed my birthday last week, I planned to rub it in a little extra.

My smile faltered as I took in the room. Papa sat hunched on the settee, head in his hands. Mama perched next to him, rubbing his back. She and Rochelle turned to me with tight, bewildered expressions.

"What's happened?" I asked, disquieted.

"Your father says he has terrible news, but wanted to wait for you," Mama answered. She turned back to my father. "Maurice, dear. Belle has come. Tell us what's weighing you down, so we can share your burden."

I lowered myself into a chair across from them as Papa exhaled forcefully. He patted my mother's hand, looking up at her, then across to me and Rochelle.

"My girls. My dear girls. You've put up with so much from me over the years. Chasing all over the countryside after the secrets of the Lady. Burying myself in books for days on end, helping me organize my notes for publishing with the academy." He coughed into a handkerchief.

"I never tried to regain our wealth. It would have been futile! I knew Belle would marry Eddie and be mistress of Croiseux again. I've hoped recently that Chelle was making plans to become a Marchand as well."

I glanced at Rochelle, momentarily surprised, but quickly turned my attention back to Papa as he sighed deeply.

"I was happy with what we had, knowing your future was

secure. I should have tried harder." He put his head back in his hands.

"Papa, don't say that!" Rochelle pleaded, "we're all here, and well, and happy! There's no need for self-reproach. Besides, while you were away, word came that the Beast War has ended. Eddie will marry Belle, and all will be as you said. We never mind when you're off researching, so long as you come home to us."

My father gave a sharp cry, and my mother hushed him gently. After a moment, he straightened up and clutched her hand.

"That's exactly what I have to tell you. That future will *not* come to pass any longer." Papa glanced around in anguish. "Don't worry Belle," he directed at me," I'm sure Eddie will marry you as soon as he comes home. But there can be no thought of you being Mistress of Croiseux any longer."

My mind went blank as Mama gasped.

"What do you mean?" she urged. "Has something happened to the Marchands?"

"No, Halette, something has happened to us. And through us, the Marchands will lose much."

Hazel clattered through the door with the tea tray. She hesitated on the threshold as she noticed the scene of misery before her.

Mama looked over, a bewildered expression on her face. "Hazel, my dear. Come put the tray down here and pour out for each of us. It seems we will need it."

Papa thanked her when she handed him a cup. "You may as well pour yourself one too and sit down, Hazel. You're almost one of us, after all, and your family may be affected just as much." He waited as she poured herself some tea and sat down between me and Rochelle, then continued his story.

"As promised by the Prince, I arrived at Asileboix Castle without incident. His mother, the Dowager Princess Mathilde, welcomed me cordially. I settled in quickly and was allowed partial access to their library."

He turned toward me, the hint of a spark in his eyes. "It was a wondrous place, Belle. You would have loved it. Manuscripts older than anything in Pelerin! An entire section on magical processes. In the open for anyone to read!" He sighed and gulped some tea, hand trembling. "But I'm getting away from myself. I studied without interruption each day, and was welcome at dinner with the Princess and her companion each evening."

Mama interrupted, her voice strained, "That much we know from your letters, darling. You said you made great strides in your research."

"Yes. I discovered an ancient genealogy book of their House, and was making headway translating it from what seemed to be an obscure dialect of Romany. Highly interesting, as the older entries recorded supposed interactions with the Lady of the Woods, along with other myths and legends. It was slow work, however, so I was only just beginning to get underway when the Prince arrived back from his trip. At first, he was very cordial, if a little brusque. Then at dinner two days ago, he inquired about my research. Before I could explain even half of it, he just erupted, slamming his cup down on the table and asking what right I had to go researching his family line. He ended dinner and stormed out. I have never witnessed the like. It made me wonder if there was some scandal in their recent family tree. The Dowager Princess apologized for his behavior, but suggested that I should prepare to go home. As if I had any interest whether there were changelings in their ruling family or not!"

"Maurice!" Mama interjected." Not in front of the ladies, *please*."

"My dear, it's been known to happen. In fact, Belle helped me research the subject within our own royal family a few years ago. Not that we submitted *that* piece for publishing of course."

Mama shot him a quelling look. Papa cleared his throat before continuing.

"Yes, well, as I was saying. The entire evening was

in turmoil. After breakfast the next morning, the Prince summoned me to his throne room. He was there with his mother and someone who turned out to be his attorney. He informed me, in the coldest manner possible, that he had recently become aware of my sale of Croiseux to someone outside my family, and though it may not be common knowledge, the estate was originally Asilean, not Pelerine. In the original deed of gift there exists a clause prohibiting sale outside any descendants of the family member it had been gifted to, without written and recorded permission of the ruler of Asileboix."

Papa's voice faltered, and Mama covered her mouth with her hand, white as a sheet.

Rochelle, looked from one to the other of us. "But what does that mean, Papa?"

"It means," Papa intoned, wearily, "that if the Prince wishes it, he can undo the sale of Croiseux and demand penalties from both our family and the Marchands for all the intervening years." He swallowed audibly. "It seems he very much does wish it."

Hazel squeaked in her chair. I closed my eyes. *This can't be happening.* After all the dreams I had sacrificed, the plans I had made to benefit my sister and our family: all swept away by the temper of a foreign Prince. It was like something from those grim fairy tales Hazel's father used to tell on summer nights.

Papa continued weakly after a moment. "It's all in order. I looked at the evidence the attorney brought with him. You know that I don't love reading law, but I am fully capable. Their case is water tight."

"Surely the King won't allow it!" Mama protested.

"I hold no hope of that, my dear. We've fallen so low I doubt he will lend us support, especially as we're still extricating ourself from the Beast War. We aren't worth the trouble.

"I fear what is to become of us, and the Marchands." Papa's voice wavered, and real fear struck my heart. "The rent arrears and fines the Prince proposed are enormous, and although my old friend Thierry has amassed a fortune, it may be more than he can take."

I heard him draw in a long breath and release it as I stared at the carpet, my mind racing.

"My dear Rosebelle," he murmured, placing his tea cup down on the table and reaching to take my hands from my lap. "You mustn't worry. When Master Eddie arrives home, you two will marry immediately. He will have his officer's pension, enough for two young people in love. No doubt he can find work from his contacts in the war. As for the rest of us," he continued unsteadily, dropping my hands and turning to put an arm around my mother, "we will find our way somehow." His voice broke, and Mama shushed him softly.

A frown creased my brow and pulled at my lips. I certainly wasn't going to marry Edouard just to live on an officer's pension, and my parents and sister couldn't be thrown out on the street. They deserved better. *There has to be a loophole somewhere, or some leverage we could use to stop this.*

"Do you think he would turn us out of our house as well, Lord Montanarte?" came Hazel's voice softly. I looked over, noticing her stricken look, then glanced beyond to where my sister sat near the fireplace, silent tears coursing down her cheeks. The fire crackled merrily, it's cheer almost offensive in the subdued atmosphere of the room.

"Not if he knows what's good for him," Papa replied, with a small, humorless chuckle. "Your father is highly skilled. I know he's one of the few that has occasional contact with the woodsmen of Asileboix, so his reputation may have reached the Prince and protect you. But I cannot say for certain. After the Prince takes possession of the Croiseux estate, the surrounding lands and even the town will become a part of Asileboix once again. He may want to turn management of the woodland over to his own people. I will come down to your father's house in a day or two to discuss it with him."

My sister gently dabbed her cheeks with her shawl. "Croiseux in a different country? It seems hard to imagine.

What about the townspeople?"

"They will either have to move or accept their new citizenship. Although it hasn't happened in this part of the country for hundreds of years, it used to be common for towns to be taken and lost along our borders with Snowdonia and Charmagne in the Border Wars. In fact, when the Beast Wars broke out fifteen years ago, the King granted several disputed towns to Charmagne in exchange for soldiers. It's never an easy process, but it changes things for the average residents very little. It's the local nobility and their retainers that bear the brunt of it, and that means us." A spasm of despair shot across his face. He kissed my mother's cheek, then creaked to his feet.

"I'm sorry for the terrible news, dear ones. We will find a way to face it in the days to come." He stared at the floor for a moment before shuffling out the door, treading slowly in the direction of his study. My sister rushed out of the room as well, the front door slamming a minute later.

"Let them go," Mama cautioned, as I watched them leave. "He needs time to collect himself, and your sister always prefers to do her thinking out of doors." She set her cup down and tried on a worried smile.

"Hazel, please clear away the tea things, and let Mrs. Comfry know that lunch should be served late today. You may then go home. Tell your parents if you wish, but ask them to keep it to themselves until Lord Montanarte has a chance to visit with your father. We can manage without you until after Chapel on Sunday."

"Yes, Lady Montanarte." Hazel got to her feet and slowly cleared the tea things.

Mother sighed and stood as well, wrapping her shawl tightly around her shoulders, her movements slow and deliberate. I felt her eyes on me for a moment before she stooped to kiss my forehead.

"I find myself in need of a walk as well. I'll go find Chelle. Things will work themselves out, dear." Her footsteps drifted out of the room.

I couldn't fully suppress my resentment. *Things never work themselves out, we have to work them out ourselves. And by We, I mean Me.*

As much as I loved my family, none of them were ambitious. My father had rare spurts of activity, but only in regard to his research. Mama ran an impeccable household, but never looked outside the family sphere. Chelle was only eighteen, too young and sheltered to make things happen. It was inevitably down to me.

What drives this Prince? Every person has a goal or desire, or even a secret, that ultimately drives their actions, including the Prince. It was simply a question of figuring out what would make it more attractive for him to leave us alone than to enforce his rights.

If I were a princess of our realm, I could offer some other border cities in exchange, like the King did with Charmagne. But the only asset we had of any remote value was Croiseux Dower House, and the Prince already had rights to it. Even though the Dower House had many little secret hideaways, none of them were likely to contain a fabulous and long forgotten treasure, valuable enough to buy the Prince's sanity back. The only other thing of any value were our titles. And of course you couldn't sell them. They transferred through blood, marriage, or not at all.

An idea flickered into my head as Hazel reached for my teacup.

"Are you heading to your parent's cottage right now?" I asked, trying to quell the hope rising in my chest. She nodded. "Would you mind delaying that trip for a day or two?"

Her mouth formed a grimace. "Not one bit. There doesn't seem to be much we can do, and I don't look forward to containing the panic it will send Ma into. Besides, Da was supposed to take my brother out to practice setting snares, so he won't even be home yet. Why?"

"I may have an idea," I said hesitantly. "Actually—I do have an idea, but I'm going to need your help. Meet me in my room as soon as you're done with the tea things, and don't mention anything to Mrs. Comfry."

* * *

Hazel slipped into my room just as I opened my wardrobe door.

"So, what is this idea you mentioned?" she asked, skeptically. "You're a veteran schemer, but the forces at work here are beyond even your capabilities."

I lifted my eyebrows at her and pulled a bag out of my wardrobe, throwing it over to the bed. "Thank you for that glowing recommendation. With encouragement like that, I can reach for the stars."

She put her hands on her hips and pursed her her lips. "Belle, be serious."

"I am serious." I put my hands on my hips, mirroring her pose. "You know me better than anyone. You know what parts of my heart I've sacrificed to benefit my family." I rubbed my forehead with both hands before pressing them against my heart.

"I have wanted to travel—to see our country, the royal court, and other countries and royal courts. I want to publish research in my own name alongside Papa. I want freedom, and security, and respect. I was raised to expect it as a child. My parents taught me to anticipate that the possibilities for those things would come my way eventually." I threw my hands in the air in exasperation.

"Well they haven't. I'm *twenty-five*, and none of those dreams are in sight. The only option in front of me is to marry that *paragon* of manliness, Eddie Marchand, when he returns; a hero, no doubt because he would conduct himself in no less a manner at all times."

I rolled my eyes in disgust. "All to regain what should have been ours to begin with, and provide enough money for my parents to live a life of ease as they grow older instead of writing and sewing every hour of the day in hopes of a few extra pennies. Not to mention provide Chelle with a dowry to find someone of our own rank instead of dying a spinster, or worse, marrying someone who can barely keep a roof over her head." I let lose a frustrated breath and started throwing stockings and handkerchiefs into my bag.

"Belle, I know all this," Hazel replied firmly. "But your parents and Chelle have never asked that of you. I don't think they want the same future that you do."

"Well they should have wanted it. And they should have wanted more for me." I shook my head and turned to face her. "None of it matters. I had resigned myself to my fate. But now, that future doesn't exist anymore. We'll all be out on the street soon, except for me because I will have married Saint Eddie Marchand, destined to make do on a small income and be a saintly little wife, mothering saintly little children, supporting her saintly husband. He's expecting to marry a paragon of womanly virtue to match his own perfection, and though I may be a Lady, you and I both know I'm no saint. He would do better to search out the Lady of the Woods and marry her instead," I muttered waspishly. Turning back to my wardrobe, I pulled out a petticoat and dress, shoving them into my bags as I continued my tirade.

"No. I will be on the streets with the rest of you after the Prince turns us out, unless we do something now. We have to! Just think, if your family is thrown out, which Papa said seems likely, you would have to move in with your sister in town, which would be ruinous for Holly's constitution. If she has another turn like she did last year, your mother wouldn't be able to forage in the woods for medicine. The Creator only knows how my family would survive." I gave a mirthless laugh as Hazel watched, concern growing on her brow. Silence stretched between us as I gathered my resolve.

"Someone has to do *something*, and that someone is me," I declared in a low voice, setting my jaw. "I have a plan that will work. It's a bit dangerous, and we'll need a lot of luck, but I *need* your help. Will you help me?"

She took a deep breath and let it out slowly. "You're right. You're especially right about Holly. I'll help. What do you have in mind?"

I let out a breath of my own, relief flooding my limbs. A Lady would never travel without a chaperone, and I needed to draw on every ounce of breeding I possessed to pull this off.

If I'm even reading the situation correctly. I released that thought quickly. There would be time for self-doubt if my gamble failed. *Thankfully, I hail from a family with centuries of haughty self-assurance to rely on in times of crises.* Even if it seemed to have skipped my parents and sister, I had it in spades. It just might help me brazen things out long enough to secure our future, and some of the dreams I had long thought dead.

"Grab your overnight bag and cloak and ready the farm horses," I directed Hazel as I went back to my wardrobe to retrieve a pair of shoes. "I'll meet you at the stable in a few minutes and tell you everything once we're on the way."

She nodded and stole away, closing the door inaudibly. I sent a prayer to the Creator—whether asking for blessing or expressing relief, or a little of both, I don't know—and continued packing. Just as I closed my wardrobe door, Mama peeked through the door.

"Darling, we're taking lunch in our rooms..." she trailed off, staring at my bag with wide eyes. "What on earth is going on?"

"Mama, I don't have much time to explain, but I need you to listen." Securing my bag, I fixed her with my most authoritative look. "I think I can save Croiseux, but I have to leave immediately, before anything else happens."

"But where are you going?"

"To Asileboix Castle."

She gaped at me in shocked silence. Crossing the few steps

between us in my cramped room, I grabbed her arms firmly and stooped so I could look directly into her eyes.

"You must let me go, Mama, and you must *not* tell Papa until tomorrow at least. I have a plan, one that might work." I turned away to retrieve my gloves from where they sat on my writing desk. Mama followed close behind, protesting in a hushed tone.

"Rosebelle! You can't be serious! Even if you are, I can't allow you to go alone. It's too dangerous." Her hands fluttered uselessly as she spoke.

"I'll follow Papa's map. He just traveled there without incident so there's no reason to fear it's not safe. Besides, I won't be alone, Hazel's coming. They're people, Mama, not beasts. The worst they'll do is give us a room for the night and send us on our way tomorrow. In fact, I plan on being back by dinner tomorrow in any event. I don't think it will take much time for the Prince to change his mind, and knowing I'm expected home will be a deterrent for anything unchivalrous."

I gave her an encouraging look as I pulled my cloak over my shoulders. She reached out to fasten the clasp, resignation on her brow.

"What do you know that will sway his mind?" she entreated quietly.

"I think I've figured out what he wants more than Croiseux. I won't say more now because I don't want to get your hopes up." Hunching my shoulders, I looked her in the eyes again. "Please don't tell Papa until I'm too far away for him to go after me. He's in no state to be reasonable, and I need to move fast if this is going to work. I know what I'm doing, Mama. Can you trust me?"

"I do trust you darling." She wrinkled her brow. "As your mother, I really shouldn't allow this." She smoothed the shoulders of my cape and kissed my cheek. "Just don't promise something that isn't yours to give."

"I won't, Mama," I replied, then kissed her back and proceeded down the stairs, slipping out the side door unseen.

* * *

Hazel was finishing with the horses' tack as I made my way into our small barn. She turned to help me stuff my pack into a saddlebag and load it on my mount, Star.

"The horses are ready. Are you sure they won't be missed?"

I cinched the saddlebag tight and stroked Star's mane. "No, we should be fine. I ran into Mama. She said she'd cover for us. Besides, the ground has been too hard to finish plowing. We just need to leave without Papa noticing." Grabbing Star's reins, I led him out of his stall. Hazel followed suit with the other horse, Firefly. Once through the gate, we mounted, walking the horses toward the path in the woods my father had so recently traversed.

Star and Firefly technically belonged to the Marchands, but we borrowed them frequently for work on our small farm. They wouldn't be the fastest mounts, especially as Hazel wasn't a good rider, but they were reliable and would get us to our destination.

I couldn't help looking back over my shoulder, worried that we would been seen. My fear lessened as we entered the woods, and I started to relax. Smoke from the gamekeeper's cottage was visible through the trees, and my stomach grumbled at the thought of Mrs. Veneur's rabbit pies. For a moment I imagined tying the horses to the gatepost and bundling into the kitchen, warming our hands at the fire and snitching a pie when no one was looking—just as we had done countless times as children, with Eddie Marchand and Henri LeFeu in tow.

Instead, we continued single file down the old horse trail, foregoing warmth and kindness for a bitter ride to an uncertain welcome. As expected from Papa's map, the horse trail dumped onto an ancient carriage path between Croiseux and Asileboix. We slowed to a halt as we stepped on to it.

To the East, trees gradually began to thin, the highest tower of Croiseux barely visible in the distance. To the West, the woodland became thicker and dotted with pine, gloomy even in the middle of the day. If we took that road, and made good time, we would reach Asileboix Castle well before sunset.

I looked back toward Croiseux, memories dancing across my eyes. Childhood games of Knights and Maidens played in its gardens, Hazel and I running as Henri played the Beastman of Asileboix, Eddie the Knight swooping in to save us. Now, I was about to enter the land of our game's villain, to see if if he could save us instead.

I shook my head, clearing cobwebs. Time to move on, not daydream over what was already lost. Nudging my horse into a walk, I guided him to the west, Hazel following in my wake.

The disused cart path we followed suddenly turned into a well maintained lane as we passed into Asileboix. Hazel and I looked at each other in surprise. Croiseux hadn't had visitors from Asileboix for generations. Surely there was no reason for them to maintain the path. I shrugged. It didn't matter to me if they wasted money on such things. We urged our horses into a trot on the smooth, wide path.

As we rode I strategized my upcoming conversation with the Prince. The main problem I foresaw, assuming my father's sketch of his character was accurate, was correctly assessing whatever mood he happened to be in, and whether my arrival worsened his disposition to see sense. I couldn't rely on a purely rational conversation with him—I couldn't rely on a purely rational conversation with *most* people on *most* days, actually—so I would need to maneuver my way into it. Growing up in Pelerin, I had learned quickly that people responded better if they felt they could play the hero. I would need to temper my habit of appearing self-sufficient.

The forest passed by, gloomy and quiet. We met no one, not even when our small path converged on a main road. The shadows were lengthening by the time we saw towers peeking out of the trees ahead. I signaled to Hazel and we slowed to a stop.

"I need your help changing into my Sunday dress and getting my hair into some sort of order," I told her as we dismounted. "I can't show up looking like country mouse."

She snorted as we led our horses to a stand of trees near a thicket. "You are a country mouse. Your best Sunday dress isn't going to change that."

"I know that, and you know that. I suppose the Prince knows it too since they met Papa. However, that doesn't mean I have to look like it," I shot back.

Hazel laughed, securing our horses as I pulled my dress from the saddlebag. Slipping behind some bushes to screen me from view, I brushed as much dust from my petticoats as I could and stripped off my cloak. Hazel helped undo the buttons of my work dress, holding it steady as I wriggled out of it, frosty air biting exposed skin as I rushed to pull on my sky blue skirt and jacket, usually reserved for Sundays and special occasions. Shivering, I fumbled with the buttons along the front while Hazel settled my cape back around my shoulders.

"So, will you finally tell me your plan?" she asked as she unraveled my usual severe bun and brushed out my hair with her fingers.

"It's fairly simple," I answered, drawing in a breath of wintry air. "I'm going to propose marriage."

My long hair thumped against my back as Hazel dropped it in surprise.

"What?!" Hazel yelped, her voice echoing in the trees.

"Hush!" I hissed back. "I know how it sounds, but the Prince has been trying to marry a Pelerine noblewoman for years." I shot a look over my shoulder. "You may recall that I'm a Pelerine noblewoman. Supposedly he wanted a duchess. Since he couldn't get one, I'm hoping he'll settle for the daughter of a Marquess, which is almost as good. I'll demand that he retroactively approve the sale of Croiseux in writing as part of marriage articles. Voila! All our problems solved, and I become a princess as well."

My hair lifted off my back again as Hazel started working it into a braid.

"You've forgotten one thing," she murmured wryly as she coiled it into a bun, tying it off with a ribbon.

"I've probably forgotten any number of things, my shawl being one of them," I laughed.

She grabbed my shoulders and spun me around. "Well this one is important: you're already engaged!"

"I haven't forgotten that. But you've forgotten that it was never formalized. We've been expected to marry since the sale of the house, but it wasn't a condition of the deed!"

Hazel frowned at me for a moment, pulling tendrils of hair out to frame my face. "I know you've never been crazy about Eddie, but he loves you. Are you sure you want to give up marrying him for a man threatening to take everything away from you?"

I snorted. "Well, to be perfectly honest, I would rather marry neither and instead be swept off my feet by one of the Princes in the capitol! But since that isn't an option, then yes, I would rather take my chances as a Princess of Asileboix, knowing my family and friends are safe, than as the wife of Captain Marchand, my family and friends suffering and knowing I hadn't tried everything to spare them."

Hazel flattened her mouth into a straight line but said nothing as we walked back to the horses. I folded my everyday dress as neatly as I could before tucking it in my saddlebag.

"Not long now, my lucky Star," I whispered as I untied my horse's reins. "I'll need all the luck you can give me today."

I could hear Hazel mumbling to Firefly behind me, no doubt unloading all her worries about her crazy friend on him. She probably wasn't wrong.

Ten minutes later, we were hailed by the first person we had seen since leaving the Dower House. A large stone wall crossed the path up ahead, a uniformed soldier standing by the gatehouse.

"Travelers, state your business," he called as we approached. I cleared my throat nervously, preparing my haughtiest aristocratic voice.

"I am Lady Rosebelle Montanarte of Pelerin. I seek an audience with the Prince of Asileboix on an urgent matter."

He looked us up and down, and apparently deciding we wouldn't be a threat, moved aside to let us pass. He yelled over his shoulder to someone inside the gatehouse, then turned his attention back to us. "If you wait a moment Lady, my squire will take you to the castle."

A youth appeared through the gatehouse door a moment later, grinning up at us, his face wide and honest. He scrambled up on a nearby pony, motioning us to follow. We passed by several fields, mostly barren except for a few winter crops. A walled city loomed in the background, dominating everything surrounding it. The guards at the next gate exchanged greetings with our guide, staring at us with open curiosity.

Hazel and I exchanged a glance as we passed into the city. *A very country mouse indeed,* I thought ruefully.

I had expected filthy, cramped alleys, like I remembered from my last visit to Pelerin's capitol. Instead, we traversed clean, winding streets lined with cheerful shops. People scurried about their business, well-dressed and busy. An ancient castle rose above everything in the distance, strong and impenetrable.

Our squire stationed us by a roaring fire in the entry hall of the castle before jogging over to a servant on the other side of the room. After a brief discussion, he hurried back in our direction.

"Someone will show you up soon, milady," he told me, stopping only long enough to sketch a short bow before trotting away, starting up a cheerful whistling tune that was at odds with the cavernous grandeur of the castle.

A footman appeared as if from thin air. "Follow me, please," he intoned, treading toward a large open archway. Following a few steps behind, we hurried to keep up. After a dizzying labyrinth of corridors and twisting stairs, we arrived in front of a pair of small but ornately carved wooden doors. My throat felt dry as he stepped inside to announce us.

"Lady Rosebelle Montanarte, requesting an audience with Prince Andrus."

As the footman stepped back out, he ushered us into a long, low room. An immense table dominated the space, a map spread across it. Late afternoon sun streamed in from a row of small windows. Fires burned in grates at either end of the room, making it markedly warmer than the hall.

A man stood at the far end of the table, holding a cup in one hand and a stack of papers in the other. He was dressed simply, but his air of command was unmistakable. Two other men, civil servants by the look of them, made to leave, but the Prince stopped them with a flick of his eyes. I dipped into a perfect full curtsy.

"Lady Montanarte," the man observed evenly after letting me sit in my curtsy for a minute, "why are you here?"

I rose and settled my skirts. Taking a fortifying breath, I looked him in the eye. "Your Royal Highness, thank you for seeing me. I've come in response to some distressing news I have lately heard from my father." His eyes narrowed and my pulse ratcheted up. It took every ounce of control I possessed not to let it bleed into my voice.

"Just this morning, he relayed a conversation he had with you regarding the sale of our beloved Croiseux many years ago. It seems Your Highness should have been consulted for approval before the land and manor left my family's ownership. By a strange chance, that technicality was missed, and the sale to the Marchands completed. Upon realizing that your rights had been overlooked, you of course notified my father that you would be enforcing them, to the effect that we will all be turned out onto the street."

The Prince shifted, a frown forming on his face as the other men shot him questioning glances. I rushed on before he could interrupt.

"My father assures me that you are completely within your rights to do such a thing. Quite simply, I am here to implore you on behalf of my mother, my younger sister, and myself, whether there is anything we can *do* or *give* to change your mind."

I ended this speech by pressing my hands to my stomach to emphasize my poor womanly nerves. *Not exactly an act at this point*, I thought to myself. If I had misread the situation, I wasn't going to get another opportunity to paint a picture of feminine vulnerability that I calculated would appeal to a prince.

As I watched him from across the room, I wasn't sure my speech excited any empathy at all. The body language of the civil servants standing near him was tense. *In reaction to my sad tale, or in anticipation of the Prince's reaction?* Hazel fidgeted a few paces behind me.

Prince Andrus moved finally, frowning as he put his goblet and papers down before bracing himself on the table in front of him.

"My lady", he addressed me, his tone clipped," I'm not usually inclined to put gently bred ladies out of their homes, but the law is clear in this instance. Your father laid out your family's situation in detail. He lost all his wealth in the Beast War. What else could you offer me?"

I breathed an internal sigh of relief. *Thank you for stepping neatly into that opening.*

"Then take me."

Shock hit the prince's face and left so quickly I almost I missed it. Out of the corner of my eye, I could see his servants' startled movements and knew I need to press my advantage.

"As you mentioned, I don't have any great wealth or property to offer you in exchange for approving the property settlement. But I *am* the oldest daughter of the Marquess of Montanarte and Earl of Croiseux. The property associated with those honorifics has diminished, but the titles remain. My father is still active in parliament and his duties to the crown, so a connection with our family would secure you a line to the Pelerine royal ear."

A slight exaggeration, but I didn't expect the prince would know that. I took a deep breath, clutching my forearms, and pressing my advantage.

"A marriage between us could build further relations between the two countries. I have almost nothing, but my blood and lineage could offer you much."

His eyebrows quirked up as I said the word blood, and I wondered if these supposed "beast men" were more squeamish than I thought. A giggle threatened to escape but scolded it back down.

"A marriage alliance? In exchange for your family's home?" The prince folded his arms, looking thoughtful.

My heart hammered in my chest, and I felt faint around the edges, having missed lunch during our long ride.

He examined me appraisingly, raising color in my cheeks. "I'm surprised you're not married already."

I could hear the '*at your age*' hanging off the end of his statement, and stiffened.

"In a spirit of transparency, I must tell you that I have been *informally* engaged to the eldest son of the Marchand family for the last five years. However, he's been away in the Beast War —it was never formalized."

I looked down at the floor and clutched my forearms even harder. This was the biggest hurdle to my position right now. I didn't want to look as though I was a promise breaker, but I wanted to make it clear that there was no impediment between us. "It was never made legally binding. He and his family would not stand in my way if you desire an alliance between us."

The Prince studied me with a furrowed brow, then barked a sudden laugh. "I'm beginning to wonder if anything ever stands in *your* way, Lady Montanarte. So, you would break your engagement to the man you love, leave your family and country, and marry someone you've just met. All to secure the property agreement between your father and the Marchands."

"Indeed, Sire," I responded, my eyes rooted to where his

hands leaned against the table. Not precisely correct in his assessment of what Eddie meant to me, but close enough.

"Of course, you would also become a princess."

My eyes flew to his, registering a slight sneer on his face. He bowed his head and adjusted a stack of papers.

"And perhaps it wouldn't be so bad for her," he muttered to himself, almost inaudibly. He looked up at me again. "It's late. A journey through the woods at night can be dangerous. You will stay here tonight."

I inclined my head, wondering at the change in conversation as he turned to one of his servants.

"Have a room prepared for Lady Montanarte and her attendant, then inform my mother that we will have a guest at dinner." Looking toward the other servant, he issued instructions regarding the papers on the table in front of him before directing his gaze toward me again. Straightening up, he strode purposefully around the room, offering me his arm when he reached my side. "Allow me to escort you to a drawing room while your chambers are prepared."

With a nervous swallow, I assented, taking his arm with as much composure as I could muster. Hazel followed as we swept out of the room and down the hall. He was *much* larger up close. I took after my father in height, so I was used being eye to eye with most men. Prince Andrus had to be half a foot taller than I was, and as broad and tan as the field laborers in summer. Now that I thought about it, although he was well spoken and had an air of authority, he didn't have nearly the royal polish and finesse I remembered from court visits in my youth.

Hazel and Mama's warnings sounded in my ears, but I tuned them out. It was a little late now.

The Prince stopped at the door of a formal drawing room, motioning us inside. Hazel followed swiftly behind as I entered, my eyes flitted over a sumptuously furnished room before I turned back to the Prince.

"You've given me much to think about, Lady Montanarte,

but I won't keep you waiting. I'll have answer for you at dinner tonight, if you will join me and my mother in an hour's time."

"I would be honored. My own family is expecting me back tomorrow evening. I would like to return with your wishes made known."

He stared at me impassively for a moment, then sketched a bow, closing the door behind him as he left.

Turning, I lurched over to the fireplace, a long breath escaping as I threw myself onto a small sofa. My head tipped back to recline against the back rest.

"Dinner in an hour. I'll waste away of hunger and nerves by then," I moaned, closing my eyes.

Hazel flopped into a chair next to me. "Belle, if we make it out of here alive I'm going to shoot you with my bow at the next deer hunt and claim it was a tragic accident."

"I feel like I've heard that threat before," I teased with a grin, my eyes still closed. "I always convince you to refrain from murder in the end, don't I?"

"I've always said you could talk your way into anything," Hazel shot back, stretching her feet toward the fire. "I guess we'll know if that's true by tonight."

Opening my eyes, I looked at the flames dancing over glowing embers in the fireplace. *After dinner, my fate will be sealed one way or the other.* Suddenly, I wasn't hungry any longer.

CHAPTER THREE

Andrus

The drawing room door closed with a click. I stood unmoving for a moment, considering the ladies I had left inside. In truth, just the one lady. The other had been a short, nondescript shadow behind a brightly burning torch.

Lady Rosebelle Montanarte.

She was irritating; complicating a mess I had already cleared up. Slight too, compared to most of the women in Asileboix. *Although, not nearly as small as her tiny maid.*

Catching a passing footman, I directed him to track down my attorney and request his services in my study after dinner, then climbed to my tower chambers.

When I had reviewed my schedule this morning, I had briefly wished that some interruption would save me from Manciple's onerous thrift reports. Not the noblest thought a Prince has ever had, but my patience had become increasingly thin these last few days.

Never, not in my wildest dreams, would I have imagined someone like Lady Rosebelle coming to my rescue: in the form of a marriage proposal, no less.

I clenched my fists. *After all those years chasing an alliance with Pelerin, here was a woman practically handing me the opportunity on a silver platter.* A laugh escaped me. No, this wasn't how I thought my afternoon would go.

Entering my chambers, I passed directly through to my dressing room and began changing for dinner. Just a small family dinner, but especially now that we had a guest, I wanted to look a little more like a Prince and less like a woodsman masquerading as a Prince.

Lady Rosebelle's image flashed into my head. Even in the relatively plain clothes she had worn, she was beautiful. Striking amber eyes, high cheekbones, a long straight nose. Her shiny light brown hair had strands of gold in it, reminding me of the morning sun streaming through the trees. A welcome sight at the end of a full moon patrol.

I shook my head. *Am I really mooning over her obvious beauty?* It irritated me that I had even noticed it. What she had proposed was a simple business transaction, and I needed to treat it as such. Besides, what sort of woman rides into a foreign castle and proposes to a stranger? *A brave or foolhardy one*, I thought as I tugged a comb through my hair.

Or a desperate one. I stared at myself in the mirror hanging over my washbasin. She *was* desperate to save her home and her loved ones. I had been the one to put her in that position.

My reflection stared back at me. *Not exactly the type of man my sixteen-year-old self imagined I would be at this age, am I?* He would never have entertained her proposal—forcing her to leave her home, parting her from the man she had been waiting for. He wouldn't have put her in such a situation in the first place. Could I?

Undoubtedly, and with little remorse, I told my reflection sternly as I continued my preparations. Besides, my sixteen-year-old self hadn't been through half the horrors my thirty-one-year-old self had been. Nor did he have the future of Asileboix hanging on his shoulders. A future that depended on making a match almost exactly like the one that had landed in my lap. We needed allies. I needed heirs from a clear bloodline. The solution to both those issues was tied to the Lady waiting for my response at dinner.

What will she be like as a wife?

I snorted. As long as she was sensible and good-hearted, that was more than I could wish for beyond being of the right status and bloodline. She seemed a little haughty, but was sacrificing her own future for the benefit of her family. I couldn't think of a more good-hearted action.

I ran back through our conversation in the cabinet room as I put my arm in the sleeve of my dinner jacket. For all of her apparent altruism, I was a bit skeptical with her image as a damsel in distress. She was certainly in a unfortunate situation, but she seemed... more intelligent and tightly controlled than desperate. At several points in the conversation, I had wondered whether I was the one holding all the cards after all. I had all the power to decide her future, but I couldn't shake the feeling that she was the one leading me down the path to my own fate.

A quick shiver went down my spine and I rolled my eyes, pulling my jacket on fully. *What has gotten into me?* I needed to get out of this suffocating castle and back on patrol in the woods. Still, my defenses were on high alert. There was something about her that I couldn't quite place. Something familiar. Something that made me feel wistful. And that made me irritated.

As I attempted to button my jacket sleeves, a knock sounded at my sitting room door.

"Enter!" I shouted, leaning partially out of my dressing room to see who it was. My mother strode into sight.

"Andrus my boy, I hear there are schemes afoot!"

"Ah, Mother. Help me button my sleeves. They're in danger of being ripped off soon." I held up my wrist as evidence.

Reaching through the dressing room door, she quickly buttoned the offending articles, putting her hands on her hips when she finished.

"I've come to see you amidst rumors of a beautiful girl in the castle, declaring her fortunes as destitute and proposing marriage to all and sundry, and all you can talk about is sleeves that won't button themselves?"

She clucked her tongue. "Your mother obviously didn't take the time to teach you any manners. Oh wait, that was me— well, I did my best, you can't blame these things on the parents you know!" She leaned in and kissed my cheek, laughing at her own joke.

"If you're done amusing yourself, Mother, I will indeed address the elephant in the room. Or Lady in the castle, if you prefer."

"Comparing your potential bride to an elephant? Not an auspicious start," she shot back, raising her eyebrows.

Shaking my head, I looked in the mirror to start wrestling with my cravat. "What did Lueren tell you?"

"Only that a woman claiming to be Lady Montanarte—the daughter, not the wife of the person we had staying with us last week—had waltzed into your meeting and proposed marriage."

"In essence, yes. Although I don't seem to recall the waltzing. She *is* his daughter. I recognize her from the portrait he showed us at dinner the other evening."

I ceased my efforts with my cravat, looking over at her. "She seems familiar somehow though. Did we meet their family when I was in Pelerin?"

She shrugged. "Not that I recall. I must say, I admire a woman who can charge into a castle and take ownership of it in one fell swoop. Perhaps you should hire her to lead the army. General Morvan could retire!"

I chuckled and turned back to my cravat as she continued. "But seriously, my dear, I would like to have a say."

"You can have it. Proceed."

"Impertinence! I mean I'd like to have a talk with her at dinner before you tell her yes."

"Of course I want your opinion first, and Clement's too. I can't make a decision like this without a little guidance."

"Nonsense, you've already made your decision." She folded

her arms and I looked up in surprise from where I stooped to change my shoes.

"You forget I'm your mother. I've known you since before you knew yourself. If it was a 'no' you would have thrown her out in the streets for interrupting your precious time with Manciple's thrift reports. Instead of buttoning your sleeves, I would be out on the streets too, begging her pardon and asking her to kindly and quietly stay the night before returning home to spread tales of our inhospitality."

I laughed in spite of myself.

"Well?" she pressed, triumphantly. "Tell me I'm wrong!"

"You're not wrong about my decision. I can't pass this up. She has enough political connection that Pelerin will be forced to give us an ear now and then, and of course she's of a clear bloodline. That's the most important thing." I stood up, jamming my heel into the sole of my shoe.

"There seems to be a matter of a prior betrothal with the heir of the family that bought Croiseux. Apparently it was never formalized. Even if it was, we could surely buy him off since he's facing eviction as well."

My mother reached out to brush lint off my sleeve as I frowned in thought.

"I wish I had more time to get to know her. You and I both know any Princess of ours doesn't have a life of ease. But we need to get this done quickly, especially since Pelerin is withdrawing from the Wasteland. Her intended may come home to remind her that it's possible to survive on love alone or some nonsense, and I'll be left without options again at the worst possible time."

Smoothing the front of my jacket, I closed my wardrobe door and stepped out of my dressing room. "I admire her bravery at least. She would be another in a long tradition of brave Asilean Princesses."

"Well, now I'm bashful," my mother joked, moving toward the door and waiting for me to open it. "Assuming you include me in that long line. For all I know, I'm the only one not on the list." She shot me a mock scowl before settling back into a smile. "In all seriousness, let me chat with her for a few minutes before you say anything. It sounds too good to be true. But I warn you, unless she's part troll, I'm going to approve. After all, I expected to be knee-deep in grandchildren by now, but they've been curiously slow to arrive."

Growling as I opened the door, I ushered her out into the corridor. "Do not *dare* mention grandchildren at dinner, Mother. You said yourself that this is too good to be true. I can't have you scaring her off before she's properly ensnared."

Mother laughed and took my arm. "I make no promises! You'll have to take your chances. And you had better lighten up before *you* scare her off." She shook her head. "By all means, let's see what we can make of her. As long as she's sensible you have as good a chance at happiness as any. Whether you've known your spouse since you were children, like your Father and I, or for only a few weeks before marrying, like the Manciples, it's more about choosing to say yes to your vows every day afterward than anything else."

She squeezed my arm as we walked down the passageway. "Enough pearls of wisdom from your aged mother. Let's hurry! I'm eager to meet her. Clement left to escort her to the dining room when I came to find you. They're probably waiting on us."

* * *

They were indeed waiting outside our private family dining room. Wearing the same blue and white dress she had arrived in, Lady Rosebelle stood in front of a portrait of my grandfather with his hunting hounds, her hands clasped demurely around her forearms. Clement stood next to her, gesturing toward the painting. A ghost of a laugh escaped her and one hand flew to her mouth. Clement grinned. He was probably relating the marriage proposal story.

Grandfather's hounds had made off with his formal court wig when he knelt to propose to my grandmother. Clement's family used to live next door her, and Clement's father had actually witnessed the event, which had taken place in the back garden. I remember Clement's father laughing over it with my grandmother when I was a boy. Now, Clement loved to trot the story out to newcomers any chance he got, which wasn't often.

Mother let out a laugh as well. "He wasted no time besmirching our family's dignity, I see."

At the sound of her voice, Lady Rosebelle and Clement turned toward us. Mother let go of my arm and stepped ahead of me, kissing Clement on the cheek before turning to our visitor.

"I'm Dowager Princess Mathilde De Vermeille," she announced, stretching out her hand, "but you may call me Mathilde."

Lady Rosebelle took her outstretched hand and dipped into a deep curtsy, saying gravely as she rose again ,"It's an honor to meet you, Your Royal Highness."

Mother shot me an amused smile. "Ah yes. I can see I've shocked you with my informality. But we're having a family dinner tonight, and I don't allow anyone to fling 'Your Highness' at me in such circumstances, not even the servers. You may call me "Madame", and we shall approach Mathilde if my son agrees to your recent request."

Lady Rosebelle flicked her eyes toward me as she dropped my mother's hand. She looked even more grave than she had before. *Does she disapprove of my mother's friendliness?* That thought raised my hackles. She was the one who had come to our castle asking for help. Now she was looking down her nose our Princess? And after all we've done for Pelerin over the centuries?

My shoulders began to tighten. Balling my hands into fists, I flexed them discretely to mimic letting go of my anger. No one in Pelerin knew of the protection we provided them, so I couldn't fault her ignorance, and her pride was hardly surprising, given my other interactions with the Pelerine people.

Mother had continued her stream of words while I wrestled my irritation under control.

"Etiquette is much more formal in Pelerin, is it not? I shouldn't be talking of proposals and waiving away titles in our first conversation." She laughed and smiled kindly at Lady Rosebelle. "I'm glad we're only having a family dinner tonight. It will be much easier to get to know one another than at a formal affair.

She turned toward Clement, taking his arm, and looked back at me. "I shall leave you to escort Lady Rosebelle in, Andrus. And do blow that thundercloud off of your forehead. Your glowering will put us all off of our appetites." She leaned in to whisper an aside to Lady Rosebelle, "He gets very moody if he hasn't eaten in awhile. He'll be as gentle as a lamb by the end of dinner."

I let out a huff of annoyance as Clement guided my mother into the dining room. She was being tactless on purpose, trying to see the effect of it on Lady Rosebelle's character, but I wasn't exactly in a mood to indulge her. I tried to loosen some of the tension apparently still showing on my face and held out my arm to Lady Rosebelle.

She dipped a small curtsy and murmured, "Your Highness," glancing up at me briefly with a small, forced smile. Her face was definitely tinged red, I noticed, as I led her into the dining room. She had obviously been embarrassed by my mother's speech, no doubt wondering how she would get through an entire dinner with us. If she aimed to become a Princess of the Asileans, she would have to let go of some of that Pelerine delicacy.

I snorted quietly as I imagined her hosting her first reception for our allies from Sherwood. She would faint dead away at *their* manners.

Nodding at the server as I pushed Lady Rosebelle's chair in

for her, the first course was placed on the table just as I settled into my own chair. Clement glanced at me as he served my mother some of the delicious looking vegetable stew.

"Did you have a chance to ride today, Andrus?" he inquired, then turned to serve Lady Rosebelle, giving her a friendly smile.

"No, unfortunately. I was embroiled with Manciple's reports half of the day. Our patrol will be the next chance I have for fresh air." I moved to serve myself as Mother beamed across the table at Lady Rosebelle.

"And you have this young lady to thank for relieving you from your meeting, don't you Andrus?"

She addressed our guest as she turned toward her soup. "Do tell us about your family. Your father talked of you all with obvious love and affection, but he soon wandered into discussing books again. You have a younger sister, I believe?"

Lady Rosebelle settled a reserved smile on her face as she set her spoon down. "There isn't much to tell, Madame. We live simply. My mother runs our household. My sister takes after her, and they devote much of their time assisting anyone in our parish who is in need." Her eyes seemed to soften for a moment as she talked of them. Then she picked up her spoon again.

"You've met my father. He dotes on us all, but can easily be caught up in the details of his work." She let out a small breath and smiled. "I heard you speak of taking a ride earlier. Are you all fond of riding?" she directed to the table in general before taking a bite of her stew.

The conversation continued much the same as dinner progressed. My mother attempting to draw her out, Lady Rosebelle giving concise, polite answers. Clement was more focused on eating than conversation, as was his wont, but spoke now and again to assist my mother. I contributed little. Lady Rosebelle's reserved, and to my mind, cold demeanor irritated my restlessness.

As the dessert plates were being cleared away, my mother

caught my eye and gave me an obvious nod and wink. I glanced at Lady Rosebelle to ensure she hadn't seen, closing my eyes in relief to find her focused on folding her napkin instead of Mother's stage-worthy theatrics. Opening my eyes again I shot my mother a frown. Far from repentant, she smirked, her eyes harboring a mischievous glint.

Setting down my cutlery, I settled back, resting my hands on the arms of my chair. There was no need for a flowery speech, considering Lady Rosebelle's own directness in her earlier proposal. As I cleared my throat, my dining companions each glanced over at me.

"I told you I wouldn't be long in answering your proposal, Lady Rosebelle, and I have already come to a decision," I declared, looking directly at her. Her face was curiously emotionless as she held my eyes.

"In exchange for your hand in marriage, I agree to retroactively approve the terms of your father's sale of Croiseux and file such approval at the property archives in Asileboix and Pelerin, but I have a few conditions of my own."

Lady Rosebelle's eyes watched me from an expressionless face, betraying no reaction whatsoever to my acceptance of her request. I continued on, ticking off my stipulations on my hands as I spoke.

"The wedding must take place directly after the New Year celebrations. Although you will be allowed to make regular visits to your family after our marriage, you will only be permitted to bring one or two trusted servants with you. They must be approved by Clement, my senior Guardsman, in advance of the wedding. Finally, your father, Lord Montanarte, must immediately abandon his research of my family's genealogy as well as the Lady of the Woods in general for the remainder of his life. He may not write or publish on the subject."

Her polished mask cracked at the last requirement, eyes widening and mouth dropping open in horror.

"Give up his research?! Why?!"

I crossed my arms before responding. "It's offensive to me, and is an absolute requirement of our marriage. That's all I'm prepared to say. But know this: if he were to break his word, you would all suffer immediate and severe consequences. So long as he keeps to it, all will be as you've asked. Will you accept?"

Her mouth pressed flat as she struggled to conceal her anger and disbelief. *This is the first real emotion I've seen since she walked in here.* I had thought she would be puzzled and perhaps suspicious, but I expected more concern over the quick wedding date and restriction on servants.

"My dear," my mother prompted softly, as silence stretched on for several minutes while Rosebelle and I glared at each other. We both started in our seats and looked over at her.

"I do apologize, I was—well I was listening out for hounds, as you can imagine," Lady Rosebelle replied, surprising me with a reference to my grandfather's proposal. Offering the barest hint of a smile as she glanced between Mother and Clement, all traces of it had vanished by the time she looked back over at me.

"I would be honored to accept your conditions, Sire. But I must tell you, I'm wholly surprised by the last one. In ceasing to publish his research, he would lose a portion of his income. In exchange, I must ask that you provide him with a bride gift, or, perhaps settle a dower portion for me, which I can use to assist my family."

A flash of exasperation shot through me. She was just like the other Pelerines I had encountered: expecting an Asilean "Beast Man," as they called us, to act utterly without honor. I tried to suppress my temper, but couldn't help the bite in my voice as I responded with a mocking smile.

"Yes, Lady Rosebelle. I will pay your family a bride *price*, in addition to the concessions over their property."

She flinched at my use of the ancient term for the groom's financial obligation, but it seemed appropriate to me. I was essentially buying protection for my family's secrets, in exchange for her family's security and wealth.

Although she seemed to waiver between embarrassment of the directness of our conversation and bewilderment of what must seem like strange conditions, she certainly understood that as well. Again, I had the brief impression that although I was in the position of the power in our negotiations, she seemed as if she held all the cards. Other than her astonishment over my stipulation regarding her father's research, she gave off a barely concealed air of satisfaction.

She threw me a flinty smile, which didn't quite reach her eyes. "You have my gratitude. May I impinge upon you further and ask that you prepare the wedding contracts as soon as possible? I would prefer to take them with me when I leave tomorrow."

"You will have them at breakfast," I volleyed back, then stood abruptly, giving her a slight bow. "I'll take my leave to make sure they're prepared."

She stood up as well, curtsying deeply. Mother and Clement sprang out of their seats, as if released from a spell. Based on Lady Rosebelle's surprised expression, she had forgotten their presence as much as I had during our sharp exchange. Mother went over to Lady Rosebelle, grabbing her hands and kissing both of her cheeks.

"Welcome to the family, my dear," she murmured softly. She made a shooing motion at me. "Begone, dear boy. Closet yourself up with Webster to finalize the contracts. I shall escort our future princess to her chambers. Oh and Andrus," she walked over to me, taking my hand, "congratulations." She squeezed before letting go, then turned back to Lady Rosebelle.

Heading toward the door, I took one last glance at my future wife. She was listening to my mother, her brow furrowed, clutching her forearm in what seemed to be a customary posture. I turned away and left to search out my attorney.

❖ ❖ ❖

In spite of a late night completing the marriage contracts with my attorney, Monsieur Webster, I was the first down to breakfast in the morning. Webster joined me soon after, his joints clicking as he made his way around the room and settled his lawyerly accoutrements out on the table.

"Sit," I ordered him, and quickly got his usual plate of biscuits, jam, and bacon from the sideboard. He had been at breakfast with us often enough over his decades of service that I knew his habits well enough.

Mother and Lady Rosebelle joined us not long after, and I acknowledged them with a short bow. Mother shepherded Rosebelle over to the sideboard, stopping along the way to inform me quietly of Clement's departure to Montblanc, our northwestern outpost. I looked up at her in concern, opening my mouth to question her further when I noticed Lady Rosebelle watching us curiously. Instead, I just nodded and turned back to my food.

Once the ladies had a chance to sit down, I introduced Monsieur Webster, who bowed his head at Lady Rosebelle from his seat. "May I offer you my congratulations, milady. Under the direction of Prince Andrus I have drawn up your marriage contract. He indicated that you may wish to review them this morning."

"Yes please," she replied, her face a mask of indifference, eyes flicking toward me as she took the proffered stack of papers.

I ground my teeth at her look. Why was she so hard to read? *She probably thinks we left something out.* I shifted in my seat as she slowly read through the documents. Mother and Webster chatted now and again over inconsequential things. I finished a second cup of coffee and tried not to focus on every movement Rosebelle made.

At last she looked up. "Everything seems in order, thank you. My father may take issue with your requirement of regular access to the Dower House woods for your patrols, but

I will speak to him about it. I would, however, like to make one small change."

"And what might that be?" I asked, exasperated but also curious to see what sort of concession she would be bold enough to try and squeeze out of me.

"I would like the phrase directing the inheritance of the Croiseux Dower House to be changed to 'being in accordance with the deed of sale' instead of 'being in accordance with Pelerine law of inheritence'," she explained, glancing at Monsieur Webster and then back to me.

"Ah, I see, Milady," Webster noted, suppressing a smile.

He was the one who had suggested we write in the phrase to begin with. Pelerine inheritance laws specified that in absence of a male heir, any property would go to the oldest daughter's husband. That technicality could have acted as back up in enforcing her father's compliance over his research, but now that she had caught it, I would have to concede. So long as her father stopped prying into our family's secrets, I didn't really care who owned the Croiseux Dower House.

I nodded at her and then glanced over at Webster. "Make the change as quickly as you can, then I'll sign and seal them."

He bent over the contract to comply.

Intrigued that she had caught the technicality, I looked back at Lady Rosebelle. She was examining me, condemnation playing across her pursed lips. *She knows we did it on purpose.*

The corners of my lips turned up involuntarily and she lifted an eyebrow. I had to admit a grudging respect for her ability to follow Webster's labyrinth of legal jargon.

After a moment she managed to form her mouth into something approaching a believable smile and continued eating her breakfast. As Webster finished his alterations, I quickly signed and affixed my seal, directing him to ride with Lady Rosebelle to collect her parent's signatures. He nodded and bowed to the company before exiting the room.

"Well," my mother chimed as she put her napkin down on her empty plate, "I must congratulate both of you, again! And myself, come to think of it. I shall be gaining a daughter-in-law." She smiled brightly at Rosebelle and then at me. "I suppose I should leave the two of you alone now that things are official, but instead I'm going to take Lady Rosebelle to the sewing room to discuss her wedding dress."

We all stood up from the table and I returned Rosebelle's curtsy with a formal bow. Mother walked around and linked arms with her. "I would like to come pay a visit to your family the week after the contracts are signed, would that be agreeable to them, do you think?" Rosebelle nodded and she continued, guiding their steps toward the door.

"Perfect. Now, I have a bolt of fabric that I think would be stunning on you for a wedding dress..." She continued chattering away as they left the room, and I watched their retreat.

Rosebelle glanced back surreptitiously as they passed the threshold of the door, her bright amber eyes questioning and slightly vulnerable. They shuttered again as they caught mine, and she turned away.

* * *

Some time later , stood in my study watching her enter our carriage with her maid and Monsieur Webster. The squad leader I had tasked with her safety latched the door after them and mounted up, directing the forerunners to start toward the castle gates.

As they rode off I mused over the sudden intrusion into my life. Rosebelle. *Does she prefer Rosebelle or Rose, or something else?*

My breath caught. "Rose? Could *she* be what the gypsy queen meant?" I turned to stare as the last of the riders left the courtyard. "Even if she is, I'll never abandon my kingdom. It's still *my* choice," I muttered, clenching my fists.

The doors to my study opened, and Manciple bustled in, a

pile of papers in his arms.

"Sire, good afternoon!" He nodded a greeting at me, placing his files on my desk. "Clement sent a messenger back to tell you that situation at the northwestern outpost was resolved. Apparently the missing rider was taken ill between way stations, but has been recovered." Manciple cleared his throat and puffed out his chest, his voluminous cravat sticking out importantly.

"Apparently the rider carries reports that may require you to restructure the next patrol. I've taken the liberty of pulling the most recent incident files from that outpost for review after we finish our thrift reports."

"Thank you Manciple," I replied, casting one last look out the window.

No, there's nothing I wouldn't sacrifice for my country. And if she's going to be our Princess, she'll need to learn that duty as well.

"Let's finish these reports so I can move on to restructuring our raid. We only have a few days left, and General Morvan is in the field." Turning back to the table, I opened up the first of the files and began to read.

CHAPTER FOUR

Belle

Hazel and I arrived back to a house filled with nervous panic. Rochelle flung herself at me before I could take off my cloak. Mama wasn't far behind, searching my face to assure herself that I was well. Papa took my hand with a halfhearted scolding. Most of his attention was focused over my shoulder as Monsieur Webster tottered in after me, followed by the more decided step of the captain of the guards. Motioning everyone forward into the sitting room, I dispatched Hazel to beg a late supper off of Mrs. Comfry and arrange accommodations for our guests.

My family took their accustomed seats around the fireplace. The exact chairs that had supported us through Papa's revelation were now going to support us through my news. Monsieur Webster sat down in the background. The soldier settled himself as unobtrusively as possible near the door.

Everyone looked expectantly at me and I opened my mouth to explain, but suddenly, I didn't know what to say. The events of the last two days jumbled together in my head. I couldn't find the beginning because all I could think of was the ending. In a month's time I would leave them, live in a different country with a new name, new position, and new expectations on my shoulders. *How can I explain it all?* I cleared my throat and smiled.

"Mama, Papa, Rochelle," I addressed each in turn, "I have some news that will surprise you."

They glanced at Monsieur Webster, then back at me, not troubling to disguise their bewilderment. *Cutting to the point worked well with Prince Andrus. May as well try the same tactic here.*

"I have just become engaged to marry the Prince of Asileboix."

Rochelle gasped and Mama gaped in horror. My smile wavered slightly but I pasted it on all the stronger.

"In exchange, he agreed to approve our sale of Croiseux to the Marchands. He will also settle a bridal gift you, so not only has everything been returned to its normal order, but we will be much better off than before." Everyone stared at me, except Papa, who gazed at the fire.

"I am very pleased, and of course honored," I ventured again, with a glance at Monsieur Webster. "The wedding will take place directly after the new year, but there is one more thing.

"The Prince is requesting that Papa..." I trailed off. Monsieur Webster cleared his throat behind me.

"The Prince is *requiring* as part of the marriage contracts, that Papa stop his research into the Lady of the Woods. Forever."

Mama whipped her eyes to my father and Rochelle let out a little cry. Papa didn't move a muscle, just stared at the carpet near my feet. A long moment passed, filled only with crackling logs and the ticking of the little clock on the mantelpiece. Without a word, he turned back to stare into the flames.

I was at a loss. I had expected more, an angry refusal perhaps, or at least surprise. His tired indifference scared me.

"This is Monsieur Webster," I stated finally, looking over at where he blinked slowly, watching the scene unfold from behind his glasses. No doubt he would have an interesting report for the Prince. *It doesn't matter.* "He has brought the marriage contracts which I reviewed with the Prince this morning. Monsieur Webster, allow me to present my mother and father, Lord and Lady Montanarte."

Monsieur Webster rose to his feet and bowed to my parents. "I shall be ready to discuss them at your convenience, Lord and Lady Montanarte. May I propose a meeting after breakfast tomorrow morning, when we've all had a chance to prepare?"

I gave a brief nod while my parents stared at him in shock. I should have realized my family would be in no state to go through paperwork this evening. A burning desire to have everything legally enforceable was making me inconsiderate. My mother mustered enough of her sense of duty as Lady of the House to give Monsieur Webster a regal nod.

"You must excuse us Monsieur, this has all come as a bit of a shock. We shall certainly be ready to discuss matters with you in the morning," Mama announced, her voice only quavering a little.

To my intense relief, Hazel bustled in just then. She went to my mother's side, whispering about guest arrangements as my mother nodded. Glancing at the soldier still standing by the door, Mama addressed the attorney again.

"Monsieur Webster, Hazel will show you and your... attendant to your rooms for the evening. I trust they will be comfortable, although we had little time to prepare. If you have need of anything, please let Hazel know."

She stood and, although I could see it trembled, offered Monsieur Webster her hand, which he took and bowed over. I felt a surge of pride at Mama's gracefulness. Hazel shot me a quick look of sympathy, then lead our guests from the room.

All was silent for a few moments after the door shut behind them. Rochelle moved to the chair next to me, recently vacated by Monsieur Webster.

"But Belle, what about Eddie?" She asked in a low, urgent tone, a worried frown marking her brow. Mama's eyes flew to mine. I grimaced

"I'll write to Eddie as soon as the marriage contracts are

signed. He has no legal claim on me, or us. I know he'll be good enough not to stand in my way."

"Good enough to not stand in your way?" Papa's voice burst out, thick with emotion. He turned from the fire. It's heat seemed to have seeped into his skin and traveled to his eyes, igniting embers in them.

"He will be too good to allow you to sacrifice yourself, and him, in such a way, if you think I am not. Don't you think we care about you at all?"

Mama tore her gaze from my own and put her hand on his arm instead.

"Papa, you're mistaken. It's truly very little sacrifice on my part. You know I have wanted to regain a position fitting my rank since we lost it. Now that dream is coming true. I know..." I paused as my voice wobbled, "I *know*, it will be a wrench for you to let go of your research, but after you grieve, you'll pick up a new topic and devote yourself to that."

The embers in his eyes blazed into fires at my words. "You think I care if ever read another book about that forsaken Lady of the Woods?! You think *that* is what upsets me most?" He raised his hands to head, pulling at his hair, a gesture he made only at his most distressed. He rounded on my mother, still clutching his hair. "And you! You allowed her to slink away from the house to throw herself into the clutches of this monster?"

Mama pulled his hands down gently. "Maurice, be rational. I didn't know that she was planning *this* when she went. She asked me to trust her, and I did. I do." She gave me a sad smile, tears in her eyes. He scoffed and opened his mouth to argue, but she held up her hand in a placating gesture.

"Hear her out. She knows her own heart and mind."

Leaning toward him she added in an undertone, "And you know my thoughts on her match with Eddie, dear though he is to us."

I looked at her in surprise. I had wondered once or twice if she was really as happy with my engagement to Eddie as she had professed to be, but never asked because it hadn't mattered. There had been no other options for me until yesterday. She had always been the sort of person to allow someone make their own choices; a listener instead of an advice dispensary.

I stirred in my seat. "Papa, please listen." He turned his face away but didn't stop me.

"I know you've thought of Eddie and me as very much in love, but if I had loved him as you love Mama, I would have married him long ago." I took a deep breath. "Now I have an opportunity to obtain real security and comfort for us. I'll be a princess, after all! My only heartache is that you must give up the Lady."

"The Lady means nothing in comparison with my own ladies," he protested, squeezing mother's hands and looking at me and Rochelle with tears in his eyes. "But I cannot allow you to marry this *Beast.* He doesn't know you at all, and he's acted abominably. I wouldn't be worthy of being your father."

"You say you cannot allow me to marry someone who doesn't know me, but Papa, Eddie knows me hardly any better than this Prince. It's true!" He scoffed but I pressed on.

"Eddie has always built me up in his head as someone other than I am. A better version of myself, perhaps, but still not me. I know he would've treated me well, and I was willing to be as good a wife to him as I was able, but it would have ended in disappointment for both of us. Not a tragedy, just a constant let-down of expectations until we found a way to tolerate each other.

"I admit, the Prince must have a ruthless streak to take advantage of our position. But he was respectable in his interactions with me, and is obviously respected by his mother and servants." Stilling my hands, which had been twisting the edge of my shawl while I spoke, I clasped them in front of me instead.

"He can't be so bad if people like them so obviously care for him. Besides, Hazel ingratiated herself with the servants on purpose to find out about him. You know if there was something terrible, at least one of them would have gossiped about it."

My father grimaced, Mama by his side. Rochelle sat frozen, eyes wide, looking back and forth between us. I waited for Papa's response.

"As your mother said, you have always known your own heart and mind." He sounded weary, the fire having burned down in his eyes again. "I admit, your arrangement seems to repair everything. If you're determined, I don't suppose I can stand in your way. But I cannot be happy about it."

A swell of relief passed over me, and I surged out of my chair, coming over to kneel before my parents. "I can't force you to be happy for me, but I would very much like it. And I am absolutely set on my course. I'll need your support in the days to come. Although I'm excited, I confess I'm also a little nervous that I won't be up to the task," I admitted, my voice breaking slightly.

Rochelle came to sit next to me on the floor. "Of course we'll support you, goose," she teased, wrapping her arms around me and squeezing. Tears spilled from Mama's eyes as she smiled down at us.

Papa reached out a trembling hand to take one of my own. "We will be here for you, always."

I kissed his hand, then hugged Rochelle back, raising her up with me after a moment. Thinking it best to leave my parents on a positive note, I bid them good night, pulling Chelle with me as I left the room.

"Give them some time alone together. They've been dealt a bit of a blow, and I need them to come to terms with it by tomorrow."

"Oh Belle, even in the midst of chaos you're always so focused on the practical," Rochelle joked with a damp sort of laugh, clinging to me.

"Darling Chelle, I can always count on you to throw my best character traits in my face as accusations," I replied, making a face. She stuck out her tongue.

"That's more like it," I encouraged, squeezing her back. We let go and set about rearranging our shawls while we walked toward the stairwell.

"You go on up and I'll bring you a warming pan for your bed. Mr. Comfry is sure to have sent most of our usual allotment of firewood to the guest chambers. Hazel probably had to give up her room for Monsieur Webster. If she's sleeping on the trundle bed in my room, she'll heat us up nicely with all the hot air she blows out, so you'll need it more than we will."

Chelle snorted and started up the stairs. Trudging down the hall and into the kitchen where Mrs. Comfry was still cleaning dishes with Hazel, I communicated my request. Mrs. Comfry clucked her tongue at me, obviously having heard the whole sorry tale from Hazel while they worked.

"I'll have it up for her in a minute, dearie. It's already heating in the fire."

She motioned to a plate of food on the counter near the cook fire, and I descended on it, ravenous. As I ate, I watched the two of them wash dishes and listened to their oddly soothing gossip about the miller's daughter's latest escapades. When I handed my plate off to be cleaned, Mrs. Comfry smiled.

"I'll send up some tea with Hazel, don't fret. Off you go." After a quick peck on her cheek, I slipped out of the warmth of the kitchen.

Hesitating for a moment in the hall, I listened for sounds of anyone moving about. All was quiet. I turned toward Papa's study slipping silently through the door.

The nearly full moon cast a pale glow inside. I was able to see my way around without lighting any lamps. Working quickly, I gathered together several manuscripts on the Lady, as well as some of Papa's main body of notes. It wasn't easy. Everything was stacked haphazardly, piled around furniture and bric-a-brac. Papa had never been one for organization, scattering things again even after I had put them to rights. I had to be careful not to take anything that would be missed.

Floorboards creaked nearby, and I froze. *Just the house settling,* I scolded myself. Gathering a smaller pile than I had hoped for, I grabbed a blanket hanging off the back of a sofa and wrapped it around my treasure.

Taking a breath, I edged my way back out of the study. When I stopped by Rochelle's room to tell her about the warming pan and tea, I found it cold and empty. I hurried across the small landing to my own room. She was there, already snuggled into my bed, reading a book.

"What are you doing?" I questioned as I stepped inside, opening my wardrobe to deposit my bundle and start changing for bed.

Chelle made a face at me. "Reading a book in bed."

"I can see that. But you're reading the book in *my* bed!" I shot back pulling my nightgown over my head.

"Belle Montanarte, I've never known you to be so perceptive!" she teased, closing the book and turning on her side to face me. "It's too cold in my room. Half the fire had gone out already. Hazel came up with the warmer and I told her she could use it if she helped me move all the firewood over to your room. I thought we could have a sleepover like we did when we were little! Besides, now we have enough firewood for a real fire all night, instead of waking up as a block of ice."

I laughed. "Well I won't mind the extra warmth, but there will hardly be enough room for the two of us. We'll have to think skinny thoughts!"

Hazel flounced in, ready for bed and bearing hot tea. We all quickly downed the soothing beverage and snuggled under the covers: me and Rochelle in my bed, Hazel down below on the pull out mattress. She shoved an extra pillow that had fallen down back up to me and Chelle.

"Don't be having any nightmares, you two. If one of you falls down on me in your sleep I'm going to be crushed!"

Chelle laughed and pushed her closed book off the edge of the bed, onto Hazel's lap.

"Oof," Hazel wheezed, then launched the book back up onto

our bed, hitting me in the feet.

"Ah yes," I said dryly, nudging the book over the edge and onto the floor. "How I shall miss the comforts of home when I am off playing Princess of the Castle." I had meant it as a joke but it sobered us all instantly.

After a moment, Chelle elbowed me in the stomach. "You're not a Princess yet, Miss High-and-Mighty. Scoot over and give me more of the cover!"

I laughed and made more room for her, pulling a battered doll from under me as I did so.

"Chelle, do *not* tell me you still sleep with Little Chip."

Chelle blushed and snatched the doll from my hand, squeezing her in a quick hug. "I don't sleep with her! *She* sleeps with *me!*"

I rolled my eyes and flicked Little Chip's soft head, right near the crack in her porcelain face. She had once been my doll, bearing a magnificent and long forgotten name. When we moved to the Dower House, Chelle had trouble sleeping, so I gave her my doll for comfort. She had instantly renamed her Little Chip, with typical toddler simplicity, because of the doll's chipped face, but also as an homage to Mr. and Mrs. Comfry's son, Chip, who had been an idol to little Chelle before he went off to the Beast War.

It made me oddly happy to see that she had kept it after all these years. My sister was much more tender-hearted than I, even to silly things like dolls. *And silly things like myself.*

Smiling at Chelle, I bid her goodnight as she closed her eyes, Hazel's light snores already reaching us from the trundle bed below.

* * *

The next morning, we awoke to Hazel softly berating herself for sleeping in so late. Sunlight streamed through the windows. With guests in the house, Hazel would normally be up early to help Mrs. Comfry finish breakfast. The three of us rushed to get ready and head downstairs.

After a brief and awkward meal, Mama, Papa, and I repaired to the study with Monsieur Webster. To my surprise, my parents had few questions. Papa asked once more whether I was sure, then reviewed each page quickly and signed with little fuss. I signed my own name eagerly, and Monsieur Webster requested access to Papa's research as soon as my ink was dry.

We spent the rest of the morning combing through his study, piling papers and books into trunks that the soldiers had brought with them, no doubt to be burned as soon as possible.

As the soldiers hefted the last trunk out the door, Monsieur Webster peered around, seated in one of the chairs near Papa's desk. "Is that it?"

My father followed his gaze miserably.

"Yes. Everything pertaining to the Lady. Well, except maybe..."

I interrupted him quickly. "Ah yes, Papa has published several books on the subject already, and those are at the bookseller's. Will you be needing those copies as well?" Papa looked at me doubtfully but said nothing.

"That won't be necessary," Monsieur Webster intoned, glancing between us. "My master is eagerly awaiting my return, so I must take my leave. Allow me to offer my congratulations once again." With a stiff bow to each of us in turn, Monsieur Webster followed after the guardsmen. Mama accompanied him, leaving me and Papa to contemplate the desolation of the study.

* * *

The following week passed by in a haze, until once again I found myself sitting at my father's desk. I had meant to write Eddie the same day the contracts were signed, but it slipped my mind as preparations for Winter Solstice and my wedding began in earnest. I was reminded of the necessity when Madame Marchand slipped me a note at chapel on Sunday with a smile.

"From Eddie," She squealed. "He's returning!"

I felt the blood drain from my face at the reminder of the bitter task ahead of me. As far as I knew, Papa had never communicated the peril we had all been in. They were happily looking forward to their oldest son returning in time for Winter Solstice, not a thought troubled by how close we had been to ruin. Madame Marchand moved on before she could note my discomfort, and my family left for home earlier than usual, eager to escape to the quiet of the Dower House.

Eddie's note was a trial to read, as usual. If I had been any other young woman, I'm sure I would have been glowing. It was full of good cheer and a discreetly phrased assurance of his love. But I was inescapably myself, so it only served to make me hate him for making my task even harder.

Not very charitable, especially for a future Princess. But I've never been able to find patience for those who naturally had good fortune fall into place around them. Eddie had been living that reality his entire life.

Not that I could fault him for it. He never shirked his responsibilities, working harder than anyone I knew. I had overheard Madame Marchand telling someone at chapel about a medal, but with his usual modesty, he hadn't mentioned it in his letter to me. He shone with glorious, oblivious goodness. I was glad I would be free of it.

Nothing I could write in this letter would convince Eddie that I was truly breaking off our engagement of my own volition, I knew. No doubt he would ascribe some wonderful virtue to me. If he learned of the real reason for this change, his sense of honor would never accept my supposed sacrifice. While I had been desperate to present myself as a martyr to Prince Andrus, I was determined to pour cold water on the same notion to Edouard.

The real truth of my motives lay somewhere between a martyr and an opportunist. Eddie didn't realize that while I had accepted my fate with him at Croiseux as necessary to support my family, it would have always tasted of ashes in my mouth. Ashes from the life of freedom and security I had known as a child. I was always seeking an echo of it, attainable only through a man.

Hypocrite.

I was attaining my larger dream of wealth, prestige, and a high title, only through another man. But that was the way women achieved things in Pelerin. Marriage or children. Some of Papa's more salacious books recounted a very different state of affairs in countries that hadn't banned magic. Pelerin didn't interact with them. *Do the Asileans practice magic?*

I gave myself a shake and sighed. My letter writing had been put off long enough. Although he irritated me and at times I hated him, Eddie had been prepared to offer me a future. He had always been a friend. He was owed the truth directly from me.

Dashing off a few lines to explain the situation, I wrote that I hoped he could be as happy for me to start a new adventure as I was for him to come home safely from his. The phrase seemed likely to stick in his mind. Maybe it would convince him that he *was* happy for me. *After that, he'll quickly get over me and find a suitable wife for his provincial plans.*

Signing my name, I sealed it, then ran it to Mr. Comfry to deliver with the farm horses this afternoon. That task finally complete, I rushed upstairs to prepare for our visit with Dowager Princess Mathilde.

* * *

The Dowager Princess arrived in a small but stately red brougham carriage, emblazoned with the Asilean crest of a crowned roaring bear with red eyes on a field of midnight blue.

Mrs. Comfry had bundled Mr. Comfry and Hazel out to the entrance to make their curtsies and bows, despite the chance that the food for tea would scamper off with no one to watch it.

"I know how to treat esteemed guests, even if we haven't had any in ever so long," she declared when Mama protested. Mama smiled and gave in, but the rest of us waited in the warmth of the vestibule.

Princess Mathilde was just as friendly and exuberant as she had been in the castle. Her manners were almost insultingly informal in contrast to our own customs. Instead of being upset, Mama was pleased by her warmth toward me as we settled into our shabby chairs in the sitting room.

Hazel arrived with tea, and Mathilde drew everyone into conversation by the time Mama was done pouring. Papa managed an amusing anecdote from his last visit to the capitol, eliciting an appreciative laugh from our guest. After he finished his tea he seemed worn out, excusing himself abruptly. Mama couldn't hide her concern over him, and whether our guest would be offended, which Princess Mathilde interpreted correctly.

"Don't mind about me, Lady Montanarte. A daughter's marriage is a difficult thing for a father under the best of circumstances, and these circumstances have jumped up at us in the most alarming manner. I can't help that I'm grateful: I'm gaining a beautiful and intelligent daughter-in-law! But I can imagine you and your husband are still trying to find your way toward peace at sharing her. And after such a lot of turmoil from my son!" She shook her head, shifting in her seat, and placing her teacup on a side table. "Well, that will soon be in the past. No doubt you take great comfort in knowing your *younger* daughter is still with you."

With an encouraging smile, she turned to Rochelle and managed to draw her into conversation about the garden, Chelle's passion. My sister waxed lyrical about some experiments with vegetables she had been trying over the last year. To my surprise, Princess Mathilde offered a few suggestions.

Princess Mathilde was nothing like what I imagined a woman of her position would be. Our own royal family had a reputation for grandness and majesty. Princess Mathilde was kind and ebullient, as ready to converse with a farmer as with a King. None of that damaged her air of graciousness or made her seem less deserving of respect.

"Now," Mathilde continued, taking a quick sip of tea and looking at each of us in turn, "when she was at the castle, Lady Rosebelle picked the *most* beautiful pink satin for her wedding dress. Our head seamstress has started working on a pattern, but I wanted to discuss sleeves." As she spoke, Mathilde pulled out a swatch of the fabric I had chosen, and my sister's and mother's faces lit up. They chattered about design ideas for some time after that, occasionally consulting me. I had few opinions. It only mattered that it looked well on me. My mother and sister, however, were in their element, and I enjoyed watching them discuss the details animatedly with the princess for the rest of her visit.

As we walked toward the entrance, Princess Mathilde peered out the window at our gardens.

"I find I need to stretch my legs before shutting myself back up in the carriage. Lady Rosebelle, would you show me around your gardens? I'm sure they're a treat to behold in summer."

I agreed, and soon found myself pointing out my sister's experimental vegetable plot in the frosty air. As we approached the stables, waving to Mr. Comfry as he returned from the Manor House, Princess Mathilde put a hand on my arm.

"Dear Lady Rosebelle, I must say how enchanted I was by your family. I hope they'll feel comfortable enough to visit at the castle after the wedding. I would love to get to know them more. You must take tea with me the Tuesday after Winter Solstice. You'll need a gown fitting, and your mother and sister are invited as well. We could show them around your new home together."

I thanked her and accepted her invitation to tea with a

smile. She squeezed my hand, then swept into her carriage and back to the forest.

Making my way toward the house, I reflected on her visit. *Mathilde is making an effort to become a friend.* She left me feeling more confident than ever in my decision, and sure that I would find a way to be happy after the wedding. *Maybe I've always felt out of place here because I belong in Asileboix.*

As I stood unwrapping my outer layers in the foyer, Hazel appeared, a grim look on her face.

"What's the matter?"

She grimaced as she folded my cloak. "Mr. Comfry just got back from delivering the horses—and your note."

"I know. I saw him while I was sending off Princess Mathilde."

Hazel shifted my cloak under her arm, looking uncomfortable. "Eddie arrived home as Mr. Comfry was leaving."

My fragile confidence left me in a rush. "I thought he wasn't due back for another week!"

Hazel shrugged.

Was he on his way over? He would be full of questions and a broken heart. Angry even. That thought flamed my own anger back to life and with it, my assurance. I looked Hazel in the eye.

"Let him come. It won't be pleasant, but I'm ready. There's nothing he can do to stop me now."

CHAPTER FIVE

Eddie

After seeing off those men in my company who lived elsewhere, I rounded up the soldiers from Croiseux and we started back together. Not all of them had horses, making it slow going, but we had become used to marching all day and sleeping rough at night. The inns we passed periodically tempted me with the promise of a real bed, but I resisted. Most of my men couldn't afford their rates, and it didn't seem right to be warm inside while they slept in tents in the frigid December air. So I camped with them, and we all froze together.

As we climbed the last hill before Croiseux, we were down to myself, LeFeu, and about fifteen others who hailed from the town of Crioseux itself, the others having peeled off at various points for the outlying villages and hamlets. The late afternoon sun acted as a guide, sinking down ahead of us behind the town walls. I could just make out the highest tower of Croiseux Manor beyond.

Home. It was just as I had dreamed.

The chime of the town clock ringing the hour reached out to us. I counted five peals and grinned over at LeFeu. I hadn't missed that noisy clanging until now.

LeFeu grinned back as one of the men yelled out with glee,

"Was that old Mother's Helper?"

We boys had bequeathed the nickname soon after my father had installed it; a gift to the town as his trade network grew ever more profitable. Every last one of our mothers had used it as the supper bell, woe betide any of us running through the door after the last chime had rung.

I turned back toward the speaker. "Why do you ask, Oger, was that your curfew? There'll be no supper for you tonight!"

Scattered laughter rang out, everyone no doubt remembering their own scoldings. Stories flew back and forth, each more ridiculous than the next We made good time down to the town gates, our attitude buoyed by the sight of our longed for home-fires.

One last handshake and slap on the back sent everyone hurrying home. A few were met with joyful surprise by loved ones who happened to see us coming down the hill. I stopped in with LeFeu at the forge for a minute, turning down an offer of refreshments eager as I was to get to my own home. His younger siblings clamored around him as I left, his father's arm around his shoulder. It was a rare gesture of affection from the normally stoic blacksmith. His mother was all smiles, trying to reign in the younger ones. A few grandchildren had sprouted since we were last home—the first signs of change. Otherwise, everything was just as we left it; as I had told LeFeu it would be.

My own welcome at home was much less exuberant. A groom stopped mid-conversation with old Mr. Comfry, taking my horse and bags off my hands. Mr. Comfry doffed his cap, wishing me well, and I waved cheerfully. The servants who crossed my path bowed and murmured.

I shook hands with each person I knew. There were a few new faces, but most were people I had grown up with, simply a little older and grayer. Upon reaching the front hall, our butler, Lazard, bowed formally as a footman took my hat and gloves. His eyes twinkled, the only betrayal of his usual adherence to strict standards.

"Welcome home, Sir. Would you prefer to see your family first, or go directly to your room?"

"My family first please. They'll have to put up with a dusty hug this time."

"As you wish," Lazard intoned. "Your father is at Stone Farm, but is expected back for dinner. Your mother is reviewing the household books with Mrs. Bellamy. If you will wait for her in the green drawing room, she will be with you shortly."

I chuckled, slapping him on the shoulder, "Lazard, old friend, it's good to be back. I've missed you. And Croiseux."

"If I may be so bold, Master Edouard, Croiseux has missed you too." He bowed me into the drawing room with just the ghost of a smile.

I only had to wait a moment or two before my mother burst through the doors. Her head swept frantically this way, missing me by the fire several times in her haste. Finally she caught sight of me and threw up her hands, rushing over.

"Eddie! My Eddie!" After hugging me fiercely, she held me at arms' length to get a good look. "You're days earlier than we expected! How glad I am! And you'll see Trinette tomorrow! She's dropping off the children on her way to visit Clair. But you haven't even met your niece and nephew yet, I forgot!"

Linking arms, she drew me over to a small sofa, her other hand gesturing nonstop as she chattered. "They're fine, strong children. They remind me of you and Trinette at that age! Never ill and full of loud fun. Did I tell you in my last letter that Clair will have her first child this spring? I can't remember if I wrote or if I decided to wait until you came home. Well now you're here, so now you know." She paused to brush at the front of her blue dress and sleeves.

"There now, you've gotten dust all over me when I hugged you. Reminds me of helping at my parents' bakery before I married your father. Flour all over my dress despite my apron. Do you know I actually miss getting up early to make bread?"

I laughed as Ma rattled everything off while giving my arm

little squeezes, as if assuring herself I was truly there.

"Yes Ma, I know you do. You always woke up early to make bread in the kitchens when we were little, even after we moved here."

She laughed and kissed my cheek, giving me a conspiratorial look, her rosy face beaming.

"I still do you know! Every week before chapel. It helps prepare my mind to think on things above." She laughed again, her face breaking into more lines than I remembered, and rang a nearby bell.

"Your Da will be home soon, don't worry. He's at Stone Farm checking on how the cattle are doing in their new barn. Or is it some new cattle in an old barn? I didn't quite catch that part. Oh, but you missed Thomas! He's at the office in town today and will stay at the old house. But if he catches wind of your return he'll come back here instead. I had better tell cook. Oh, there you are." She turned toward a parlor maid I didn't recognize, who looked vaguely like one of the men in my company.

She must be his his little sister, I realized with surprise. She had been a small child when we left.

"You can see dear Eddie is home at last!" Ma exclaimed, addressing her enthusiastically. "Please make sure there's a bath ready in his room. Look at my dress! He's covered in dust from the road." She issued a stream of instructions to the maid, who took them stoically and then left to carry them out.

Ma continued the flow of conversation, her stream of cheerful words covering me like a blanket, warm and familiar. Every so often, she would get up and up fuss over me—pouring a glass of water from the sideboard, settling a pillow behind my back. She had always been like this, talking a mile a minute and keeping her hands just as busy too. When we lived in town, that meant getting the chores done. Once we moved to the manor house it meant suitable projects for ladies of the manor—and sneaking off to help with chores when she could manage it.

I smiled. *She and Da are two of a kind.* Both were busy, cheerful people. They had worked hard to build up a fortune, but still lived mainly the way they always had, just in nicer surroundings. They preferred doing things themselves instead of being waited on.

I know the feeling. Even sitting here in the warm, familiar drawing room, waiting for the servants to finish readying my room and bath, I felt twitchy. We had lived in a tiny house in town until I was ten. After moving here, my parents didn't allow us to become used to the life of the gentry. We learned all the rules of polite society, but hard work was the order of every day.

It was an upbringing I was thankful for after I joined the infantry. There hadn't been anyone going around airing out my sheets and filling a tub with water on the front. Still, a hot bath sounded good to my weary muscles and a short time later, Lazard entered, informing us that my rooms were ready. Ma sent me off with a kiss and a laugh. As I climbed the stairs, I heard her murmuring to Lazard about sending a messenger to Thomas, as well as his more measured reply that a groom had already been sent.

"Oh Eddie!" Ma's voice rang out, "I completely forgot! What good timing you have."

I took a few steps back down the stairs as she hurried up them, slightly out of breath. "This came for you today. From the Dower House, from Mr. Comfry. I mean, from dear Lady Belle, but Mr. Comfry brought it." Her words rushed out along with her breath, jumbled and just barely coherent in her excitement.

A small, sealed envelope addressed with my name was placed in my hand.

"I gave her your note at Chapel, discreetly of course! It's probably in response to that. Such timing, as if she knew you would arrive. Ah, hearts in love are never apart, no matter how far."

She laughed, noticing my smile at Belle's unmistakable

flourish on the envelope. "I'm sure you can ride to her after dinner if you wish. Although, if you could discipline your heart one more day I'd like to have you to ourselves tonight."

"I'll ride to her tomorrow Ma, thank you." Stuffing the note in my pocket, I pecked her cheek before continuing up the stairs. "Just let me get off the dust from the road before Da and Thomas arrive. I'll be back down soon."

She hummed as she went her way, and I continued on mine. A few steps down the hall, I paused by a closed door. Hesitating a moment, I turned the knob and peeked inside. My Da's office.

I glanced around. Light streamed through its west-facing windows, overlaying everything with a yellow-orange sheen. The scent was exactly as I remembered—leather, paper, dust, and ash from the fire. My younger self appeared before me. Standing before my Da during a dressing down from a prank gone wrong, head bowed in shame. Slouching at my desk, my mind numbed into boredom from paperwork for our estate and businesses. My mouth crooked up in a smile. My younger self could have used a few days in a cold trench for perspective.

Before the call had gone out for more soldiers, Da had suggested that I use the room as my own office as I took on more responsibility from him. I had never had the chance to convert it. Now looking around, I couldn't imagine it as mine.

There was too much of Da in it. The framed firebird feather he and Lord Montanarte discovered at an archive when I was twelve. Neat stacks of books with note cards sticking out for easy reference. The inevitable piles of estate and farm work waiting by the door for his assistant to file. Models of various machines, realistic or not, that he liked to dream up. It was almost a physical representation of his soul. I couldn't imagine the room accepting me instead. Glancing at the small corner desk where I had worked before enlisting, I noted signs of recent occupation with surprise.

A stand filled with the new style of metal pens and nibs told me all I needed to know. My younger brother Thomas preferred them to the usual quills and ink, even though they splattered more often. I was painfully aware of that defect, having received regular letters from him. Ink splotches had dripped over his detailed explanations of work projects and experiments they were trying at one of the farms, making them almost unreadable. Thomas' handwriting betrayed his mind. His guiding characteristic was curiosity, and I looked back over at the models wondering how many of them were his.

A beam of light refracted off the crystal inkwell on my father's desk, momentarily blinding me. The sun was sinking down, reminding me of the time. Closing the door on the office, with its mix of familiar and new, I continued down the hall. *The cost of all that woolgathering will be cold bathwater, no doubt,* I scolded myself.

After a hurried wash, I pulled on a clean uniform from my pack. Rumbling sounded from my stomach as I combed my wet hair, and I grinned at myself in the mirror. *I can't wait for one of Cook's meals!*

When I arrived at the sitting room, I found it curiously dark and cold, and looked around for a servant to help me find my bearings. Lazard's steady tread announced his approach, and as he rounded the corner he caught sight of me. "Ah, Master Edouard. The family gather in the parlor before dinner, if you would follow me."

"The parlor?" I asked as I followed him back down the hallway.

"Yes. You knew it as the music room before you left. It was converted into a parlor during Madame Clair's season."

"I see." I followed him even though I knew where the old music room was, theoretically. For all I knew, they had knocked down some part of the house and reconfigured it while I was gone, forgetting to mention it in their letters. I had received regular letters from all my family, but some were inevitably lost, and only Clair had ever written with much detail on the mundane routine of the house and family. That had changed once her season began and she quickly became engaged and married. A prickle of dissonance itched between my shoulders.

"There he is!" Ma called, craning her neck to see as Lazard opened the doors ahead of me. "Did you go to the sitting room? I just now remembered that we used to go there before dinner when you were children. But when I ran out to send the maid after you, she said that Lazard had already thought of it, of course. This room is so much more cozy now that it's just us and Thomas. And Thomas is in town half the week anyway, so then it's just me and your father."

While Ma chattered on, Thomas stood to shake my hand, clearly having just come from town. He grinned widely.

"Welcome home, Eddie."

I pulled him into a brief hug, slapping his back. "You've grown up!" I laughed. He was seven years younger, and had grown into a man since I left.

"Yes, old timer, it's me. I'm sorry I missed you in town. We could have ridden back together."

Just then, the door opened and Da rushed into the room, still in his coat and gloves.

"My boy!" he shouted, pulling me into a cracking hug. "Home safe! And in victory over those mangy Beasts too!" He dealt me a few slaps to the back, even harder than the ones I had imposed on Thomas, grinning from ear to ear. Lazard entered again discreetly, nodding to my mother and taking my father's outerwear as soon as he had an opening.

"Let's go in for dinner everyone," Ma said, raising her voice to be heard over my Da's commotion. "They've obviously been starving poor Eddie." Standing and ushering us toward the dining room, she batted my father away, to his amused chuckle, and took my arm instead.

Dinner was lavish. Cook managed to put several of my old favorites on the table, and we all lingered over the food, joking with each other and telling stories. Ma was surprisingly quiet, chiming in only now and again when Da told a story wrong, or to ask one of us a question.

BELLE & BEAST

The last crumb of dessert cleared from my plate, I couldn't help breaking the spell of warm-hearted companionship, excusing myself to bed. Da walked me to the door.

"Eddie, you've been running yourself ragged. Well, you're home now. Instead of a battlefield at the border, you'll soon be in the battlefield behind a desk with me and Thomas. We've been looking forward to having you take on some of our paperwork, eh Thomas?" They laughed and Ma shooed me off with one more kiss.

Da's words bounced between my ears as I prepared for bed. Although I was glad to be home and looking forward to peacetime, I had done well as a soldier. Secretly, if I was honest with myself, I had enjoyed it. Not the killing, exactly, but the camaraderie, the discipline. Seeing what needed to happen and just doing it.

I was good at fighting. Good at commanding my men. I had become at home in the battlefield, at home sleeping out of doors and constantly on the move. The thought of sitting behind a desk and negotiating trade deals made me uncomfortable—a suit that didn't quite fit.

I puffed out a breath. *There's bound to be a period of adjustment. And adjusting to running a successful business isn't exactly a hardship.* Some of my men were going home to very uncertain circumstances.

I'll ride back to town after breakfast to check on some of them. Maybe we can offer them positions here at the Manor House. I sunk down on my bed—the first real mattress I had slept on in over a year—and passed into sleep.

* * *

I awoke with a start, disoriented by warm darkness. *Where am I?* My ears reached for sounds of the battle nearby but met with silence. *Have they pushed the line forward while I slept? I need to get back out there.* My hand reached for my bayonet but encountered heavy blankets instead. Disoriented, I cast around, eyes starting to adjust to the gloom.

My room. Home.

Pale light was starting to leak around the edges of heavy drapes in the windows, highlighting splashes of color on a new rug. Another change. Most of my room was as I remembered it, but Mother had obviously been updating pieces of the house here and there. The little changes bothered me. It was disconcerting to walk into the setting of a memory, and find it just different enough to make you doubt.

Dreams of home were a steady anchor for a soldier camped in cold and mud. Or dreams of a sweetheart. Many of my men would ramble on and on about not minding much as long as they knew their special someone was safe and waiting for them.

I yawned, swinging my legs out of bed. The softness of an actual mattress was so foreign it was almost uncomfortable. I wasn't exactly rested, but I had more energy than I was used to, and I itched to be doing something.

Perhaps a ride to Stone Farm to surprise Trinette. And I should ride with Thomas back to town and check in on my men. A laugh escaped me as I thought of poor LeFeu. He was probably out of words by now, having used up his usual meager supply to satisfy his family's curiosity and become acquainted with his new nieces and nephews. A flash of white caught my eyes. An envelope lay propped against a vase on the mantle.

My note from Belle! Whichever servant had taken my travel stained clothes for washing yesterday must have put it there after finding it in my pocket. *Yes, I'll stop in at the Dower House first to feast my eyes on her, and pay my respects to her family.*

Although the changes at home had been disconcerting, Belle was as steady as a rock. It would be soothing to be in her calm, cool presence again. Eagerly, I prepared for the day, grabbing her letter from the mantle as I left for breakfast.

My appetite had returned tenfold while I slept, even after the enormous dinner Cook had sent up last night. I shoved my note into my waistcoat pocket, right next to my good luck charm. I could read while I ate.

Tinkling cutlery reached my ears as I entered the dining room. Thomas was buttering toast, stopping mid-yawn to grin at me sleepily.

Da stuck his head out from behind his newspaper. "Cook sent up all your favorites. You have your work cut out for you, my boy!"

Filling my plate and pouring myself a cup of coffee, I got to work filling my belly. I couldn't help wolfing down the first half of my plate as I had been used to doing over the last few years. When I stopped to wash it down with a drink, I caught my father watching with an amused smile.

"Nothing like home cooking, eh son?"

I chuckled and shrugged before continuing at a more sedate pace. Da and Thomas discussed business in between sips of coffee. Just as I finished the last drop of my own cup, Ma sailed in, radiating happiness. She swooped among each of us like a sparrow, planting kisses.

"All my boys together again! Well except little Jean, but he'll be here later! And of course my sons-in-law. But we shall all be together for Yuletide and then my heart will be bursting! Now, Thomas, Cook has a lunch prepared for you so mind you stop in for it before you go. Unless you're staying here for the day?" She looked over at him inquiringly as she filled her own plate from the sideboard.

"No, unfortunately," Thomas answered, looking apologetically at me. "We have a meeting with our best trading partner from Charmagne this afternoon. I need to finish preparing."

"Would you like to join us?" Da asked, slapping his hand down on the table. "You can ride over with me after lunch. Thomas will have everything ready. We could take a turn around the estate beforehand. I can show you the changes we've made."

"That suits me, Da, although I'm not sure I should sit in on the meeting. All I have to wear are my uniforms until I can meet with the tailor. A grim looking soldier might make your partner nervous." I laughed. "But I would love to ride around the estate, or even out to the farms, as long as we have time to stop in at the Dower House. Oh, that reminds me."

Setting down my coffee cup, I fished the letter out of my pocket and broke the seal. Ma smiled fondly as she sat down, murmuring something about being young and in love, squeezing Da's hand as she did so. Skimming through the letter, my own smile vanished.

It was short. They always were. But while she started out as usual, I couldn't comprehend the rest of her note.

Dear Edouard,

Thank you for the note informing me of your release from your military unit and plans to arrive back home. Your mother was kind enough to pass it along at Chapel last Sunday. I must express the gladness of my entire family that you will be returning to Croiseux safely. We look forward to welcoming you.

I have news that will surprise you. You have been kind enough to consider yourself engaged to me these several years, and I know that our families have long expected us to marry. I must now release you, and them, from that expectation, as I have recently become betrothed to another. My father and I signed the marriage articles just a few days ago, and I expect to be married in the new year. I am very happy, and I flatter myself that this news will not cause you any undue dissatisfaction, and perhaps may come as a relief. I hope you will be as happy for me to start a new adventure as you must be to come home from your own.

Sincerely,
Lady Rosebelle Montanarte.

I sat perfectly still. *Belle, the one I had been planning on marrying for the last decade at least, betrothed to another?*

That she would be happy doing so I discounted

immediately. *We've been in love since childhood.* True, we had never had a grand romance like my sister Clair enjoyed reading about in novels, but she had always been my Fair Maiden, and I her Knight.

None of this makes sense. If Belle had been courted by another, surely my parents would have given me notice of it. She must be under the delusion that I had changed over my long absence and desired a release from our engagement. It was just the sort of selfless consideration I knew her to have in her heart.

She would have had no trouble capturing another's regard, or course. She was the most beautiful woman in town, and of noble blood as well. But it would be simple enough to make this fellow understand my prior claim once he realized her love for me.

Looking up, I caught my mother's eyes. "Ma, what do you make of this?" I asked, handing her the note. She read it through, turning to stare at me with shock.

"That answers my question. So, you haven't heard anything that would make you think she had fallen in love with someone else?"

"No, dear, not a thing!"

My father and brother started asking questions, but I stood up, ignoring them all. Questions could only be answered by one person, and she wasn't here. Leaving Ma to explain, I stalked out to the front door, calling for my greatcoat and hat.

Instead of waiting for my horse to be saddled, I practically ran to the Dower House, just as I had done hundreds of times in my youth. Stopping to catch my breath as I reached the front door, I straightened up and knocking as loudly as I could. It opened a moment later, and Hazel Veneur cannoned into me, hugging me fiercely.

"Eddie! Oh hang propriety!" Her voice was slightly muffled by my shoulder. "I know I'm supposed to welcome you in discreetly and take your things with a curtsy, but forgive me once for old times sake. I'm so happy you're home safe and sound!" I hugged her back just as fiercely. Although Belle had always been the object of my affections, Hazel was one of the best friends anyone could have.

She pulled back to peer around me. "Is Henri not with you?"

I shook my head at her with a slight grin, despite my inner turmoil. She smiled up at me for a moment, then seemed to note my tenseness and nodded, her expression becoming more serious. She was no doubt aware of the circumstances conveyed in Belle's note.

"I see. Well, let's get you out of the cold." She ushered me in to the sitting room without offering to take my coat. Before I had a chance to voice my desire to see Belle she turned back toward the door.

"Everyone is mostly still asleep, but Belle is in the dining room. I'll fetch her for you." She hesitated for a moment as if to say something more, then turned and left.

Time seemed to stretch on, although probably only a few minutes passed until Belle was before me, offering me her hand with a pale, inscrutable look on her face. I stood and clasped it between both of my own.

"Welcome home, Edouard. I am so glad you've returned safely."

I didn't know what to say to such an opening.

"Did you receive my note?" she inquired, and I nodded, releasing her hand as she turned to sit by the fire. "You must have questions."

I remained standing, surprised by her calmness. *But she's always calm. She masks her thoughts and emotions, never wishing to burden others. It doesn't mean she isn't under terrible strain.* I did detect signs of tension in the set of her mouth.

"Belle," I finally croaked out. "What did you mean by it?"

A small laugh escaped her and she looked at me with almost harsh amusement in her eyes, but quickly resumed her usual grave demeanor.

"I apologize, Edouard. I thought I had made myself clear in my letter, but perhaps not. What I meant was simply this: I have become engaged to another."

I sat down quickly. It was one thing to read a note, and quite another to hear it from her directly.

"This can't be what you truly want. We've been in love for years! I can only think that you doubt my continued affection —which hurts, but is understandable after so long an absence." I slid forward in my chair. "Your goodness always puts others above yourself, but for once, take what you desire instead!" I considered reaching out for her hand again, but dismissed the urge. Belle had never been very demonstrative and I didn't want to distress her further.

A brittle laugh escaped as she arranged her mouth into a small smile. "Edouard, thank you for such kind words. I'm sure you're eager to marry and settle into your new life. But as you know, we never formalized our engagement. As it happens, in the interim, I was given the opportunity to attach myself to another person. I have done so, taking—as you phrased it— what I have desired most."

Confusion swept over me. Not wanting to look at her air of calm unconcern anymore, I studied the floor in front of me, considering her words. I felt no pain. Surely that would come later. But the world no longer made sense around me. Belle's voice chimed out again, a little softer.

"I know it isn't what you expected. I hope you will come to see that this is the best possible outcome for us. Perhaps someday you will wish me joy, just as I shall whenever you marry."

That was so like her. I looked up, a pulse of warmth threading through my bewildered heart in response to her goodness.

"You're always thinking of others before yourself. What pain I might feel means nothing if you're truly happy. I wouldn't be so low as to try to keep you if you loved someone else. How could I look at myself in the mirror with any honor?" She didn't meet my eye, smoothing her skirts repeatedly. Curiosity overtook me.

"Who is this lucky man? I may not shake his hand at Chapel on Sunday, but I'm sure I'll bring myself to do so by your wedding day." I managed a short laugh. She frowned in response.

"You won't see him at Chapel. He's not from our parish. In fact, he's not even from our country."

"Then who?"

She drew a breath and straightened in her chair. "I am engaged to Prince Andrus of Asileboix."

For the second time that morning my head was cleared of all thought. Slowly, her revelation trickled its way into my overtaxed brain.

"Asileboix. You will move to Asileboix. To marry the Prince." I stared at her with wide eyes as she gave a terse nod.

"How did you even meet him? And when?"

Belle lifted her chin gracefully. "I met him only recently, as a result of my father's last research trip. Papa had been granted access to the Asilean library and archive. The Prince and I..." She trailed off and a rare, faint blush appeared on her cheeks as she thought over her next words. "I'll just say that all my happiness and wellbeing is inextricably linked to becoming his wife. It was all very sudden."

Her blush shook me even more than her words. She never lost control of her emotions, yet this stranger stirred her so much that she was blushing over him? A tendril of jealousy snaked into my heart and took root, blooming with anger and disbelief.

"Your father's research trip? But Belle, my Da—my Father, I mean—wrote to me about that. That was only a few weeks ago! You mean that you met this Prince, fell in love, and became engaged in only a few weeks?!"

She just pressed her lips together, as unreadable as ever. I stood up and paced the small room, needing movement to think.

"You would throw away everything we have for someone we know nothing about? Even if he is a Prince, there will be so many difficulties! I know that you've loved me too. I cannot have mistaken your heart all this time..."

She pushed out of her seat, walking toward a window overlooking the forest, her hands wrapped around her forearms. Her form bristled with anger. For someone who presented a universally collected demeanor whenever she was in company, this was the equivalent of a shout. I had rarely seen her this agitated since we were children. I pressed my advantage.

"You say you'll be happy to see me with someone else: just imagine another woman as mistress of Croiseux! You could never stand it. Your place is there, by my side. You will always have my heart, always. You've been in it so long there isn't room for another." Her only response was to change windows, leaning against the windowsill in front of her.

"I have no wish to anger you," I said softly to her back, wishing she would turn and run to me, saying it was all a mistake and asking for my help untangling it all.

She did turn from the window, but instead of softness, her eyes held fire.

"If that is so, please do me the courtesy of believing me. I have made my choice and I am happy with it." Her tone stung like a whip and I flinched.

She took a deep breath and smoothed her skirts before looking back at me.

"There's no going back to the way things were. Meeting Prince Andrus has opened up...well I believe my place is by *his* side. You'll discover someone who is much better suited to you than I am. She will preside at Croiseux and establish the Marchand family there, and you will bless me for having averted our marriage. I'll think of the two of you with happiness when I hear of it, whoever she may be. In any event, as I mentioned in my note, the marriage contract was signed. The wedding date is set. There's no question of undoing it."

A sudden image popped into my mind. A faceless woman, relaxing next to me under a shade tree in Croiseux's back garden, a number of children running wild through the hedges. A picture of peace and untroubled tranquility.

I shuddered at it. A Montanarte should be mistress at Croiseux after my mother, I knew it in my bones. It wasn't truly our house. We were merely keeping it until Belle could take her rightful place. In some of my more fanciful days as a child, I had imagined the house merely tolerating us until the Montanartes returned. Now Belle was trying to rewrite the only fate that made sense. I needed time to think this through.

"I know of old that once you have made up your mind, no one can sway it. It seems you have legally bound yourself to this person already, no matter what may be going on inside your perfectly composed exterior. If you truly love him, I'll wish you joy on your wedding day. But I'm sorry to say I can't do that right now. There's no one better suited to stand beside me than you, Belle. This man—prince though he is—hasn't loved you half as well as I have. It's a mistake. You must know that I will do all I can to save you from it." Casting one last look at her stoic face as my chest heaved, I stalked outside.

* * *

The cold air was refreshing on my overheated face. Gravel crunched as I stomped away from the Dower House. When I reached the end of their drive, two paths diverged at my feet. *Back to the Manor House to answer everyone's questions, and perhaps immerse myself in business? Or head toward the gamekeeper's cottage, my only inquisitors the apathetic trees?*

I took the path through the woodland. After such a disastrous conversation, I needed time to consider Belle's revelation, and plan a campaign to fix it. *It wouldn't hurt to say hello to the Veneurs, and maybe soothe my soul with some of Madame Veneur's cooking.*

The stillness of the woods settled my jealousy as I strode toward the Veneurs, puzzling over the events of the morning.

Belle, not at Croiseux? Impossible. Her affection had never been as deep as my own, but that had never bothered me. Her selflessness didn't allow her to give way to her own feelings. I couldn't see her falling deeply in love with someone else—an Asilean, no less—after all this time.

Besides, she had exhibited none of the lovestruck sighing I had seen some of the other girls display over romances while growing up. Even my ever-practical sister Trinette had displayed a softness toward her husband when she wrote of him to me. I certainly remembered scoffing at her blushes and giggles when they were first courting. Other than an errant flush of color, which was probably due to our indelicately direct conversation, I had seen nothing of such emotions from Belle.

There was a piece to this situation that I was missing. *Whatever it is, I'll fix it. Just another campaign to fight.* I nodded to myself and continued briskly toward the Veneur's cottage.

As I turned from securing the garden gate behind me, Madame Veneur opened the kitchen door of the cottage.

"Eddie!" she yelled, opening her arms wide. Two of their ever-present hounds spilled out of the house around her. I laughed as they charged me, sniffing and jumping up to lick my face once they satisfied themselves that I was neither prey or predator.

Monsieur Veneur's face appeared over Madame's shoulder with a grin. I hurried the rest of the way down the path and was enveloped in Madame's hug, succeeded quickly by a bruising handshake from her husband.

Holly appeared, bumping into her mother as Madame tried to get out of the doorway. The rest of the dogs wriggled their way through everyone's legs, barking joyfully as they escaped out to the yard. After several minutes of chaos we restored ourselves to order, and I found myself at the kitchen table in the same chair I used to sit in as a child.

"Just make yourself comfortable, Master Eddie. I'll heat up a pie for ye." Madame Veneur scurried around, issuing stern but ineffectual commands to the hounds as they settled around the warm kitchen.

Nothing much had changed in their small cottage. Same furniture; same warm, tidy kitchen with food in various stages of preparation.

The occupants were a little older, of course. I had been mildly surprised to see that Holly was no longer a toddler. She had been born years after the rest of her siblings, and had always stayed at her mother's side instead of running around with us older children. It seemed that was still true.

I soaked in the familiar scene. Madame chatted with me while she put a meat pie over the fire for me and started back to work on the other food she was making. Holly settled into her father's side with a blanket and a book, blinking sleepily. Monsieur Veneur was sorting through a tangled mass of pegs and cords to be used as snares. With Winter Solstice quickly approaching, he would need to provide a large batch of wild game for the Soltice Day Feast and other parties my mother would host.

Sixteen-year-old Rowan peeked his head through the door, his face red with cold.

"Welcome home, Master Eddie." I nodded at him as Holly grumbled about the breeze he was letting through the door.

"Da started me as apprentice 'bout two years ago now! I've taken over almost all of Hazel's chores since she went to work for Lady Belle."

I called my congratulations to him as he pulled the door shut, beaming with pride.

The oldest of a pack of girls until Rowan came along, Hazel had helped her father manage the Manor House's vast woodland growing up. Gamekeeping isn't a suitable occupation for a Pelerine woman, so she had started training as a ladies' maid with Belle once Rowan was old enough to help. Since he was a full apprentice now, Hazel probably only had to assist in pulling in game during hunts and feasting seasons. *I wonder if she misses it. She always loved hunting, improper though it may be.*

Her mother's voice broke into my thoughts. "Came from the Dower House, did ya, son?"

I nodded in response.

"You've heard the news then. Probably feeling a bit lost, eh pet?" I offered a weak smile as she put a cup of hot cocoa down in front of me.

"Don't fret yourself about it. That Lady Belle was born to be a princess, in charge of everything and everyone. And them Asileans ain't so bad. My Matthieu always said that they're a sturdy, dependable people, haven't you Matthieu?" She put her hands on her hips and glared at her husband. He nodded without looking up.

"That Prince o' theirs tis said to be fearsome, but I expect our Belle will have him in hand before the year is out, and that will be that. Even so, she needs looking after, is what I says to my Hazel. Always got a few pots bubbling on the stove, that one. Needs someone to make sure she don't burn herself. So I told Hazel that she's bound to go with Lady Belle and look after her. 'Cept Matthieu said she 'as to come home and help during feasting seasons until our Rowan's fully trained. Said those Asileans have women hunters, if you can imagine, so they're sure to let her." She looked doubtful.

"Woman or no, she's a solid hunter, and helped me train Rowan, too." Monsieur Veneur interjected quietly so as not to disturb Holly, who had fallen asleep next to him.

"Hmm," replied Madame Veneur, looking at me before turning back to her cooking. "We won't say anymore about it Master Eddie. I'm sure you've got your own thinkin' to do since you only jus' heard. But my Hazel will be looking after Lady Belle if I have a say in it, so don't fret. Besides, if Hazel goes too, they'll have an opening for my Holly at the Dower House. She'll train as lady's maid to Lady Rochelle, which would just be perfect, and close to home. She's of an age to start apprenticing but I can't bear to part with her yet." She smiled with satisfaction as she stirred the pot in front of her.

I drained my hot cocoa, the heat warming my chest as it went down. "Thank you for your kind words, and your delicious cooking."

"Yes indeed, Master Eddie!" Her eyes creased at my compliment. "Now, hand me that mug so I can do the washing up, there's a good boy."

Handing over my empty mug, I relished the last few bites of pie before standing up. "I need to be going, loathe though I am to leave this haven. You have no idea how often I dreamed of eating a game pie in this very kitchen when I was freezing my toes off at the border. LeFeu and I kept ourselves from starving imagining it!"

She laughed, her eyes bright with sudden tears and came to give me another cracking hug.

"My poor boys! Well, it's better than mulberry pudding to have you both home again. Tell Henri to come and see us soon. I'll be stopping in town next week so I'll have to bring him a pie then—I can't have him complaining I'm playing favorites. Although I seem to remember more than one being stolen from my windowsill by some troublesome youths back in the day. Perhaps I should punish the both of you!" She winked at me, then turned back to her sink.

"Stay a moment, Master Eddie, and I'll walk you out," Monsieur Veneur urged in a quiet rumble. Placing his work down gently, he picked Holly up with care. After depositing her in their snug little sitting room, he donned a coat and hat and we filed out the door. We turned deeper into the forest, walking side by side on the narrow path.

After several minutes in companionable silence, the gamekeeper cleared his throat. "Won't take up too much of your time, Master Eddie. I've kept your father up to date o' course, but he weren't at the Manor last time, so he don't seem to think anything of it." I looked at him curiously, stuffing my hands in my pockets.

"It's like this. Sixteen years ago, just before that war started up, I was finding strange signs in the woods. Now I see a funny thing here or there, bein' next to the border of Asileboix as we are, and I know the Romany still traverse those northern woods now and again. But this were different. Animals torn apart as if by a bear, but when any bear with sense would be hibernatin'. Or flung up in the trees. Strange totems and markings. Dead spots in the woods—areas where nothin' grew at all. It were just one or two things now and again, but they got worse as the war started, and worst of all just before that princess' wedding in Asileboix. The older sister to the current prince. She and her new husband were attacked by beasties in their own castle. Some of the Asilean huntsmen I knew from meetin' about herd migrations over the years were slain that day. They're funny folk, but they care for their woods and animals, which tells me a lot about 'em." Monsieur Veneur sighed heavily at the memory.

"Anyway, after that, the strangeness stopped suddenly. The Asileans started patrolling their woods much more heavily, and have done since. I seen totems on their side of the border more than I did as a lad, but that's their business, not mine, so I've left it alone. But now I've seen more and more charms and sigils on our side. Last month, there was two deer, slaughtered just like they were all those years ago. Now I finds a dead spot up at the northern edge of the Dower Wood. It ain't natural. After you and yours destroyed all those Beasties in the war, I thought we were safe. But the woods have changed. I can feel it. Somethin's there, or somethin's coming."

A prickle of unease crept up my spine. My eyes darted between the trees. Nothing felt strange to me, just the same woods I had tromped around in as a child. But I was used to battlefields now, and like everything else here, the woods had continued growing while I was away.

Veneur's talk troubled me. If he was seeing the same signs that he had witnessed before the outbreak of the fifteen-year war we had just concluded, it deserved attention. It reminded me of something General Des Concordes had mentioned when we spoke together after the award ceremony, and I thought back to my interaction with him.

The general had been greeting the officers who had received medals that day, including me.

"Captain Marchand, from a place called Croiseux?" I nodded as he shook my hand.

"I stayed there once with Lord Montanarte before his troubles. Grand manor, as I recall, and charming town too. But very near the border with Asileboix, those snakes. Wouldn't send us reinforcements at all during the war. Prince of their's was sniffing around for a bride a few years ago. As if we would put any of our daughters into his clutches!" The general made a noise of disgust and folded his arms. "He had the nerve to approach my older brother about an alliance with my niece. Duke of Bentien, you know. And my niece is heiress to a large estate in the west. Wouldn't even lend us an army unit as part of his marriage articles, which I suggested to my brother. If we were overrun, where would that leave Asileboix, I ask you? Perhaps they wouldn't be troubled by it, eh? More beast than man, the old tales say. Well, may you go home to well earned peace, Captain. But keep one eye turned toward those Asileans. We depend on soldiers like to you to keep us safe. Just send me word if they cause any trouble." He had turned toward another officer at that point, and I had tucked his little speech away as an interesting foible from an otherwise brilliant general. Now it seemed that he may be on to something.

"Keep me apprised as well, Veneur. If it's the same pattern from before, that's enough to worry me. I planned on reviewing the estate and town's defenses now that I'm home, but maybe I'll start by organizing a regular patrol in the woods; if it won't affect your game quotas, that is." I looked at Veneur enquiringly.

"Aye, that would do," he said, scratching his beard. "So long as they isn't going through my usual huntin' grounds, should be fine. I'd feel better with more eyes and ears out. If Hazel were a boy she'd be my assistant by now, could take some of the load. All I have is Rowan, good lad. Not enough eyes 'round for my likin'."

"Right. I'll talk to LeFeu and let you know what we have in mind after Chapel."

He nodded, shaking my hand one more time before we parted ways. He, back to his warm cottage and family, and I, back to the Manor House with a bit more confidence in my step. I still had no idea how to win Belle's heart back, but here was I a problem I knew how to meet.

A sense of purpose rooted within me, filling some of the space left by all the changes and Belle's defection. I quickened my pace to a jog, eager to get to work.

CHAPTER SIX

Belle

"How much longer are you going to be, Hazel?"

She grinned down at me from her perch, slowly sawing through a moderately sized pine branch. We had already gathered swags of holly, juniper, and fir, but just before we started home, an idea had occurred to her.

So far, her idea consisted of leaving me to twiddle my thumbs in the middle of our already over-filled baskets. I was secretly hoping her younger brother, Rowan, would stumble upon us as he checked snares or something. I would coerce him into carrying my share of the baskets back. I couldn't help grumbling as I rubbed my hands together to keep warm.

"If Henri could see you now, he'd never have you!" I yelled up to her, grumpily.

"What a rude Lady you are, Belle. I thought you were supposed to be composed and gracious at all moments of the day," she shot back, making me grin.

"There's a loophole in the nobility rules. We can be as ungracious as we like if we're stuck in the cold, waiting on our friend to come to her senses."

"Ah, well, you're not wrong about that. And I doubt Henri would have me even if I wasn't prone to climbing trees."

She tossed me an exasperated look. Hazel had fallen in love with Henri the year before he left for the war. She had tried everything we could think of to make him fall in love too. In typical LeFeu fashion, he proved to be as observant as a rock and left without giving her any hope. Despite my advice, she had never wavered during his absence.

The sawing stopped.

"Are you okay?" I peered through the branches.

A disgruntled sigh drifted down. "Yes, fine. Just thinking. When I was in town yesterday, the cooper's daughter was sitting at the forge while he worked, chatting cozily. He was actually answering her! But when I stopped in to welcome him home, he barely gave me the time of day. Said he couldn't talk because of his work! Although, he was helping his father with some beautiful iron scrollwork at the time, so that was true, I guess. And he was only working on nails when the cooper's daughter was blabbering on, but still. If he's looking for attention, couldn't he look *my* direction?" A few pine needles drifted down as Hazel shifted her footing above.

"If making nails is as boring as I imagine it is, I'm sure he'd be happy to talk to anyone. Even though he has the personality of a brick, Henri is good enough to deserve better than Justine, and smart enough to know it."

I sighed. "But Hazel, if he isn't smart enough to realize you've been waiting for him, maybe it's time to move on. You said you talked to him about it before he left, didn't you?"

She stopped sawing to look look down at me. "I told you I did." Her gaze turned thoughtful. "At least I think I did. Looking back maybe I wasn't completely clear. But he's impossible! It's not as if I could just declare my love and propose to him; it wouldn't be proper!"

I shot a glare in her direction.

"Oops! Present company excluded. There's a loophole in those nobility rules for that too obviously." She grinned and started back to work again.

A loud cracking noise split the air. The limb Hazel had

been sawing dropped to the ground, sending pine needles everywhere.

"There!" She declared, tossing the saw a safe distance away before dropping down on the other side of the tree. "Urgh, I have pine sap on my skirt, but it's worth it."

"Worth what, you insane woodland creature?" I demanded through my scarf, having ducked my chin down into it to keep warm.

"The scent! At home, we always have a section of pine branch in among the logs on the fire. It spreads the scent throughout the room. Since it's our last Yuletide here, I thought we could do it at the Dower House too!" Grabbing her saw, she started splitting the limb into sections.

I put my foot on one end of the branch to help keep it steady. "We have enough branches to ensure the house smells of pine until the new year. Besides, Mama says—wait a minute. Did you say 'our' last Yuletide?" I looked at her over my scarf, not daring to breathe. She stopped what she was doing to grin at me.

"Yes, I did. I've decided to go with you, if you'll have me."

I let out a very unladylike whoop, jumping up and down.

"But I'll be needed to help my Da at feast days for a couple years until Rowan is trained to become his full assistant. Do you think that will be a problem?"

I rushed over to squeeze her. She laughed, holding the saw away from us gingerly, and I gave her a kiss right on the top of her strawberry blonde head. Although we had been the same size as children, she had stopped growing when we were fourteen, just slightly over five feet. I had continued to grow almost another half a foot and towered over her. Stepping back, I pulled my scarf down from my face.

"I'm sure it'll be fine. I'll write to Princess Mathilde. Since you'll be the only person I'm requesting to bring with me, and your father already knows their huntsmen, I'm sure they'll approve. Oh Hazel, if you're there I'm sure I can face anything. Even my own husband!" I couldn't help beaming as I held the branch, while she continued working. My heart felt like soaring into the clear blue sky above us.

"Here," I ordered, holding out my hand for the saw when she took a break after a few minutes. I finished the small section of branch that was left and we distributed the branches between our baskets. We began trudging back, following a meandering game trail.

Just before we made it back to the main path, Hazel came to a standstill. I barreled into her.

"Are you okay?" I asked, adjusting my hold on my basket.

"Look."

She pointed to our left, and I peered in the direction of her hand. Just an arm's length away hung a wooden ring. Small animal bones, teeth, moss, and several charms dangled from it. One I recognized as an ancient depiction of the Lady of the Woods, carved in a small amber figurine, dangling by her raised hunting bow. The huntress stylization. The Lady was more often shown grouped with forest animals or women and children, expressing her protective nature. But this was beautifully worked, and seemed to glow when the light caught it.

I stepped off the path to get a closer look at the other charms, but Hazel dropped her basket to grab my arm.

"What are you doing?!" she hissed shrilly, her eyes darting all around us.

"I want to look at the charms. The darker ones are hard to see." I moved toward it again.

"Leave it," she ordered. Leaves crunched in the distance and a branch snapped.

My eyes snapped to hers. They radiated fear. *Just a deer. Or maybe Rowan?*

I stepped back onto the game trail and she snatched her basket off the ground, hissing, "Let's go, *now*."

Once we left the tree line she let out a breath, and slowed down, shuddering as we stepped from the gloom of the woods into the sunshine behind the Dower House.

"Belle, I need to go tell my Da about that. Do you mind if I run to my parents' house now instead of after lunch?"

"That's fine, but what was it?" I panted, coming alongside of her as we continued walking. The baskets were making my arms ache and I was too warm from the swift pace we maintained.

"It's a hanging charm. I don't know what it's for, but they have magical properties. Da said I was to tell him immediately if I ever came across something like it."

She was breathing heavily too, and shifted her basket onto her hip. "The Asileans post hanging charms on in their side of the border, but they just have depictions of the Lady and their Prince's crest. This was different."

"But if whoever made it was trying to invoke the Lady, surely it was benign..." I trailed off staring at Hazel. "Wait, you said Asileans use charms in their territory, but that was our land."

She nodded. "That's why I have to tell my Da. If someone saw it, your family could be accused of harboring magic. Da can ask one of the Asilean huntsman to move it next time they meet."

After unloading our baskets by the kitchen door, I waved her off to her parents' house and made my way upstairs, my mind racing. Grateful to be out of the cold, I changed into dry clothes, and carefully extracted the papers hidden in my wardrobe, wrapping myself in a blanket by the fire to look through them.

Near the bottom of the pile I found the one I wanted. An index of depictions of the Lady, including sketches. There were two pictures of her stylized as a huntress. One of the sketches looked similar to the amber charm I had seen. A small note at the bottom of the page caught my attention. *This style is similar to one noted in Hermier's Magical Instructions, Bestiary, and The Lady, for uses in spells supposed to give warning or draw evil.*

I shivered and pulled the blankets close. Hermier's book held the reference Papa found to the Asilean royal family. It was the one which sent him to their castle and changed our fates forever.

Magic had been outlawed in our country for generations, and most people, my father included, didn't believe in it. Some claimed that as long as you didn't *believe* it held power over you, it wouldn't.

How they reconciled that with the resurgence of the Beasts —abominable creatures that had more power and stamina and cunning than any usual animal predator on our continent— I didn't know. Papa claimed they were predators from the continent beyond the high mountains that had found a way here and were multiplying without the presence of whatever force checked them in their own territory. I was inclined to agree with the prevailing theory: that they were twisted by whatever magic had created the wasteland, the origin of which had been lost over the centuries since their first appearance.

It had never mattered much since the war had been contained to the border and our plains to the east. Magic had mostly been an academic topic we stumbled across in research on the Lady, or sometimes in newspaper articles, when the police had uncovered some bumbling magician or sorceress, hawking love or wealth potions.

The charm in the forest was tangible. The time taken to craft the tokens and collect the broken bits of bone and feather and moss spoke of something wilder and more vibrant than I had imagined. *Somehow, it's connected to the Asileans.*

Maybe I am making an error in judgment, as Eddie claimed. I shrugged. It changed nothing. And just because the Prince's family lineage may have been up to their eyes in magic, or even blood magic, it didn't mean they were currently. Mathilde was much too warm and sensible to be involved in something nefarious. The Prince didn't seem evil—even if he reminded me of a disagreeable bear.

Besides, as you're at pains to convey to Eddie, the marriage articles are signed and legally binding. If I were to back out now, we would be in a more ruinous position than before.

I would find my way forward. But I was more determined than ever to figure out what my father had been so close to discovering. *How can I smuggle these notes into the castle with me?*

Looking around my chamber, my eyes lit upon the old, inlaid writing desk in the corner. *That's it!* As Princess, I could assuredly commission a new, grander one, but this one held several secret drawers that would do the trick. Stuffing my papers inside them, I rushed downstairs for permission to take it with me.

✽ ✽ ✽

The Yuletide season passed quickly. As news of my new engagement became widespread, we received more visitors than usual, and paid more calls in return.

The most painful visit had been to the Marchand family for our traditional Winter Solstice celebration at Croiseux Manor. We arrived to the usual joyous chaos. Madame Marchand looked at me very gravely from her seat by the fire.

Monsieur Marchand stood to greet us, hugging me with tears in his eyes.

"Congratulations, my dear. To think our Belle will be a Princess!" I couldn't help smiling as his attention was captured by my father's entrance, the two of them quickly heading up to Monsieur Marchand's study to discuss some new idea or another.

Trinette stole a few moments from shepherding her children and husband, and most of her other family members too, to take me aside and offer me sincere congratulations.

"I never thought you and Eddie would suit. If you've found your match, I think everyone involved will be happier—no offense."

I *was* a little offended by her frankness, but having known her so long, I recognized the compliment she was trying to give me and thanked her.

After a while, Madame Marchand had warmed up again, saying to Mama, "What will Eddie do now that Belle is off to foreign parts? How he let her slip through his fingers, I'll never know."

Mama made a noncommittal noise. "And how is he settling in?" She asked, successfully diverting Madame Marchand and nodding at the waterfall of words from her friend, who was interrupted frequently by her grandchildren.

I caught my mother looking longingly at them and I felt a sudden pang, wondering how often she would be able to see any children I might have. My nerves fluttered momentarily thinking about what was necessary to create said grandchildren, but I quickly banished the thought from my mind.

Eddie's other sister, Clair, offered me a sweet smile. "I'm so happy you've found your own true love, just like I have with my dear LeRoy." I murmured my thanks as Rochelle linked arms with her, pulling her away to discuss her own impending motherhood.

Thomas sketched a quick bow as he followed after them. He barely spoke to me the entire day, but that was due to his preoccupation with blushing at my sister—and receiving her blushes in turn—than any disapproval at my choices. I was surprised by the two of them, but decided to leave it for now. It was Yuletide after all. Although my sister was destined for finer things, there wasn't much harm in receiving attention from a nice boy like Thomas at a party. If only he had been the sole Marchand brother paying attention to a Montanarte sister!

Eddie was the worst of it to my great annoyance, but not my surprise. He was a perfect gentleman, of course, but he attached himself to me like glue on a vellum binding.

"Come sit by me at the fire, Belle," he entreated. I could hardly refuse or the tentative bridge what was being built between our families after my defection would be crushed.

He waxed lyrical of yuletides past, our games with Henri and Hazel as children, and on and on. He plied me with treats, attending to my comfort in all the little ways a lifelong friend knows, a futile attempt to sway my heart.

Being at beloved Croiseux Manor for what was probably the last time was a bittersweet trial, but having him gently wooing me with such solicitude was nauseating. I was the closest to being the saint Eddie always claimed I was, bearing with him patiently, and only snapping frosty replies a few times.

"I'm going to lock him in the coat closet," I hissed to Hazel as she passed me at one point.

"Behave!" She retorted, laughing. Her smile turned bashful as the LeFeu family entered, Henri in their midst. She quickly drew the children into a game, pretending not to want LeFeu's attention as he stood watching. Although he laughed at Hazel's boisterousness, I didn't see him paying any special attention to her, and whenever she addressed him directly, their encounters seemed painfully awkward.

Obviously Henri's heart was not in the same place as Hazel's. It would be good to get her away from Croiseux. *She'll have a chance at finding someone new.*

Despite those trials, I tried my best to treasure the day, as well as our own quiet family festivities at the Dower House. Before I knew it, Winter Solstice was over and we were heading toward a new year—and my new life.

* * *

The conclusion of Yuletide festivities saw me bumping along in one of my future husband's carriages, headed to the Asilean castle for tea and a dress fitting. Mama and Chelle had both contracted a cold after Winter Solstice and remained at home. Hazel dozed in the seat across from me instead, having been approved as my attendant by letter from Princess

Mathilde only a few days before.

We passed straight through the outer wall, gatekeeper bowing instead of asking our business like last time. Mathilde stood in the Great Hall to greet us.

"Happy New Year, and welcome back," she greeted, kissing both cheeks. "My son is still in his cabinet meeting unfortunately, or he would be here to greet you as well. He'll join us at tea. Do you need any refreshment before we go to the fitting?" I shook my head and we started toward the seamstresses rooms, Hazel trailing behind us.

As we entered a small fitting room just off the main workshop, Hazel and I gasped at the gown laid out on a nearby table. Clothilda, the head seamstress, whom I remembered from when we picked the fabric during my last visit, looked up from where she was working, smiling at my astonishment.

"How exquisate!" I gushed as I looked it over. The beautiful rose wool-silk blend had been sewn into a wide skirt. It split in the front to reveal a delicate white underskirt, sewn with horizontal flounces. The waist was fitted around the front and sides, but was allowed to hang loosely in the back, from the shoulders, down to the floor, creating a small but regal train that would be beautiful and easy to manage. The neckline was wide and although not very low, looked lower than what I was used to wearing—perfect for displaying jewelry. It would easily be the most beautiful dress I had ever worn. *I can't wait to try it on!*

Hazel and the seamstress helped me change, and I was soon standing in front of a full-length mirror, an excitement approaching giddiness stretching my lips into a wide smile.

"Absolutely perfect. I knew that color would suit you to the bone," Mathilde pronounced, appearing next to me in the mirror.

"It will be nice to have a Princess of Beauty reigning over the castle, eh Clothilda?" she joked with the seamstress, the two of them laughing at the strangled expression on my face. Mathilde squeezed my arm, "You'll get used to us soon enough.

And you really are a vision in this dress. You'll send Andrus into a fit of vapors when he sees you."

Banishing the image of the stern prince that suddenly popped into my head, I gingerly stepped out of the gown with Hazel's help. She and Clothilda carried it over to the work table again, chattering about beadwork as they went. They seemed to be well on their way to friendship.

I felt a pang as I stepped back into my own gown. It was the same one I had worn the first time I was at the castle, being far and away my best winter gown. The quality was only marginally better than the work gown the seamstress was wearing and vastly inferior to the Dowager Princess' rich-hued day gown.

I pulled the sleeves of my mitts a little tighter, hoping the seamstress hadn't noticed how rough my hands were from assisting with housework all these years. Vanity on my part, I knew, but it was a painful reminder of how low our family had fallen, even though I actually enjoyed working alongside Hazel as we chatted. *True beauty comes from within*, I reminded myself sternly.

As I stepped from behind the changing screen, Princess Mathilde linked her arm with mine and led me from the room. Hazel stayed behind to receive instruction from Clothilda on how the dressing would be managed on the day of the wedding, and if I knew Hazel, a good gossip all around about castle life and who was who.

Mathilde and I paced toward the family wing, stopping periodically as she pointed out notable rooms and artwork. Just as we entered a corridor I recognized from my first visit, a servant called to Princess Mathilde.

"Your Highness, a shipment for the Forest Guards was delivered to the kitchen by mistake. It's causing problems for the cook staff. The guardsman are here to move it, but are saying it won't fit in their storage area. They don't know where to put it," the servant relayed, slightly out of breath.

"I see. I'm assuming it's for the…" Mathilde's voice stopped abruptly and she glanced at me.

"Dear Lady Rosebelle, I hate to leave you on your own, but it will be much easier if I attend to this in person. It should only take a few moments. Would you mind waiting for me in the drawing room? You'll find it just through that door at the end of the corridor."

"Of course. I believe I used it the last time I was here, so I'm sure I can find it."

"Thank you, my dear. Go ahead and pour tea without me, just in case it takes a little longer than expected. I'll be back in a moment!" She turned back toward the way we came, head bowed close to the servant, clearly discussing the shipment and storage logistics.

Surely the steward would deal with such a thing. Then I remembered that Prince Andrus was in a cabinet meeting which may include his steward. *Besides*, I thought with a grin, remembering household lessons from Mama, *the cook staff's needs override all else in a house, whether it's a humble cottage or a grand castle.*

Ambling down the corridor, my feet slowed in front of a portrait of what was probably a long dead Prince and Princess of Asileboix. The Princess was beautiful: pleasant features, a soft smile, and long, loosely styled hair,crowned by a magnificent tiara. Not as extravagant a display of wealth as favored by the Pelerin royal family, but still regal. My eyes lit upon a sword belted on her waist. What I took at first to be openwork gloves covering her forearms were actually bracers. One hand was clasped in the Prince's next to her, the other rested on what I realized in wonder must be her own bow. The man next to her, crowned and obviously a Prince of the realm, held similar weapons. *She's a warrior.*

A strange thrill buzzed through me. Such a thing would be unthinkable in Pelerin. Sword fighting didn't exactly interest me, but Hazel had taught me to shoot with a bow in secret when we were younger, and I wondered what a Lady proficient with both could accomplish in her own power. She wouldn't be like me, seeking advancement only through marriage.

Of course, the warlike lady in the picture was holding the hand of the Prince next to her, so maybe a partnership could give strength after all.

The sound of raised voices reached me, and I realized that one of the doors near the portrait wasn't fully shut. A deep voice broke in over the others, causing a thrill to shoot up the back of my neck.

Prince Andrus.

Not wanting to be caught eavesdropping, I hurried toward the drawing room. As I passed the door, a few words became intelligible and stopped me in my tracks.

"If anyone is to die, let it be them, and let it be in droves!" the prince shouted.

My breath caught. Voices murmured and I strained to hear. I could only make out a few words, "Lady... Romany ... hanging". None of them were exactly soothing.

A fussy sort of voice called out over the others, much closer to the door than I had expected. "As Lueren has mentioned, Sire, there is nothing to cause concern. Adjustments have been made among the servants and guards."

The nearness of the speaker startled me into action. Picking up my skirts, I hurried down the hall and through the door to the drawing room. Glancing back toward the cabinet room, I was relieved to see that no one had come out. Quickly, I stepped inside and pulled the door shut behind me, breathing a sigh of relief.

I rushed over to the same sofa I had flopped into the last time I was in the room, sinking onto it a little more primly, hand on my chest. Every thought in my head was jumbled.

The Prince had obviously been angry about something to do with an attack. From the sounds of things, his advisers were riled up too. I hadn't heard of any attacks on Asileboix, but in Pelerin we received almost no information about our neighbors to the west.

An image of Papa's map depicting the entire continent of

BELLE & BEAST

Istoire formed in my mind. Asileboix was bordered by the wasteland to the north, Pelerin on the east and south, and the Grand Duchy of Sherwood to the west. *Maybe they're at war with Sherwood?*

My thoughts drifted back to the three broken words I had overheard. They had reminded me of the charm Hazel and I discovered in the woods, which reminded me of the mystery that led me here in the first place—the connection between Papa's research and the Prince. *Will he tell me after we're married, or will I need to dig it up on my own?*

Pushing out of my chair, I meandered to the sideboard, pouring out a cup of tea as the Princess had suggested. To my surprise, the teapot was quite warm. The servants must have been in here only a moment before I entered. I selected a few of the delicacies laid out on silver platters and settled myself back into my chair near the fire.

Princess Mathilde breezed in, pausing to fill a cup and grab some biscuits from the sideboard before settling across from me near the fire. We chatted about the wedding menu and schedule while sipping tea, and I relaxed.

Some time later, Prince Andrus entered the room, kissing his mother's cheek and sketching a bow in my direction, expression closed. His presence dampened the mood, at least for me. Princess Mathilde, of course, continued in her witty banter as she always did. *Does Andrus take after his father?* If the former Prince had been just as taciturn, I couldn't see what would have attracted the effervescent Mathilde to her now-deceased husband in the first place.

The prince settled down at the far end of my settee. He sipped his tea quietly, interjecting comments every now and again, but mainly alternating between glaring at the fire and glaring at me when I chanced to talk. It was unnerving at first, but soon became more of an annoyance than anything else. *Who glares at a person just for talking?* It's not as if I was saying anything shocking. *What would he do if I started spouting off some of Papa and Monsieur Marchand's fringe parliamentary*

109

ideas? Given the informality I had witnessed quite often amongst the staff and the royals in this castle, maybe those ideas wouldn't be radical at all.

I snuck a sidelong glance at him as I sipped my tea, noting signs of weariness that I had missed earlier. There were shadows under his eyes and he looked a little pale, even though his skin was still more bronzed than I was used to seeing on a nobleman. His eyes flicked toward me and I quickly turned my attention to my last biscuit, a flush creeping up my neck.

Now he would assume I was admiring him. Wonderful. Really, he was very good-looking, although not in the debonair way Pelerine men favored. I felt my blush spreading, and sent a prayer to the Creator in hopes that Prince Andrus didn't see. Thankfully a clock chimed soon afterward, announcing the time for my departure, and we all rose to leave.

"Lady Rosebelle, will you allow me to escort you to the carriage?" Prince Andrus addressed me with a small bow.

"I—well—yes, of course," I managed to respond, surprised. Princess Mathilde gave me a light kiss on my cheek and bid me farewell. Prince Andrus offered me his arm, guiding me through the door and toward the front hall. The carriage hadn't arrived, so we entered a small waiting room off the main entrance hall. It was just large enough to house a few seats and a small fireplace, the air cozy and warm. Delivering me to a bench nestled in amongst the windows, we both sat down on it to wait. As I took in our surroundings, he reached into his jacket pocket and pulled out a small box, withdrawing something from it before re-pocketing the box. He turned to face me.

He held his palm out to me. Laying in the center was a gorgeous ring. A band of shining gold crowned by a large, brightly-hued ruby in a high setting. I couldn't help but gasp a little, and he turned his glare from the ring to me.

"Will you do me the honor of accepting this token of our betrothal?" he asked, his tone flat.

The setting was designed in a leaf pattern, tiny emeralds

studded close together to give the whole thing an effect of a flower. *A rose, like my name,* I realized, with a little dismay. I opened my mouth to ask if the wedding band would be inscribed with a bell motif to complete the metaphor, but stuffed the words down before they could escape.

How very literal. It was amusing to joke with my family about the connotations of my name, as well as Chelle's, but it was a bit of a let-down to realize I would be wearing such an obvious token for the rest of my life. *Maybe I can change it later.* Although, tacky name reference aside, it really was a thing of beauty. Maybe I would grow used to it.

"I would be honored, Your Highness," I responded finally, blushing as I realized he had been watching me critically the entire time. He plucked the ring from the palm of his hand with two fingers and held it out to me. He meant for me to take it, instead of putting in on my finger himself. *How strange,* I thought, but was actually glad as I slid it on my own finger, feeling the callous under my knuckle. No need to reveal to him how unfit my roughened hands were to bear such a jewel.

"It's a rose," he announced, still eying me without so much as a hint of a smile, "like your name."

I wondered how to respond to that. *Is he looking for a reward for making that connection?* I bit my tongue. His glares made me sarcastic, and I was having trouble keeping my usual "public" demeanor.

Ice, I told myself. *Your blood is full of ice. It's cooling everything down. You're as cold as ice.* I felt my oddly erratic heartbeat slow down marginally under my efforts. Before we had to let her go, my last governess had taught me the trick as a way of calming myself in public—something I often struggled with as a child. The imagery had carried me through trying times ever since.

"Indeed. Perhaps it will be a useful reminder to all of your subjects as I am introduced," I replied evenly, imagining that my words were as cold as my blood.

A smile ghosted across his face. He turned to look out the window.

Did he really just smile at my sarcasm? Surely not—I'm seeing things in the lengthening shadows.

"It really is quite beautiful. Thank you, Your Highness," I murmured, mustering a little more warmth.

He looked back at me, his usual hint of a scowl dispelling any notions of smiling. "I'm pleased you find it so, Lady Rosebelle."

A rattle on the cobblestones outside our window drew both our attention. Prince Andrus stood, offering his hand. I rose as well, a little flustered, and took it. We swept into the courtyard without another word.

I glanced up as he handed me up to the carriage. He held my gaze for a moment, and I was startled to realize that he had beautiful eyes. Green with flecks of gold scattered throughout. They were rimmed with red. *He's exhausted. He needs a break,* I mused as he finished handing me up.

He closed the door without another word, stalking back into the castle. I watched him for a moment before turning to Hazel. She sat on the seat across from me, staring at my ring with huge eyes. I laughed and held out my hand.

We spent the rest of the ride comparing notes about our time at the castle, gushing over my dress, and talking about some of the changes we would need to navigate once we moved. After such a strange afternoon, I was glad to be settled back into the happy chatter I was used to with my friend.

❖ ❖ ❖

After my visit at the castle, Mama and Rochelle recovered quickly. We were soon so consumed with preparation for the wedding I could hardly keep track of the days. The castle seamstresses were making most of my trousseau, enough gowns and outfits to see me through until I was settled and could give them directions as to the rest of the items I required.

I had no need for furnishings or decorations to be moved other than my writing desk, which Papa had agreed to give me. Since the wedding would be held at the castle, our house and servants didn't need to prepare for guests. I would have thought that there wouldn't be much to do. In fact, I was afraid I wouldn't get the necessities completed in time.

We walked to town on several occasions, ordering local fabric and other odds and ends I wanted to bring with me from my hometown, including books. We also used some of my marriage settlement to pay for new dresses for my mother and sister, made by the town seamstress instead of sewing them ourselves. We procured new clothes from the tailor for Papa as well. Mama insisted on sorting through nearly every item in our house, most of which I elected to leave of course, but several items I ended up taking as security against days of loneliness in a new place. We finished our list the day before my wedding, and after an enormous lunch filled with some of my favorite foods, I escaped for a solitary walk to my favorite outdoor haunts to say goodbye. We were turning in early that evening in order to leave for the castle at first light. I wouldn't have another chance for a last walk at the Dower House.

My feet took me first to the empty stables, missing Star and Firefly. They were being housed in the Manor stables to make room for the horse and carriage that would convey us to the wedding the next day. Next I meandered through the kitchen gardens, mostly empty except for a few winter vegetables. I could see the spire of the Lady's shrine in the small hamlet not far from our house as I walked by our front gates. I had spent time at the shrine earlier in the week, praying to the Creator for protection and guidance as I started my new role, even leaving a ribbon tied to a mother of pearl button as a token to the lady. It was an old custom for brides that I had read about years ago. Placing it near the altar fountain, I couldn't help wishing she were real and could protect me while I continued my research into the Asilean mysteries.

My walk ended around the back of the house amongst the

beehives, just as the sun began to sink behind the trees. I would miss honey from our own hives once I moved. Did they have an apiary at the castle? I would think that would be easy enough to arrange if they didn't.

Walking toward the tree line, I reached out to touch a barren branch of the nearest tree once I was close enough. A rumbling of hooves reached my ears and I looked around, wondering if it was an outrunner from Asileboix.

It wasn't. The hoofbeats slowed, and two figures on horseback emerged from the wood line a few yards away. Eddie and Henri. They stopped when they saw me, turning to each other for a whispered conversation. Henri gave me a long look and doffed his cap before riding back into the woods. He had already given me a gruff but heartfelt goodbye when I passed by the forge during one of my trips to town this week. The sight of him made me miss our childhood. He had been woven into the fabric of my days, an inevitable part of any games or adventures I would be getting into. As much as the thought of him irritated me in general these days on Hazel's account, I would miss him. Eddie nudged his horse into a walk toward me. I rocked on my heels, fighting the urge to run back toward the house. *Your blood is ice.* It wasn't difficult to visualize in the frosty air.

After picketing his horse, Eddie walked the rest of the way, stopping about a foot in front of me with anguished eyes. I felt my blood boil in response. *Ice. Cold as Ice.* It had only been a few weeks since I had upended all of his plans. I owed him patience.

"Belle. You *cannot* do this," he pleaded, the torment in his eyes permeating his voice as well, making it thick and gruff. "I've tried to be patient, to win you back gently. I haven't seen any evidence that you love this Prince more than you love me, but you're persisting in your course! There is something you're not telling me. Whatever it is, we'll face it together. Why won't you trust me?!"

I turned from him, attempting to hide the censure that was surely creeping onto my face, but he grabbed my hand, stilling me.

"Belle, please. I'm begging you not to go through with it. I'll spend my life waiting for you to come back. I could never love another."

"Don't touch me!" I exclaimed, whirling around and unable to hide the venom in my voice. He dropped my hand with a look of surprise and I glanced at the Dower House. If anyone happened to look out the windows, they would be able to see me yelling at him. I stalked out of sight behind a nearby blackberry thicket. He trailed after me, as I knew he would.

"You idiot," I hissed. "You absolute fool. I've tried to make myself clear, but you keep pushing and pushing. You're right. There is something you don't know, so allow me to enlighten you."

As succinctly as possible, I described what had occurred just before he came home. He was stricken, his hands balled his hands into fists by the end of my tale.

"So you see, *dear Eddie*, I had a greater reason than you, or I, or even love, to make this match. But I didn't lie when I said I was happy. I *am* happy. I will be a Princess, and even now, my parents' and sister's fortunes have turned for the better because of this. Just leave it alone, and move on."

I waited for a response but he seemed at a loss, so I brushed past him.

"No," his voice rasped, just as I was turning the corner around the blackberry patch. Stopping in my tracks, I turned and stalked back to him.

"Excuse me?" I spat at him

"No," he repeated, his face utterly calm, but with a touch of iron in his voice.

Somewhere, the back of my brain appreciated how magnificent he was. *This is what he must be like in the heat of battle.* I could see him strengthening his soldiers' resolve in a lost cause, inspiring determination and winning the day by force of will alone. It was jarring to see a character trait buried so deeply emerge after all of these years. *Is there more buried inside that I missed?*

I was jolted back to the moment as he continued implacably. "I will not allow you to sacrifice yourself, even for the sake of my family."

He paused and I noted his clenched jaw, the tension cording his neck. "This man must be a monster to manipulate you in this position and force your hand in marriage. Force you to marry him when you don't love him! I won't allow you to throw your future away in misery—just so we can live in comfort and ease. No. I *will not* allow it."

That small back corner of my brain acknowledged that his speech displayed the type of character he had, the one that won medals of valor and sacrificed for his men.

The rest of me boiled in anger. I was surprised steam wasn't rising from my skin. Because although I had had similar thoughts about Andrus myself, I recognized my own image in the monster of his words. A monster who would sacrifice and manipulate situations to win their own goals and comfort. When I compared my own character to the heroic Edouard Marchand, well, I simply lost my composure.

"You. Won't. Allow. It." I bit off each word. "How funny it is to hear those words from you, Edouard. What a kind, benevolent dictator you are to issue such a proclamation, protecting my poor, feeble person. Unfortunately, it isn't *your* choice whether it will be allowed or not. It's mine. And I choose Prince Andrus. I choose him in spite of the so-called sacrifice I'm making. I choose him in spite of the fact that I'm not in love with him. I choose his country over Pelerin, and his castle over Croiseux. In fact, were the circumstances that initially necessitated my betrothal to him removed, I would choose him still. I don't deny that it's been a wrench, letting go of my family, but mark my words. He can—and will—give me things you could never give me. Do you see this?"

I yanked my left mitt off and showed him my crimson engagement ring. It sparkled in the final rays of the sun, sending splatters of deep red over the snow like blood. His eyes grew wide at the sight of the enormous jewel, then distant.

"It's just a token from him. A small reminder for me that he and I are bound. And I adore it." I yanked my mitt back over my freezing hand.

"We were engaged for five years, Edouard. Yet I never received a ring from you. Did you even have one? I'm curious—tell me!" I glared at him, my eyebrows raised in question. The air around us seemed to vibrate with anger. He pressed his lips into a grim line before giving a short shake of his head. "Just as I had thought," I retorted, my voice dripping with scorn. I shook my head.

"You speak of loving me, Eddie, but you don't. You created a shadow Belle whom you adore, but she was never real. I have always been just as I am now. If you knew me at all, you would see I'm perfectly suited to be the wife of the monster you just described. The thing is, although he's the one who put us in an impossible situation, I'm the one who maneuvered him into marrying me."

I put my hands on my hips as he frowned at my words. "Me! The poor daughter of an obscure nobleman. Past my prime. No wealth, no vast tracts of lands, no relation to the king of Pelerin. Just me. And I've seized the chance I've been given. So you *will* allow it, Eddie, because I wish it—and I've made it so." I huffed a scornful laugh. "If you can't face it, then don't come to the wedding. Believe me, if you make so much as a hint of trouble to ruin my happiness, I will find a way to crush yours."

I pushed him lightly along with the last of my diatribe, and he stumbled backward, a look of surprise on his face. I spun on my heel and walked a few paces, calling out as I left, "I told you one day you would thank me for being released from our engagement—now you can see why. You always land on your feet Eddie. Find someone else. Forget us—forget me."

CHAPTER SEVEN

Eddie

My feet stumbled a few steps toward Belle as she stormed away, but when I rounded the edge of the blackberry bushes they slowed to a stop. There were no words to bring her back after that speech. My hand strayed to my waistcoat pocket, as it had a habit of doing all on its own in times of trouble. I pulled out my good luck ribbon, silently counting off each little token that had been looped over it and rubbing my thumb along the frayed silk.

A door slammed in the distance and the urge to chuckle overtook me. My mind reached back to a hot summer's day, fifteen years before. I had stood in almost this same spot, rubbing the smooth silk of this same hair ribbon after she had given me an equally acidic tirade. Only time separated the adult versions of us from our childhood selves. She had completely flummoxed me then. *She still does.*

Her accusation darted across my mind. *Had I fallen in love with a shadow Belle?* I was a bit too raw to examine such an idea impartially, so I pushed it away until later.

A benevolent dictator. I turned the idea over as I pocketed my charm. A few of my men had joked with me using the exact same term. It had come from some battered philosophy book one of them had been unaccountably reading in between battles. I couldn't remember which philosopher. No doubt Belle had read the same book and recognized me in its pages, just as the men had done.

My horse whinnied in a friendly way as I approached her. The sun had fully sunk behind the trees and darkness approached. I needed to get back to the Manor House before my men arrived for dinner.

Our uneventful patrol hadn't distracted me from the state of misery I was in over Belle's wedding. When the chance to dissuade her one more time had presented itself, it felt like divine intervention.

I thought she had felt drawn to me as I approached through the trees, her heart knowing my presence even if she couldn't see me. I was hoping she would agree to elope. Instead I found her not only as determined as ever, but accusing me of never having known her! *She's inexplicable.*

Pulling myself into the saddle, I turned my horse toward the path to the Manor House. My mind insisted on sliding back to my encounter with Belle as I rode. *Can she really be happy in such a decision?* I didn't think any person could be truly happy without loving their spouse deeply. I knew it wasn't fashionable among the aristocracy, but Belle had been free of those expectations since she was young by virtue of her family's circumstances.

Truthfully, I couldn't help feeling a little triumphant at discovering that there *was* another layer to everything, just as I had deduced. But to allow a woman—let alone my beloved *Belle* —sacrifice herself for me went against every honorable bone in my body. I longed to swoop in and save her, but she wasn't exactly making that an option. The feeling of restlessness I had been pushing away since my return home surged over me again.

The rational part of my brain agreed with one part of her description of herself. Not that I would have said she was past her prime, but I agreed that she was a mature woman, not some flighty debutante. Even when she had been the age of a debutante, she had never been flighty. She had always been ten steps ahead of the rest of us, figuring out a way to make the best of every situation. *How can a man prove his love to a woman who doesn't want his love?*

I was struck suddenly. She told me how to do so in our first conversation after my return. "*Please do me the courtesy of believing me when I say that I have made my choice and am happy with it.*"

Could I do it? If I really loved her and respected that she was capable of making her own decision, then I suppose I had my answer. I sent a prayer to the Creator, something I had previously only done on the battlefield.

Tell me what to do. Show me somehow.

The sound of my horse's canter suddenly seemed to organize itself into the echo of a response. "Let her go, let her go, let her go." I chuckled at my foolishness, but turned the thought over in my mind.

Let her go? In all but the physical sense, she was already gone. The decision was already made. I had to respect her, and let her go.

A stab of pain went through my heart, but my mind felt clear. I would release her, knowing that meant I would never have her, knowing that I would never stop loving her. But I would be ready to assist her always. Whenever she needed shelter from the storm she was surely stepping into, I would be ready.

❊ ❊ ❊

I arrived back at the Manor House with just enough time to stable my horse and change before the men began to arrive for dinner. Most of them hadn't been to the Manor House before, but my mother's cheerful ways soon set everyone at ease. Conversation veered from some of the less gruesome war stories, to difficulties in picking up their trades or crafts again, to stories of children—or in some cases grandchildren—who had grown during our absence. Even LeFeu was talkative, for him anyway. He exclaimed over his younger brother's progress as apprentice to their father, pride coloring his voice.

After dinner we removed to the library. Ma left us after ensuring we were all settled, and I steered the talk toward the purpose for our gathering.

"Thank you all for coming. I brought you all here, not just to maintain our bonds and talk of the war, but to discuss the future. Our recent victory has secured peace for now, hopefully for the rest of our lives. But we didn't wipe out every Beast in the wasteland. Because of that, we know—we *know,* that they'll come again one day. It's only a matter of time."

I paused, evaluating each man. Some nodded, others looked at the table. Da met my eyes, a glass of port in his hand and a serious look on his usually smiling face. LeFeu was silent, arms crossed, surveying the men as well.

"We have to look to the defense of our town and villages," I continued. "The majority of that responsibility falls to the Manor House, and my father and I have already spoken about repairs to be made. The town walls have been kept in good order, although the Shrine in the Dower Hamlet has fallen into some disrepair. But we need to stock the armory. We must be prepared in case we are called upon to defend what's ours." Some of the men nodded, others looked blank. I pressed on.

"As I said, I hope and pray that our fighting days are over. But the fact is, our beloved Croiseux sits right alongside the ancient woods of Asileboix, a country we know nothing about except for the old tales."

Pausing for a moment, I could feel my anger at their Prince grow. I attempted to tamp down my ill will before continuing to speak, but couldn't rid myself of it entirely.

"The woodland to our north extends to the border with the Wasteland, and isn't well patrolled. If we aren't vigilant, the beasts could wreak havoc on us while we sleep. You know what they're capable of, and I know what each of you is capable of.

Can I count on you?"

A chorus of "Yes, Sir!" rang out, each man nodding. I expected no less. My former company had contained the best soldiers in our regiment.

Da and LeFeu pulled out a map of the estate, unrolling it on a table, and I motioned for everyone to gather round. We debated exhaustively about strategic points and time frames for patrolling borders. By the time I sent everyone off, either in carriages back home, or guest rooms for those staying overnight, I was satisfied with our plans. For the second time that day, I found myself thanking the Creator. It felt a little strange to be talking to a being I couldn't see and wasn't sure would care even if he or it existed.

Da went up to bed, but LeFeu and I wandered down to the kitchens in search of a snack. We were surprised to find Hazel there, speaking with one of the kitchen assistants about some venison she had just delivered on her father's behalf.

"Hazel, what are you doing here so late?"

She turned toward us with a smile as the kitchen attendant took the meat away for storage.

"I came to deliver my father's quota for the week," she replied, her eyes flickering between us. "I couldn't sleep for nerves about tomorrow, so I told him I'd take it over tonight. Save him a trip in the morning. I'm sleeping at my parent's house one last time," she added wistfully.

"Shouldn't have let you go alone so late at night," LeFeu said in his scratchy, deep voice. Sometimes I wondered if it was scratchy because it was rusty from disuse—although tonight he had talked more than he had in years.

Hazel frowned. "The path is on estate parkland, which couldn't be safer. And I think my Da can trust me to keep my virtue long enough to make a delivery and come back." Her skin was starting to match her hair color as her anger spiked at the perceived affront. LeFeu just glowered more darkly than usual.

"I don't think that's what he meant, Hazel. We're just

concerned about you, that's all," I interjected. The problem with these two was not lack of sparks, but that they caught and burned too quickly for either one to sort out what the other meant. Hazel was leaving with Belle in the morning, and I didn't want her last memory of us to be a bad one.

Henri may never get another chance to sort this mess out. I suppose I should give him a push since he allowed me my own chance with Belle earlier. Hopefully he has more luck. I cleared my throat.

"Hazel, I'm glad to have seen you, but it *is* quite late. You should head back or you won't be any help to Belle in the morning. Why don't you allow Henri to escort you?" I suggested nonchalantly. She opened her mouth but seemed torn between protesting her competency without being rude. I spoke again before she could make up her mind.

"LeFeu—run up and get your overcoat and gloves. I'll wait with her until you're back."

LeFeu looked at Hazel for a moment, then left before she could protest.

"Just let him walk you home," I counseled as she watched him go, eyes conflicted. "It will make us both feel better. Plus he's staying here tonight, so it's not as if he'll be going out of his way in getting back home."

She turned and gave me a wry grin. "Fine, *Master* Eddie, it shall be as you decree. I suppose I'll be glad of the company anyway."

Her joke prodded the still tender wound Belle had left. *Was I really more overbearing than I thought?*

"Hazel, I spoke with Belle earlier today. It didn't go well."

She rolled her eyes at me. "I know, I helped her with her things after she stomped into the house. She mentioned that she saw you—and that you were being a blockhead—but nothing more than that." Her sympathetic smile did little to ease my discomfort. "I'm sorry things haven't gone the way you wanted. But you have to realize that she really is happy with her choice, even if the circumstances aren't perfect."

"You know, then, how it all transpired?"

"Of course! I was there, wasn't I?" She sighed. "Just so you know, I did try to talk her out of it; but she has her mind set. If you think about it logically, it does sort of make sense. She's getting everything she's ever dreamed of since she was a child." She looked up at me, her nose wrinkled. "Or maybe you don't know that. She doesn't share much of herself outside of her family, so people sort of fill in the missing bits with ideas of their own. Trust me—she's content. And I suppose I am too." Her voice wobbled slightly, and she fussed with her cape as a distraction.

LeFeu entered and marched over to the kitchen door. He glowered at Hazel, ready to escort her out into the night. I chuckled internally. He can't help but look the typical taciturn blacksmith, with his dark hair and deep set eyes. But really, he could learn to lighten up a little.

No wonder Hazel hasn't been as responsive as he'd like since he returned. No doubt she thinks he's angry all the time. Hazel grabbed her empty game bags and gave me a quick hug before ducking under LeFeu's arm and out the door.

"And don't dawdle," I called to him with a smirk, earning me a glare of my own before he stomped out after her.

Grabbing a bread roll and a glass of water, I turned my steps toward my chambers. As I prepared for bed, my eyes caught sight of the clothes laid out for the wedding tomorrow. I had decided to attend—if only to prove to myself how far beyond my grasp she has gone. It would also be an opportunity to show her that even though I may not understand her as well as I thought, I'm still her stalwart knight, ready to champion her will, whatever her course. As I climbed into bed, I heard LeFeu's door across the hall open and close with a thud.

I smirked to myself. Well he either declared his love in short order and received a decided no, or he chickened out and just deposited her safely home before haring it back here. My money was on the latter.

Somehow, both of us had chosen to fall in love with the only two girls in the kingdom eager to leave it all behind.

CHAPTER EIGHT

Andrus

A rare free afternoon presented itself as I finished lunch. Lueren claimed it was to be used in contemplation of my wedding the next morning. What was more likely was that there was simply no one available to meet with me. My mother had called in every castle attendant, and even some of the townsfolk, to make sure preparations were completed on time. Not being used to such freedom, I spent some time going through the endless paperwork in my study. I was receiving more reports than usual from our border with the wastelands, but the activity wasn't as alarming as it had been almost two weeks ago. The Beasts were no longer harrying Pelerin. They had to go somewhere to sate their appetites. It was either our direction, or to the east.

I suspected it would be our direction. The worst of their activity always seemed to be concentrated around our country and Sherwood. Clement had reported in that same meeting that patrols were finding powerful charms scattered throughout the wood, concentrated towards our border with Pelerin. Romany make, and spelled to draw out and contain evil. I shivered. The Romany hadn't been to our lands in many years.

Pushing to my feet, I dropped my quill and walked out of

BELLE & BEAST

my study, attempting to leave my worries behind. My steward, Manciple, had reassured me that proper precautions had been taken for defense in both our outposts and at the castle. I could either trust the competent staff I had put in place around me or tear myself apart trying to do everything myself.

My feet carried me toward the castle chapel. It was a sunny space, quiet except for the tinkling of water from the altar fountain. I often took time in the mornings to sit and center myself with my place in the world. As I turned into the corridor leading to one of its side doors, I suddenly remembered why I hadn't done so this morning.

No longer calm, it was the center of activity in the castle. Doors thrown open, a buzz emanated from within, everyone working to clean its nooks and crannies and hang decorations. An enormous mound of greenery peaked over the top of one of the pews. I recognized several scribes from the library sitting in another row, chattering as they transformed yards of ribbon into bows.

I backed away. Not exactly the atmosphere of tranquility I was seeking.

I took myself instead to the stables and readied my horse, Ironheart. A bruising ride through the woods was exactly what I needed to burn off these nerves.

I made a quick circuit around the walls. Everything was exactly as it should be according to Manciple and Clement's revisions. I came across two patrols during my ride, both of whom challenged me before they recognized me, just as they were trained.

Manciple had been right, our security was perfect. Turning onto one of the main paths east of the city, I passed over a small river and rode toward Pelerin. It was one of the flatter and best maintained paths due to the easy terrain, and I wanted to gallop. I gave my horse her head for some time, and just focused on breathing. Whizzing scenery passed us by, and I lost myself in in the ride.

After several intervals of running and walking, I stopped to

127

let the horse drink from a nearby spring, taking note of our surroundings. We had come further than I had realized over the last hour or so, close to the border of Pelerin.

A sudden curiosity to see the Dower House rose within me, now that I was so close. No doubt it was just as busy as the castle. After my horse had her fill, I mounted again, following a footpath leading toward Croiseux.

I wonder what Lady Rosebelle is doing right now. Probably something efficient and logical if I had taken her measure correctly.

Her face flashed before me, her gasp when I presented her with an engagement ring. I had instructed our goldsmith to shape the setting so that the entire ring bore resemblance to a red rose. He had assumed it was in reference to the future princess' name, Rosebelle. Certainly, her name created a pleasant consistency, but that wasn't why I chose such a setting. The symbol of a rose had long been one I held before me as a reminder of my duty to my people's security above all else. A reminder that I was the master of my own fate.

Coming upon the boundary between Asileboix and Pelerin suddenly, I pulled up short. Dismounting, I tied my horse to a nearby tree before continuing on foot. It was improbable that anyone else would be here at this time, but getting caught in Pelerine territory would be unwise.

My desire to catch a glimpse of Lady Rosebelle's house was proving stronger than my common sense. It was as if I was being pulled there by something beyond my knowledge. Seeing with my own eyes that her house was secure seemed paramount.

As the edge of the trees came into view I stilled. Two figures stood next to a barren fruit tree, deep in conversation. I recognized Lady Rosebelle after a moment and chuckled softly. So, I wasn't the only one in need of a walk today. I turned to pick my way back to my horse, not wanting to stoop to the level of an eavesdropper, when Lady Rosebelle's voice rose in pitch before abruptly cutting off. I whipped my head back in time to see her pull her hand away from the other person, then stomp closer to the tree line.

She stopped behind a large thicket, the man following stiffly. I settled down on my haunches, screened in the deepening gloom of the woods, determined to stay in case she needed assistance. *No doubt she hasn't had any sort of defensive training.* It would be highly scandalous for a Pelerine lady. *I'll have to convince her to learn after our wedding.*

Their conversation was too quiet to hear, for which I was glad, but I closely scrutinized their body language to be sure Rosebelle wasn't in any trouble. My posture relaxed after a moment. She was clearly in control, and looked like she was haranguing the poor man at her side. It was amusing to watch since I wasn't the target of it. Rosebelle stomped back around the thicket, calling once more over her shoulder to the man. This time she yelled loud enough that I could hear clearly.

"I told you one day you would thank me for being released from our engagement. Now you can see why. You always land on your feet Eddie. Find someone else. Forget us—forget me."

Her words put a damper on my amusement. My eyes snapped back to the man she had left behind. He had taken a few steps after her, but then stopped and pulled something out from beneath his coat. I moved forward several paces, heart suddenly in my chest in case it was a weapon, but stopped when he made no further move.

His hand dropped to his side and I couldn't quite make out what he was holding. It almost looked like a hanging charm, with several tokens dangling from a ribbon. *Some sort of protection charm?* A shaft of sunlight hit it through trees and suddenly I could see it clearly. A faded blue ribbon. I sat back, shocked, a twig snapping underneath me causing the man's horse to whinny.

He stirred himself and finally climbed into his saddle, the hood on his cape falling back as he did so, confirming everything. These were the two children I had witnessed arguing, in almost this exact spot, all those years ago. I could see the resemblance in the man's face, and the feeling of having seen Lady Rosebelle before suddenly clicked into place.

It was them.

I shook my head, pushing the memory aside. *It doesn't matter. Forget it.*

The scene I witnessed spoke of a long and intimate history. That must be the man she had been betrothed to, the engagement she had severed in her bid to marry me.

I'll need to be sensitive to that once we married. She would need time for her heart to heal from the looks of things. I had already planned on taking things slow so that we could get to know one another, but I needed to remember to give her time to grieve as well.

* * *

Once I was alone again, I focused on making my way back to my horse, obscuring my tracks as best I could. But after I was mounted and on my way back to the castle, the monotonous pounding opened the door to a memory I had been desperately trying to keep locked away. A memory that seemed to be repeating in the present. It flooded around me, blocking out everything else. I was retracing the very steps I had taken fifteen years ago.

I had been on patrol with Clement in this sector the night before my sister's wedding. I had witnessed those two argue, then ridden my horse back to the castle to prepare for her ceremony the next afternoon.

The wedding had been beautiful. Marguerite had been resplendent as she walked down the aisle in the throne room. People from all over Asileboix had poured in to see our beloved Princess marry her childhood sweetheart, the romantic tale known to all Asileans. Our capitol city and castle had been stuffed to the gills to accommodate everyone. During the ceremony, she formally renounced her hereditary right to rule as firstborn, passing that duty to me, her sixteen-year-old brother.

I had been standing across the ballroom from where Marguerite and Devon led the line of dancers later that evening. They were standing right next to an ancient stained glass window, waiting their turn to dance down the line when the first of the Beasts broke through it. I watched in stunned horror as it took down my sister. The one following it took her new husband. The screams of nearby dancers broke through my shock and my sword leapt out from its sheath on sheer instinct. I tried desperately to find my mother and father in the crowd, pressing my way toward the fighting.

Clement found me a moment later, and attempted to steer me toward the side doors.

"Prince Andrus! Come with me. Your father charged me with taking you and your mother to the Old Keep."

I pulled my arm from where he was holding it, glaring at him. He pushed me toward the door again.

"Your father has Forest Guards with him. They're rallying to fight. We need to secure your mother!" I tried to push back toward the fighting, but Clement collared me.

"No, lad. I know you want to help, but you're not your own. You're a Prince. Your duty now is to find your mother and help me secure as many citizens in the Old Keep as we can. You cannot ignore your father's commands to follow your heart right now, as agonizing as it may be."

I nodded grimly, trying not to cry as we turned away. We ushered as many people as we could back with us to safety.

Mother was already there, her gown torn and hair coming undone, a grim expression on her face. She hugged me fiercely for a moment before looking to Clement questioningly.

"He's still alive, Princess. He's rallied the guards and they're gaining ground."

She let out a sob, hugged me tighter, then pulled herself together. What followed was a long night of clearing the castle and then the town. We reunited with Father briefly after daybreak, sharing breakfast and information. He gave us both a kiss before riding off at the head of his best forest guards to track down the rest of the hoard and ensure the safety of our people.

He fought valiantly. He died valiantly.

The guards brought his body back after ensuring our lands had been rid of the enemy. We buried him alongside my sister and her husband in the royal tomb, and I went from being second in line to the throne of Asileboix to the reigning Prince of Asileboix in just a few wretched days. Witnessing the childhood fight between Rosebelle and that boy had been the last thing I had done before my entire world changed. I clenched my hands, my thoughts jumping to my coronation before I could stop them.

It had been short. Somber. We held it in the throne room after the castle had been cleaned up enough to allow visitors. After the recent violence, few had attended. Other than a few representatives from Sherwood, there was only one other set of foreign dignitaries: the Romany.

A few had been in attendance for the wedding, but a caravan bearing the Romany Queen arrived just before I was crowned. At the end of the ceremony, when most of the attendees had filed out, the Queen offered to read my palm.

It was said that the Romany people had been gifted by the Black Prince to see a person's fate as it lay in the palm of their hand. Many sought them out to learn their fates, but the Romany rarely offered a reading of their own volition. It was an honor and not to be refused lightly.

She had taken her time, silently studying every line. Her head bent over my hand, curly brown hair streaked heavily with gray. A young boy clutched her skirts, fidgeting now and then. Finally she closed her eyes and delivered my fate.

"Prince of Beastmen, Prince in Darkness; true love's kiss unravels the curse. Look for the sign of the rose and flee Asileboix in its darkest hour."

She looked up, her dark brown eyes boring into my

hazel ones. I'll never forget their expression: implacable, emotionless, full of certainty. She nodded once, then picked up the child and left. We hadn't seen them since, and I had been glad of it.

Is it her? Is it her? I couldn't help crying out to the Creator in rhythm with my horse's hooves. After the fortune telling, I had cleared our gardens of roses. There was only one plant left in the whole palace. I grew it in a pot on the window of my study. A reminder to myself that my destiny lay in my hands and that I would never choose to forsake my country.

The Creator sent no answer to my plea, and I tried to clear my head as the castle walls finally came into view. I felt reassured to see the watch fires burning steadily. All as it should be. But I couldn't shake the cold feeling in the pit of my stomach.

Mother found me as I came inside, scolding me for having missed dinner before noticing my mood.

"Andrus, what is it?"

I couldn't bring myself to put all that I was feeling into words, so instead I said the first thing that came to mind.

"It's the first royal wedding since hers."

"Oh, my dear." She slipped her arm around me and I could see tears gathering in her eyes. "I know. I've been thinking the same thing. Or trying not to. It was so long ago, but some days…"

I pulled her into a bear hug. "I didn't mean to make you cry, Mother," I admonished gruffly. "I've just been remembering her wedding and everything that happened—even though I know it's not the same."

"Poor child." She squeezed me back, then pulled away to look me in the eyes.

"You're right, it's not the same. I should have checked in with you before now to make sure you were okay." She sniffed heavily, trying to pull herself together.

"I'm fine, Mother. You know I am. I just needed to ride away from the ghosts of the past for awhile. Tire myself out so I can sleep. I must be getting soft in my old age," I joked gently.

"Well. If you're old I don't know what that makes me!" My mother grinned color returning to her cheeks. "I'm glad you said something. Now it's out in the air and doesn't have a hold over us. Although if there are ghosts around, I hope the ghosts of your father and Marguerite and poor Devon are here with us tomorrow." She laughed shakily, patting my arm.

"I'll have someone send up a tray since the dining room has been cleaned up. You really did give me a turn when you didn't show up, you wretch. Although, not a big enough one to stop Clement and me from eating." She shot me a waterlogged grin.

I smiled back. "Thank you. But send it to my workshop. I think I'll do a little work before I turn in tonight.

"Don't stay up too late," she scolded, waggling her finger at me as she started toward the kitchens. "Make sure you read through the itinerary again before you go to bed. And when you wake up, for that matter. I left it on the desk in your study."

She disappeared around the corner as I jogged up to my rooms. After taking a quick bath and changing out of my riding clothes, I ran down to my study to take a look at the itinerary. Lueren was there, filing papers.

"Lueren. It's the night before your illustrious Prince's wedding. Go to bed! Or at least do something more fun than filing papers," I reprimanded as I strolled over to my desk.

"Hmm. Do I hear the pot calling the kettle black, Sire?" he quipped, looking at me with raised eyebrows.

I barked out a laugh. "A Prince is always working. Comes with the job. Besides, my mother told me to review the itinerary before I turned in." I found it placed neatly in the center of my desk. "By the Lady! Is this it?" I held up a sizable stack of papers bound in a beautiful cover embossed in gold.

"Yes, Sire. All of the guests will receive one, although yours is a little longer since it has more information." He grinned down at his filing.

I sat down heavily. Hunger gnawed at my belly. *My food is probably waiting in my workshop.* Flicking through several

BELLE & BEAST

pages, I found a schedule of events. It looked the same as every other wedding I had ever attended. I glanced at Lueren speculatively.

"What's your job tomorrow?" I asked, dropping the itinerary back onto my desk.

He snorted. "Same as every day—assisting the illustrious Prince of the realm."

"Your use of 'illustrious' wasn't very convincing—you need to work on that. Have you read this thing?" I demanded.

"Of course. I helped create it!" Only a hint of pride threaded through his voice.

"Perfect. I'll trust you to guide me where I need to go tomorrow." I stood up as he rolled his eyes at his filing.

"Never fear, Sire."

Smirking, I turned to leave with a little more spring in my step. I was halfway to the door when my eyes hit upon several crates next to his pile.

"Lueren, are those the boxes we took from Lord Montanarte's house?"

"Yes. I'm holding them until you tell me whether to file or burn them," he confirmed, looking up.

I hesitated. I hated to burn them as they represented years of work and may be interesting to examine. But I didn't want them sitting where Rosebelle could stumble upon them somehow and be upset.

"File them in the archives in the Old Keep. And move them tonight. I want them out of the way before tomorrow."

"I'll do it immediately." He stood up, carefully placing the project he was working on back in its box and moving toward the Montanarte research. The potted rose in the window beyond Lueren caught my eye for a moment. Turning away, I thanked him and left, feeling a little less burdened. Everything and everyone was prepared. I was as well. No rose, no matter whether it was a beautiful flower or a beautiful bride, would cause me to betray my country. My duty had been drilled into me since I was a child and was something I believed in wholeheartedly. I would treat my wife with respect, and love her the best that I could, but she would never be first. As the last remaining heir to the throne, I couldn't afford to put anyone before my people.

A servant was stepping into my workroom with a tray of food as I finished climbing the stairs. I sped up, the scent of Cook's roast beef and potatoes reaching my nose and drawing a loud rumble from my stomach. Good food and a few hours focusing on the tests I was conducting was just what I needed.

CHAPTER NINE

Belle

I kept as still as I could while Hazel and Clothilda examined something on the hem of my dress. I was standing in front of a mirror while we made final adjustments to my bridal finery, just a little too far from the lovely fire I could see in the reflection. I shivered slightly and my mother pulled her shawl from around her shoulders.

"No thank you, Mama," I told her with a small smile.

"Are you sure, dear?" she urged, holding it out to me.

"I'm sure. It's not really that cold, I was just woolgathering."

She patted my cheek, then turned as we heard the door open. Rochelle swept around the corner, grinning widely.

"It's time! Princess Mathilde sent me in to get you, Mama. We're to be seated now, and you too, Hazel. Papa will be in to collect Belle in a moment." She giggled, running up to give me a kiss before pressing my small floral bouquet—roses of course —into my hands and rushing back to the hall. Mama turned to me as tears gathered in her eyes. She gently squeezed my upper arms.

"Rosebelle. I've only ever wanted good things for you. For you to be happy. I know this marriage is starting out a bit bumpy, but you are even more beautiful inside than you are on the outside. If the Prince has any sense, he will soon see that and grow to treasure you deeply. I love you my dear." With a soft smile and a quick peck on the cheek, she glided from the room.

Hazel stood and winked at me, whispering, "see you when you're a Princess!" before following my mother out of the room, Clothilda on her heels.

Clothilda had truly worked a vision. It was the most beautiful gown I had ever seen. The color brought out a rosy undertone in my cheeks and contrasted with my hair perfectly. Numerous pink diamonds twinkled at me from my tiara. Mathilde and my mother had helped me put on matching drop earrings, bracelets, and a single strand necklace of perfectly matched diamonds. I had never glittered so much in my life.

The ruby in my engagement ring winked at me in the mirror. I still hadn't gotten used to it over the last few weeks. As annoying as it was to be given a ring shaped like a rose—proof that my betrothed was capable of thinking about only the most surface level, obvious, cliche—I had to admit it was beautiful.

I resisted the urge to shrug and instead eyed the trail of tiny roses wired into my elaborate hairstyle, spilling out from behind the tiara. My hair wasn't so much styled, as it was engineered. Teased as high as possible, it was an elegant backdrop on which to anchor the tiara, rosebuds, as well as half a dozen snowy white feather tips. I was still getting used to balancing everything and hoped I wouldn't wobble during the ceremony.

Despite my fear of messing up, when I looked in the mirror I saw a princess. She looked back at me: beautiful, poised, and elegant. Happiness bubbled up, and I watched a small smile form on my lips. I couldn't help a triumphant laugh escaping me after a second. All those nights as a child in a cold bedroom, or days helping my mother mend our dresses, or assisting Hazel or Mrs. Comfry with the chores because we couldn't afford a proper team of servants. They were over forever. Instead of the faded and patched blue gown I had worn when

I first arrived in this castle, I was resplendent in rose—my mother and sister were secure and dressed in finery, Papa too.

My smile drooped a little. It's true that his circumstances were better, but the passion that lit up his life had been ripped from him. I squared my shoulders. There wasn't much I could do about that now. *And it would have been ripped from him regardless. Besides, I've secured the most important parts of his research already and I'll continue it secretly—in his name.*

"I'm glad to see you so happy."

My father's voice cut in over my whirling thoughts. He appeared in the mirror just over my shoulder, and I turned to face him, being careful to make sure my small train followed properly. Shifting my bouquet to my right hand, I held my left out to him.

"Oh, Papa, I *am* happy. I only hope you can be happy *for* me!" He took my hand and squeezed it before tucking it through his arm. His eyes caught on my engagement ring for a moment, then lifted to meet mine.

"If you're happy, then I am too, my dear. Don't worry about a dusty old scholar like me. And if you see me with tears in my eyes, it's only because I'm remembering my own wedding day with your mother. The best day of my life, seeing her come down the aisle to me, knowing she was mine forever." He winked. "Except for the days when you and Rochelle were born, of course."

I laughed. "You look very well, Papa." New, expertly tailored breeches and coat, along with a pair of shining buckled shoes. His graying hair was combed neatly and held back in a pink ribbon instead of being in his usual state of tidy disorder. It lent him a regal air.

"Thank you, Rosebelle. And you look glorious. I don't believe anyone will notice me next to your twinkling splendor —which is as it should be." He kissed my cheek and led me carefully from the room. The castle steward, Monsieur Manciple, was waiting by the closed doors and bowed as we approached. We paused—my nerves jangling but my heart full of excitement—until the organ music changed, signaling the bride's entrance. Manciple opened the doors and we entered the chapel.

My first impression was of a fairyland. Flower petals had been strewn along the green aisle runner. Sheer pink and gold fabric was draped along the pews and around archways. Small trees had been brought in pots to line the wall, and lights were twinkling from their branches. Two larger trees looked as if they were growing into the floor near the altar fountain, and upon closer inspection, I could see that they truly were. Their branches were bare, but the sun was shining softly through stained glass windows beyond, and more flowers and fabric and lights had been draped around their branches. I couldn't help smile a little wider at all the beauty.

My eyes finally lit upon my groom. It took all my effort to keep my smile from sliding off my face. He was dressed in a beautiful green jacket with black breeches and white hose, looking very handsome. But he was wasn't smiling—or even pleased. In fact, his face was as expressive as the stone fountain at the altar. Less so, actually, because the fountain evoked a feeling of calmness and serenity.

At least he isn't glaring. I felt color play across my cheeks and cursed my fair skin. I hoped anyone who noticed just thought I was the usual blushing bride instead of embarrassed. *Even at my most beautiful I can't capture my groom's interest.*

My father handed me off to Prince Andrus and the Prince helped me place my bouquet on the altar and kneel. I met his eyes briefly as we got down on our knees, wondering if he was nervous—or if he felt anything at all—before turning my attention to the priest.

* * *

What seemed like moments later, we were finishing our vows, completing the somewhat disturbing blood ritual essential to an Asilean marriage. It wasn't as painful as I had imagined. The priest simply pricked both of our thumbs and pressed them together as we spoke our commitment to each other and the Creator. We washed our hands in the altar fountain and dried them together on a handkerchief embroidered with our initials. With a chaste peck on the lips from Prince Andrus, the ceremony was complete.

As we turned back down the aisle together, I noticed our witnesses for the first time. My family was there, sitting on one side, with the entire Marchand family behind them, including Trinette and her children. LeFeu was there, sitting with Eddie. The four men of the royal Pelerin delegation were sitting behind them. Otherwise, my side was empty.

On the groom's side there more people, but I didn't know most of them. I knew Princess Mathilde, of course, and Clement. I recognized Prince Andrus' personal secretary, Lueren. He was sitting near an older woman with a kind face. I was relatively sure she was Madame Manciple, the castle steward's wife. Her youngest children had been my attendants and were now sitting with her in the pews. Monsieur Manciple was probably still at the door, in charge of making sure everything ran smoothly today. The rest of the people I assumed were close friends and attendants from the major families of the realm. Lifting my chin marginally as we walked down the aisle, I let my eyes and heart soak up the beauty of the chapel one last time.

The doors opened ahead of us as if by magic, and Prince Andrus steered me to an area just off the entrance where we prepared to greet our guests.

The Prince's subjects were joyful and effusive. The Marchands were warm—even Eddie—and LeFeu managed a half-smile and bent to kiss my hand, which surprised me. Two rough-looking men dressed in plain but obviously costly garments offered hearty congratulations, and the Prince introduced them as representatives from Sherwood. I looked at them curiously from the corner of my eye as they moved down the line, but was soon distracted by the delegation from Pelerin, whose congratulations seemed distant and cold to my ears after the heartfelt wishes we had received from the Asileans. *Do all Pelerines seem this way to outsiders?*

We sat down at a large head table in the banquet hall, presiding over a decadent feast. The room had been decorated in much the same style as the chapel, but even more luxuriously. A large, gilt cage housed white doves, several musicians playing stringed instruments, and lights twinkled wherever I looked. Around the edges of the room were placed leafy potted trees, creating the effect of eating in a meadow in the middle of the woods. *One would think that the Asileans would be sick of trees, located as they were in the middle of a forest, but apparently not.*

In between courses I drank in the beauty and generally ignored my new husband, who was sitting stiffly to my left. Instead, I spoke with my family and Princess Mathilde, when she wasn't occupied with the Pelerine diplomats.

As my eyes wandered, I sought out the strange Sherwood delegation. They were seated with what looked like some senior officers from the Asilean guards. *Shouldn't they be at the head table with us?* After observing them for a few minutes, I decided they seemed perfectly happy where they were, laughing uproariously with people they clearly knew well.

"The people of Sherwood are not generally as refined as the people of Pelerin," Andrus murmured, "but I know many of them personally, and they are stalwart allies." He spoke in a tone low enough that only I could hear.

I turned to him, feeling unwanted heat rising on my cheeks —whether from being caught staring or because it was the first time he had spoken to me other than to give terse directions since the completion of our ceremony.

"I—" I faltered, a little flustered at his hazel eyes looking so directly into mine, an inscrutable mask on his face. "I had wondered if there was a mistake in their seating since they aren't at the head table. But they seem happy where they are."

BELLE & BEAST

Something like surprise flashed across his face before his features settled into the grim mask I was becoming accustomed to. "Yes, they requested to be seated with the senior Forest Guards instead of the head table. My mother thought it would be easier on both them and your family to acquiesce."

"I see. Well that was probably for the best." I gave him a small smile.

He looked at me steadily. Just as I was about to turn back to my food he took a quick breath. "I wanted to say—you look beautiful today. Radiant, actually," he murmured—so softly I could barely hear him over the noise of the banqueters.

I beamed at him, a little surprised at how much the complement delighted me. "You look quite handsome yourself, if you don't mind me saying."

His eyes drifted from mine down to my probably too-large-to-be-ladylike smile. His lips curved up slightly in answer. The sight of it warmed my insides like a cup of tea on a cold day. As his eyes met mine again, the smile dropped off his face. Returning to his usual serious expression, he nodded in an approximation of a bow before turning back to his food.

I followed suit, slightly bewildered, but quickly triumphant again. *I made him smile!* A *real* smile. Not bad for a loveless match made in desperate circumstances.

In no time at all, our celebration was at an end. There was no dancing, which would be an unthinkable omission at any Pelerine wedding, but Mathilde had been insistent.

I couldn't help but cry a little as I sent my family off. Hazel arrived at my side again and helped me dry my tears discreetly.

We were waving at the departing carriages when a shadow fell over us. Prince Andrus stood on the step above me. He had seemed twitchy during the send off, glancing up at the ramparts and delivering rather curt farewells. He cleared his throat and held his arm out to me.

"Allow me to escort you and Hazel to your chambers."

I swallowed, suddenly nervous, and placed my hand on his

forearm. He practically hauled me up the stairs after him, setting a brisk pace up the stairs until we were almost at the top of one of the tallest towers of the keep. After walking in a tense silence, he cleared his throat again and indicated a set of doors down the hall.

"My rooms are there. Yours are here." We stopped in front of a set of carved wooden doors and he pulled them open. Motioning us to enter, he followed after us.

It was lovely. A cheerful fire crackled in an enormous arched fireplace in the center of a sitting room, the walls painted in greens and blues. A row of large windows overlooked the main courtyard. An open door to the right revealed what was clearly a bedchamber, decorated in cream and blue, and a door to the left offered a glimpse into a dressing room.

"I hope everything is to your liking. Hazel has a room in a nearby corridor and she will be able to show you which bell pull links directly to her room." Prince Andrus looked over my shoulder to Hazel. "Would you please wait in the dressing room?"

She nodded and shot a look at me before dropping a curtsy and shutting the door behind her. My heart suddenly caught in my throat and I went over to the windows to collect my thoughts. Prince Andrus followed. After a moment he spoke.

"These rooms are not the royal suite. Our suite is a shared chamber and is being renovated. It won't be completed for several months." He paused and I glanced up at him. His shoulder lifted at my curious look.

"I didn't move into it after I ascended to the throne. I chose to live here instead. Until the royal suite is done, we will maintain separate rooms. Your bedchamber connects to my own through a set of doors. I will keep mine unlocked, but I ask that you keep yours locked unless there is an emergency."

I turned to him in surprise.

"You must always feel that you can come to me for help if you need it," he continued, "but I mean for us to use the time before our state chambers are completed to get to know each other. Does that suit you?" His face betrayed no emotion whatsoever.

"Oh yes!" I agreed—a little too enthusiastically. I scrambled to soften my eagerness. "I mean, not that I wouldn't be more than happy to...well. Although I'm not completely ready to—" I blushed furiously, knowing I sounded like a complete fool. I took a steadying breath. "What I'm trying to say is, I think that would be very wise, Prince Andrus."

"Just Andrus," he responded, as serious as ever. He hadn't even cracked a mocking smile while I bumbled through my last words.

"What?"

"Just Andrus. Not Prince Andrus. We're of equal rank now —not to mention married. So you should address me as just Andrus."

"As you wish, Just Andrus," I quipped, trying to provoke a smile. I received an eyebrow twitch. *I'll count it as a win, even though it was probably a product of scorn instead of humor.* "You may call me Rosebelle—or Just Belle—if you wish."

He bowed—no eyebrow twitch. A loss then. I looked at what remained of the afternoon sunlight outside the windows. I was too relieved at his announcement to let his stoicism dampen my spirits.

"It isn't yet very late. Shall we take a walk in the gardens together? I could be ready—"

He held his hand up. "No. Not today. I have business to attend to and don't have time, nor will I be available for the rest of the evening. I must ask that you remain in your room for the rest of the evening." I gaped at him as he continued. "A footman has been stationed at the end of hall in case you need anything, and Hazel has been instructed in how some of the conveniences of your room work. I must stress—it is of utmost importance to me that you remain in your room. Will you give me your word?"

I stared at him in shock, struggling to compose myself. It had been a long day even though it was still early. I was losing some of the happiness that had buoyed me up.

"Yes, of course, if it's so important. But, do you mean I must be confined to my rooms every evening?" I inquired haltingly.

"No!" he replied, startled. "Not at all. It's just that tonight—well, for tonight it's just important that you remain here, safely." His eyes twitched toward the window briefly.

"Breakfast starts at seven in the morning." He hesitated. "I could escort you there, if it isn't too early."

I furrowed my brow at his vacillating manner. "No, it's not too early. I would be happy for an escort. Thank you."

He bowed again, bid me good night—then was gone.

I stared at the door for a moment, a mixture of confusion and relief and something approaching disappointment that I didn't dare examine further.

Suddenly I remembered Hazel stashed away in the dressing room, probably wondering what was happening. I ran to the door and pulled it open, my eyes skimming over dressers and wardrobes until they lit on her.

She had climbed up on a stool and was shielding her eyes to stare down into a wall sconces. I froze, hovering between amusement and bewilderment.

"Hazel? What are you doing?"

She looked around at me in surprise.

"Oh, Belle!" Carefully, she climbed down from the stool, blinking the strong light out of her eyes. "Where is Prince Andrus?"

"He left. He has things to see to apparently. Which is fine. I mean, I'm fine."

I realized I was probably starting to babble and took a quick breath through my nose. "What I mean is, we are going to be taking our time getting to know each other before... well, you know."

My cheeks flamed. I fought the desire to roll my eyes. I had never—ever—been someone who blushes. Now I seemed to be doing it several times an hour. *What a nuisance.* Maybe I should begin wearing heavy face powder like the fashionable people at court do. *Pelerine Court*, I corrected myself, wincing. I needed to lose my Pelerine mindset as quickly as possible.

"Oh, okay. I mean, is that okay? I would prefer that if it were me, but are you all right?" Hazel asked, breaking me out of my thoughts.

"You're kidding, right?" I scoffed. "Yes—I am definitely content to postpone all—*that*—until I know him a little better." She waggled her eyebrows at me and I shook my head. "Anyway, why were you staring into that light?"

"Right! I'm glad he's gone because now I get to show you all the fun stuff!" she gushed, turning back toward the stool she had been standing on. She stopped short before she could climb up again, then peered over her shoulder at me, muttering to herself.

"What has gotten into you?" I demanded, smothering a giggle.

She turned to face me. "Okay, instead of just launching right into things, let's get you changed. You may want to be sitting down for some of this anyway. I can run you a bath, too. It's been a long day."

I stared at her for a minute, puzzled, then nodded. I stole a glance at her as I made my way to the enormous vanity on the other side of the room.

"That's fine. Although I'm getting a little bit nervous now so be quick!"

She came up behind me in the mirror and started working on untwisting the wires securing my hair ornaments, organizing her thoughts as she did so.

"I haven't said anything because Clothilda asked me not to. She told me that Dowager Princess Mathilde would be going through everything with you personally, and that we should just leave it to you two since you're both Princesses of the castle. Since you didn't mention anything to me, I assumed that you wanted to keep it to yourself." She caught a glimpse of my puzzled frown and gave me a half smile. "Anyway, all I'm trying to say is—don't be mad, I thought you knew."

I raised my hand to still her right wrist as she worked on my hair. "Hazel. You're rambling. Just say whatever it is you're trying to say," I demanded, giving her an exasperated look in the mirror. She pursed her lips for a minute, then took a big breath.

"They use magic here—lots of it—all the time." She let her breath go and stared at me as if gauging my reaction, then squeaked as my hand tightened involuntarily on her wrist.

"Sorry!" I exclaimed, releasing it before spinning around on the bench so I could face her. "Sorry—that was an accident." I screwed my eyes tight for a minute than looked at her again, "Did you just say *magic*?"

She nodded, grinning as she absently rubbed her wrist. "Yes! For everything! It's *so* amazing! That's why I was trying to look into the lights. They're all magic—not lamps! Well, they *are* lamps, but they're not lit by candles. I mean—okay, actually they *are* candles, but the flame is magic, so the candles never burn down. They use them all over the castle!" A frown passed over her brow momentarily. "Though, not in the Great Hall —or the guest areas. But even there, apparently the candles and fires are spelled for safety, so they don't have to worry as much about it when they have guests here. It's incredible!" She beamed at me, bouncing on her heels.

I sat still, staring at her dumbly. *Magic. All around us.* I peered over at the nearest wall sconce skeptically.

"I know, I know. It's strange. I've had several weeks to get used to it, so I don't feel as scared as I did at first. And we knew that the Asileans used magic at least some. Remember? My Da told me they put charms along their border sometimes for protection, like I told you that day in the woods. He always said the Asileans were good people and everyone we've met has been wonderful, so I've had time to adjust." Words tumbled from her quickly, no doubt in response to the whiteness of my face which was visible in the mirror from the corner of my eye.

I turned back toward my vanity and leaned my forearms against the surface of the table, then snatched them up, wondering what sort of magic the vanity itself held. A second later, I realized that if the vanity held magic, the beautiful matching bench would too, and I jumped off of it, staring down to make sure it wasn't going to collapse from under me.

Hazel looked at me in astonishment, then burst out laughing.

"They're not going to spell a chair to bite you!" she choked out between laughs. I glared at her—to no effect—and gingerly sat back down.

After a moment, she got herself back under control and put her hands on my shoulders, squeezing gently. I considered shrugging her off in irritation, but was actually grateful for the solidarity. Without her, I would be alone in a new residence, a new country, and apparently surrounded by magic.

"From what I've seen, everything they use it for is to help," she assured me. "I know it's a lot to take in, especially since we grew up with the notion that magic is bad. But it really does make things easier. Just wait until you see your bathroom. Remember the room we stayed in when we visited before today?" I nodded slowly.

"Well, it was one of the guest rooms they keep for people not from Asileboix, so it was pretty much like we'd expect," she gushed excitedly. "This room isn't meant for foreign guests so it has everything the Asileans use on a daily basis—like your own taps with hot and cold water! The water is heated somehow by magic, so you don't have to wait for a servant to lug it to your room! You have your own bathtub, but there's something called a shower closet too! The water comes down from the ceiling. It's almost like a waterfall. One of the servants showed me how everything works and it's amazing!"

I listened distractedly as she continued to describe conveniences throughout my room and the palace. Excitement began to rise in spite of my ingrained suspicion of the magic itself. There was lots of evidence that the ancients had technologies we could hardly dream of, but the secret of them had all been lost hundreds of years ago. Papa and I had discussed the theory that the ancients used magic to achieve such wonders, but it was a banned topic and not widely believed among scholars. Now I was apparently going to be living it out in my life every day. I felt strange inside. I was being bombarded with so much new information, but I didn't know how I should think or feel towards it.

Deep breath in. Like most things, I would adjust. I had no choice but to adjust. Right now I needed to focus on reality, and the reality was I would be dealing with magic every day. Better to gain as much information as possible and sift through it all later.

The Prince was a mystery. But people like Mathilde and Clement, Clothilda, and the Manciples certainly didn't seem evil. They had all been kind, not just to me—their future Princess—but to Hazel and my family members, and even to each other. If they used magic often, it didn't seem to be affecting their sense of right and wrong.

My head ached. *What I really need is rest.* After a good breakfast in the morning, I could begin figuring it all out. As Hazel continued to talk, I asked questions here and there. She helped me take down my hair and put the jewels away properly before removing my wedding gown. While I changed from my underclothes into a luxurious dark red velvet dressing gown, she went through a door to my bathroom and began running the bath water for me. After dropping the rest of my clothes on a chair, I followed her in.

It was a beautiful room. White and gray marble floors and paneling created the effect that you were in the midst of a cloud. To one side, a large porcelain bathtub was being filled with steaming water from a set of silver taps. Hazel flitted around the room as the tub continued to fill, showing me how each item worked.

An ornate black and silver woodstove sat along the wall on one side, heating the room. The marble floor was cold, but a cushiony dark blue rug had been placed in the center of the room with a settee and small table. I was stunned. This bathroom was as large as my bedroom at home and I had never dreamed of such luxury. The blatant magic use, evidenced by the hot water streaming from the wall into my bathtub, still made me anxious, but it would make Hazel's duties much easier and reduce the number of maids required to keep things clean and orderly. Besides, I was looking forward to soaking in the the bathtub and washing away the day.

After shutting the water off, Hazel gave me a quick tour of the rest of my chambers, pointing out where the bell pull to her own room was located and showing me how to turn all of the lights off at once by putting my hand on one of the sconces and saying, "Lights, off," or "Lights, on," if I wanted them on again. It was dizzying.

"Oh, can you come help me wake up and dress before seven tomorrow morning? I know it's early, but Andrus will be escorting me to breakfast. You can go back to sleep if you want afterward," I asked her, remembering my conversation with Andrus.

"Of course!" she replied with a smile. "I'll be up anyway. I wanted to get down to the servant's breakfast and start making friends."

"Perfect. If you can show me where my nightgowns have been stowed, it looks like I'll have everything I need and you can take the rest of the evening off. We could both afford to turn in early."

She tossed me a relieved look. "If you're sure, that sounds great. If you end up needing me, just ring the bell!"

I gave her a hug. I was so glad to have Hazel with me amidst all these changes. After a few last instructions and extracting a promise from me to ring the bell if I wanted company at all, she hugged me again and left for her own rooms.

Making sure my door was locked, I headed back to my heavenly bathroom. The water was still hot, so I slipped into the tub and lay back so only the moon of my face broke the surface. All I could hear was the pounding of my heart, and the muted thump of my limbs hitting the side of the tub every now and again. Once the temperature began to cool, I scrubbed my hair and limbs quickly. The water was cold before I got out, and I rushed to put on my nightgown, dressing robe, and a pair of velvet slippers.

Inky blackness hung outside my windows as I wandered back into my sitting room. I padded over to one of the floor-to-ceiling windows set into the south wall of my sitting room.

Pulling a sheer curtain aside, I expected to see a view of the large main courtyard but instead looked out onto a large stone balcony. I exclaimed in surprise. Small chairs and tables dotted the space.

Stepping back to look for the door I assumed I had missed earlier, my eyes lit upon bolts at the top and bottom of the last window in the row. It looked like a window, but functioned as a door.

Grabbing a blanket from the back of a nearby chair, I wrapped it around my shoulders and fumbled with the latches. I breathed in deeply as I stepped into the cold night air. A gust of wind rifled through my hair, eliciting a shiver.

My eyes tested the limits of the balcony in the dim light. It seemed to extend along the length of my chambers. Just beyond where I estimated my bedchamber ended, there was a hip height railing of thick stone. The floor of the balcony extended beyond it into the darkness.

That must be Andrus' balcony. I stepped away from his end of the balcony, and followed the railing around. Over the edge, I could see a picturesque view of the main courtyard, and further out, a view of the entire walled city. Lights twinkled here and there cheerfully in the distance.

The courtyard was mostly empty since it was cold, but I could just make out the sounds of the stables on the ground floor. I gazed across to where I knew the ballroom was located and pushed down wistful thoughts of dancing there with my handsome Prince. A sigh escaped me before I could help it and I shook my head at my dramatics.

My eyes drifted across the main gate, which was shut at

this time of night. Beyond it were rooms in what Mathilde had called the Ministry Wing of the palace. One room along the middle of the wall was a blaze of light, and I leaned forward to see.

A figure was seated at a large desk, writing. After a moment, the person got up and started pacing, coming near the window. I could see enough of his face to recognize him and was startled to realize it was Andrus.

He really is working. I was surprised. Not that it exactly soothed my ruffled feathers at being abandoned, but it was better than some of the alternatives I had imagined. I watched him pace for a few more minutes, then sit down suddenly at his desk again, rifling through piles of papers in front of him. Watching him work so late in the evening made me feel idle and insignificant. I had nothing to occupy myself with as far as I knew except for lessons with Mathilde at some point, and of course, my secret research once I could find a way to continue it safely.

I thought wistfully of my parents and the Dower House. I hoped my family was in the sitting room right now, drinking some tea and discussing the day.

I walked down the balcony toward the portion that faced the forest to take my mind off of them. I was feeling very sleepy, and the view was beautiful. The trees waving back and forth slowly, almost hypnotically. Relaxing finally, I wrapped my blanket more tightly.

I startled more fully awake after a moment—my hand going to my chest. *What was that?* A crouching shape, almost like a man but with too long arms and oddly shaped legs.

I shook my head to clear the sleep from my eyes, then gave myself a stern talking to. *The woods are just woods. There's nothing there.*

I shivered and pulled my blanket even tighter. No reason at all to be scared, but it was definitely a sign that it was time for bed. Making my way back into my sitting room, I turned the lights off then snuggled into my soft, warm bed with a weary sigh. I had everything I had ever dreamed of and more. Tomorrow the future began.

PART II – THE PRINCE

CHAPTER TEN

Belle

I flopped onto a cushioned window seat near the entrance to the Royal Wing. All was quiet here at the back of the castle—for the moment at least. Arranging my patterned brocade skirts around me, I patted the top of my hair to confirm that my pearl circlet was securely in place. It was, so I relaxed a little bit—leaning back against the wall and tilting my head to look outside.

I had been Princess of Asileboix for an entire week. The only times I had seen my Prince during that week were at breakfast, and briefly at dinner the evening before. I saw Mathilde and Clement at both breakfast and dinner each day, but they all seemed to take their lunches in their offices. Instead of sitting in the dining room in solitary splendor, I had taken to eating lunch in my room with Hazel for company. It was quickly becoming my favorite time of day.

Having just finished lunch a few minutes ago, my full stomach was making me sleepy. I was scheduled to take a tour of the the castle and town with Monsieur Manciple. He seemed to be a kind but slightly stuffy character. Supposedly he was a stickler for regulation which, according to Mathilde, made him an excellent castle steward. Andrus, who had been present at breakfast this morning while Mathilde and I were discussing him, had actually snorted at her observation, although he tried to hide it with a painfully obvious cough.

My eyes followed the activity in the back courtyard below my window seat. Servants hurried to and fro on the paths below. A few brave souls sat on a bench under barren trees, bundled up and chatting as they watched a cluster of children run wild in the bitter fresh air. I observed with interest as one little girl toddled toward my side of the courtyard, no doubt attracted to the stables situated roughly below me. After a moment, one of the older children scooped her up and plopped her back with the adults, one of whom delivered a scolding before giving her a hug. I smiled as she flopped down into a short temper tantrum, distracted from it easily enough by one of the other children racing by.

Loud thumping came from somewhere over my head. Above me, renovations were being completed in the Royal Tower, which housed the Prince and Princess' suite, a nursery for their children, a solar, and a rooftop garden. The tower apparently hadn't been in use since Andrus took the throne. Although it wasn't in disrepair, it was certainly in need of updating and redecorating.

I winced as a particularly loud crash came from upstairs. My eyes drifted toward the door to the Royal Wing on the opposite side of the lobby I was sitting in. Dowager Princess Mathilde occupied rooms there, but to my understanding, she was the only one.

The royal family had dwindled significantly in recent generations. Few now had close enough ties to warrant a dedicated guest apartment in the Royal Wing, let alone live there year-round. That fact made me sad and apprehensive at the same time. I knew from a brief royal history lesson that Andrus had only one cousin. She lived in Sherwood and wasn't eligible to inherit the Asilean throne. She and her mother were the only people who kept rooms in the Royal Wing now, but hardly used them. They had such an ancient lineage but it seemed to be on the verge of collapse.

And I was now his wife. I was in a position to bring life back to the royal line and create a foundation to revive his bloodline. There was a part of me that longed to be the source of establishing that lineage and filling these halls with children and grandchildren. But there was a larger part of me that hadn't thought extensively about having children and whispered that I would be a terrible mother.

The doors leading to the Ministry Wing clicked, creaking as they swung open. Monsieur Manciple stepped through in his usual stately manner. To my surprise, he was followed quickly by Monsieur Lueren in his more staccato tread.

I had met Monsieur Lueren a few times, but had not spoken with him very much. He was Andrus' personal secretary. My main impression was that of a competent windstorm. He always seemed to be rushing off to do something, but instead of spreading chaos like a true windstorm would, he spread order.

In contrast, the middle aged Monsieur Manciple was more ponderous. His movements reminded me of a slow-moving river, flowing inevitably toward the next item on his agenda, not to be rushed along no matter how quickly you wished to get something done. He wasn't the sort of person who would embrace change or quickness, but I was sure that it was his hand—under Mathilde's guidance—that made the running of this castle appear so seamless. As Manciple closed the doors, I rose from my seat to greet them. Lueren caught sight of me and bowed in my direction.

"Monsieur Lueren! Are you here for the tour as well?" I inquired, walking across the lobby towards them.

"Yes, Your Highness. Prince Andrus asked me to assist Monsieur Manciple in case he was called away by one of the servants. Having grown up here, I could fill in at any point if needed."

Based off of Andrus' behavior at dinner last night, I suspected he had actually sent Lueren to help chivvy Manciple along and ensure the tour didn't extend into a week-long lecture. The gesture was simultaneously rude on Manciple's behalf and thoughtful on my own. Typical of Andrus, from what I'd seen so far.

After slowly and quietly closing the doors, Monsieur Manciple made his way towards us, bowing as he stopped beside Lueren.

"Good afternoon, Madame. May I say what an immense honor it is to be allowed to show you around the castle? If you would condescend to take my advice, let's start with the Royal Wing." He motioned me toward the doors and I caught Lueren trying to hide a grin as he rubbed his nose.

After the Royal Wing, he took us briefly through the Ministry Wing. I tried to catch a glimpse of Andrus when we passed the cabinet room and his study, but I didn't see him in either place.

We walked through the Old Keep, Manciple pointing out the armory, treasury and the archive. We didn't go in any of the rooms, but it was fascinating to see the oldest part of the castle. I made sure to note the location of the archive in case I needed it for my research.

While passing through the breezeway back to the main castle, Manciple stopped to answer a question from a passing servant. Lueren made me laugh by encouraging me to drop a pencil nub out of the window and into the moat below. It bobbed along in the current, dropping finally over the weir and into the river flowing toward the city. Lueren earned a stern look from Manciple as he cheered quietly.

Manciple's domestic issue resolved, we turned along the front of the castle, crossing a lengthy gallery over the main gate and into an enclosed balcony overlooking the throne room.

The throne room was long and high-ceilinged, facing almost due east. Tall, narrow windows of plain glass lined the alcove behind the thrones as well as the other walls, suffusing light throughout the room and affording beautiful views of the city.

We wound down the staircase to the grand ballroom on the ground floor. It, too, had high ceilings. Enormous stained glass depictions of Asilean history lined every outward wall. The sun cast rich jewel tones onto the inlaid wood floor.

If I had known the ballroom was this beautiful, I would have negotiated for a ball with Mathilde! I could easily picture the room lit up with music and dancing. But Manciple didn't allow me to sit and dream for more than a minute, continuing our tour relentlessly.

We passed through the great hall to stop at the entrance to the kitchens. Since it was between meals, I couldn't hear the normal clatter I would have expected from beyond the double doors. Lueren slipped inside while Manciple droned on about the dining services and banquets hosted at the castle. Lueren eased back through the door after a few minutes, surreptitiously handing over a napkin full of grapes and cheese as Manciple expounded on something to do with vaulted ceilings, earning a whisper of thanks from me.

We directed our steps toward the stables and our waiting carriage. After making ourselves comfortable, Manciple signaled the driver and we passed through the castle gates— the first time for me since my wedding.

Nibbling on a few grapes from my bundle, I wished I could hang my head out of the window to see everything. Instead I settled for waving serenely to anyone who noticed the crest and bowed.

Town was fascinating. Winding lanes with cobblestone streets. Houses with small gardens provided splashes of color among the gray stone buildings. Shops and stores were mostly located along the main road or in a large town square towards the southern end of town. Scattered everywhere were tall trees providing shade for pedestrians.

The market was in full swing in the square. Colorful stalls sold produce and goods from all over Asileboix—and beyond, by the looks of things. I saw at least one magical goods stall doing a brisk trade and a magician performing in the town square to the amusement of a group of children.

We ended our tour in the western portion of the city, located beyond the small Fountain River. The name, as Manciple informed me, was not only a nod to the Creator, but also a literal moniker derived from its source: the multiple fresh water fountains that sprung up around the castle and city. Their streams came together to form the upper course of the river itself.

Driving by the River Chapel, I had a glimpse of an outpost in the distance just inside the city walls. It had a distinctly militaristic look to the layout, but we turned back toward the palace instead of continuing on. I turned to inquire about it from my guides, but Manciple anticipated my question.

"That, Madame, is the Forest Guard Headquarters. They are under the direct command of General Morvan and are not to be approached. His Highness has ordered that their portion of the city be accessed only by those with direct business or with permission from the Cabinet alone." He paused at my frown, but continued on steadily.

"You must understand, Madame. Their headquarters is not to be approached without express permission, even by you."

I stared at him, shocked by the directness of his orders to stay away, before looking toward Lueren for confirmation. Lueren's uncharacteristically grim look told me everything I needed to know. I snapped my snapped mouth shut. They had obviously been charged with ensuring I knew not to approach that sector of my new realm and wouldn't be forthcoming. My first lesson with Mathilde was scheduled for immediately after this tour. Perhaps I could try pumping her for information instead.

"I see. Thank you for informing me of the restrictions." I said instead, allowing a look of concern to cross my face. I *was* concerned after all. If I recalled from my conversations with Mathilde, the ruling couple of Asileboix shared responsibility equally during their partnership. The one who married into the partnership was not considered of lesser power than the one who was born to it. That meant I should have access to any part of the princedom, or at least access to whatever sensitive information that I desired about it. It was true that I hadn't yet been crowned, but that was a formality. The power transfer was considered complete during the blood ritual of the marriage. That I was being blocked from understanding more about the Forest Guard was concerning. Another mystery to add to my pile. I didn't like it.

A quiet tiredness settled over us during the ride back as we had covered a lot of ground this afternoon. Although my body was tired, my mind was abuzz. I hoped the tea at Mathilde's apartments was strong. I was going to need it.

* * *

Mathilde's parlor was warm and comfortable, smelling of lavender and chamomile despite the presence of several hounds basking on the carpet near the fireplace. Large curtains in a faded floral print hung by the windows, which overlooked the ramparts at the back of the castle and into the woods beyond. Paintings had been hung here and there, including a portrait of a younger Mathilde in her wedding finery with Andrus' father, and a portrait of a young girl and a baby, whom I took to be Marguerite and Andrus.

I looked around with interest, as it was the first time I had been in her private apartments. She had chosen the suite of rooms right at the back of the royal wing, at the northernmost end of the castle.

"I love a bit of quiet at the end of the day!" she answered when I asked if she was lonely on her own in this wing. I could understand, but preferred the wide balcony and views of the busy courtyard from my current rooms. Once I took over my entire array of duties maybe I would crave peace and quiet as well.

After a few minutes of light conversation, Mathilde finished the last bite of her scone before turning to look at me with a businesslike air.

"Now that we've each had some tea to fortify ourselves for our first lesson, let's begin. First of all, how are you doing, my dear? This entire affair has been a whirlwind, and I'm sure you're feeling a bit turned around in it all. I married Andrus' father very young and felt just the same. We had fallen madly in love, so that was our foundation, but I had to take over all of the duties as Princess almost right away so that his mother could marry again." She crooked a smile at me. "You're a little more mature than I was, but I had more training, and had grown up here besides. I still remember being a little overwhelmed for the first year or so."

I smiled at her look of genuine sympathy. "I must admit to feeling—a little windblown, if you will. But I trust that I'll learn quickly. I've had training from my mother on running a large estate, since that was expected of me—before. The role of Princess is obviously a much larger scale, and of course you do things differently here, but I hope my background will make for an easy transition."

Princess Mathilde smiled at me. "Indeed! Now, funny you should mention doing things differently here, but that's just one of the things I wanted to talk to you about. I think our first lesson should be on magic!"

I froze, my cup of tea hovering by my mouth. My eyes hit hers and she smiled even wider. Carefully, I placed my cup of tea on a side table and turned back to Princess Mathilde.

"Pardon me?" I choked out, trying desperately not to show my lingering discomfort over one of the biggest changes I had been adjusting to.

"Magic, I said." She was grinning now. "I believe it's outright banned in Pelerin, is it not?"

I cleared my throat delicately. "You're correct. It's been banned for generations now. Most people in the capitol city don't even believe in it, as far as I'm aware," I answered cautiously.

"I can see I've shocked you," Mathilde chuckled. "Perhaps I dove in a little too quickly. I believe Hazel showed you some of the common magical items in your room?"

I nodded and she continued.

"We usually keep them out of sight or disguised when we have guests. We don't like to make any visitors uncomfortable. And of course, if visitors from countries like Pelerin or Charmagne were to realize how much we use magic, it may make our relations even more strained."

I nodded again, not sure where she was going with her comments.

"Engineered artifacts are one thing, but we also have to manage use of other magic as well. We aren't a large enough country to have separate guilds for each type of magic user, but they have formed a guild for users of magic in general, and Mrs. Manciple is actually their head liaison." Mathilde smiled at my raised eyebrows before continuing on.

"The ruling consort of Asileboix is expected to spearhead the support efforts for healers during times of military crisis. Beyond that, the most important role you will need to fill as Princess will be in leading our monthly Vigils. Those are the times we come together as a community to recite a liturgy for protection of our Forest Guard and citizens. They're the most important events in Asilean society and are held all over the princedom. I'll continue to oversee these efforts for some time, but we really must have you involved as soon as possible."

"Hasn't need for that sort of thing diminished since the end of the most recent war?" I asked, confused.

"No, indeed," she replied firmly. "If anything, it's increased. Andrus believes—and I agree—that the focus of the hoards has been shifting back toward Asileboix. We, along with Sherwood, have always borne the brunt of the efforts to keep the Beasts at bay, but we haven't had any major incursions since the start of the last war. There's been an increase of activity at the border recently. So far it's been manageable. If it continues, I'm afraid you will need to become very competent very quickly or lives will be lost. I hate to be so bleak dear but it comes with the territory."

I put my cup of tea down on a side table and turned over everything in my head before responding. "This is all going to take some getting used to, I'll admit. I'm only just beginning to feel comfortable knowing I'm surrounded by spelled objects! I suppose the place to start would be getting to know some magicians better. You say Madame Manciple is their leader?!"

"Yes, and absolutely first rate. She is technically a Shaman, since she has a degree in healing magic and used to work in our castle infirmary before she married Monsieur Manciple. Now she fills in at both the castle and city infirmaries when the Doctors there have time off. Between that and her duties as Guild Liason, and of course her five children, she doesn't have time to run our own infirmary. But she did an excellent job training Doctor Moreau so it's all worked out in the end." She smiled encouragingly at me.

"I would have never guessed that she was a magician! Is there any way you can tell?"

Mathilde let out a gale of laughter, to my annoyance. "Oh no, my dear," she finally responded, wiping away a few tears with her handkerchief. "No, they're just people whose skills happen to involve handling magic." She chuckled again to herself and I had to smile a little too.

I suppose that's a good way to look at it. Just another job. It was an interesting idea. Mathilde was looking thoughtful as well.

"Actually, any magician that has received a degree is required to wear a medallion marking their rank. If they're attached to a military unit, they're required to wear its uniform and a patch when on duty as well, so you would be able to pick them out. But no, dear, otherwise they're just ordinary people living their ordinary lives." She grinned at me once again.

"I'm sorry to have laughed at you, but it *was* a bit humorous. You always seem so thoroughly reasonable I forget that you've grown up being told the most amazing falsehoods about magic. Remember this—magic is just another talent given to us by the Creator. Some of us have more, some have less, or even no aptitude at all. Some may have skill and choose not to develop it, or not have very much skill at all but work hard to become an expert. I, for one, am glad to have such a tool to combat the evil times we are living in. If the Lady were still here it may be different, but although we keep her memory sacred, she hasn't offered help as she used to in ancient times."

She sighed and leaned back in her seat. I was a little taken aback to her reference to the Lady, but my head was so full of magic and the sights I had seen during the tour, I didn't think I could follow anything else. Mathilde must have have seen my bewilderment because she stood up suddenly, nudging one of her dogs out of the way.

"Let's end our first lesson today, Rosebelle," she suggested, gathering her tea things to put them on the sideboard. "Our next ones will be more structured and cover more ground. In the meantime, it will be quite helpful if you read this biography of some of our most recent Princesses at the castle and the difficult times they have faced. It's very interesting material, although it does give one pause to think—one might be included in it some day."

With a quick thank you, I picked up my new book and left to mull things over until dinner.

* * *

Tucking my book into the crook of my arm, I wandered slowly out of Mathilde's chambers and down the long empty hall of the Royal Wing. Shadows slanted across the walls. A few last rays of sunlight were being swallowed up by the forest before they could reach the row of small windows to my right. Thick carpeting muted my footsteps. As I reached the middle of the corridor, I paused, realizing this was the first time I had truly been alone since moving to the castle. Even when I was by myself in my chambers, I was constantly aware that there was a footman or two stationed in the hallway, that my door and balcony connected to Andrus' rooms, and even that a glance out my windows would show people hurrying to and fro across the courtyard below. Here, in the underused Royal Wing of the castle, all was silent.

The row of windows showed only still, murky trees, and I was cognizant that the dozens of rooms nearby were all empty. Unused save for the one at the end which I had just left. Increasing darkness seemed to press in on me. I had been busy every day since my wedding, and even in periods of unscheduled time, I was preparing for the next item on my agenda or trying to understand some of the overwhelming amounts of information I had been given about my new role.

The hallway was quiet and cold—smelling of stone and dust. I felt as if I was standing in the ancient heart of the castle. Time no longer passed in its unmoving, solid existence. My eyes fluttered shut, and I stilled, listening—a sudden fancy convincing me that perhaps I could hear the castle's heartbeat if I was quiet enough.

A vision of the Dower House flickered into my mind: the image of my parents and sister gathered around the fireplace in the sitting room, discussing the day's activities before dinner. I wondered if Hazel's younger sister, Holly, was sitting with them as my mother had often asked Hazel to do. I had such a strong yearning for Mrs. Comfry's tea in that moment that I felt quite thirsty, even though I had just taken tea with Mathilde.

But I wasn't just thirsty for tea, I admitted to myself. I was thirsty for my family's love. Thirsty for connection. The feeling of being treasured and respected, of being mistress of my own situation. My eyes flicked open. I pressed my hand against the cold stone wall and rested my head on it, peering out the nearest window. The peak of the chapel roof blocked any views of the city but I could just see a waxing moon rising above the dark trees. It cast a cold light along the treetops, illuminating their shape in ghostly silver.

I was mistress here in name—the Princess of the realm. But I didn't belong. There was so much I didn't know or understand. Areas of expertise I could never have dreamed existed when I was in Pelerin were important functions of being a Princess of Asileboix. Ideas I had long held as truth were seen as silly here. Mathilde was patient and kind and I was growing to love her. Hazel was as stalwart and cheerful as ever, having won over half the staff as dear friends already, no doubt poised to conquer the remaining half whenever she could find the time. And Andrus was there. Mysterious and prickly, but there.

Everyone was kind, really, but I had never had an easy time forging real connections and I felt a sliver of despair stab my heart, shaking my confidence in myself. I craved a refuge, something familiar to cling to as I adjusted to my new role —not only as princess, but also as wife. I was half drowning in things I didn't understand—my husband, magic users, the forest guards; it made me breathless.

Lights flickered on along the length of the hallway. I straightened, startled, and looked around. I had missed the sound of door opening as well as the spoken command for the lights. A tall figure stalked toward me—Andrus.

His face was stern, as always, and he seemed to be looking directly at me as he strode down the hall. He was as serious and distant as he had been the first evening I had spoken with him, and I was ill-equipped to know how to bridge that gap. The week that had passed since our wedding had done nothing to strengthen our relationship or even build a foundation for friendship. One more duty in which I was coming up short.

I released a breath I didn't realize I was holding. *Ice. Your blood is ice. Nothing touches you*, I thought to myself, mentally smoothing any lingering emotion off my face. He didn't slow down as he approached. Wildly, I wondered if he actually hadn't seen me or, with an erratic thump of my heart, whether

I had become invisible. Perhaps there was a spell here in the hall that caused a person to become invisible if they stood in the dark during a rising moon. It sounded like a something I had read in one of my father's dusty old spell books. I let out a strangled laugh and looked to Andrus to see whether he had heard it, wishing I was back in Papa's study instead of here.

Andrus stopped abruptly, about a foot in front of me.

"Are you well?" he asked, bluntly.

I stared at him blankly, surprised that he had seen me, and wondering whether I looked as if I was going to faint or something.

"Yes," came my brilliant reply after a moment.

"You were in the dark. Alone. Leaning against the wall," he recited. "Are you sure you're well?"

"Yes, yes. I'm well." I mentally shook myself, casting around for some excuse. "I had my tour of the castle today. I was trying to remember the fastest way to get to the library. I would like to find something new to read before dinner."

His eyes dipped to the biography in the crook of my arm and I forced my lips into a small smile. "Something a little lighter than this, I mean."

He looked back up at me, as sternly as ever for a moment, before answering with a perfunctory smile of his own.

"I've just returned from a patrol ride and thought you would still be at lessons with my mother. I was coming to see how your tour went," he explained, offering his arm.

Surprised, I reached to take it, noting as I did that he was still in his riding clothes, which showed traces of dirt and even a leaf or two. His hair was more windblown than I had been used to seeing it. He smelled of cold air and fallen leaves.

"It went well. But a ride sounds wonderful," I answered as he turned us toward the entrance of the hall. "Although I am sure a patrol leaves little room for enjoyment."

We walked at a measured pace and I was surprised at how nervous I felt. The entire day was becoming jumbled in my mind and I wasn't exactly sure what I was saying, or even where he was leading me. I felt like a little lamb being led along on a string by a large wolf. I realized Andrus was speaking and I hadn't been paying any attention.

"It's the hot meals that I miss the most, really," he was saying. "Although since I took the throne that has occurred much less often." He grinned down at me—actually grinning—which made my thoughts scatter again.

No wonder I don't often make him smile if he finds missing meals and camping outside amusing. I tried to focus on what he was saying again.

"Did you know that Clement was in charge of my forestry training?" he asked, still smiling at me. I shook my head. "He took great pleasure in denying his young Prince the comforts of royal life."

Andrus chuckled and stopped to open the door at the end of the corridor for me. After I passed through, he latched it behind us and offered his arm again. We continued on in silence before stopping in front of a nondescript door just inside the entrance to the Ministry Wing. I looked at Andrus skeptically as he opened it, revealing what looked like a storage closet and motioning me inside.

"I'm sorry, where exactly are you taking me?" I asked finally.

"The fastest way to the library, of course," he replied with another ghost of a smile. He was giving smiles away faster than I could think tonight. Stepping into the closet, he held the door open in invitation. I hesitated only a moment, then gathered the skirts of my green wool gown and followed him inside.

There wasn't much room in the narrow walkway between supply shelves, and I was glad I was wearing a more common Asilean style dress with fewer petticoats. If I had been wearing a fuller skirt, it would be knocking carefully stacked quills and paper everywhere. I held my book down by my side as Andrus reached around me to close the door, plunging us into darkness.

"So did you enjoy your tour?" he asked from somewhere to

my right.

"I did. Very much. The castle is fascinating and I loved seeing the city. Although I confess nothing as interesting as this occurred."

"I told Lueren to do his best, but with Manciple in charge I'm sure it was more informative than illuminating," he replied, and it sounded like he was smiling again.

"Speaking of illumination, would you care to shed some light on how standing in a dark closet will get me to the library?" I asked with a befuddled laugh.

"Here."

I felt his hand grab mine. He pulled it gently toward a section of the wall and as he pulled me forward, I could just make out a glowing symbol.

"It's a quill!" I exclaimed in surprise.

"That's right. It's easier to find in the dark. Press on it." He guided my hand toward the faintly glowing symbol.

I pressed against symbol, which was warm under the palm of my hand, then gasped. The wall panel slid away silently. A narrow set of stairs was revealed, lit by small orbs of light next to each step. The orbs cast a golden haze just bright enough to illuminate the way forward.

"A secret passage!" I exclaimed in excitement. "Just like at home!" I realized my telling slip and looked at him a little guiltily. His smile was gone but he didn't seem upset.

"I meant at the Dower House. Home is here now, of course. We had two secret passages and little secret compartments everywhere. I don't know why the builders put them in, but they were wonderful fun for Rochelle and myself growing up."

His smile returned faintly. "I think that's an interest shared by children everywhere. My sister and I used to play in all of the secret passages and rooms in the palace, much to the annoyance of our parents and tutors. The urge was always strongest when it was time for lessons."

I chuckled at the image, then stopped short. "Andrus, did you say secret passages? As in, more than just this one? And rooms? Those weren't included on the tour today! I thought I was seeing all the inner workings of the palace!" My excitement returned in full force. "Will you take me to see them?"

"What, now?" he asked with a laugh.

"Yes! I mean, if you're available. Or you can have Manciple show me I suppose. Or anyone. Does Mathilde know them all?" I realized I was starting to babble. A combination of tiredness and excitement—mixed in with close proximity to a smiling Andrus—was starting to erode my composure.

His smile dimmed. "No, Manciple only knows a few. My mother knows more of them, but there are others that Marguerite and I kept to ourselves. I would be happy to show you all of the ones I know about, but it will have to be another time. I don't want them becoming general knowledge, so we would need to be discrete."

"It would make me feel more at home, I think, knowing all the castle's secrets," I murmured, more to myself. Andrus held his hand out for me to proceed him into the passageway and we were soon making our way down the long flight of stairs.

They ended abruptly and I stopped at the bottom step, just in front of a panelled wall. I didn't see a doorknob or a latch, so I looked back at Andrus questioningly.

"The sign is difficult to find in the light. Can you see it there?" He pointed to a part of the wall panel, but I couldn't see anything different about it. I shook my head, feeling one of the curls Hazel had pinned in a chignon at the base of my neck working its way loose.

In reply I heard Andrus mutter, "Lights, off," and we were plunged into darkness again. Disoriented while my eyes adjusted, I was more alert to the rapid pumping of my heart, and the scent of dust mixed faintly with horse and dirt from Andrus' riding clothes.

"There it is!" I said after a moment, then reached toward it. "Shall I just press on it again?"

"Wait," he commanded, grabbing my shoulders to hold me

in place. "Listen for a moment. It opens into an alcove near the back of the library, but sometimes people wander into it." We strained our ears, but rather than listening for potential witnesses, I focused instead on his quiet breathing, right near my ear. His hands spanned the length of my shoulders easily and I was reminded again how tall and broad he was.

I was considered tall for a Pelerine woman. Prince Andrus made me feel as dainty as my mother and sister had always seemed to me. It felt strange, this new perspective on myself. I started slightly when he released my shoulders.

"It sounds clear. Go ahead and press it."

My hand crossed the remaining distance and the panel in front of us slid open noiselessly. I stepped into a dimly lit alcove littered with supplies. I could see a row of books through a gap at the edge of the curtain covering the exit of the alcove. Taking a few quiet steps, I peeked around it to make sure no one was nearby.

Smiling, I turned back to tell Andrus only to find myself staring at a blank wall. The entrance had closed and I was standing in the alcove alone. Clutching my book to my chest, I rushed back to the panel but couldn't find a symbol anywhere. I crouched down, not caring that I trailed my skirts in the dusty floor.

There! Just the faintest glow, an outline of a quill. I glanced around and pressed it quickly, rushing through the door and up the first several steps. My feet stuttered to a stop. Andrus was there, about fifteen steps above me. He looked down at me, having half-turned at the sound of my shoes on the stairs.

I stared up at him, taken aback. "I thought you were..." I had thought something had happened, that the door malfunctioned and closed before he could follow me out, or that he was trapped. Now I realized he was merely making his way back to the top floor again, to continue on to his next appointment. I had assumed he was going to come with me into the library and felt a little silly at being so abruptly abandoned. His easy smiles not long ago had lulled me into a feeling of friendliness much earlier than I usually allowed for new acquaintances, and it chafed to see that he obviously hadn't felt the same.

"Do you need assistance?" he asked, his brow furrowed.

"No, not at all. I just—well, you didn't say goodbye."

I cringed at the vulnerability I heard in my tone. "Not that you have to say goodbye exactly. I just thought something was wrong." I cringed again, wishing he would say something.

He just stared at me, his usual solemn demeanor firmly back in place.

I felt exposed. I had opened up to him, thinking we were making a connection, only to find that he was simply escorting me to a different room, like you would a child. It made me irritable and a little angry with myself.

"Nothing is wrong. Enjoy the library," he said finally, turning to continue his way up the steps.

I scoffed. "Thank you, Your Highness. I'm sure it will answer every expectation."

His footsteps continued on uninterrupted.

"I hope my concern over your sudden departure wasn't an inconvenience." I layered as much sarcasm as I could muster into my tone, hoping I could needle him into feeling as irritated as I did, but he merely called down, "It wasn't, don't trouble yourself," without even slowing his ascent.

"I'm not troubling myself," I muttered under my breath. "*You're* troubling myself."

He stopped suddenly but didn't turn around. After a second or two he continued on his way and I wondered if he could possibly have heard my soft remark. I watched his measured tread with resentment, wondering how he made my blood boil so easily. Hopefully I quickly became used to whatever it was. Keeping my composure under any circumstance was the skill I had worked on most as a child, and of which I was proudest. If that was changing, there's no telling who I would become.

I huffed out a breath and turned back to the library. Maybe I could locate some items to assist in my research while I was there, especially since Andrus was obviously going to be too busy to observe what I was doing. I smiled at the thought and flounced through the alcove with a little more purpose. It looked like I didn't have much aptitude for being a good wife, and learning my duties as Princess was requiring a monumental effort. But effective and efficient research was something I knew how to do. It was time to figure out what Andrus had been so desperate to hide.

CHAPTER ELEVEN

Eddie

L etters on the page in front of me stared up, blurring together. The steady scratching of the clerks' quills as they filled their ledgers reached my ears through the door. It added to the sleepy fog I was fighting to make sense of a trade offer I was reviewing. My limbs felt lethargic and I caught myself yawning frequently.

I had been back at Da's office for several weeks now, slowly re-familiarizing myself with everything I had been taught before I left. I had missed it in the trenches. Missed the calculations and projections. Missed the management of the storehouse and our small staff. I had excelled at it when I was younger and those skills had helped me become a better officer once I bought my commission.

Now, I found myself devising strategies to keep awake. I itched to be moving instead of sitting at a desk. A pang of guilt pricked my conscience. I was lucky to have a profession and secure future ahead of me. My father and brother had been working industriously to ease me back into things. I wanted to put my former roles and talents back on like an old coat, but the more I tried, the more it felt like this coat didn't fit anymore. Something was missing. Or someone.

Belle. I allowed my mind to wander in her direction. *Belle is gone, and with her, the reason for everything I've been building all these years.* It had been two weeks since her wedding. I had attended to show support to my dearest friend, and to show my family that they didn't need to be concerned about me. Also to give LeFeu a reason to go so he could see Hazel one more time. Since she hadn't come home with us, I assumed he hadn't worked up the nerve to talk to her—again.

Her wedding had been beautiful, if short. I had seen the Prince and Belle smiling at each other during a portion of the banquet, which made me jealous and simultaneously a little hopeful. If the Prince would come to love her as she deserved, then she would be truly secure. But other than that one exchange, they had hardly interacted at all.

Everything had been done in high style and with utmost correctness, but the quick resolution of festivities,and the armed guard dispatched to escort us all out of the princedom that same evening were unnerving. There was something more going on, and I couldn't put my finger on it.

I frowned at my papers. It was also off putting that the Asilean people were so tall. Most of the women there had been almost my height, and at six feet, I was quite tall for a Pelerine man. The Asilean men had been even taller. What's more, I had seen women among the guard units. *Disturbing to say the least. They could never be actual warriors.* I assumed they were included keep visiting emissaries unnerved. If that was their tactic, it certainly worked on me. I wondered briefly what Belle's reaction had been the first time she saw the lady guardsmen—or guardswomen, I supposed—and chuckled. She was a stickler for propriety. *She probably has sorted that out already.*

My brother's voice broke in on my thoughts. "I never knew Charmagnian equine reports could be so amusing."

I glanced toward the door, realizing that the clerks had stopped their scratching and were already gone.

"I'm afraid I was lost in my thoughts," I answered, a little ruffled at how unfocused I had become.

"Well, it's the end of the day. That trade agreement is one of the most convoluted I've seen yet. The Corienne family is hoping we have a line to Asileboix after the wedding and want to use us to extend their trade into a new territory. It will be interesting..." he trailed off with a laugh as my eyes glazed over again. "Never mind. It's after six. We can discuss it at home. Didn't you hear the bell?"

I shook my head and put the contract in an envelope. "I must have missed it. I guess I need a break."

Thomas held his hand out for the envelope and I gave it to him with a sense of relief. "Let's go, Da's already on his way to the stables," he urged, tucking my paperwork into his bag.

Standing up and stretching, I grabbed my greatcoat and followed him down through the offices. My lungs filled with crisp evening air as he locked the doors behind us, shaking off the daze I had been under. I reveled in the open sky fading to black above us.

"I'll walk you to the stables, but I'm going to meet LeFeu for dinner and stay at the townhouse tonight," I told him as we started toward the stables. He looked at me with surprise. I shrugged.

"I want to check in with my men tomorrow,to make sure they're all settling in okay. Most seem to be doing well, but there are a few that haven't quite found a place for themselves again. I'm trying to convince them to come work for the estate." Thomas nodded with understanding.

"I should be back for lunch tomorrow, though. And I wanted to go over to the Dower House afterward to visit." The memory of Thomas tripping over his words to Rochelle at our Yuletide party surfaced. "Would you go with me? I'd like to check in on Lord Montanarte, so it may be useful to have someone to entertain Lady Montanarte and Lady Rochelle." I glanced at him out of the corner of my eye and smiled at the dull flush creeping up his neck. Although my recent mess with Belle had me doubting my understanding of women and love in general, even I could see the attraction between him and Rochelle

BELLE & BEAST

whenever they were together.

"I'd be happy to help," he agreed with studied nonchalance.

I grinned to myself, glad the lengthening shadows would hide it from Thomas. We cut through the town square, taking the most direct route to the stables by the main gate. Soon we could see our father chatting with the stable master, who let loose a guffaw of laughter in response to whatever joke Da was telling him.

After giving me a quick farewell, he and Thomas mounted up and steered their horses through the gate towards Croiseux Manor. The blacksmith forge was just a few yards from the main stables, so I found myself waiting on a stool in the warm forge not long after. Henri was cleaning up his work station while his father and younger brother were hammering away at something at the anvil. I watched with interest until Henri was ready.

We made our way towards The Cat On The Wall, a small pub in the southwest corner of Croiseux—or as it was known to locals—the Caterwaul. It was nestled up against the town walls between the laundry and the cooper, not too far from the smithy. Smaller and more out of the way than the larger Pilgram's Cross Tavern on the eastern side of town, it had better beer, in my opinion, and catered mostly to locals. Once we had a pint and bowl of steaming mutton stew, we hunched around a table in the corner. News was exchanged in between bites of piping hot stew, each of us ravenous. Once we had eaten, Henri settled back with a sigh. I leaned forward, sliding my bowl toward the end of the table.

"Have you heard anything from Hazel?" I asked, my voice low. Henri looked at me with a frown.

"No," he muttered. "You?"

"Of course not. Why would she write to me? I haven't heard anything of either of them. Although Belle would have no reason to write to me now. I'm going to the Dower House tomorrow to see what news they've had."

"Don't like it," he replied after a minute. "Them being so far away. We came home only to lose 'em again. Not right."

He leaned forward as well, taking a sip of his beer. "Saw more of those charms on my last ride. Closer to the Dower House."

I nodded. "Me too. In the large stand of birch to the north?"

"Yeah. And some closer to the Shrine. Still think we should leave them hanging?"

"I don't know. I'm hoping to ask Lord Montanarte about them tomorrow. There's a chance it's some research project he's working on, but I doubt it." I took a sip of my own beer. I knew Lord Montanarte was involved in some not entirely legal lines of research from time to time, but I figured my Da would have told me about it if he was up to something.

We compared notes on each of our last patrols, speaking quietly so as not to be overheard. Thankfully, a group of regulars were arguing loudly over a game of dice, so there wasn't much chance of that.

"Think it'll stop soon?" LeFeu asked later as we walked back toward the forge. His parents lived in a cottage facing the smithy, but Henri was sharing the small living quarters above the forge, along with his next youngest brother, to make more room in the cottage for their younger siblings.

"Stop what?" I asked, bewildered.

"That voice that keeps telling me I don't belong here," he answered, pausing at the entrance to the smithy. The fire had been put out for the night, but I could still feel warm air blowing out from the main work area. I looked around it for a minute, able to see most of the forge over the half wall that separated it from the street.

"LeFeu. You belong at the smithy. I couldn't imagine you doing anything else. What else would you want to do?" I asked.

"Not the forge. I mean here, Croiseux." He spread his arms wide. "Thought it was just a reaction to all the changes when we first got back, and then all the mess with Belle and Hazel." His face was thoughtful for a minute. "I dreamed of living over the forge until I could take it over, of convincing Hazel to marry me and live there with me. But now it does seem like a dream. Even if Hazel were here with me, I think I'd still hear it. The voice." He shook his head with a rare smile. "Guess I got a taste of the road in the war. Never thought I'd say that. How many nights did we talk about settling down in peace? But now —nothing fits here anymore. Feels like I need to take my life and put it in the flames to reforge it. If only I could."

He laughed and stepped over the threshold, calling back over his shoulder as he made for the stairs, "Nevermind. Caterwaul's brew must be stronger than usual tonight. Better sleep it off before I start writin' poetry or somethin'."

I watched him stomp up the stairs and turned toward the townhouse. His words brought back my thoughts from a few hours ago.

Maybe we didn't fit here anymore. I shook my head, the fuzzy feeling I had from a belly full of good stew and beer going away in the brisk night air.

It wasn't that we didn't belong, it was that there was something going on around here that didn't fit. Those charms in the woods. The dead spot we had come across, as if something had burned everything in a perfect circle, ten feet in diameter. It was surely witchcraft. And it was more close to the Asilean border. Surely Asileboix was the source of it. And Belle was in the middle of their capitol, chained to their Prince.

The house was cold so I hustled upstairs to my tiny bedroom and lit a fire. I made myself ready for bed but instead of going to sleep, I pulled my writing desk close to the fire and wrote a letter to General De Concordes' office. I hadn't forgotten his warning about Asileboix, nor his instructions to write if anything unusual occurred. I didn't want to report anything currently, especially since there was a small chance it was one of Lord Montanarte's experiments. But I did want more information about Asileboix and about whether we had seen an increased movement along our border with the Wasteland. It hardly merited the General's attention, but I figured an aide-de-camp in his office might be glad of the change of pace in answering my inquiry. I completed the letter and prepared it to go out with the mail carrier tomorrow, then banked my fire and went to bed.

* * *

The pre-dawn sky reached through my window to awaken me—as I had neglected to close my curtains properly the night before. Rushing through preparations for the day, I walked down to the tavern in search of breakfast. My letter was passed to the innkeeper while I took a quick meal and a strong cup of tea. He would give it to the royal mail rider that stopped by every Saturday.

Stomach full, I set off to visit members of my old unit. Making my way around the town, I spent time with each man and his family, ensuring myself of their wellbeing. Private Oger concerned me the most. His parents had both died during the war, so he didn't have an occupation readily available. I spent the better part of an hour persuading him to take a position at Croiseux Manor. He was a cheerful sort, but didn't like to feel as though he was a charity case. There were a number of other soldiers looking for work as well and I promised to help them until they found something that suited them.

The tension between my shoulders soothed as I rode back to the Manor House. Sun streamed down without a cloud in sight. The air was warmer today than it had been all winter, although still frosty enough. I made it back in time for lunch, which consisted of venison, artichokes, buttered potatoes, and a great deal of cheerful conversation. Ma had been visiting Trinette at Stone Farm the last two days and had an abundance of amusing tales to tell about my niece and nephew. My heart warmed as I remembered some of the silly games we played all those years ago.

After lunch, Thomas and I started off to the Dower House.

We were greeted by Holly and a great deal of noise.

"There's workmen puttin' up wallpaper in the sittin' room right now, so you can't go in there. And they have workmen in the kitchen puttin' in a brand new range, so don't expect much for tea if you stay that long," she warned us, her eyes sparkling with excitement. "Lady Montanarte said they don't get many guests so as no need to put a fire in the drawing room since it's so drafty, but you're the second set today! The first was the priest and his wife so I don't know if that counts actually. They have to visit everyone. I had to make 'em wait here in the entry way before I could settle 'em with Lady Montanarte.'"

"Are they still here?" Thomas inquired, grinning at her excitement.

"Oh no, they left before lunch. They've all finished eating by now." Holly bounced on her feet, looking back and forth between us cheerfully.

"Should we wait here while you find Lady Montanarte or Lady Rochelle?" I asked, trying to speed her along. She had only been working as their ladies' maid for the last few weeks. It seemed like she had a lot to learn if she was divulging this much information to every guest that came by.

"Oh, no need to find 'em," she replied cheerfully. "They're in the drawing room, of course."

"With no fire?" Thomas demanded skeptically.

"Of course they have a fire, Mr. Thomas. Tis too cold to be sittin' somewhere without a fire. I'll take you to 'em. I mean, this way, please, Sirs," she declared with sound logic, never minding the fact that she had just told us there was no fire in the drawing room.

Thomas opened his mouth to argue the point but I grabbed his arm and shook my head.

There was indeed a roaring fire in the drawing room. Lady Montanarte and Rochelle sat close beside the fireplace, working on their sewing, when Holly announced us. They greeted us warmly and we all settled back down to exchange news. After the pleasantries were out of the way, and Thomas and Rochelle were discussing whatever item Rochelle had been sewing, I inquired of Lady Montanarte about her husband.

"He's in his study, tucked away from all the racket." Her smile dimmed slightly. "I'm sure a visit from you would do him a world of good if you would like to see him."

"I would, thank you. I know you're all feeling the loss of Belle, but I imagine he's missing her the most."

"Indeed." She shot a quick glance at Thomas and Rochelle. "Would you mind if I walked you there?"

"Not at all," I agreed, little surprised. I followed her from the drawing room, leaving the door open to ensure propriety for the beet red Thomas and Rochelle, who suddenly had nothing to say based off of the silence of the room as we walked away.

"Thank you, Eddie. I just wanted to warn you before you go in that he's quite changed. He's been lost without Belle. Usually he would confide in your father, but Thierry has been a bit busy with you home and business booming since the war ended. Seeing a friend will help. Besides," she added with a twinkle coming to her eye, "I simply had to give Thomas and Rochelle a chance to be embarrassed with one another without anyone else looking on. I hope I'm not too forward."

I burst out laughing at her sheepish look. "Not at all, Lady Montanarte. Will it surprise you to learn that Ma is hoping for a spring wedding?" She gave an answering chuckle and left me for the drawing room again.

After my knock on the study door went unanswered, I pushed the door open. A fire crackled in the grate, but I didn't see Lord Montanarte in his usual chair. Abnormally bare shelves jumped out at me as I surveyed the room. *Maybe his office is next in line for renovations.* My eyes caught on Lord Montanarte's figure, rooted in place at one of the long windows overlooking the north lawn. He didn't turn to acknowledge me so I took a few moments to study him.

He stood quietly, shoulders hunched. He was dressed in his usual careless manner, but was somehow even more rumpled than usual. I could make out his profile from my position, and noted a general pallor. Instead of the usual whistling or muttering to himself over his notes he was silent—threadbare, and worn. The sight pained me. Lord Montanarte was the one who could make my jovial father laugh loudest and longest. The man before me looked as if he had never known what a laugh was.

I marched over to his side and gazed out the window. Grey clouds were rolling in from the north. The lawn was a mottled beige and the ornamental garden was barren. A bleak picture.

"Your refuge from the improvements to the house?" I inquired finally.

He turned to me with a start, obviously having missed my entry into the room.

"Eddie, my dear fellow. What a surprise! When did you arrive?" He blinked at my outstretched hand before shaking it.

"Not long ago, Lord Montanarte. I visited with your Lady and Lady Rochelle first. My brother is keeping them company so I came to seek you out, Sir."

"Very good, my boy. And do call me Maurice. At least here at the house. Belle would have my hide but never mind all that. You're family, whatever else may have happened," he mumbled the last part more to himself.

"Thank you, Lord—Maurice." I corrected myself with a smile, corralling him gently toward his desk near the fire. "Will your study by taken over by the workmen next?"

"Hmm? No, I don't think so," he replied, looking around. "Well, possibly. My dear Halette is in charge of all that so perhaps you're right."

"I assumed that's why you packed up all your books and research. I've never seen your study so empty! You must be going mad not having everything to hand," I explained as I settled myself into a chair across from him.

He sighed. "No, Eddie. It's been packed away, but not for that. Condition of the marriage, you know. The Prince was most adamant. Nothing about the Lady, or his family, or magic, or the history of his people, etc. etc. Didn't leave much for me."

My mind was blank as I tried to comprehend his meaning. "Are you saying that the Prince made it a condition of Belle's marriage contract that you cease your research?"

His unfocused eyes stayed trained on the fire as he replied. "Yes, quite. Didn't leave a scrap of it. His lawyer fellow was very efficient. I suppose they burned it all before the wedding."

"Lord Montanarte—Maurice, I mean—how can that be? That's your life's work! Belle never would have agreed to it! She knew better than anyone..."

"No, no, Eddie. None of that. Couldn't be helped. Besides, it's not as much of a wrench as you'd think. The worst of it was losing Belle. A few pages of my boring drivel don't count for much when you think of that. You understand me." He glanced at me, an expression of kindness in his eyes.

"Here I am pottering on about my loss, when you have it even worse. Now I won't say much, as I suppose you're not the type to talk about these things, but I *am* sorry for the way things turned out. You loved her with a constancy few young men seem to have these days. Only you know the depth of your sorrow, but you're not alone, my boy. It was our greatest delight, your father's and mine, to see you two promised to each other." He shook his head and turned back to the fire. "I'll say no more. Don't mind me."

Several moments passed with just the crackling of logs interrupting the quiet between us. I was still turning everything over in my mind when he shot me a look of concern.

"Forget I said anything about the research, young man. Can't have it getting back to the Prince that I've been complaining. I wouldn't want to make things difficult for Belle as she's trying to settle in." He trailed off again, eyes slipping back toward the flames.

My sense of honor bristled at his request. Not that I would have a problem keeping his business to myself, but the idea that rumors of his reasonable complaint would make things *difficult* for Belle rankled. What sort of man was this Prince and what sort of difficulties was Maurice contemplating for her?

Trust me, she had asked. I did trust her. I had given up my right to fight for her and allowed her to walk down that aisle, next to a father who was more broken than I thought, and pledge herself to a man we knew nothing about. *She* knew nothing about. It may have been right to trust her, but I should never have trusted her groom.

The blood ritual at their wedding flashed before my eyes. It spoke of an underlying brutality in their culture for which Belle was ill-prepared. Her training was for running a prosperous Pelerine Manor House, directing its servants, arranging entertainments, and raising a family. A shudder passed through me. *All the more reason to find out more about Asileboix and continue to guard our border closely.*

Instead of asking about the charms we had found, as it was obvious Lord Montanarte wasn't involved, I inquired about news from Belle and Hazel. A few letters had been received from Belle. She reported that they were both settling in slowly, but missing home. Nothing to worry over, but nothing very personal either. Not enough to reassure me, at any rate.

We visited for some time and although Lord Montanarte chatted with me over various topics, I wasn't sure that I had done much to lift him out of his general malaise. Finally, I collected Thomas from the drawing room. We practically ran home in an effort to make it before rain from the gathering clouds burst upon us.

❈ ❈ ❈

Another week passed and I found myself settling into a routine of work and patrol rides, and checking on the estate and my former soldiers. I still itched to leave my desk at the end of the day. The paperwork was tiring, but I told myself that all work comes with it's difficulties. Besides, I had my patrols to look forward to.

A reply to my inquiry at General des Concordes' office arrived with the next mail. I had stayed at the townhouse on purpose to wait for a note and was doubly rewarded. To my surprise, the General had written back himself. After a few pleasantries, he recounted a story that struck horror within me.

No doubt you've heard the tale of the Beast Bride of Asileboix. It's a story told to many children in Pelerin. You may know more than most since you hail from near that accursed country, but I will recount it here; having been privy to a report on the actual affair which occurred when I first took the rank of General.

The events happened about fifteen years ago now, in the summer. The Asilean crown passes to the eldest child, male or female. It seems to be more complicated than that, as there have been a surprising number of abdications of right by the eldest child from what we know of their history. While one might expect that as a natural occurrence when the eldest is female, as that delicate sex is not suited to bear the weight of an entire country upon their slight shoulders, it appears to happen as frequently with the male children as the female. An example of the strangeness of their society.

The present Prince of that realm was, in fact, the second child of its former rulers. He had an elder sister who was heir to the crown by right. She had just celebrated her eighteenth birthday and was set to marry her betrothed only a few days later. Our King considered sending ambassadors to the wedding, but declined as the Beast Wars had broken out only months before and we had no envoys to spare for a foreign maiden's wedding. Our information was received instead from the newly crowned King John of Sherwood, whose representatives had actually attended the wedding.

What he reported was horrific. The bride and groom were bound in marriage in their strange ceremonies. A celebratory ball

*had hardly begun when suddenly, all devolved into chaos. Beasts
had stormed the castle, somehow being let into the ballroom with
hardly a challenge at all. Many of the guests died that day,
including the bride and groom. Some have said that the groom
himself was turned into a beast and he murdered his own bride and
called his brothers to him. What our envoys at King John's court
believed, and I think most likely, is that the overlooked younger
brother saw his chance to claim the crown. One can understand
his frustration, and perhaps a desire to put a fit male ruler on
the throne in place of one of the weaker sex, but it cannot be
condoned. She may yet have provided male heirs to steer their
country correctly. And to do so with such violence! He would have
been better served to lock her up the way Prince John of Sherwood
had done with his own female pretender. No, it speaks to his greed
and an inhumanity inherent in their society.*

*Long have tales been told that their citizens are more beast
than man. Could it be that the Prince is one of those and led the
attack himself? I cannot say with certainty, but we do know this:
by the time the atrocities at the wedding were complete and order
restored, both the reigning Prince and the Princess Heiress were
dead. Young Prince Andrus was ruler of the entire country.*

*That is the truth of the matter. What level his own ruthlessness
may be, I have no personal knowledge, but I take notice of this:
when he decided it was time to take a bride, he looked to Pelerin
for one. He did not seek a bride from his own country, as has been
the custom of their royal family for generations. I believe that none
would have him, knowing better the details of how he came to his
throne. I only hope you didn't know the poor girl he ensnared so
recently. She was the daughter of an ancient line that had fallen in
ruin, or so I've heard. Probably a sacrifice to restore glory for the
family. I'm assuming they were well paid for it, which speaks well
of her dutiful nature. One cannot imagine the father knew all. The
only good to be done for her now is prayer to the Creator, if you
believe in that sort of thing.*

*Enough of that. My office has been charged with security at our
borders, and most of our effort is in securing the north, although*

we must give thought to our other neighbors as well. I rely on you to send word of potential concerns from Asileboix. The brutality of their current Prince is a black cloud in my mind. Write again with any news - General des Concordes.

The letter drifted down to my desk as I put my head in my hands. *What had I let Belle walk into?* We had allowed her confidence in herself dictate our actions. She was used to getting her way, especially since she was generally right. But at the time she most needed guidance and protection, I had failed her.

Now she was chained to a despot who, from the General's account, had killed his own father and sister to gain the throne. I crumpled the letter in my hand and threw it to the floor. She was beyond my grasp, but not entirely beyond my help.

At the first hint that all was not well with her, I would call upon the General's office even if the consequence was something I had only recently escaped—war.

CHAPTER TWELVE

Andrus

Boots hit the ground around me as I slipped from my horse. I had just returned from a patrol with a squad of Forest Guards and Clement. All had been well on our circuit. I had enjoyed the quiet of the woods, working in tandem with my mount and the other guards. The changes we had made to the castle's outer defenses over the last months had been seamless, and I was encouraged to see it.

After a few words with the squadron leader, we deposited our armor with an attendant and left our mounts to be cared for at the stable. Clement found a pair of fresh horses for us, so we began to make our way back to the castle keep.

As we wound our way through the quiet western bank, the Royal Tower caught my eye. Even now, craftsmen worked busily, redesigning the layout to the specifications my wife had made. *My wife.* We had been married for almost a month but I felt no closer to knowing her.

Immediately after our engagement I had ordered major renovations to the tower we were destined to share and then left her to make changes and choose the details as she pleased. They were needed, but I had also used that excuse as a way to delay our inevitable closeness. We needed time to get to know one another, which she had seemed relieved about.

She was beautiful—intoxicatingly so. Even that first night —dusty and rumpled from the road, obviously tired—she had possessed a backbone of steel that made you forget about everything else and just see *her*. It was as if I had recognized an old friend—or maybe an old foe. Our meeting seemed inevitable. Fated. Its outcome, too. I had sensed her manipulating the conversation so skillfully I doubt it was apparent to anyone else, save perhaps my mother. Normally that would have put my back up, but instead I was only impressed and intrigued. She was like a hawk masquerading as a dove.

Her outward beauty matched her name—that of a rose. Her skin was fair. She seemed to blush at the drop of a hat, which was amusing considering what I had seen of her haughty personality. Her light brown hair was streaked with gold in places, and her eyes were the same amber that we saved to work images of the Lady into or use in protective charms— warm, with flecks of gold to match her hair. They were living charms, and I found myself entranced when she looked at me.

I disliked it. Not her beauty but my reaction to it. I knew no more of her than that she was a predator. A trait that would serve her well in a country that was always on guard, and certainly more interesting to have in a partner than the docile bride I had envisioned when I first set my sights on marrying a Pelerine. But although she seemed to be taking her new role seriously, I wasn't sure whether she would ever consider herself Asilean. Especially once she learned our secrets. If she considered herself an opponent of what we stood for, she would be formidable. Better to keep her in the dark for the foreseeable future.

Clement's voice broke in on my brooding. "Looking forward to seeing Princess Rosebelle?" He had obviously noticed me staring up at the Royal Tower and made assumptions, apparent by the grin on his face.

"I was thinking of her, yes," I replied, not wanting to answer his question fully. "She is still a bit of a mystery to me, I'll admit. We've both been busy with our duties since the wedding, and it hasn't left much time to get to know one another."

"Ah yes. Duty is the first love of most Asileans. We never quite get over her all our lives. Not a bad thing, of course. But there's a season for everything, and the Creator made us all to be known for ourselves, especially in a marriage. That's the duty of partners in a marriage. Knowing each other—and celebrating that knowledge."

We rode in silence for a few minutes while I considered his words. As Prince of our country, duty was my shadow. It never left me. There was no one who could shoulder my job for me. *Save, of course, for my wife.* I grimaced. I knew I had a duty to love my wife, provide for her, and honor her, but I hadn't considered myself under a duty to *know* her, let alone celebrate knowing her. What if she ended up hating our country? Hating me? I couldn't live vulnerable to hatred. It would degrade my ability to lead.

"Course, knowing someone doesn't happen in a day, or even a month. And love often takes even longer," Clement ruminated, once again interrupting my chain of thought. He laughed. "Look at your mother and me. I've known her longer than you've been alive! But I've only really gotten to know who she is inside these last few years, and that's when the opportunity for love arose."

I observed him thoughtfully.

"Now don't be looking at me like that, son," he scolded with a sad chuckle. "Not a day goes by when I don't wish your father was still alive. And if he were, your mother and I would be different people because of it. But as it is, we've both been alone and tied to duty for these last decades. We found a way to each other in that."

He concentrated on the road ahead of us, lost in his own thoughts and memories. I felt my lips curve into a smile as I observed him. I missed my father terribly some days. He had been strong, intelligent, and comfortable with the responsibility of our kingdom. My clearest memories were of him stopping to pray whenever he felt led, even in the middle of a sentence—which was sometimes confusing for the person he was talking to. His connection to the Creator was deep and made him seem fearless. He never hesitated in being the first to fight or serve, or apologize. I had always wanted to be like him. That desire only heightened after his death.

Although I inherited his own penchant for action, I never felt like I measured up. Not that I imagined he wouldn't be proud of me. I knew he was. I tried every day to do my best to serve our people. But I knew fear. I didn't let it stop me from my duty, but I felt it in a way I my father's strong faith never allowed him to feel.

He used to tell me, "If you've sought the Creator's guidance and given your plans over to Him, your confidence and faith will leave no room for fear, son."

I did have confidence in the Creator's power and faith in His love for us, but I could also see the all the other players on the board. I was the last of my line. I knew that in other countries, Sherwood's recent history being a prime example, people were constantly struggling to gain more power and land. Our land was different. Each person worked for the good of the one beside them and to protect and guard the Lady's ancient stronghold. It was the very basis of our country's formation over a thousand years ago, and our people had not failed in that trust. As Prince, I was responsible for ensuring that each citizen had their place, the ability to fill it, and the security of our borders. No one in their right mind wanted to take that responsibility on their shoulders if they didn't have to.

Clement was right, our people did consider duty their highest calling. He and my mother above all else. They had patiently, if not quite cheerfully, waited for me to find a wife all of these years. Our laws demanded that the in absence of a consort, the dowager consort must fulfill the role, remaining unmarried until the ruling monarch chose a consort. Breaking from tradition going back centuries, I had insisted on finding a wife outside our borders or those of Sherwood. It had taken longer than expected. I turned my gaze back to Clement.

"Speaking of you and Mother, have you decided when you will be married? I'm surprised she hasn't handed me an outline for her own ceremony yet."

He let out a loud laugh as we navigated the stone bridge uniting the western bank with the main city.

"Not exactly, Sire. That is to say, she's already completed the outline, but we'll be settling the actual date with the priest soon. We're giving you and Princess Rosebelle a year to settle in, considering you've done your courtship a bit backwards." He shook a finger at me. "But when that year's up we'll be down to the altar before you can blink, and you'll be on your own."

I rolled my eyes at him, then focused on traversing the busier stretch of road we had come upon. Buildings soon gave way to a small stretch of fields that acted as the castle's kitchen gardens and provided some green space for the walled city's inhabitants. I always enjoyed riding through the quiet peace of the fields before ascending to the main castle keep.

"She hasn't been raised to believe that the Lady was real," I confided in Clement, with a sigh. "She thinks of the her as a character in a book." Clement looked over, waiting for me to continue.

I huffed, irritable that he was making me explain my thoughts. "I knew that was probable for any wife I took from Pelerin, but now that I'm actually married, it seems like a big obstacle."

He nodded and looked up at the castle for a minute before answering. "She's a canny one, Andrus. Being surrounded by the Lady's stronghold will give her proof she didn't come across much in Pelerin."

I grunted in response and stared at the road.

"You leave her belief in the Lady to the Creator, Andrus. It's His business anyway. Your business is learning to be her friend and her husband, and supporting her as Princess. Stick to that and it will all get sorted."

I glanced over, giving him a nod when he caught my eye. He was right, as he often was.

A bluebird swooped in front of us, landing on one of the trees lining the path. I watched it hop up and add something to a small nest being started on one of the higher branches and smiled. Although winter still chilled the air, spring couldn't be far away if birds were nesting.

A sign from the Creator, perhaps, to focus on building my own nest? I shook my head in silent laughter at myself. *Pretty egocentric to assume the Creator is rearranging nesting patterns to nudge you into being a better husband,* I thought ruefully. Whether it was a supernatural sign or not, I could acknowledge the wisdom in it. I didn't think falling *in* love was smart. I had my own reasons for being wary of Roses. But it was my duty to her as my wife, and to my country towards their Princess, to build a cohesive family and legacy. *I'll start today... right after my cabinet meeting.*

✲ ✲ ✲

My meeting dragged on for hours. General Morvan showed up not long before we were scheduled to conclude, throwing me a salute as the Minister of Agriculture continued with her report. He was still dusty from the road and pulled Clement aside to review his latest maps. As soon as the other business was finished, I gestured for them to discuss their findings with the room.

General Morvan was succinct. "Sire, I just arrived from Montblanc. They've continued to see heavy action these last two weeks. I had to send relief units much earlier than we expected. I've set up an increased rotation schedule, but we'll need to monitor it closely."

My eyes flicked to Clement, who looked stone faced at the map in front of him. I gestured for General Morvan to continue.

"On my return, I rode through Le Moyeu. Waiting for me was a missive from Captain Hood, which included a note for you." He passed a letter to me, along with a copy of our boundary map.

He continued on, a grim set to his mouth. "The message was written in spelled ink, so it vanished as soon as I read it. It was short, informing us that they had seen a light increase in activity at their own border. The bigger blow is that several of their undercover operatives have gone missing in the last month, presumed captured or deceased, including an elite unit from Spindle."

Gasps echoed around the room. The Sherwood military contained a specialized branch of trained warriors. They routinely went into the wasteland to collect intelligence. Their operatives had been working over the last several years with a near perfect success rate. To hear that some of them had been captured was a blow.

"When did this happen?" I asked apprehensively.

"Captain Hood was assigned to retrieve the operatives when a distress call was issued. She returned two days ago having failed to locate any of them, and losing several of her own team members in the attempt. Lord Hood directed her to forward a report to us. He thinks we should prepare for increased pressure on our borders. The missing operatives were all assigned to missions closest to our territory."

My eyes lingered on the note he had passed to me as the General sat down and the ministers buzzed amongst each other. The misplacement of intelligence operatives was shocking enough, but failure on the part of Captain Hood—the famous Red Rider—was just as unbelievable.

The spelled ink on her note was a jumble of symbols and shapes. I breathed on them to verify my identity. As I did, they rearranged themselves, forming a few short sentences. I read silently.

"*Bear,*" it began, referencing my childhood nickname, "*the news is grim I know. I'm generally uninjured. Don't worry over me, and tell Mathilde I'm fine. I hear congratulations are in order, so congratulations. All my love, Red."*

Some of the tension between my shoulders eased as I read her quick note. *She's fine.* I rarely worried about Red. Her fearsome reputation was well-earned and as a warrior, she was unmatched. But she was one of the few that I loved dearly, not just as a Prince to his subjects. The thought that she had been injured in her mission had worried me as soon as General Morvan spoke of it. I took a steadying breath.

"The Red Rider is well," I announced, breaking into my minister's chatter. "Although the news of the missing agents and her failure to retrieve them is grim. You know my thoughts have been turned toward a resurgence from the Wasteland, despite the Pelerine certainty that they dealt the enemy a grave blow." I leaned forward in my chair.

"This proves it. I will not wait to prepare for an onslaught until after the Beasts have moved against us. If anyone has any objections, present them now. Otherwise, I will be ordering General Morvan to prepare our northern borders for war."

I sat back, observing every cabinet member in turn. Each of them nodded or murmured their agreement. I looked at Clement last of all. His posture was ramrod straight. As Chief Royal Guard, he was in charge of castle security, and specifically the security of the royal family. He held my eye for a minute, then nodded his assent.

I glanced to General Morvan. "You know your orders. Go. I'll be down tomorrow morning before you leave."

He stood and saluted, then strode out of the room, Clement on his heels. I excused the rest of the cabinet and watched them go, their apprehensive murmurs fading as they walked down the hall. The room was soon empty.

I sat in the quiet for a few minutes. Dust swirled through beams of sunlight streaming from a row of windows next to me. It was quite peaceful. You wouldn't have thought I had ordered preparations for war in such a sunny, tranquil spot only moments before.

Abruptly, the double doors leading into the hallway banged open and my mother marched in, stopping as she caught site of me.

"Clement told me," she announced, walking around the table to stand at my side. "He said Red was unharmed?"

"Yes," I replied and she closed her eyes in thanksgiving. "Although, she told me she was 'relatively uninjured' so who knows what that means."

My mother's eyes snapped open with horror. "Do you think she is hurt after all?!" she cried in alarm.

"No! Mother, calm down." I covered her hand with mine briefly. "She wouldn't lie to us. If she was gravely injured, she'd say so. She probably just received a few bites from one of the Beasts and is embarrassed." I laughed and she rolled her eyes at me.

"Dear girl. She does take her profession so seriously. I wish she had come to the castle more before she became this Red Rider person. It would have been good for both of you." She sighed, a bone weary sound, then muttered to herself, "Too late for that now."

I looked at my mother with a sad smile. She loved Red as much as I did and had tried her best over the years to get us together as often as she could. I remembered long, carefree visits when we were very young, but once Prince John had taken custody of her, those visits stopped. After the revolution in Sherwood we had seen each other slightly more, but Red had an obligation to her own family and country, as I had to mine. Although we were close, duty conspired to keep us apart over the years.

Mother turned and studied me with a sad smile of her own. "I'm sorry I missed the cabinet meeting again. My lesson with Rosebelle went long. I figured you would send someone if you needed my input on anything."

I nodded and stood up from my chair, gathering my notes, Red's letter, and the map General Morvan had given me. Mother trailed behind me through the door and out into the hall.

"I'll see you at dinner?" she asked my back as I walked toward my study.

"I had planned on it, but now...I may have to skip it. I'm not sure," I responded, stopping briefly to turn toward her.

"Alright, son. I'll see you at breakfast then. But you should try to come." She hesitated for a moment before continuing in a lowered tone. "And, I don't want to overstep, but you really need to make more of an effort with Rosebelle. She's doing well in her lessons, but she actually asked me today if you were on a mission somewhere. She thought you weren't even in the castle!" Her voice was practically a hiss.

"It's a little difficult to get past her armor, but I really think she's a lovely person underneath that aloof exterior she puts on. One of you needs to let down your guard first, and I really think it should be you. She's in *your* country and you're six years older and *supposedly* more mature..." she trailed off as someone stepped out of one of the offices down the corridor.

"Hmph," she sniffed once they were out of sight. "I'm really not trying to pry, but the more I get to know her,the more I think you two are well-matched. But nothing's going to happen if You. Don't. Show. Up." Jabbing her finger with each word, she poked my arm harder than I would have expected.

A growl slipped out before I could help myself and her eyebrows shot straight up.

"Did you just growl at me?"

I let out a small laugh, the tension I felt at her advice dissipating slightly.

"Sorry, Mother. I'm a little stressed. I hear what you're saying," I answered, pulling her into a quick hug.

Her own frustration at my manners disappeared with my hug and she smiled wryly as she took a step back.

"I know it's not easy to open up. With war on the horizon, it may seem like the worst time. But our time isn't a given. All your plans for this marriage will unravel in ways you couldn't fathom if you overlook *her*. I can guess that you feel you've done enough in promising to uphold your vows and making her a Princess, but you need to choose her every day of your marriage. If for no other reason than the fact that she's your counterpart in ruling, make your relationship as solid and stable as you can. The princedom will benefit, and both your lives and your children's lives will be richer."

I grimaced at her. I could hear truth in her words, or rather, feel it like an itch in my soul, but I didn't want to think about it right now. "I know, Mother," I replied, hearing the impatience in my voice and cringing slightly.

"Alright, my dear. I'll leave it at that. See you at breakfast, if not before."

I could hear her muttering as she left and couldn't help but chuckle softly at her words "*...actually growled at me. I thought we were done with that when he was ten but here we are, two decades later, and apparently the Prince feels he can growl at his mother...*"

I turned my feet the opposite way, continuing toward my study. After placing my paperwork in a tray on my desk I tapped my nails thoughtfully for a moment. My intent had been to continue working through some petitions I hadn't had time to review yesterday, but my mother's words continued to bother me. I kicked the sturdy leg of my desk, failing to budge it even an inch. The petitioners wouldn't be back until next week. I could leave their requests until tomorrow. Instead, I swept out of the room and headed toward the chapel. The demands of the day had me craving prayer and reflection.

The chapel was quiet and smelled of incense. Hushed tinkling sounded from the fountain, soothing to both my ears and soul. No one else was in sight, not even the priest. I was glad of the quiet. It forced me to be honest with myself, and the Creator.

I know she's your child, Creator. I know your Book says to outdo one another in service to the other and to love your family more than your own self, but I can't do that without making myself vulnerable, can I? I need to be strong now, more than ever. The *enemy is at our door. I can't be distracted by her. I will **not** abandon my country to become heartsick over my wife!*

My logic seemed sound to me, but my thoughts felt cowardly. Wearily, I sighed, the peace of the chapel failing to seep into my heart. I needed food and bed so I could get down to the Forest Guard headquarters at first light before General Morvan rode out.

Taking a quick drink from the fountain before I left, the crisp, cold water cleared the fog in my head momentarily. The full moon was close and it was getting harder to keep my thoughts, as well as my temper, in any sort of order. An extra reason to be vigilant.

As I exited the chapel I felt—rather than saw—movement at the end of the corridor. Only disused storage rooms were located down there. There was no good reason for anyone to be in them at this time. I tensed at the thought and whirled, nerves already wound tight. After a moment I relaxed, but only a fraction.

Rosebelle hovered by an ancient statue, her color high and her breathing shallow and rapid. She clutched a light cloak around herself.

"Rosebelle," I greeted her through gritted teeth, my spike of adrenaline slowly coming down. "What are you doing here?"

She frowned at my words for some reason, stiffening her spine. "I was examining this statue." She gestured toward the carving next to her. It was ancient and crumbling, one of the reasons it was in a disused corridor.

"I see." I breathed in through my nose to dispel the rest of the sudden strain I was feeling.

She released the grip she had on her cloak, letting it pool around her, and instead clasped her hands around her forearms as she started walking towards me. I watched her graceful steps as my heart rate slowly returned to normal.

"Were you in the chapel?" she asked coolly, stopping a few feet in front of me.

"Yes. I find it peaceful, especially when no one else is

around." I wondered how she could sound so frosty when her amber eyes looked like honey warmed in the sun.

I winced at my own thoughts. I had better things to do than to compose poetry over a pair of eyes. "Would you like me to escort you to your rooms?"

"Yes, thank you. I need to prepare for dinner."

I offered my arm and she stared at it for a moment before taking it. Her light touch always surprised me. The only other woman I escorted on my arm with any regularity was my mother, and she had no qualms about squeezing my arm or leaning her weight on me. Rosebelle rested her hand as if it were a butterfly ready to fly away again at any moment. Pelerine training, no doubt. It gave me the urge to either flick it away or squeeze it mercilessly between my arm and my side. I resisted both and instead started back towards the main castle, towing her gently in my wake.

After walking in silence for several minutes, Rosebelle looked up at me. "Will you be at dinner this evening?"

I shook my head. "No. I have work to complete, and I need to be up earlier than usual to meet with one of my generals. Speaking of which…"

We had reached the door to a common area connecting the Chapel Wing, the Ministry Wing, and the stable block. There were several workers inside chatting while they ate dinner after a long day's work. I drew her along the wall, mainly unnoticed by the current occupants, and slipped out a side door which opened into the back courtyard. Outside it was still and quiet, the temperature having lowered with the sun. Rosebelle hunched against the frigid air, pulling her cloak tight. If she had been cold enough inside to wear a cloak in the castle, she must be entirely freezing now.

"I won't keep us here long," I assured her, maneuvering so she was out of the wind. "I wanted you to know. I gave an order tonight for our guardsman to prepare for war."

Her eyes snapped to mine, expression revealing little else of what was going on in her head.

"It won't mean too much change here at the castle yet, although Clement has his own set of protocols that will tighten security in the coming days."

She nodded, her jaw clenched firmly. A violent shiver wracked her body.

"There's no need to be concerned. I'm not telling you this to worry you, but you'll need to know since you have certain duties as consort in wartime. Hopefully this is all for nothing and my concerns are unfounded."

She shivered again, and I gingerly pulled her closer.

"I understand," she replied. "Mathilde and I have been discussing my duties in wartime and reviewing the increased infirmary inventory she's been stockpiling since the end of the Pelerine War. I had asked her to go over that information first instead of our foreign relations history. Now I'm glad."

She grimaced, teeth chattering. "Still, I'll have to put in extra effort to be sure I'm competent enough if something does happen. I've never even met the field hospital corps so mobilizing them may tricky the first time, and that would have dire consequences." She trailed off, eyes focused on one of the barren trees littered throughout the courtyard. Her body trembled with cold again and she unconsciously stepped closer, seeking the heat rolling off of me.

I looked at her with surprise. Not so much because of our physical proximity, but because of her matter of fact acceptance of the situation and immediate response as to how she could help.

"Could we go inside now? I'm in danger of becoming an ice sculpture. Although, you don't seem to be much affected."

A laugh escaped me and I pulled her out of the corner we had been standing in, toward the stables.

"No, I'm not much affected, Rosebelle. But I shouldn't have kept you out in the cold." I put my arm around her as we walked, knowing it would probably shock her sensibilities, but feeling guilty for her shivers. She tensed, but then eased even closer into my side.

We separated as we reached the entrance to the stables. The heat charms in the stable lanterns rolled a wave of warm air over us as we crossed the threshold. Rosebelle didn't make eye contact as I held the door into the castle open, but she took my arm again as we started toward the staircase to our rooms, her butterfly touch making me want to roll my eyes again. It felt as though she would float away on a stray breeze.

I paused at the door leading to the kitchens. She continued toward the staircase, momentarily pulling my arm along with her and then jerking to a stop. She looked back at me in bewilderment.

"I need to order a tray for dinner. Would you like to go on to your rooms?" I asked.

She shook her head slowly. "No, I'll... actually, I've only seen the entrance to the kitchens during my tour for a few minutes. Would it be alright if I came in with you?"

In response I turned and opened the door, ushering her in before me.

Once we were in the cavernous room, I collared a nearby attendant. He took my order for a tray as Rosebelle looked around, astonishment plain on her face. She didn't notice when the attendant walked off with my order, and I watched as she took in the busy staff and the magic fueled items they used to assist in preparing dinner.

I glanced around too, trying to look at it from her point of view. It was a massive space, taking up the entire ground floor of the guest tower. There were two great fireplaces roasting meat on spits that turned themselves. Tall windows normally let in ample light, but since the sun had already set, candles set in simple iron-worked chandeliers and lampstands were lit, casting everything in a bright, warm glow and reflecting off the whitewashed walls. Three long tables stood to one side of the room, various assistants cleaning and chopping produce for the next meal. In the center of the room was a giant support pillar, upon which the Chef had hung her menus for the day next to assignments and charts organizing the workers and their duties. Her desk was covered in cookbooks and orders. She had a separate office on the floor above, but the majority of her working day was spent down here. The other side of the vast room held a row of bread ovens for the pastry chefs and bakers.

I reached for Rosebelle's hand, tucking it onto my arm and startling her out of her trance. She blushed, whether from my rough touch on her warm hand or at being caught gaping, I didn't know. We stepped away from the roaring sizzle and clatter of the kitchens into the quiet stairwell beyond. She laughed softly as I led her up the stairs.

"I have *never* seen a sight like that in my entire life! When I came on my tour it was between meals and Manciple didn't want to disturb anything. He just showed me the entrance!"

I snorted in amusement. "More like he didn't want to disturb the Chef. They're constantly at odds over the kitchen budget and I know he was on her bad side over our wedding banquet. He just didn't want to receive a scolding in front of his new Princess."

"Oh, well, that's not necessarily a surprise. My mother always said that the cook rules the house, whether it's a humble cottage or a grand palace," Rosebelle remarked thoughtfully.

We climbed the remaining stairs to our rooms in silence, she contemplating the kitchens, no doubt. I was contemplating the slightly tighter grip on my arm—more like a kitten than a butterfly—and wondering whether it was because she was forgetting herself in the trek up the stairs or whether she felt more comfortable touching me. A rebellious part of me wanted the latter.

We stopped outside of her rooms and I unlatched the door for her.

"Will I start sitting in on cabinet meetings now?" she asked, her tone low so it wouldn't reach the footmen.

I looked down at her in surprise. "No, not at all. My mother knows well enough what you will need to do. It would be too overwhelming for you to attend the meetings so soon. Better to wait until you've adjusted."

She observed me steadily for a moment, her thoughtful expression smoothing into an inscrutable mask as I spoke.

"I see." The sparkles of gold in her eyes seemed to flash as she walked into her chambers. Turning, she bowed her head slightly. "Thank you for escorting me safely to my room. I hope to see you again soon, Andrus." The door clicked shut between us.

I had bowed my head back but could think of nothing to say before she closed the door. *Just stared at her like an idiot.*

Her sudden shift in moods bewildered me. I was irritated at how much so, and how much thought I was allocating towards trying to understand why. *Time to focus on work, not a woman,* I scolded myself. I continued down the passage and turned into my workroom, which was just across the hall from my bedchamber.

Sighing, I closed the door and turned on the lights. The familiar sight of test tubes, distillery jars, and neatly stacked notes was soothing to my ruffled soul. *You can't say I didn't make an effort!* I scolded the Creator, wrapping an apron over my tunic and washing my hands in a nearby basin. I continued preparing my workstation, but I couldn't quite shake the feeling that I had missed something during my interaction with Rosebelle—an opportunity or the right words to say. It served to further my annoyance. Just as I was opening my notes to review what I had been working on when I last left off, a kitchen server arrived with my tray. *Perfect timing,* I told myself as he set it down on my desk and left again. I dug in to my dinner, throwing off a lingering sense of guilt as I prepared to start my experiments once again.

CHAPTER THIRTEEN

Belle

"Creator, do not turn your eyes from our enemy's pursuit. Keep us from despair. Let us sing praises at the Lady's Stronghold on her return." As I finished reciting, I cracked open my left eye to peek at the page in front of me, hoping I hadn't missed a portion of the prayer.

"Absolutely perfect," Mathilde praised, beaming at me from where she was sorting order forms for the infirmary that I had written out. "I believe you couldn't be more prepared for your first vigil tomorrow night. Remember, although the consort usually leads the vigil in the ballroom or throne room, Manciple will do that in our stead tomorrow. You and I will hold a separate vigil in the Chapel until you're used to the liturgy. Why don't you run through it one more time with the motions?"

Pushing off of the cushion I had been kneeling on, I blew out the candles at our makeshift altar and fountain, then turned toward my mother-in-law.

"Mathilde," I considered my words carefully, not wanting to give offense but feeling burdened by my reservations, "could we go through the importance of this ceremony again? It's just all so foreign to me, if I'm being honest. At chapel in Pelerin we often pray to the Creator to protect us from the Beast hoards, but—I suppose I'm just having trouble understanding it all. If I'm supposed to lead this liturgy, I want to fully appreciate what I'm doing."

Mathilde's eyes followed the forms she was stacking as she listened. After a long moment—where my discomfort at my own disbelief warred with my desire for truth—she looked up at me, her usual glance of gentle amusement replaced with complete earnestness.

"I *do* appreciate how unusual this must seem to you. After all, you were raised to think of the Lady as a fairytale. I think the only thing that will help you is time, my dear. That's one reason why we are holding a separate vigil for now. It would be too overwhelming for you to bear the scrutiny and hopes and fears of the entire palace while you're still working through your own understanding of the Lady right now. We've discussed the Asilean belief that the Lady of the Woods held her stronghold here in Asileboix, although we have little written evidence to present for it. I believe the Creator will show you the truth if you just keep your mind open. Otherwise, I wouldn't worry about it too much if I were you. Just try to be as sincere as you can, and pay attention to anything the Creator is telling you." She smiled as she looked down at her desk.

"It's perfectly fine to feel a little apprehensive. The first time I lead the vigil, I was completely overwhelmed! I'm glad we have time to ease you into it together."

Her words reassured me as I turned back to the practice altar. I felt a bit like a fraud, learning the liturgy when I didn't even really believe the Lady was real. But I recognized that it was my duty to perform it as consort and threw myself into one last round of practice. By the time I was finished, Mathilde had sorted the paperwork. Together, we cleaned up the candles and ceremonial elements I was using to practice, placing each one on a side table for a servant to send to storage.

We were laughing at our attempts to fit the pretend altar cloth into its tiny carrying bag when the door swung open and

Andrus strode in. An arrested look passed over his face as he took in the sight of us: Mathilde kneeling on the floor holding the bag open and me trying—and failing to cram the cloth inside—and let out a storm of laughter. It was the first time I had heard him laugh so freely. The joy of it took me by surprise.

The sun was high, throwing beams of light across Mathilde's office. Fine white scars on Andrus' face and hands stood in stark relief against the darker shade of his skin. Laugh lines crinkled around his eyes instead of the usual frown etched there by degrees. Varying hues of brown and bronze and gold shone through his hair in the sunlight. His whole being radiated joy for a few minutes as he doubled over in laughter—he was magnificent.

As he straightened back up, his eyes fixed upon me for a moment and I realized with a start that my mouth was hanging open. A flush shot from my neck to my hairline and I snapped it shut. I turned away to compose myself under the guise of re-folding the cloth. My blush receded by degrees as I ruthlessly pushed the image of him laughing in the sunlight from my mind. His words filtered through my embarrassment as he spoke with his mother.

"...expecting grim history recitation but instead I find you two wrestling a drop cloth into a bag like two guilty children caught hiding something."

"Well, really, Andrus, we're not exactly guilty children," Mathilde chided him with a chuckle. "We just can't seem to get the knack of how to fold that cloth. Hazel brought it up to us in the bag so I know it fits, but it's not fitting now!"

"It reminded me of the time Marguerite and I ripped your favorite silk cloak playing Knights and Shieldmaidens." Footsteps sounded in my direction and I tensed, sensing his approach. "We only realized it when we were sneaking to put it back, and tried stuffing it into one of your bags in the hope that you'd think you had done it."

"Darling girl always did want to look her best, even if she was pretending to be a warrior. I believe I just about bit your heads off over that, if I remember correctly," Mathilde responded, a smile coloring her voice.

I kept my face angled down, fussing with the cloth.

"Yes, but we were expecting to skip dessert as punishment, so I think we counted it as a win." A tanned hand reached around me, scars and callouses crisscrossing the palm. "Allow me?" Andrus asked just over my shoulder.

Pretending to myself that my blush hadn't returned, I admitted defeat and twisted to face him, offering the offending cloth and its bag. Daring myself to look up at him, I hoped my brain would remember its function some time soon.

His wide grin was gone but laugh lines crinkled around green and gold eyes, softening his expression. As he took the items from my hands, my eyes trailed down a slightly crooked nose toward his full mouth, just the hint of a smile curling the edges.

He turned away and I realized he had caught me ogling him again. I clutched my forearms with my hands, giving myself a stern mental berating. *Some fine Lady he must think he's married. I mean, it's certainly not a bad thing to be attracted to your own husband, but he's a person—not a picture to be admired!*

"Will you help?" Andrus' voice cut across my self chastisement. I realized he had included me in that request, and I joined Mathilde at the opposite end of the cloth, which he had rolled out on the floor. Folding the edges in at various points, he made quick work of it as we helped keep it straight. The technique he used was similar to one I had used when helping Hazel with laundry at the Dower. If I had just thought about it for a minute, I could have done it on my own. I wondered how Andrus knew the trick of it. *I wouldn't put it past him to do his own laundry.* As if in answer to my thought, he looked over as he placed the now closed bag next to the other items on the table.

"That's how we fold our tents when we're on patrol. They've got to fit into their carrying bag or else it's a nightmare lugging them around."

I nodded, part of me wanting to connect with him by offering my own experiences with the laundry at home, the other part wanting to hide the fact that we had been so poor that I had needed to help with the laundry. Logically, I knew enough about Mathilde and Andrus to know that they wouldn't scorn me for it, but I still couldn't shake my own feelings of inadequacy.

Instead I said nothing, and turned instead to collect my gloves and hat. Mathilde bustled around her office, getting ready to leave, and Andrus volunteered to step into Clement's office next door to collect him for our appointed ride.

Mathilde and I were both dressed in our riding habits already. She was busy tying an embroidered purple scarf around her head and neck to block out the wind once we were outside. I smoothed my cranberry dress, adjusting the cream colored blouse and cravat just peeking out over my waistcoat, before pulling on my own overcoat. I had a row of shining gold buttons in the shape of—yes—roses,down the front of my jacket, which buttoned from the neck down to my waist. I reveled in the slightly shorter cut of my skirts and fewer layers of fabric. As freeing as some of the Asilean fashions were, I wasn't quite ready to wear riding breeches like Mathilde.

Andrus and Clement collected us a few minutes later and we all trooped down to the stables together, the men reminiscing over camping stories as we walked. Andrus pulled me aside as we walked through the stable doors.

"I have a surprise for you. I hope you like it." He nodded to a corner of the barn.

Following his gaze, I watched a groom lead an elegant palomino toward us. I glanced back at Andrus, eyebrows raised.

"He's for you," he said warily, answering my silent question. "His name's Lodestone. I just purchased him from one of the best stables in Charmagne though our broker. I've examined him myself, and he's an excellent trail horse."

Lodestone came to a stop in front of us and I rubbed his nose gently. "Hello boy." He snuffed my hair in greeting.

I glanced back at Andrus, my heart warmed by his thoughtfulness. "He's beautiful. Thank you!"

"You're welcome," Andrus replied with a small smile, moving around to help me mount. "Let's see how you two get along."

Andrus indicated that I ride in front with him as we passed through the main gate of the castle, descending sedately down the old motte and into the city. As we started through the city I could see why. Once word of our presence began to spread, citizens lined the street, shouting and welcoming their new princess. Andrus and Mathilde called out greetings, but I didn't know quite what to say so I just nodded and waved from time to time, my smile growing ever larger at the genuine expressions of interest by the people. I could feel Andrus' eyes on me every so often and wondered if I was doing something incorrectly, but when I caught his eyes once and raised my eyebrows in question, he just grinned at me.

Lodestone was a dream to ride and we quickly got used to each other. After passing out of the city gate and into the enclosed pastureland beyond, Andrus patted his horse's neck and shot a devious grin at us all.

"Anyone up for a race? Ironheart is itching for a challenge."

Mathilde's response was to take off immediately, Andrus yelling his objection as he followed a moment later leaving Clement to continue in a more dignified trot beside me as we trailed behind.

They stood laughing with some guards by the huge curtain wall when we caught up to them. Instead of going through to the woodland beyond, Andrus led us along a riding track that followed the inside of the wall.

We soon relaxed into a comfortable chatter as fields passed us by. None of us could contain our enjoyment of the spate of slightly warmer weather that had tempted us outside, and Clement and Mathilde bickered about some seedlings they had planted in the rooftop garden above the Royal Wing. Andrus rode his horse out in front a few times to "stretch Ironside's legs," as he claimed, but then fell towards the back with me.

Clement and Mathilde gradually pulled ahead of us, engrossed in the minutia of their discussion. To my surprise, Andrus and I had no difficulty maintaining conversation without their interference. By the time we had traced the entire curtain wall and started back toward the city, both of us were laughing over my astonishment at my first trip to the kitchens. As we caught up to Clement and Mathilde, Andrus recounted the entire scene to their amusement. I found I didn't mind their laughter very much. Usually I intensely disliked being the source of anyone else's amusement, but they were so quick to relay with stories of their own silliness that I forgot to maintain my sense of aristocratic dignity. I could hardly remember feeling so relaxed.

The sun began to sink as we made our way back through the city streets. They were largely empty, as most people were at the dinner table by now. After the afternoon of warm companionship, I hated to say goodbye to Lodestone when we returned. A growl from my stomach reminded me that time was marching on.

We parted company with Mathilde and Clement at the stables. Sudden awkwardness descended between me and Andrus as we walked up the stairs to our chambers. He broke our silence as we reached my door.

"Can I escort you down to dinner this evening?"

His invitation flustered me. I had gotten used to his absence at dinner, and the new friendliness between us seemed as delicate as some of the ancient manuscripts in the archives of the Old Keep: liable to crumble into dust at the slightest careless touch.

"I would be honored. How long do we have?" I hoped he assumed the breathlessness of my voice was due to the stairs and not the fluttering in my throat.

"Half an hour. I'll wait for you just outside your door."

I watched his broad back disappear down the hallway, then

turned into my own rooms to prepare.

* * *

Hazel was inside, reading a book and lounging by the fire. She looked up with a smile as I entered.

"How was the ride?" she asked, following me into my dressing room.

"Wonderful, actually. It was so nice to get outside of these walls. Andrus was surprisingly pleasant as well," I replied, not making eye contact as she helped me out of my riding habit.

"Prince Doom and Gloom?" she teased, "You shock me, milady!"

I giggled as I pulled off my jewelry. "Also, he asked to escort me to dinner tonight. Ugh, I sound like Lena from the Dower Hamlet, gushing over her latest crush, don't I?" I moaned putting my hands over my face.

"No, Highness, not at all." Hazel's tone was polite and formal.

I finally made eye contact and she stuck her tongue out at me. Laughter bubbled up from my chest.

"Don't lie to me Hazel Veneur! I've known you too long." I clicked my tongue at myself as I stepped out of the rest of my clothes and wrapped myself in a bathrobe. "What is wrong with me?! I'm altogether too giddy. Maybe I just need dinner."

Hazel called out from the bathroom where she was starting the shower closet for me. "Are you sure that's what you need? I was thinking maybe you needed something else, like a tall, dark, handsome Prince who conveniently lives just down the hall, and who's conveniently married to you, and just so happens to have a door that connects..."

"Hazel!" I yelled, storming into the bathroom. "There are footmen stationed just out in the hall!" Laughs tumbled from me despite my embarrassment.

"Belle, don't be a ninny," she scolded as she pulled out some towels. "Just in case you didn't realize, the entire castle knows you're married. It's not a secret."

I shook my head as she flounced back to my dressing room, smirking impishly. I rushed through my shower. The warm water was soothing but did nothing to help the butterflies in my stomach. I dried off quickly, pulling my robe back on and sitting down at my vanity for Hazel to start on my hair.

"I changed your dinner dress to the blue and white velvet and pulled out some different jewelry to match," Hazel announced as she brushed my hair dry with a spelled iron and twisted it into a simple chignon. "I'm styling your hair so you can take it down yourself," she continued, waggling her eyebrows in the mirror at me.

"Hazel, stop!" I replied. "We really aren't at that stage yet. We're in separate rooms still for heaven's sake.

"Well, sure, but your bedrooms have a connecting door. One that *he* keeps unlocked."

I rolled her eyes at her again.

"Alright, I'm just saying. I'm not planning on coming back tonight unless you ring for me. So your hair and clothes are styles that you can take down yourself, or you know, with a little help from someone—"

I tossed a hairbrush back at her and she burst into giggles.

While I put the rest of my jewelry on she tidied up the rest of the room, humming to herself quietly. After a quick hug, she left to go to the servant's dinner and, knowing her, an early bedtime. She was a morning person and usually quite tired after dinner. I usually tried to make sure I didn't need her after dinner for that very reason.

My preparations took less time than usual, so I decided to cool the flush Hazel had raised on my cheeks with fresh air from my balcony. Pulling a light cloak around my shoulders, one that I used when exploring bits of the palace in my free time, I stepped outside, drifting over to the edge of the balcony to observe the busy courtyard below.

To my surprise, Andrus stepped out of his own balcony door

only a minute later. I had never yet seen him use it.

He hesitated when he noticed me. "Were you looking to be alone?"

"No, not really. I'm just watching the last of the sun go down since I finished early," I replied, walking toward the banister separating our two balconies, leaning my hip against it. After a moment he closed his own door and made his way over, sitting down next to me so that his eyes were on the same level as mine.

"I enjoyed our ride today," he ventured with a polite smile. "You're an excellent horsewoman, although I can't imagine why you ride aside."

I shook my head. "I was never taught another way and with everything else I'm learning, it hasn't been a priority. Although, seeing you and Mathilde race off at the drop of a hat has moved it up on the list. I would love to do the same! I'm sure my mother will faint to hear about it."

He grinned even wider, displaying his canines. "There's a lot about my country that would make a Pelerine Lady faint. You seem to be resisting the urge so far, which I'll admit has impressed me."

I couldn't help but laugh at the slightly backhanded compliment. "I'm glad I'm impressing someone. I'm working as hard as I can to take it all in, but everything is so different!" I clutched my cape around me to ward off the temperature, which was lowering in tandem with the sun. My smile dimmed as I considered my transition to the Asilean way of life.

"I'm glad Hazel agreed to come with me. She's as captivated by Asileboix as I am and it's nice to have someone who understands what I'm experiencing."

Andrus tapped his first two fingers on the side of his leg as a thoughtful silence stretched between us. I took a look over the edge of the balcony and into the courtyard below. It had been busy a few minutes ago, but it was almost empty now. No doubt the workers were all going to their own dinners.

"What's been the most difficult adjustment since you arrived?" Andrus asked rather suddenly. I was taken aback at the personal nature of his inquiry and blurted out the truth without stopping to phrase it carefully.

"The Lady's Vigil," I replied, glancing up at the waxing moon as I thought. "I'm struggling with my part in it. I'll need to lead the vigil month after month. Be a symbol of strength and unity for the people who attend and instill hope, devote myself to 'protecting the Lady's stronghold,' as Mathilde phrased it. But I don't understand why! I comprehend the benefits of gathering together as a community, but isn't it counterproductive to reinforce ancient fear of the full moon? As for the Lady... there's no evidence that she's even real. There's no point in protecting her if she's not even around."

I trailed off, mumbling more to myself. Realizing with a start how much doubt I had revealed, I glanced over at Andrus, hoping he hadn't heard my last few words.

He radiated tension. His hands fisted at his side and his spine was so straight I could hear the voice of my governess praising him from across the years. A wild urge to giggle passed over me at the thought, but left me as he sprung up, heaving in a great breath of air. He strode toward the edge of the balcony, cold night air sweeping into the distance between us.

"That vigil," he rumbled out, knuckles white as he gripped the balustrade, "that vigil is the lifeblood of our people. The protection it affords our country..." He whirled around, eyes gleaming even though his face was cast in shadow.

"We have protected your own country, your own life, countless times over the years. The Lady's Vigil is what protects our own warriors and border."

He stalked back over to where I was standing, my hands almost frozen to the stone railing separating us. My eyes were wide at his change in countenance.

"I will not allow you to weaken it—to weaken us—because of your ignorance. You don't get to question our duty or what keeps us strong. You're here to serve and do what it takes to see that we remain strong. If not for Asileboix, then for the sake of your own country."

He glared down at me—more angry than I had yet seen him. I had been shocked when he first started talking, but the more he said the more I felt my own anger rise up within me until it rushed out of me.

"I don't recall laying my brain down as one of the vows at our wedding. So don't act as if it's a requirement for keeping *your* country safe." I pushed off the railing that still separated us, squaring my shoulders.

"You may have missed it while you've been off every day, running around doing who knows what, but I've been working every minute since our wedding to understand my place here, to make this the country of my heart even if it's not the country of my birth."

His face remained icily stoic, which only irritated me further; as if everything I said just bounced off of him. "I'm not stupid. I know that you all think I lack something basic, something important. It's why you've distanced yourself from me even though you said we were supposed to be getting to know one another. I can see it in Clement's kind politeness, the frantic way that Mathilde is cramming information into me from one day to the next. Even the servants treat me differently, as if I'm somehow fragile compared to you and Mathilde."

He finally reacted to my words, scoffing, "Fragile? Yes, you're fragile. You may be tall for a Pelerine woman, but you must have noticed since coming here that you're small for an Asilean. You have no self-defense training, no notion of magic, no understanding of how the charms work or how they might react to your presence. Of course the servants treat you carefully. They honor you but they also have to do their jobs, particularly if that means saving you from yourself!"

"Saving me from *myself*?!" I hadn't raised my voice this far in ages, not even in my last argument with Eddie. I was practically out of control. All of my pent up frustration was bubbling out to the surface: my haunting sense of failure at lessons and with Andrus; the discord in my heart from years of slowly strangling my dreams, only to have them suddenly come true; and the overwhelming feeling that those dreams were now exploding in my face. I couldn't stop even if I wanted to.

"So everyone here has nothing better to do but toddle after the idiot Princess?! I haven't needed saving in ... well, *ever*, actually. And when I do, I save myself, thank you very much. I don't need servants, or teachers, or "friends," or *you* to run after me cleaning up whatever messes I'm supposedly making. And here's the thing—I don't think I *am* making messes. I think I'm doing better than you expected and it scares you! Because you've been alone, or because you don't like me, or because there's something else keeping you from wanting me to do well. But I will spend every last breath I have proving you wrong, and smiling as I do it!" My hand reached out in a shove, but stilled inches from his chest as I came to my senses. I curled my fingers into a fist and hit my leg with them instead.

He was a cold statue, every inch a disdainful Prince. I spun away, my own chest heaving as I tried to get my whirling emotions under control. My loss of control made my head whirl. My fingers scraped stone as I leaned on the balustrade to anchor myself.

Something like a growl issued deep within his chest behind me. "I will leave you to collect yourself. Be outside your door in three minutes and I will escort you to dinner."

I grabbed my forearms with my hands, a gesture of habit, and squeezed to try and keep a lid on my temper.

"I am not—" I turned to face him as I spoke, only to watch his back disappear through into his apartments. "Beast!" I hissed to the empty balcony. I felt like a child again, my emotions a tempest tossing me in choppy waves. I could never sit down to dinner without erupting again.

Stomping back into my room, I strode across and locked

the door to the corridor. My feet took a few paces towards my bedchamber, then stopped. That direction would be going towards Andrus, even if walls separated us. I was too angry to move even a foot closer. *He's supposed to be the one giving me the most support. Instead, he's the one tearing me down.* I threw up my hands.

A heavy rap on my door rang out followed by Andrus' irritated rumble. "We're going to be late to dinner, Rosebelle."

I cringed. "I'm not feeling well enough to go. Please give my excuses to the others." I closed my eyes, praying that he would just leave. His baritone voice barked something unintelligible down the hall. Probably an order to the footmen down the hall to leave. Sure enough, a minute later his voice rang out again through my door.

"I was *just* with you on the balcony. You're not ill. Stop the nonsense and Come. Down. To. Dinner." He punctuated every word of his order.

Does he really expect me to let that slide?!

The lid I was desperately trying to keep on my anger blew off again. Sliding the lock open, I pulled the door back violently.

He was leaning against the doorframe, one arm propping him up, the other balled in a fist at his side. The gold flecks in his hazel eyes gleamed ever brighter than before under furrowed brows. For the first time, I could see a flush of red creeping up his neck. *He's finally rattled. Good.*

Glaring up at him, I announced in tones as clear and sharp as an icicle, "I. Will. Not. Go." I made to close the door, then jerked it open again.

"And you're right, I'm not ill. But I *will* be if I have to sit through a dinner with *you*." I slammed the door in his face and slid the bolt home again, staring at the barrier between us. All was silent save the sound of my own breathing.

"Fine. You want to starve? That's your business," He growled, almost too quietly for me to hear. A few footsteps made their way down the hall, then came back toward the door again. "I'll just go ahead and tell Chef that you're *too ill* to stomach our food, so don't bother asking for a tray!"

I scoffed at his childishness as he stomped away from my door.

Kicking my shoes across the room, I threw myself into my favorite chair by the fire, pressing both hands to my throbbing temples.

Slowly, I inhaled a deep breath, listening as my pounding heart began to quiet. After my pulse reached a more normal rhythm, I cracked my eyes open. The fireplace in front of me was burning merrily. Embers glowed orange, yellow flames leaped into the air over and over not in the least affected by the storm unleashed between Andrus and myself.

Watching the fire soothed me into a drowsy stupor. As I stirred myself to get ready for bed, I realized I was actually quite hungry. *No surprise after the long ride you had today.* The thought of the camaraderie we had enjoyed on the ride made me wince. *That hadn't lasted long.*

I didn't want to request a tray to my room in case Andrus had been petty enough to make good on his threat. I didn't think the Chef would refuse to send up food, but I didn't want to put her in an awkward situation and make extra work. Ringing the bell for Hazel didn't seem attractive either since she was probably finishing her own dinner and would want to talk about everything. I was too tired for that at the moment and needed time to process—process Andrus' conduct, but even more so my own.

Trudging into my dressing room, I examined my reflection as I sat down and removed my jewelry. A pale and tired face stared back at me, a frown its most prominent feature.

It had been easy to smile since coming here, although not when I was missing my family. Everything had seemed like an adventure, each day brought new information and excitement. Andrus had seemed like a puzzle I just needed to figure out how to put together properly. I had been pushing myself hard to comprehend it all and adjusting my way of thinking, but I had loved it. Asileboix was a place where I could re-create myself away from the rules and expectations of Pelerin.

Now I just felt deflated. A little lost as I realized I still didn't quite belong. There was empty space inside where I had stretched to accommodate my new life, but I didn't know who Belle was in those places yet. I was no longer in control, not just of my options, but of myself. Sighing, I reached up to unravel my hair before changing out of the beautiful gown Hazel had chosen for me. Her expectations, if not my own, had been dashed for the evening.

Regret seeped through cracks in the armor around my heart. The afternoon Andrus and I spent together had been unexpected—the beginning of a real connection. But right when I truly opened up, he turned on me. Punished my honesty.

I shook my head. *He shouldn't have done that, Belle, but you could have realized you had hit a nerve and backed off.* I groaned, pulling my robe on as my stomach grumbled loudly.

The fruit bowl in my sitting room caught my eye and I padded over to it. There was one small pear in it. Grabbing it hungrily, the sweet tartness of it burst over my tongue relieving the emptiness in my stomach. Too soon, I finished my meal and threw the core into the fire, watching it burn; restless, but not yet ready for sleep.

A knock on my door sounded, snapping me out of my sleepy contemplation. *Andrus?* My nerves stretched taut again. I was too tired for more dramatics.

Crossing the room with a sense of foreboding, I opened the door to reveal Mathilde holding a small basket. She breezed through as I held the door open for her.

One of her hounds trailed in behind her. Settling the basket on my table, she pulled several dishes out before turning to face me.

"Do you want to talk?" she asked briskly but kindly, scratching her dog behind its ears.

"Not really." I crossed my arms, avoiding her eyes.

"Never mind then, dear. But if you do, come find me

tomorrow morning. I won't mind." She made her way back over to the door.

"Andrus didn't say much, but I gathered you two had an argument about the Vigil."

I pursed my lips, wondering how much he *did* say if she knew that. Words escaped before I could stop myself. "It may have been about the Vigil to him, but it was more about how distant he's been to me." I snorted softly. "Probably what really drove it was my own lack of self-control. I've been through too many changes since I came here. I've allowed my expectations to adjust unrealistically." I flung my hands up in the air. "I really don't want to talk about it right now. This is exactly why I didn't come to dinner."

She cocked her head and gave me a half-smile. "I understand, Rosebelle, more than you probably realize." She hesitated for the barest moment, then continued, "I married Andrus' father when we were both eighteen, and took on the role of Princess almost immediately. We had been in love for several years so I had been preparing for the role, but it was still difficult to jump right into marriage and such large responsibilities all at once. And did we both have towering tempers! The stress of that first year was enormous." She shook her head, her expression a mix of humor and wistfulness.

"I can remember one blow-up we had was just outside the kitchens during the staff dinnertime. Everyone was going to and fro to get food on the various refectory tables and there we were, going at it like fishwives in the market. That was when we realized something needed to change. It wasn't easy! But I'll tell you something my mother-in-law, Eleanor, said to me then: try to find each other every day, and trust the Creator to bring it all around for good. No matter how many fights you have!"

She laughed, ruffling her dog's ears. "They became fewer and far between as the years went on and we kept working at finding each other. I miss those days. He was a magnificent

BELLE & BEAST

Prince and Father. An irritating man to be married to, but we were passionately in love right until the end." Tears glistened in her eyes and she bent down to hug the dog.

"The Vigil really is the backbone of our society. I know that you understand that. Andrus probably knows you know it too, but he is sensitive about the meaning of it and, well, he's on edge right now."

I raised my eyebrows at the notion that Andrus was sensitive to anything, but kept my thoughts to myself.

"Enough. You said you wanted space but here I am warbling on," Mathilde declared, giving the dog one last pat on the head. "I've brought Lilac here in case you wanted some company that couldn't talk back to you. She's very much the mothering sort. Shall I leave her with you?"

"Yes, please," I said with a laugh, my voice thick with emotion. I wasn't necessarily a "dog person", but she seemed sweet. I found I rather wanted something warm and soft with me tonight.

"Very good." Mathilde urged the dog over to me with a whistled command. Lilac trotted to my side, sitting down with a thump.

"If you get tired of her, just put her outside your door. She'll find her way to the stables and sleep with whoever is on call tonight."

As she walked out the door, she paused and stuck her head back through. "I just wanted you to know that you're not alone, and we do all care for you very much already." Flashing a warm smile, she slipped out the door before I could think of a reply.

I inhaled the food as soon as she left. Feeding tidbits to Lilac as I went, I briefly wondered whether they would spoil her appetite in the morning. Of course, I didn't share any of the pralines that Chef sent up, finding a small note tucked behind them saying, *"Enjoy, and ring for more if you like."* I was touched by the gesture and ate every crumb, wishing for home and my tiny bed in my rickety room.

Lilac and I snuggled by the fire until I felt tired, then we made our way over to my bedchamber. The dog burrowed herself into the blankets, but I stepped out on my balcony again for moment of fresh air, and to banish the ghost of our earlier argument before I went to sleep. I wandered over to the balustrade separating our balconies and stuck my tongue out at it, then laughed to think of what Rochelle would say at my childish behavior this evening.

Drifting toward the edge, I leaned against the railing and looked down into the quiet courtyard. A rounded moon made the fountains below stand out in stark relief. Their tinkling spray just barely reached my ears in the stillness. Most of the castle lights were out, but here and there torches flickered. One of the offices near the library was lit up as well. Someone was either working late or had forgotten to turn off their lights.

Several windows on the top floor of the ministry wing were blazing and it took me a minute to remember it was Andrus' study. He was seated at his desk. I felt a pang to see him working so late, remembering my words to him earlier. Everything he did was for the betterment of his country, and I had mocked him for it with bitterness in my heart. My gaze drifted up to the night sky and the shining moon, a prayer tumbling out.

Help me find him, please. And really, help me find myself. After another look at Andrus bent over whatever papers currently covered his desk, I shrugged my shoulders and wandered back to Lilac's sleepy snuffling.

CHAPTER FOURTEEN

Andrus

It had been two days since our fight and I still hadn't seen Rosebelle. The next night was the full moon, which meant I was busy on patrol. Thankfully our sweep was uneventful. My route took me north so I spent the day after recovering and checking in on the warriors stationed along our border with the Wastleand. The long ride back saw me collapsing into bed as soon as I made it home last night

Lueren bustled around my room, clanging dishes much louder than necessary as he set out food in my sitting room. I could hear him humming as he did it and considered throwing something at him, but there wasn't anything at hand except pillows. Besides, if I threw something at him it would probably land on my food, and I was alarmingly hungry by now.

A groan escaped as I swung my legs out of bed.

"That's the spirit, Sire. We'll be driving the Beast Hoarde back from whence they came in no time with vim and vigor like that going around," Lueren positively thrummed with cheerful sarcasm.

I grumbled under my breath as he switched his humming for whistling, then shuffled out to the dining area and shoveled food into my mouth, wincing at the midday sunshine streaming through the windows.

"Yes, I serve the Prince directly, I tell my friends. Such grace under pressure as you've never seen, I tell them. Up at the crack of dawn, works until midnight, couldn't ask for a better master." He grinned at me when I shot a glare in his direction.

"Lueren, you're pushing forty. I feel like I hit a wall when I turned thirty and it's taking me twice as long to recover from the simplest things." I gulped some water as he sat down next to me, grinning widely, and grabbed a sandwich for himself.

"Take stretching. It's an event now. Something that used to be a warm up to something else I was going to do has now become an event that I schedule into my day." I made a noise of disgust and turned my attention back to my food, ticking off a mental note to take some time to stretch as soon as I was done eating. *Maybe that would help the strain in my right shoulder.*

Lueren spluttered around a mouthful of chicken salad. "I'm thirty-five! Hardly pushing forty. And I'm as spry as ever, no matter what you say."

I snorted. "The fact that you used the word 'spry' in a sentence proves my entire case for me."

He rolled his eyes and we made quick work of the lunch spread he had brought up.

"Now," he announced as he began clearing the dishes back onto the service tray, "you were supposed to review treasury reports with Manciple this morning. I did it instead so you could get your beauty rest. There's a summary of everything we reviewed waiting on your desk." He glanced at the mantel clock. "You have about twenty minutes to prepare for your afternoon appointment so you'd better get moving."

My brow furrowed as I tried to remember what was on my schedule for today.

"City rounds with Princess Rosebelle," he prompted with only a trace of exasperation.

I hissed out a breath. Not something I wanted to do after a taxing full moon patrol and an unresolved argument hanging between us. Still, it had to be faced. I hadn't completed rounds in several weeks and it was to be Rosebelle's first time.

BELLE & BEAST

I mumbled my thanks as Lueren headed out the door. After a quick round of preparations, I stuck my hand out the door to my balcony to gauge the weather. Chilly again. Shrugging on my greatcoat and hat, I walked swiftly down to the stables.

Maybe Rosebelle will skip our ride. I quickly dismissed the thought. She had been dedicated to learning her duties since the day after our wedding. I had been overly harsh on her the other night, and mischaracterized her. I wasn't looking forward to apologizing, but I did owe her one.

When I got to the stables I found her mounted on Lodestone, speaking quietly with the stable master. I looked at her with surprise and went over to where my groom held Ironheart.

"Good afternoon," I greeted the room at large. Rosebelle looked collected, but I detected a trace of tension in the set of her mouth.

"Are we riding today?" I directed toward her. "I assumed we would be taking a carriage."

"Mathilde assured me that the people we're visiting are within easy riding distance. I wanted to practice."

It was only then that I remembered that she wasn't used to riding astride. She gave me a tight smile. Silently, I turned my attention to Ironheart, climbing up and turning him to lead the way out out.

"Will you be alright?" I asked as we left the castle gates, passing through the kitchen gardens, still mostly barren though spring approached.

"Yes," she answered, her tone clipped, then let out a breath. "I mean, yes, thank you. I practiced with one of the grooms for several hours yesterday. It's much easier to keep your balance than riding aside, as I'm sure you can imagine. But it does feel strange to me, so it will take a little practice to become completely comfortable."

We continued on in silence for a time. I was trying to figure out a way to broach the subject of our argument and offer an apology, but I was finding it difficult. I needed to apologize for my behavior, but I was still tired and definitely irritable. Her remarks about the Vigil continued to frustrate me. It offered some of the best protection for our warriors during full moon patrols. I knew she didn't have all the information on it yet, so she *couldn't* understand. Even so, Clement had informed me on my return yesterday evening that she done an excellent job at her first one the other night.

My mind drifted back to our last ride together. She had been charming and friendly. I had relaxed in her presence for the first time—which ended with our blistering exchange later that night. I had never had such a relationship before. My ascendancy to the throne happened when I was very young, and I had realized quickly that I would never be able to marry someone within my own or Sherwood's borders, no matter how compatible we may be. So I spared myself the heartbreak by not allowing feelings to develop for any woman I knew. Now I was married to someone both intriguing and incomprehensible. I didn't have practice navigating the shades of gray this sort of relationship seemed to bring with it. Giving my head a quick shake, which made Ironheart nicker, I wrestled my mind away from her and back to the task in front of us.

The city mayor handled most issues with the town residents, but part of the rulers' duties is to reinforce the relationship between the crown and those it served on a regular basis. One of the most important parts of that relationship is reaching out to the most vulnerable members of our country.

We were approaching the first house on our list, that of an older couple without any family left in the city. They were still able to care for themselves and their neighbors helped look after them, but they weren't able to leave their home very often. I wasn't sure how to coach Rosebelle on what to expect and how to act without being insulting or appearing condescending, so I kept silent and hoped she would follow my lead.

BELLE & BEAST

The visit went surprisingly well. Monsieur and Madame Tabard were in good health and were very excited to meet their new Princess. Rosebelle blushed as much as she ever did, fumbling to find a place to put the fresh fruit we brought with us and almost sitting on a lazy cat, half-hidden under a rumpled blanket. But she recovered herself admirably and set Madame and Monsieur Tabard laughing with a quick joke. They showed her the small woodcarvings Madame Tabard was still able to create, and which Monsieur painted, before gifting her a delicate wooden rose, painted a deep red. Madame Tabard cackled as Rosebelle thanked her for it very sincerely.

"I bet you can't get away from roses, can you, dearie?" Madame asked her, leaning on Rosebelle's arm as Rosebelle escorted her back to sit with Monsieur by the fire again.

"You speak truth, Madame," Rosebelle said with a faint blush and a quick glance in my direction. "It used to be a point of annoyance with me as a child, and I insisted all of my friends and family call me Belle instead of Rose because of it. Although," she dropped her voice a little lower, but still loud enough for the old couple to hear, "between you and me, it was also because the second part of my name means Beauty in the old tongue. My vanity was such that I secretly wanted everyone to call me beautiful all day long. Looking back, I think I must have been quite an absurd child!"

Madame Tabard cackled again and Monsieur Tabard joined his own wheezy chuckle to hers.

"Well, now you're our very own Rose Princess, and we're glad of it, eh wife?" Monsieur Tabard looked at his wife, who nodded her head as she settled her lap blanket and took her husband's hand.

I watched the exchange with a smile. Rosebelle was a natural: kind, thoughtful, full of gentle conversation, and not put off by any amount of teasing or the bluntness our people favored. I had been expecting to drag her into speaking with people below her station, but she was leading the charge. I was simply in the background.

As we moved on to the other houses on our route, it was much the same. Whether we were visiting the elderly, or sick, or people in the depths of grief, she listened attentively, made conversation where appropriate, and allowed children to examine her fine dress and pull her hair. The only time she seemed out of her depth was when a new mother handed her the baby. She glanced at me with alarm her eyes as she gingerly patted the baby's back and I barely contained my burst of laughter. She clearly noticed my amusement by the quirk of her eyebrow, but I had pity on her and took the baby myself. Although I had almost no family of my own, I had hours of practice helping with Manciple's children throughout the years. After handing the baby back to her mother, we started back to the castle at a languid pace. The road took us by the East Gate and a desire to get out of the castle walls overtook me.

"Would you like to continue practicing riding astride? We could take a run through the woods."

Rosebelle assented eagerly and I directed two of the guards at the gate to ride out ahead of us and ensure the path was secure.

* * *

The outriders returned, having confirmed that the first half of the eastern road was clear. After instructing our guards to wait for us at the gate, we urged our horses into a trot, then a canter, Rosebelle proving brave enough to try it in her new seat. We alternated between walking and cantering, pulling into a full gallop at one point. Tension melted off of me the further away from the castle we went. A friendly silence stretched between us.

After reaching the main crossroad, we climbed down from our horses to let them drink and rest for a few minutes. I didn't want to disturb our tentative peace, but I knew it was time to repair the damage from our fight.

"Rosebelle, I must apologize for the way I spoke to you the other night," I said abruptly. She stopped stroking her horses mane and stood completely still, not looking at me. "I was irritable and hungry, and snapped at you when I should have heard you out. I'm sorry for it. Would you please forgive me?"

She resumed brushing her horse's mane for a few minutes, then turned and walked toward me, stopping just out of my reach and looking me in the eyes.

"I'm sorry too," she said, her mouth pressed flat. "I completely lost my temper, and I'm ashamed of the things I said. I was hurt by your reaction, so I lashed out to protect myself. That wasn't right. I hope you can forgive me too."

I looked down into her golden eyes, reading sincerity there. A huge weight lifted off my shoulders. "I forgive you," I replied simply. Then I grinned at her, "Although you didn't say that I was actually forgiven, now that I think about it."

A startled look passed over her face. "Oh! Of course you're forgiven. Although a few more compliments about my riding and successful efforts on our rounds today would be appreciated." She shot me a sly look as she wandered toward the eastern road.

A desire to encourage her flared within me. "You are doing well, actually. Very well. You charmed everyone this morning with little effort."

"Oh well, that was easy," she responded, rubbing her arm with one hand. "Everyone seemed genuinely interested in meeting me. They seemed to see *me*—as a person. Not a symbol, or a status, or a means to an end. Just Rosebelle, their new friend and Princess. It was… fun."

I watched, taken aback by her words, as she scuffed her boot in the gravel and looked off into the trees. I had certainly treated her as a means to an end when I first met her. I cleared my throat.

"I find myself needing to ask forgiveness again," I ventured, steeling myself. "I've treated you as a means to an end to a large extent, and I didn't stop to consider how wrong that was. I'm sorry if it's given you pain. I didn't think it had, which made me better able to ignore what I was doing, but even if it hasn't, I'm sorry for it."

She whipped her head around and took a few steps toward me, surprise evident on her face. "Oh no, not at all. I mean… well, yes I'm sorry as well, I suppose. We were quite clear during our engagement at how things stood. That is, I was using you too. Oh no!" She put her hands up to frame her face, not quite in time to hide the mounting flush.

I couldn't help laughing as I strode toward her. I grabbed her shoulders, noting with surprise how slight they were, and hunched down to look her in the eye. "It's all right. You've cut right to the heart of things. We were using each other for our own ends and it wasn't right." I let her go and she pulled her hands down slightly so that they just covered her mouth.

"I can't say I'm sorry that we're married, especially as I've gotten just about everything that I wanted, but I am sorry for treating you the way that I did. Can we start again as friends?"

"Yes," she squeaked from behind her hands, then winced at herself. "I really am usually quite eloquent and dignified, actually." She threw up her hands in exasperation. "Ask anyone in Croiseux—they'll tell you! But somehow lately…" she trailed off with a shrug.

I couldn't help teasing her a little. "I know. You proved that at our very first meeting. And my agents did ask around at the village."

"What? When? I definitely would have heard if there were strangers asking questions about me. I didn't have many friends but, well, I suppose I had enough—that I would have heard." She sputtered lamely. My grin widened as she muttered quietly to herself, "Not sure his end of the deal is worth a Princess who can't carry a sentence *or* hold her temper."

She was nothing like I had imagined when I first met her. "I witnessed your temper before we married, so don't be troubled about that," I teased again.

BELLE & BEAST

She looked up at me suspiciously and I pinched the bridge of my nose. I hadn't meant to reveal that.

"Witnessed my temper? I rarely lost my temper before moving here! Unless Hazel talked to your agents without telling me?"

"No, no," I rushed to assure her. "It's worse than that." Berating myself for my slip, I knew I had to explain. *She's going to think I'm so strange.*

I sighed, turning and lifting a finger to point down the road. "Do you see that path?" I asked, and she nodded. "It leads toward Pelerin."

"I assumed so," she replied, "since it's going east. But are there any towns in that direction? I've never heard of anyone living so close to Croiseux."

"No, most of our villages and towns are concentrated to the north and west. That road eventually leads to smaller game trail by the cottage where Hazel's parents live. My huntsmen trade information with him about game migration and other issues affecting the forest several times a year. We know he's a trustworthy man and not one to spread tales, which is why it was an easy choice to approve Hazel to come with you."

I shifted on my feet and put my hands behind my back, starting to pace as I continued. "I have to admit that I... well this is going to sound bad no matter how I say it so I'll just say it. I witnessed your conversation with, I believe his name is Monsieur Marchand, the evening before our wedding."

She looked at me skeptically, pressing her lips into a flat line. "How?"

"I went for a ride to clear my head. Just anywhere to get away from the preparations in the castle. I ended up taking the eastern path, and before I knew it, I was at the turn off to the Dower Lands. I don't know why, but I continued on. I wanted a glimpse of your house for some reason, just to make sure you were safe. I suppose I was curious if things were busy there too. It was foolhardy really since I was on my own and near the border." I shrugged helplessly.

235

"Anyway, I didn't notice the two of you until I was at the tree line. I turned to go almost immediately, but it looked like tempers were flaring. I stayed to make sure you were alright."

She spun away slowly, clutching her forearms as she used to do often when we first met.

"I'm sorry for intruding on your privacy. I didn't hear much. I didn't want to! But I did hear your words at the end."

She stiffened, but I pressed on, wanting her to know that I understood her pain, and that I wasn't angry over her grief, since we were on the topic. "You told him to forget you. To forget what you had." She remained silent and I searched for a way to convey my thoughts.

"I know he was your intended, the one you had been engaged to for so long. You left because of the situation I put you in. You're grieving for him, for the plans you had made."

I couldn't truthfully say I was sorry. I simply *wasn't* sorry that we were married or that her father wasn't digging into the history of Asileboix. Although she made me uneasy at times because of the Gypsy Queen's foretelling, I wasn't sorry that I had a beautiful wife with a connection to Pelerin. But I *was* sorry that I had torn up her life, and for the pain of heartbreak she experienced because of that.

"I guess I need to say it yet again today. I'm—"

"Don't." She held up her hand to forestall me. "Don't say sorry, that is." Turning, her face revealed remorse but none of the tears I was expecting.

"Don't even *feel* sorry, actually." She huffed a dry laugh. "It's a little embarrassing to think that I had a witness for such a spectacle, but if you were truly there to make sure I was safe, it's actually endearing." She gave me a sardonic smile and took a step toward me then stopped, her words coming out in a rush as if to get them over with as fast as possible.

"I'm not grieving. I don't love him—I never did. Yes, he was the one I was engaged to, but that was because it was expected between our families. It just seemed right to everyone that the Marchand heir marry me, especially as we had grown up together." She hesitated for a brief moment, her discomfort plain. "It's true that he had loved me for as long as I can remember, but I had never been in love with him. To me, he was just a means to an end that we all desired."

She stared at my shoulder instead of my face, as silence stretched between us. The concern I had felt about her pain was replace by relief. I wondered how I could ease her obvious embarrassment.

"I don't think he really ever loved me as Belle, though, just the idea of me," she continued quietly. "As we grew, he just projected what he thought my best qualities were over top of the real me. He always viewed me as this beautiful, genuine, caring 'Lady of the Manor'. As you especially have seen, that's not precisely who I am. I sound very cruel, now that I'm confessing all of this. Ah well—I suppose I am." A sheepish laugh escaped her as she wrapped her arms around her waist. "Not exactly kind and gentle—more like cruel and cunning."

I wondered at her picture of herself. She had certainly been kind and gentle on our rounds this afternoon. In fact, she had acted exactly as she described the 'Lady of the Manor': beautiful, genuine, caring, present with each person we met. I had also witnessed intelligence, shrewdness, and a subtle ability to influence people and events to meet her goals. Those qualities were just as valuable to me, especially if her own goals lined up with mine: the welfare of our people.

Our people. As much as I had accused her of being an outsider just a few days ago, I could see that she was already starting to see herself as Asilean. She had taken our use of magic in stride even though she had been raised in a society that thought it evil. She threw herself into lessons, quickly learning to perform her duties—even ones she didn't understand, like her role in the Vigil.

Even her honest admission of concern about the Vigil was a sign of how seriously she takes her role. Without the full story, she viewed it as a dangerous continuation of superstition. She had voiced her concern over the harm it might be continuing as soon as I gave her an opportunity. She didn't conceal her apprehension in a bid to just keep the peace. She did exactly what we would want our Princess to do—she voiced her concerns over something that might weakening Asilebois. *And you blew it all up in her face.* Yet another reason to be irritated with myself. *Humility is being served in large portions today.* I huffed a laugh.

She flinched as if I had slapped her. *She thinks you're laughing at her.* I took a quick step and pulled her into a crushing bear hug, chuckling. Her frame was tense for a moment, then relaxed and tentatively leaned against me. I released her after a moment, grabbed her shoulders again and looked into her eyes.

"I don't know about cruel, but I'll take cunning in my Princess any day. I've certainly seen kindness and gentleness from you toward people who deserve it. Unfortunately I don't think I've deserved much of it myself, to this point." She frowned up at me and I continued on, rubbing my thumbs along her upper arms.

"It takes an extraordinary person to be a good ruler. You have to be just, merciful, self-sacrificing, a good listener, a convincing speaker, a grand symbol, but also an approachable advocate. Shrewd enough to see what needs to be done and strong enough to make the hard choices: a decision-maker. A warrior. Not that I'm complementing myself. I've been raised to use my talents and find ways to adjust for my weaknesses since I was a child. I've built a team of people around me to make up for my failings. You seem to have come to it all naturally. There's no better partner than you to champion Asileboix with me."

Vulnerability shone out of her eyes as she listened, oddly unsettling me. I released her and rubbed the back of my neck, turning back to our horses, and she followed a moment later. Wordlessly, I assisted her in mounting. A thoughtful silence stretching between us as I climbed up onto my own and we headed home. The urge to connect with her made my thoughts tumble out of my mouth.

"At the risk of sounding completely insane, it wasn't the first time I had seen you arguing with him," I revealed, assessing her reaction out of the corner of my eye.

"How? Eddie hasn't been around to argue with over the last few years." She looked at me expectantly.

I released a heavy breath. "It's the main reason I insisted we didn't have a wedding ball. It was a little over fifteen years ago now. You were just children. So was I really, although I thought myself quite grown up at the time." I shifted in my seat.

"I had been out on patrol with Clement. He was a Forest Guard and my father's best friend. We had uncovered several issues during our patrol. On our way home, we rode by the gamekeeper's cottage to warn him, and check if he had seen anything similar. Clement left me with the horses while he went on foot to speak with Monsieur Veneur. I heard shouting, and given what we had uncovered during our patrol, I left the horses to check it out."

I chuckled mirthlessly. "It was you and Monsieur Marchand. You were shouting at him, I don't why. But I do remember you pushing him to the ground before running inside. I've never forgotten it."

She raised her eyebrows. "Ah, I see it all now. You were struck by the little termagant and vowed that one day she would be yours. You've been plotting all these years for a way to come between me and my prey, to snatch me away so I could berate you instead."

I burst out laughing at her teasing sarcasm. "I suppose since that's what has happened, maybe I *was* unknowingly moving all the puzzle pieces these years to capture you." We both grinned at each other, but my smile faded quickly.

"Actually, I didn't make the connection between you and that little girl until the evening before our wedding, when I witnessed you yell at him all over again."

She laughed. "I must say I'm a little let down that you haven't been pining for me all this time, but I suppose I'll take it." We rode in silence for a few minutes before I continued my story, hesitant to be vulnerable but feeling the need to finish it now that I had begun.

"I've remembered it all these years because, for one thing, it had been funny, but it was also the last normal, innocent thing I remember from before everything changed." I glanced over at her. She stared at the road ahead, a frown on her face.

"The next afternoon was my sister Marguerite's wedding. She had never wanted to rule. Even when she was a little girl she would go around telling people that she wasn't the Princess, her baby brother was." I snorted. "She always teased me about that. Even on the day she died."

I sighed, the memories weighty but faded for the moment. "Anyway, by law, she couldn't abdicate her right and responsibility until she came of age or was married. At her wish, she performed the renunciation ceremony in the throne room, and then immediately took her wedding vows with Devon." I paused, overwhelmed by memories of the heartfelt ceremony, and my own swirling teenage feelings at becoming direct heir to the throne.

"We had a grand ball to celebrate of course. People from all over the kingdom came, as Marguerite had been immensely popular. Even some of the gypsies graced us with their presence. The gates were thrown open, pavilions and food provided throughout the city. It was an enormous, hope-filled party."

"Sounds lovely," Rosebelle said, looking over at me.

"It was, really. Even for a sixteen year old boy who wasn't fond of dancing or weddings." I ordered my thoughts as I navigated a tree root sticking out of the road.

"She was dancing with Devon when it happened. I was watching them across the room and thinking what an idiot Devon was for marrying my annoying sister. They were directly in front of the stained glass window at the far end. It used to be of Princess Isabelle and Prince Andrew, our dynasty's founders. It shattered to pieces as a Beast broke

BELLE & BEAST

through. A beast took down my sister before the glass had even fallen to the floor. Another was on Devon before I registered what was happening.

"It was chaos. Eventually my father rallied the guards in attendance, managing to get weapons into their hands and beat the monsters back. Clement, my mother, and I secured as many people as we could in the Old Keep. We saw my father only one more time—after the castle and city had been swept and before he rode out with the guards to chase down the enemy. He died securing the border, but he did secure it. A week later, I was crowned Prince."

Our bridles jingled in the silence between us, as Rosebelle digested my story and I attempted to button the old feelings back up again.

"So, that memory of the two children stuck with me. You were a symbol of my own childhood, of innocence and security. I can tell you that I was shaken to the core when I realized who you were the night before our own wedding. And it was too similar... I was afraid of the same thing happening. Watching you argue. Riding back to the castle. A wedding. A ball. The beasts breaking through the same window, only now it would be you and I dying, and there would be no one left to secure the borders and protect our people." I shivered violently, startling my horse slightly and drawing Rosebelle's gaze. I stared stonily ahead as she considered me thoughtfully.

"I can understand that. I did wonder why we had no ball. But I thought that our engagement was too short for you to organize one. And I knew you hardly ever allow anyone to stay in your kingdom overnight." She paused, considering her thoughts. "It was for their own safety that you made the foreigners leave, wasn't it?"

I replied dully, trying not to seem as vulnerable as I felt, "Yes, among other things."

"They tell stories about her wedding in Pelerin," Rosebelle continued gently. "Scary stories for children mainly. I never thought they made sense. But I did wonder about the other

241

tales of cruelty and of Beastmen." She paused and I prepared for awkward questions or a repetition of the fantastical tales I had heard during my own trips to Pelerin.

"I knew they were all lies the first night I met you," she said instead, with a smirk.

I barked out a surprised laugh. "Really? You seem quite confident. What convinced you? Not my manners—nor my actions, I'm sure."

"No, certainly not," she agreed, her smile growing wider. "Your conversation, of course."

I raised my eyebrows at her skeptically.

"Oh yes. Don't be surprised! I could see immediately how much you love and respect your mother, and I knew that anyone who behaved like that couldn't be anything like those tales. Besides, your mother struck me as eminently reasonable from the first time I spoke with her, and she obviously loves you. Even a doting mother could never love a 'Beastman of Asileboix'." She laughed and urged her horse ahead of me and into a trot.

I matched her pace, my amusement turning to something more like dread. "And how do you know that, Rosebelle? Perhaps Mathilde is one too?"

Her laugh peeled even louder than before. "Mathilde? A Beastwoman? A Beast tamer, maybe. If anyone could tame them, she probably could. She would make them follow her around and do her bidding, just like her hounds."

She chuckled again, urging her horse faster. "Besides, I'm not saying I haven't decided that you're not a Beastman yet!" Her yell floated back to me as she pulled ahead. "I'm only saying that if you are, you can't be as bad as the stories."

Her teasing soothed the exposed parts of me, and I urged my horse into a gallop. "Well if I'm a Beast, I suppose I don't have to play the gentleman and let you win."

We raced neck and neck toward the castle walls, yelling and laughing in exultation. I called the passwords ahead of us as we raced through the gates, passing the fields in the outer bailey, and only slowing as we approached the city itself. Rosebelle's eyes sparkled as we made our way up the streets, out of breath and laughing. As I helped her dismount at the stables, Manciple found me.

"Ah, Sire, there you are. Princess, good evening." We both nodded to him as the grooms led our horses away.

"I hate to interrupt, but I have an urgent request from the mayor about the well in the Market Square. It is rather dire, I'm afraid."

I looked down at Rosebelle, an apology on my lips, feeling something like regret.

"Shall I tell them you need a tray for dinner?" she asked me, a half-smile on her face.

Manciple answered before I could open my mouth. "It is not necessary Madame, I've already arranged for one in his study."

"Well it appears I'm off," I said feebly, feeling awkward at the sudden change of events after the afternoon we had just shared.

"It appears that way, yes," she replied, still smiling. Suddenly, she put a hand on my upper arm, leaning on me as she rose up on tiptoes and placed a gentle kiss on my cheek. Warm lips pressed against my cold skin, and an ember flared to life in the pit of my stomach.

"Thank you for encouraging me earlier and sharing that story," she whispered, before sinking back down and walking slowly toward our rooms.

I stared after her, bewildered, my head turning to watch her go.

Manciple cleared his throat. "I do apologize, Sire. But the situation really is quite urgent. The charm on the well failed earlier in the day, and he's requesting approval for an alchemist or an engineering mage to be contracted to fix it as soon as possible."

I shook my head to clear my thoughts and turned toward him. "I see. That's the well that most of the businesses in that district use, correct?"

"Indeed, Sire," Manciple answered as we started toward my study. "I've pulled the relevant charter information and town codes for your review before we submit a request. They're waiting for your signature."

"Thank you, Manciple. Let's have a look. Sounds like we'll need someone from Spindle." We picked up the pace, and I turned my mind toward my problem in the city instead of my beautiful wife.

CHAPTER FIFTEEN

Belle

I walked slowly away from the stables and toward my rooms, my face heated at my boldness and feeling Andrus' eyes on my back. I wondered whether it had been something he welcomed or disliked when I kissed him. More likely something he felt nothing at all about, unless it was surprise that a cold Pelerine lady like me would do such a thing.

I dawdled as I walked, replaying our afternoon in my head. Our apologies. His admittance to having seen me argue with Eddie. The story he shared about his sister. Cringing, I remembered my flirtatiousness toward the end of our ride. Not a trace of my Pelerine birth seemed to be hanging around me now. Apparently I was already as bold as an Asilean.

My pace slowed even more as I aproached in an alcove in the stairwell. I didn't want to pass by the footmen always on duty near our rooms with my face so red. Besides, Hazel was surely already waiting for me in my chambers and would notice straight off, demanding details. It felt too personal to talk about just yet. I wanted time to sift through everything.

The most excruciating part of our conversation had been describing my relationship with Eddie. Hearing myself explain it out loud felt like salt in a wound. I was ashamed of my conduct, insecure at having exposed it to Andrus. I seemed to have a habit of embarrassing myself around him. The inner Belle that I kept so carefully hidden seemed to charge out at the worst moments.

I groaned as I remembered listing my worst qualities to him. *Literally cannot think of a worse way to build a friendship —right after he offered to start fresh!* My head dropped to my hands.

I'll take cunning in my Princess any day. His compliment thrilled as it flashed through my memory, straightening my spine. I had always thought of my tendency to manipulate things as bad, and the fact that I was so good at it meant that I was rotten somehow. It was certainly viewed that way for women in Pelerin. Andrus not only accepted that part of me, but was glad of it.

'My Princess,' he had called me. I banished that thought quickly. He hadn't meant it that way. At least not yet.

Recalling forgiveness and acceptance forced me to examine the one thing I was trying to keep out of sight in the back of my mind. I had been nudging it further away even as I brought my other memories of the day forward, hoping it would just slide off a cliff into the abyss where occurrences or people who don't merit space in your memories go forever: my conduct toward Eddie.

I folded my arms, frustrated. For once I was frustrated with myself, not Eddie. I could hardly stand to think back over my treatment of him, my thoughts toward him. I couldn't touch the memory of our last conversation—the one Andrus had apparently witnessed, of all people. I groaned again, turning toward a window into the courtyard below. Night had fallen. My eyes strayed toward where I knew Andrus would be at work in his study, but I forced them elsewhere. *No use mooning over someone you're just getting to know. Besides, you're doing it to distract yourself now.*

For years I had scorned Eddie and felt justified in it because I knew he put me on a pedestal. If I was honest with myself, he was really an infinitely better person than I had ever been, and that was why his near perfection had always grated on me. He was constantly blind where I was concerned, which made me feel superior. But was it any wonder that he was blind towards me? His own generous nature tended to see and encourage the best in people. I had stopped revealing my true self to anyone outside my family and Hazel shortly after we lost all of our property. All he had ever seen was a reserved, impoverished Lady. He knew that as a child I had been good-natured—if a little bossy and spoiled—so he probably assumed my good nature had continued to grow along with my beauty and hard-won dignity.

My conduct towards Andrus had been almost nothing when I compared it with the years of derision I had heaped on Eddie. Andrus and I had been like two chess players, scoring off each other for our own gain, yes, but at least we had been playing the same game. Eddie had been like a lamb I was leading to market.

There you go again—that's not fair to him. It wasn't really. If I could cudgel my brain into thinking about him objectively, he was actually quite a catch. Handsome, self-sacrificing, a hard worker, utterly loyal, and completely chivalrous. Any other woman in Pelerin would have done just about anything to win the heart of such a man. I had trampled on it and thrown it away. Sadness crept over me. Not for severing my connection with him: we were truly ill-matched. He was a Knight of old and deserved a Fair Maiden. I might look like a Fair Maiden on the outside, but I was full of thorns on the inside.

A perfect fit for a prince of the 'Beast Men of Asileboix' then. Andrus had already proved that it took more than a few pricks of my sharp tongue to pierce his skin—I was better off where I was. His blunt apology flashed through my mind. How surprising it had been that he apologized first. Or apologized at all.

You should apologize to Eddie. I shrank from that thought. Turning, I stomped back over to the stairs and continued up to my room. *I can't apologize, I'll probably never see him again.*

You could write.

Could I write? No, definitely not. *Out of the question. It wouldn't be proper.* A verse from the Book of Hearts flashed through my mind. *Better to be uncomfortable making amends where you've done wrong than to try and live comfortably with guilt in your heart.*

I huffed out a breath. I didn't have time to spend planning an apology to Eddie. Did I owe him one? Yes. Should I write to him? Probably not. It would look silly for a Princess of Asileboix to be writing apologies to retired army officers in Pelerin. And possibly suspicious as well, if the wrong person got a hold of it. I tucked the thought out of my head a little uneasily.

You're going to be late for dinner! I scolded myself, hurrying past the footmen before bursting into my room.

"Hazel?" I called, walking straight into my dressing room to start changing for dinner. When I didn't see her waiting for me there, I noticed a piece of paper propped up against my vanity mirror.

Andrus and Mathilde were called away on business. Clement is having a tray in his office. I've gone down to get yours as well—be back with enough for both of us! - Hazel.

I smiled and slipped the note into the wastebasket. I had been looking forward to a real dinner with Andrus, Mathilde, Clement, and myself all together, but since that was obviously not going to happen, I could enjoy some time with my best friend instead. I quickly changed and showered. I was becoming quite comfortable operating the spelled conveniences in my room, although a little sad that Pelerine laws prohibited my family from enjoying them too.

I was tentatively operating the drying iron when Hazel came back in.

"Belle?" she called over the noise of the drying iron.

"In here!" I yelled back. She poked her head around the door and laughed at my attempt to dry my mass of waist-length hair, then dipped back out to put the tray on the dining table. The scent of food wafted through to my dressing room, my stomach responding eagerly. Turning off the iron, I let my hair hang down my back, slightly damp as I hurried out to the table.

We dug in with gusto. Chef had sent up a number of small plates instead of just a few large dishes. Sauteed mushrooms in butter sauce, roasted potatoes and asparagus, venison au jus, salmon patties with hollandaise sauce, and dark colored bread that I would have disdained eating in Pelerin as it looked common, but had actually become quite fond of since I had moved to Asileboix. We chatted while we ate, and afterward, sat across from each other in front of the fire in my sitting room. Hazel worked on a torn hem on one of my dresses, and I repaired some ribbon that had come loose on one of my hats. I had hated working on such things in Pelerin, as a lady of my rank wouldn't be caught dead doing it usually. During my time in Asileboix, I found that I preferred keeping busy to being idle, especially if it gave me a chance to sit with Hazel.

"I still can't get over how beautiful that Vigil was," Hazel remarked during a break in the conversation. "I had expected it to be a little strange and maybe sad, but it actually felt hopeful. It brought everyone together. Our connection to each other just felt more apparent, if that makes sense."

I looked up from where I was tying off a stitch, considering her words. "Yes, actually, that does make sense. There are so many people in this castle and town. I know we're all reliant on each other to an extent, but you don't get a feeling for it on a day-to-day basis."

I focused on tying off my stitch and held out the hat to examine it. Everything looked in order, so I laid it on a nearby table and tipped back into my seat.

"Andrus and I actually got into an argument about the Vigil a few days ago. It was quite heated," I mentioned, snuggling in under a blanket.

"Really?! You never told me that!" Hazel glanced up from her work.

I sighed. "Yes. We had been chatting when I mentioned that I didn't understand the Vigil and was worried it would spread superstition and fear. Andrus became *very* upset. We eventually patched things up, although I'm sure the footmen overheard us yelling at one point. We were *so* loud!" Hazel chuckled as I traced the pattern on my blanket with a finger.

"Now that we've been through an actual Vigil I can see it doesn't spread fear. Quite the opposite. I think my favorite parts were the prayers."

"Oh no—the best part was the singing. It sounded so beautiful echoing off the chapel walls."

I laughed. "No surprise there! You have a wonderful voice!"

"Oh stuff. You have a lovely voice too, and you know it."

"Of course, it's expected for a Pelerine lady, and I still remember my governess clutching her heart when I went off pitch! But you're a natural. I love to hear to you sing."

Hazel stood up and began cleaning away our sewing supplies, but slowed to a stop as she put some thread into the basket. "Did you see..." she trailed off, her expression pensive.

"What?" I prodded, standing up to help look for the needle or whatever sewing article she was missing.

"This is going to sound very silly, but I have to know. Did you see the water in the fountain turn gold for a moment when the priest said the First Blessing during the Vigil?"

I thought carefully. "No. But I did see the whole room fill with a golden haze. It must have been a trick of light. The last rays of the sun lighting everything up."

Hazel frowned for a moment before turning to tidy up the rest of our sewing projects .

I watched her out of the corner of my eye. Her expression was unusually solemn; her shoulders hunched in on herself. Finally she divulged what was on her mind, her tone defiant.

"I don't think it was the sun, actually. It was down by then, and the light lasted longer than a second. I could have sworn that it lingered, most strongly around Mathilde and you! Maybe I was seeing things." She bit her lip, looking worried.

"Well, you're not exactly flighty, so if you saw something, you saw something. And I did see a haze of golden light in the room. Could it have been the light charms in the room going a little haywire?"

"Maybe. I hadn't thought of that." Relief passed over her face and she sat a little taller. "Still, there are so many strange things that go on here." My eyebrow shot up quizzically.

"Not bad," she assured me quickly, "just strange. Like that golden light, and those Forest Guards."

That comment piqued my interest. "What do you mean the Forest Guards? They're just soldiers, although they're certainly secretive."

"Well, I don't think they *are* just soldiers. There's something else about them. Something they do or are in charge of. The other servants obviously revere them. Any time they have a request for the servants, they drop everything and attend to it. Just tonight, I had to wait on your tray because one of the guards came in asking for a meal. The cook in charge of your tray stopped to make up several trays for him before getting back to your own food."

"I didn't notice any delay," I commented, sliding my slippers off and tucking my feet up on the settee beside me. "I wasn't even done with my hair when you came in."

"Yes, but only because you were dawdling with Sir Prince!" She shot me a teasing grin. "And I didn't make a fuss or anything, I just thought it strange that he was served first when she was almost done with your tray." She shrugged.

"It's definitely different around here, you're not wrong. Let's just keep our eyes and ears open. I'll see what I can dig up discreetly about the Forest Guard. Manciple warned me away from where their headquarters is located, and Mathilde hasn't covered their function at all in my lessons. It's a little mysterious."

"I'm telling you, something is strange about them," Hazel repeated as she got up from her own chair. "I'm off to bed. You've kept me up way too late, Madame Princess! I'll be missing breakfast in the morning if I stay up any later. Good night!"

"Good night!" I called as she bounced into the hall. I heard her call cheerful hellos to the footmen on duty.

Although my muscles were tired from the long ride in a new type of saddle, my brain wasn't. Hazel's comments about the Forest Guards had stirred my interest into the secrets of Asileboix again. *I could use the secret passage to get to the library and dig into the archive!* I glanced at the clock. Maybe another night. I was already dressed for bed.

"Papa's research!" I exclaimed suddenly, sitting straight up in my seat. I slapped my hands over my mouth and sat still, listening. I chuckled at my reaction. I was alone. No need to worry that someone had discovered my folders, stacked away.

Actually, what if someone has *discovered them!* I panicked, realizing I hadn't checked on them since I moved in. Jumping off my sofa, I ran to my bedroom, sinking to my knees in front of my escritoire.

I slid my hand under the central part of the desk until I hit the release mechanism. The bottom swung down several inches, a folder of papers catching on a lip at the front just before it would have fallen to the floor. A relieved breath left me.

I checked each and every compartment, confirming all was still there. Closing everything back up again, I kept the pages on the Asilean lineage out.

"You wanted a mystery," I told myself as I settled at my desk. "How have you been here a month and not done any further investigating?!"

The memory Andrus' solid arm underneath my hand as I leaned up to kiss him stole across my brain. "So all it takes is a bunch of muscles and pair of green eyes and your brain no longer functions?" I scolded. *And a humble spirit. And someone who sees you for who you are and likes you for it.*

I shook my head uneasily. I didn't like the idea of going behind Andrus' back, but he hadn't actually forbidden *me* from

BELLE & BEAST

doing any research. And now that I was an Asilean, I had a right to know what he was hiding. I pushed my conscience aside and set about re-familiarizing myself with the research.

* * *

I waved to Mathilde as I stepped into my chambers. There were several hours before dawn, and we had just finished my second Vigil in the castle Chapel. The moon had already set, which ended our Vigil earlier than my first one a month ago. I had paid extra attention to see if I could catch the light Hazel saw last time, but all I noticed was a golden haze again.

"It was even stronger this time!" Hazel had hissed in my ear when we parted ways to our separate chambers. Flashing her an intrigued look, I had continued on with Mathilde, who was determined to see me safely to my rooms. *Andrus' orders, no doubt.* I didn't enjoy feeling like I need to be looked after, but I knew it came from a place of hurt over his own sister's death in this very stronghold so it didn't bother me so much.

Instead of feeling completely drained like the last Vigil, which had lasted until dawn, I felt energized and centered. *Should I pull out Papa's research?* I had been working on it in secret over the last month in fits and starts, with Hazel's reluctant help.

I stepped out onto my balcony instead to clear my head. Stars blazed in the clear night sky. Here and there, lights sparkled around the castle and the city. The air was quite warm for early March, which only served to fuel my desire to be doing something. *If only I could get out of my chambers and do something—anything!*

My eyes drifted toward Andrus' side of the balcony. Last week we had spent several hours out on the balcony, discussing the constellations and trading stories about late night escapades with our siblings from our childhood. The memory glowed in my mind.

After our first heated fight and apology, we had had several more arguments—and apologies—but had also grown steadily closer. He was randomly irritable and prone to jumping to conclusions. I continued to put my foot in my mouth at the most inopportune times around him. My blushing problem was somehow better and worse. I didn't blush every time he spoke to me anymore, especially in private, but I would feel my face getting heated at the worst times—like if I felt his eyes on me in public, or if he caught me staring at him when he was talking to someone else. I felt heat on my face just thinking about it now.

A year ago, I would have considered his looks almost coarse, especially compared the refined features of fashionable Pelerine men. He was built on a large scale, his skin olive toned and crisscrossed with tiny scars that I hadn't had the courage to ask about. His nose had obviously been broken, perhaps more than once, and he kept his hair very short, as seemed to be the custom with the Asilean warriors. His eyes went from brown, to hazel, to green from one day to the next. Secretly, I enjoyed guessing what color they would be when next they looked at me.

Maybe it's a good thing he is out on patrol. He filled my head tonight, and although a strengthening friendship had blossomed between us, and I at least felt definite attraction, his feelings weren't always transparent. I was *decidedly* glad that the Royal Tower wasn't finished yet, which would force us to start living together. I had increasing hope that we would really grow to love each other, but we weren't there yet.

My lungs welcomed the midnight air, breathing deeply. People clattered in the courtyard below, leaving the Vigil in the throne room. The sound of their actions spurred me into my own. Hurrying to my dressing room, I pulled a light cloak over my dark blue gown, grabbed a few books that I had borrowed from the library, and slipped out of my room.

"I always need something to read in order to go to sleep! I'm glad the library is so large," I chirped to the poorly disguised soldier-as-footman on duty. He furrowed his brow so I added, "Don't worry, there's no need to accompany me. Hazel would be happy to go."

He relaxed and I shrugged my shoulders as soon as I was out of sight, attempting to shrug off the deception as well. Hazel *would* be happy to go with me—if I asked her. I just wasn't going to ask her. And I *did* usually need a book to help me fall asleep—I just wasn't returning the books tonight.

My tread was light and measured as I went down the stairs and across the long gallery that linked my tower to the drawing room of the Royal Tower. When I arrived, I strode purposely toward the working wing, projecting as much confidence as I could muster.

No one was there. I breathed a sigh of relief, giddy at my burgeoning sense of freedom. Passing into the ministry wing, I slipped inside the supply closet as quickly as I could, shutting the door without a sound. Listening, I held my breath, then slowly released it, my heartbeat returning to normal when it was clear I hadn't been seen.

I stood, giving my eyes time to adjust to the dark, before realizing that it was so pitch black they wouldn't be able to adjust to anything. Mentally kicking myself for not bringing a light, I revolved in place until I thought I faced the glowing symbol and searched the dark with my eyes. *There!* My hand stretched out and pressed the warm stone.

The faintest scrape of stone sounded, revealing glowing stairs. Excitement accelerated my heartbeat once more. Clutching my books in one hand and my skirts in another, I stepped into the light.

After reaching the last step, I slipped into the library. A cautious pause confirmed that it was truly empty, most of the lights extinguished. The dimness forced me to navigate between rows of massive shelves mostly by feel. Eventually, I stumbled into the main aisle, cursing my lack of foresight in not bringing a lamp. Although how I would have explained it away to the guardian footman I wasn't sure.

Luck was with me. Perched on one of the circulation desks was a small, unlit lantern. Snagging it triumphantly, I clutched it to my side, resisting the urge to light it immediately in case it brought curious guards down up on me.

As I hurried out of the library and toward the Chapel Wing, my excitement grew. It seemed everyone was in bed. Finally, I made it to the end of the hall just beyond the Chapel entrance. There, an ancient statue of the Lady of the Woods stood guard, covering the entrance to another storage closet. Slipping inside, I quickly lit my lantern. It's light illuminated neatly organized shelves, packed with religious objects and art. As far as I could tell, no one had been here since I had discovered its secret, just over a month ago.

I hadn't been looking for a secret passage. After sitting in the peaceful quiet of the Chapel, something that was becoming a bit of a routine for me, I had walked over to examine the statue of the Lady. To find such a large and obviously ancient example had been fascinating. After a time, my eyes had caught on the door in the wall behind her, and I peeked inside to see what it was.

Rows of more beautiful art, mostly broken or of a style currently out of fashion, had met my eyes. I couldn't resist taking a quick look around. To my surprise, I discovered a faintly glowing tower symbol etched into the wall and half-hidden behind a moth-eaten tapestry.

I had been longing to explore the passage behind it further. That first day I had only had time to press the symbol and confirm that there *was* a secret passage before heading back for fear of discovery. I had been just in time. Andrus had exited the Chapel only moments afterward. At the time, I didn't trust him enough to ask about the passageway, so I passed off my presence with a different story.

Now I had ample time to explore. No one would be looking for me, and I was full of energy. I dumped the books I was still carrying onto a shelf by the door. Eagerly, I searched the wall for the symbol, pressing it without hesitation once it caught my eye.

My lantern flickered as it slid open. Excitement bubbled up and I plunged across the threshold, the wall sliding closed behind me.

The passage sloped gently downward. After fifteen minutes of monotonous tunnel, some of my excitement began to wear off. I had been expecting secret rooms or a tunnel to another part of the castle, perhaps. So far, it had just been one long, continuous passage—heading west as far as I could tell. A few more minutes and I came to the end, disappointment rising as I couldn't find any mark revealing a secret opening. *There has to be one!* I thought back to the first time Andrus showed me the library's secret passage. We had stood together in the dark. *He said it's easier to see them in the dark!* I put out my lantern.

Sure enough, an identical tower symbol glowed into the night. Putting my hand to it, the wall scraped open. The sound of insects and rustling grass reached my ears. Blinking, I realized I could see stars. *The passage leads outside!*

As I stepped out, the wall scraped closed behind me. Alarmed, I looked back to make sure I could locate the entry mark and breathed a sigh of relief. There it was, a steady golden glow.

I squinted around in the dimness. It was very dark. No street lamps glowed nearby, although I could see some in the distance. A dark structure loomed to my left. After a moment I realized it was a chapel. There were trees here and there, interspaced by rectangular lumps at regular intervals.

With a jolt I realized that it was the city graveyard, next to the Western Chapel. A shiver went down my spine and my feet turned back to the secret passage, but pulled up short.

It's just a graveyard. The dead can't hurt you, Belle. Squaring my shoulders I looked around with new eyes, realizing that although it was a bit alarming, it was also still and peaceful. I was more alone here than I had been in months. My smile grew and I started forward, quickly finding a meandering gravel path. Breathing deeply, my body loosened and started relaxing.

Freedom opened up around me. The trees and gravestones certainly weren't expecting me to be competent or collected.

My skirts flared as I spun around in a circle laughing out loud. No need to keep my voice down. I knew from the maps in the library that the graveyard was massive, bounded by the city wall and the castle kitchen gardens. The nearest residences were well beyond the Chapel. While I wouldn't be shouting up to the sky, there was no one around to hear me.

My heart soared into the openness. I didn't bother re-lighting my lantern. Not only did I not want to risk it being seen and causing someone to investigate, but there was enough ambient light to see the white gravel paths.

Giddiness bubbled up from the bottom of my toes to the top of my head. It was cold enough that I was glad of my cloak, but so long as I kept moving, I didn't feel the chill. I mock curtsied to a few of the barren trees as I went, laughing at myself. It was a game Rochelle and I had played in the orchard as children, pretending the trees were our dance partners at a ball, since we were not invited to high society balls ourselves.

Up ahead, the path split into several branches. Just beyond the crossroads, an enormous weeping willow stood stark against the net of stars in the sky. Dancing toward the willow, I swept my lowest curtsy yet before parting the long, barren branches and passing through, straining to see through the darkness inside the bower of limbs.

I walked a circle around the inside of the tree. My hand trailed along the the curtain of thin branches, and I watched the ground outside appear and then vanish again as the branches parted and fell back into place.

Suddenly I stopped, my heart in my throat. A figure, huge and stark black appeared against the deep purple of the sky. Steeling my nerves, I forced my hand to pull apart the thin branches in front of me—just enough to peek out.

I froze at the sight before me. A hulking, vaguely humanoid shape was revealed about fifty yards away. It stood completely still and after a few minutes my heart began to slow. *Just an oddly shaped tree*, I told myself. Relief swept over me and I smiled at my silliness.

Then it moved.

My heart leapt up my throat and out of my mouth, fluttering somewhere above my head. The inky black shadow was enormous, walking on two legs like a man, but in a lurching gait. It moved toward the chapel and I watched in horror until the fear that had originally frozen my limbs, snapped my heart back into my chest. *Run!*

Edging backwards, out from under the protective circle of the tree, my feet crunched on the gravel path. A quiet curse escaped me. I prayed incoherently, desperately hoping that the figure, monster, *Beast* hadn't heard.

I lurched sideways to the grass next to the path and started running. I *had* to find my way back to the wall before that monster discovered me. Ragged gasps filled and emptied my burning lungs. The wall loomed in front of me. Frantic hope flared in my chest as I approached, then snuffed out abruptly as I stumbled over a low headstone and fell to the ground.

I watched as my lantern rolled out of my grasp, clattering loudly as it tumbled over and over on the ground. *Move! Now!* Tearing my skirts out of my way violently, I pushed myself up, lunging toward the wall as a low growl issued from behind me. Giving my lantern up for lost, I searched frantically for the glowing symbol, panic mounting as my eyes swept back and forth along the wall.

Panic closed my throat. *Did I take the wrong path back from the willow tree?* A gleam caught my eye. The tower glowed faintly, partially obscured by lichen. My hand scrabbled over it, the scrape of the wall echoing painfully loud into the night. Another growl issued from whatever it was behind me. My heart gave a painful squeeze and I stumbled into the passage, the reassuring sound of scraping stone meeting my ears as I started running in the pitch black.

Disoriented, I held my right hand out to trail along the wall, helping me keep a sense of equilibrium. I ran as fast as I could, my skirts bunched up and gathered as high as I could hold them so they wouldn't tangle.

How do the symbols work? I wished I had asked Andrus more about them. They had to have some sort of recognition spell worked into them, but I couldn't be sure. I didn't dare let myself wonder if the Beast could get into the tunnel. I couldn't face the idea.

If there was some sort of Beast attack I needed to get back to the castle to warn someone. Suddenly my left knuckles grazed stone as I pumped my arm up. I had only enough time let go of my skirts and lift my hand up to protect my face before I slammed into a wall, rebounding slightly before dropping to the floor. I pushed myself to my knees, crying out in pain when I put weight on my left hand.

I leaned against the wall to my right, panting. Waves of pain radiated out from my knuckles. I hadn't run nearly far enough to make it back to the castle. I shook my head, confused, my eyes searching for the castle symbol. After a moment they picked out the reassuring golden glow, and I leaned my right hand against it heavily, my left still stabbing with pain. I dashed through the door as it slid open, stopping in surprise after a few steps.

It wasn't the Chapel storage closet. I was back outside, standing on a path running along an irrigation ditch. *The city fields?* Panic and pain overwhelmed me. *How can I be in the city fields?*

I shook my head to clear my thoughts. The passage had seemed shorter than I remembered. Much shorter. And now that I had a moment to think, I realized it had been sloping down, not up as it should have if it had been leading back up to the castle. I must have taken a different path away from the willow tree after all, and found a new passage.

I shivered, feeling cold and exposed. Moments ago, I had reveled in the open sky. Now I wanted only the safe stone walls of my tower.

Peering into the distance, I tried to make out where my

current path led. It extended along the wall, as far as I could see to the right and left. A smaller track followed the irrigation ditch directly in front of me, lined every so often with marker stones. The curtain wall, the last barrier between us and the forest, emerged about a hundred yards ahead.

I gasped, taking a few steps forward, my left hand clenched to my side to prevent jostling. *Was that a... yes! A tower symbol!* I hurried toward a marker stone, ten yards ahead of me. A tower symbol gleamed at me. When I reached it, I pressed my hand on the warm marker and pressed.

Nothing happened. My head whipped around wildly. No sound of scraping alerted me to a secret passage. Not a doorway or silent opening in sight. Finally, my eyes caught on another marker stone about ten yards in front of me. As I looked, I could see another mark gleaming beyond that one. *A path,* I realized, half in relief, half in agony. I was afraid and coming to the end of my stamina: tired, hurt, and alone. I was desperate to be safe.

Picking up my skirts, I jogged down the trail, following the lights as they lead straight toward the outer wall. Hope blossomed again as I remembered that there was a guard tower in the rear wall. Maybe the symbols would lead me to a contingent of Forest Guards! I didn't see a tower outlined along the top of the wall, but perhaps the guard station was tucked within the wall itself. My feet stumbled along faster, the promise of other people, protection, and capable soldiers spurring me on.

I had just passed my ninth marking stone and was beginning to slow my pace as the curtain wall came into view, when the sound of scraping stone broke out into the still night air.

A sob tore out of my lips, a wave of cold fear overcoming me. *The Beast.* I lurched the final feet to the wall, my vision obscured by tears as I pushed the glowing symbol. My terror ricocheted to relief and then back again as stone scraped open in front me. I dashed into the passage beyond.

Please! Please! I screamed to the Creator in my head as I rushed forward, stumbling over my hem, my right hand held out in front of me to warn me of any obstacles in the darkness. After a minute my hand hit stone and I skidded to a stop, shoulder bouncing off the wall. Frantically I looked for the symbol, hitting it with anxious panic and rushing beyond, hardly able to think anymore.

Fifty yards of cleared scrubland extended in front of me, forest looming beyond. I sobbed again. Not a soldier or guard station in sight. I was on my own.

Hiking up my dress, I pumped my legs furiously. My left hand stabbed with pain every time I swung it through the air. I could barely hear anything except blood thundering through my ears and my breathing coming in loud uneven gasps.

I had made it most of the way across the field, stumbling now and again over rocks, terror helping me ignore a stabbing cramp in my side, when the dreaded sound of scraping stone echoed behind me. A guttural noise burst out of the night, echoing off the wall. My feet pounded heavily, my thin slippers no protection as I put on a burst of speed. *Get to the woods. Find a place to hide.* I dared not look back.

With a crash, I broke through the tree line, dodging trees and rocks. White-hot pain seared my side, stunting my gasps for breath. I stumbled to a stop near a tree for a minute, eyes wide with fear as I searched for shelter. Just ahead, beyond a small clearing, was a cluster of holly. I dashed toward it, swerving around a huge fallen tree trunk. Brushing through spiny branches, which scraped me in protest, I pressed toward the center of the holly grove. Pulling my grey cloak around me, I sank to the forest floor, trying to quiet my breathing as best as I could, tears spilling over onto my cheeks as the pain in my side sought release. I strained my ears, listening for sounds of pursuit.

Rustling. Faint lurching stomps growing steadily louder. I turned my head to listen better behind me. Disoriented, I realized that the noise wasn't behind, but in *front* of me.

Fear erased all thought. I began edging back the way I had come as fast as I could, my eyes fixed on the shaking underbrush visible between the holly branches. Faster and faster I scrambled back as the noise grew louder, footsteps sounding closer every second.

My back hit something solid and I glanced behind me to see the fallen tree trunk. The crashing in front of me became abruptly louder and I swung my eyes back in that direction, heart throbbing painfully in fear.

Three shapes burst out of the trees, one after another. The first one stopped just a yard or two in front of me, the second pulling up right beside it. The third shadow tumbled into the first, which snapped at it before turning its attention back to me.

Unlike most Pelerines, I had seen drawings of Beasts in textbooks. They didn't usually run prints of them in weekly news sheets that my father received. It was believed that the images would incite panic among the people.

I can see why, I thought critically, my mind suddenly detached from the fear that was debilitating my body. *They're more petrifying than I had ever imagined. And this is what Andrus and Eddie and Henri have been fighting all those years. How did they survive?*

The question of survival pierced the fog of terror surrounding my brain. My hands scrabbled in the dirt, my right hand happening upon a nice-sized rock, my left finding a short, thick branch. I levered myself to my feet using the tree trunk behind me, trembling with terror but determined to try and do something—*anything.*

The beasts had halted momentarily, the first one seeming to be settling some sort of question of dominance with the third. *Just as the packs of dogs on the streets of Croiseux,* I recalled dispassionately. The monsters in front of me bore no other resemblance to the town dogs.

The first one was the largest. There *was* something canine about it, but it was the size of a man and had very little fur.

Instead, its hide was crisscrossed with ropey scars. Patches of hair and fur appeared here and there along its bulging forearms and hind legs. Pointed ears sat on top of its head. A short muzzle housed broken teeth, currently displayed in a snarl.

The one it was snapping at was just as big as the first, but much thinner. Its leg bones jutted out in an odd angle, and its snout was long and tapered. It was utterly hairless. *It has a tail.* The thought turned my stomach. A long ropey tale, also hairless, flashed into view from behind it.

My eyes strayed to the other beast. It was staring right at me, the eyes unnervingly intelligent, almost human, and gleaming a dull murky red. They were set inside a small skull above an even smaller snout. This one was covered in matted brown and gray fur. Smaller than the other two, it had a rounded, muscled body. Its arms were bony in comparison, and as it took a half step toward me, I realized that there was webbing stretching from its arms to its body.

Not webbing. Wings. Terror shortened my breaths.

The other two noticed its movement and refocused on me as well. I gripped my makeshift weapons in sweaty hands, pushing my weight away from the tree trunk as the first one leaped toward me.

Time seemed to slow. I noticed its shoulder muscles bunch as it sprung toward me. Saliva dripped from its fangs as it opened its mouth to snarl. I wondered what those teeth would feel like when they clamped down on my skin.

They're quite dirty. Infection is bound to set in. The monster's front legs left the ground and I traced its arc with my eyes, knowing exactly where it would land on me.

All of the sudden, an earth shattering roar shook the air. A massive shape sprung off of the trunk behind me, leaping over my head. It caught the first monster full in the chest as it landed.

The new monster crouched over its prey, slicing its throat in a quick motion. The other two leaped at it, the second one latching onto its back, while the third one swiped at its face, landing a scratching blow before being hit with a punch strong enough to knock it backwards. Reaching behind, the new monster pulled at the batlike one before dropping its arms to defend against another attack from the one it had just hit. The batlike creature took the opportunity to dig into its back deeper and tear at it with its teeth.

The new monster fought quickly with powerful, controlled motions, using its fists mainly. I saw the flash of a long knife every now and again. It pushed back the third beast and managed to reach behind its neck and pull off the batlike one, throwing it towards its packmate. Whirling toward me, I cowered against the log as the new monster took a giant leap and landed inches from my face. I saw a flash of glowing, bloodshot hazel eyes sizing me up, flicking between the stone and branch in my hands. Then it leaned forward and snuffled my hair before turning its back on me, crouched in preparation for another attack by the Beasts.

Confused, I stood uselessly, half leaning against the tree trunk. This hulking monster had seemed almost human. Familiar even. I had been sure it was going to kill me as it had leaped toward me, but instead it seemed to check me over, not as a source of potential food, but almost as if looking for injuries.

Numb with shock, I watched as it surged forward again, its knife flashing in and out as it swung at the rat-beast. The bat creature edged around and I cried out as it vaulted onto my monster's back again, tearing with its teeth as it latched on. I pushed off the log, my foot hovering in a step forward, wanting to help but not knowing how. As the fray moved closer, I scuttled back against the tree trunk.

My Beast grappled with the rat creature, fists and knife flying against teeth and claw. Finally the rat thing stumbled, and my Beast finished it with a quick motion.

He reached around, trying to grab the remaining Beast on his back again, but it eluded his grasp, tearing at his hands with its teeth. Staggering to and fro, he stumbled backward toward me. Panicking, I dropped the stick in my left hand and spun around, half jumping, half pulling myself over the log, putting it's girth between me and the fighting monsters.

I jumped as my Beast slammed his back into the tree trunk, squishing the bat monster between his back and the tree. The bat creature had understood his plan just in time and managed to throw itself partially away from him instead of being wholly trapped. It used tooth and claw to tear at my monster's side and stomach, eliciting an echoing roar as he hunched forward in pain.

The batlike creature latched on all the more fiercely, and I could see that my monster was seriously injured. He pushed back against the log again, but weaker than before. Panic rose up again.

If my monster lost, would the other creature come for me? Without thinking, I gripped the rock I still held in my right hand above my head and strode the few paces between myself and the ongoing fight. Eying the skull of the bat creature, with two hands I brought the rock down on its head, both feeling and hearing a jarring crunch. I stumbled backwards, sick to my stomach. Dropping the rock, I sat down heavily, the world spinning as I strove to keep the contents of my stomach down.

Slowly, everything stilled and my stomach settled. Rustling sounded close by and I flashed my eyes open, remembering my situation.

A monster lurked nearby, wounded. Whatever sympathy or protectiveness I had read in his eyes had to have been a trick. Now was my time to get away. I leaned back on my hands, slipping as pain flashed from my injured left hand again.

Changing tactics, I leaned forward. Cautiously pushing myself up with my right hand, I risked a glance around. My monster was hunched on the ground, twisting to examine his injured side. I felt a pang of sympathy and quickly stuffed it down. *It's a monster. Whatever you thought you recognized in it, you were wrong. Get out of here!*

Keeping my eyes trained on the Beast, I stepped backward toward the edge of the small clearing, heart pounding. As I reached the treeline, a twig crunched under my foot and he stiffened.

Whirling, I leaped into a run. I heard the monster surge to its feet. It crashed through the underbrush behind me, and I could sense it getting closer.

Somehow, I stayed ahead of it, bursting through the edge of the tree line and moving as fast as I could toward the curtain wall. *Oh please let Andrus' patrol be nearby.* Tiredness enveloped my muscles, and I could feel how much slower I was moving than I had earlier that night.

"Guards! Andrus! Clement! Someone—please help!" I shouted, hoping wildly that someone was close enough to hear and could help.

"Rose... Rosebelle!" I heard what sounded like Andrus' growling baritone ring out between coughs from behind me. Wild hope flared within me as I whirled around, expecting to find him on his horse. Instead the only living thing in view was the monster as it broke away from the trees. A hood masked its face and its dark cape swirled behind.

"Andrus—please! Help me! There's a monster!" I screamed, looking around frantically as I continued backing up toward the wall, the scratch of stone against my palms as I bumped into it.

The monster slowed its pursuit, stalking toward me in a measured tread, one hand clutching its side. I couldn't see it's face, but its form was huge, and coarse brown hair showed under the end of its bronze chain mail sleeve, extending down onto huge hands.

Wait, chain mail? He stopped a few feet in front of me, and I snapped my eyes up to where a face was hidden inside the hood, and waited for my doom to be revealed.

"Rosebelle." Andrus' voice came again, cut off by coughing. I stared dumbly at the form in front of me. His voice had almost seemed like it came from the monster.

267

"It's me, Rose." Andrus voice sounded once more, and the monster put his free hand up to his hood, sweeping it back.

Streaks of gold gleamed out of green eyes, the whites bloodshot. The hair on his head was the same short, medium brown of Andrus', but it seemed thicker, coarser, running down into his neck. His ears were slightly higher on his head, and his chin and mouth seemed different. Longer, maybe, and narrower. His mouth was crowded, as if it was straining to contain his teeth. He wasn't any taller than Andrus, but he did seem larger, even bulkier than Andrus' already muscular frame. He gave me the general impression of a forest bear I had seen in a bestiary once. Somehow nice looking and wild all at once.

It was Andrus, but also not Andrus. My voice rang out suddenly in my own ears, loud and trembling. "You... you have Andrus voice, but you're not him. *Please*."

The glimmering eyes across from me closed for a minute, then flashed open. "It's me Rosebelle. This isn't how I wanted you to find out, but it's me. We need to get inside the wall quickly. I don't sense any more Beasts, but that doesn't mean more aren't close by.

The voice was rasping and gutteral, but it was Andrus'. The eyes were Andrus' too, just bloodshot and somehow shining, almost like the symbols demarcating the secret passages. His mention of more Beasts shot a sense of clarity through me.

"More Beasts? But you're a Beast. I won't show you how to get in." Belatedly, I remembered that this Andrus-Monster-thing had followed me out of the castle to begin with.

He chuffed a rumbling laugh. "That's my Princess." Shifting to look back towards the woods he continued. "I don't need you to show me. I know all the secret passages here. I just need you to come with me to safety so I can report this Beast incursion."

I searched his face. The more I looked at him, the more like Andrus he appeared. *And he could have killed me by now if he wanted to.*

My brain was slowing down along with my body, the fight

almost gone. I took a step forward, my body startling me with the decision to trust him just a moment before my brain agreed. Relief shot through those strange eyes and he reached out a meaty fist to grab my hand, then pulled back as I gasped in pain. He had grabbed my injured left hand, sending white hot tendrils of agony up my wrist and into my arm.

"My hand," I panted, cradling it to my side. "I think it's broken."

He growled in response, the low rumble startling at first but oddly comforting when I realized it wasn't directed at me. Glancing around one more time, he put his right arm around me gingerly, pulling me closer to him, still clutching his left side with his other arm.

I stiffened at his touch, but relaxed as he lead me along the wall at a walking pace, guiding us around rocks and divots in the ground that I could hardly see until we were right on top of them. A few minutes later he stopped and pressed his hand to a spot in the wall. I caught a flash of gold as the wall slid away before Andrus pushed me gently into the dark passageway, following closely behind. The door slid shut again, and we were plunged into darkness. Andrus muttered a command. A faint light flared behind me. I turned to look and was surprised by a gray light emanating from the broach fastening his cloak. It looked like a simple iron pin, but a large dark moonstone was set within it, surrounded by several smaller pieces of moonstone. The light was emanating from the central stone, and the hazy quality of it fascinated me.

"Rosebelle. We have to move." The growling version of Andrus' voice cut through my foggy thoughts and I swung my head around, feet shuffling forward obediently. Andrus kept his hand on my shoulder, maintaining contact as we walked through the tunnel. He reached around me to open the door when we came to the end of the passage, then tucked me into his side again as we stepped onto the path near the irrigation ditch. I was glad of it. His huge form was warm next to me, and felt safe. I wanted to go to sleep, but we were far from the castle. Far from my bed. He stopped us after a few steps, and I frowned as he let me go to fiddle with his brooch.

"Andrus, why are you like this?" I stumbled over my words a little as as I watched his movements. He didn't dismiss the light, but he was doing something to one of the smaller dark moonstones, my eyes unable to follow his movements in the dark.

"Like what?" he asked, distracted, then pulled me back to his side and forward down the path.

"Oh you know. You look like a bear. You're acting like one too. Actually, you snuffled my hair back there, didn't you? That was a bit strange. Did someone put a spell on you?"

His rumbling chuckle cut through my babbling. "No, Rosebelle, no one put a spell on me. And I don't know why, really—I've always been like *this*."

"No you haven't," I insisted, a bit cross since my brain wasn't working as quickly as it normally did. "I've known you for months now, and I've never seen you like this."

"Oh, right." He cleared his throat as he hurried us down the path, his tone becoming more serious. "Like I said, I've always been this way. Many Asileans are, at least during the full moon. There's something in us, in our blood, that responds to the moon and rises to the surface. We call it the Shift. Most of us have it to some extent, although the strength of the magic varies from person to person. It's strongest in the royal family, as well as our best soldiers. We're not beasts, not savage or out of control. We're still ourselves, just different: stronger, better senses, sometimes better magical ability."

"So you all look like bears at the full moon?" I asked, my brain working tiredly.

He barked a growly laugh. "No, no, not at all. Generally it seems that you shift towards whatever animal you have the most affinity with. The type of animal and level of transformation depends on the person. It's true that most of the royal family tends towards bears, but not always. And most people don't change to the extent that I do, they just have a hint of a physical differences with behavioral changes not being so apparent. I happen to have it very strongly."

My thoughts tumbled over each other as we approached the wall. Something clunked into place finally. "Is that what the Lady's Vigil is for, then? Something to do with the change?"

He glanced down at me as we drew to a stop. "Yes, partially. It bands us all together when the Shift magic is at its highest. And it protects those of us who go on patrol to fight the Beasts." His eyes left mine as hoofbeats sounded in the dark. Several riders came into view from the east. Behind them, the sky seemed a shade lighter. Andrus' voice rang out as they came into hearing distance.

"Beast attack, just outside the curtain wall, three of them. Their bodies are in a clearing near the holly grove. Do a sweep. Find out how they got so close. Contact me if you find anything. Oh, and send someone to inform General Morvan. He's on duty until dawn."

The leader threw a salute and peeled off in the direction of the nearest gate, her soldiers forming up behind her. One of her men took off toward the Forest Guard headquarters.

Once they were out of sight, Andrus turned toward the city wall. He pressed the symbol, his hand steady on my shoulder as he guided us into darkness.

Andrus loped relentlessly up to the castle, towing me gingerly in his wake and using the secret passages to speed our way. By the time we passed the chapel, I was stumbling over my feet with every step. Andrus was more than half holding me up, steadied against his side. He directed our steps toward the infirmary, helping me lay down on the first available bed before limping out of sight to find the doctor. A few minutes later, Dr. Moreau, followed by Andrus and her assistant, appeared around my bed. Dr. Moreau directed Andrus to the bed next to mine, speaking to him in a low voice, then turned to me.

"Princess Rosebelle." Her voice was firm, not a trace of sleep in it. "Andrus tells me that you've been injured in a Beast attack and may have a broken hand. I need to examine you, and give you some medicine to numb the pain while I set your hand all right?"

I nodded, my eyes following her assistant as she pulled rolling curtain panels around me, blocking us from the rest of the room. Dr. Moreau took a glass vial from a tray that had been placed on the bed table and held it to my lips. I drained it in one swallow, the earthy, bitter aftertaste making me grimace. The medicine slowly dulled my senses, and I felt my mind drifting as the doctor finished her exam.

"Thankfully, your hand isn't broken, but it's a very bad bone bruise. It will feel better by the time you wake up." She motioned to her assistant and began laying out supplies.

I wish. I thought hazily. The last thing I saw before I drifted off was the Doctor putting a glowing pendant on a long chain over her head and sitting down near my left hand.

* * *

My head pounded as I slowly came back to consciousness. The view screens around my bed were gone. The grayish haze of a pre-dawn sky filtered through tall windows. *I haven't slept very long then.* Turning my head, I my eyes hit upon Andrus sitting on the bed next to mine. Doctor Moreau's assistant was gathering up blood-soaked linens while the Doctor spoke to the Prince. He stretched his left arm and side and I remembered in a flash that he had been injured. I sat up quickly, my head spinning with the effort. Andrus and Dr. Moreau looked at me in concern.

"Andrus!" My voice sounded thick with anxiety. The look of concern on his face was replaced by a blank mask. Examining him closely, I could see that the changes from earlier were almost gone. His ears were back to their usual position and shape, and the thicker, coarser hair had receded. His eyes were still bloodshot, but the gleaming gold was gone, and they looked tired. Dark circles were stark against the pallor of his skin. Although he was still larger than life, he looked weary and somehow diminished.

"It wasn't a nightmare then?" I asked slowly.

He shook his head, eyes boring into mine. I swung my legs out of bed pushing myself up to stand before remembering my injured hand. I didn't feel anymore pain. Shocked, I held it in front of my face. There was no sign of any injury, no hint of pain. I shot a questioning look at Doctor Moreau.

"I was able to heal it as you slept," she answered, a small smile on her face. "It wasn't broken so it was simple enough. The small bruises and scrapes on your skin were too numerous to fix properly, so I repaired the worst. The others will have to heal on their own. Probably just a day or two if you keep them clean."

I gasped in wonder, noticing that the scrapes from the holly trees had been significantly reduced in size and number. I looked back at Andrus, who was watching me guardedly. Taking a few steps toward him, I stopped just before I reached him, wrapping my arms around my waist and wishing for my warm bed. Trembles shook my limbs as the castle's chill seeped into my bones. Andrus' eyes took in my crossed arms before traveling back up to my face.

"Your side," I said, looking from him to Dr. Moreau. "His side was hurt, badly, in a fight."

She held her hands up, a soothing expression on her face. "All fixed, Princess Rosebelle. It was more difficult than your injuries, but nothing I am not accustomed to. He should have no lasting effects."

I breathed a sigh of relief, turning to sit back down on my cot. I was utterly exhausted, a headache throbbing at my temples and shivers coming in waves. "I'd like to go to my own room now, please."

"I'll take you there." Andrus' voice sounded gravelly, but not as gruff as it had hours before. Standing, he pulled a dark Forest Guard tunic over his stained white undershirt and shrugged on his overcoat. When he reached my bed, he settled his large black cloak around my shoulders and fastened the pin to keep it closed before offering me his arm. I stood up more slowly, my head feeling quite light.

Leaning on his arm, I gathered up the excess material of the cloak, which was simply enormous on me, holding it in a pile in my right arm. Andrus walked us slowly from the infirmary, but I felt my strength draining at every step. By the time we reached the staircase leading to our chambers, I was spent.

"Can I sit down for a moment before we try the steps?" I asked, my head dizzy. He stopped walking, and I expected him to lead me toward a chair. Instead, he stooped down and gathered me up—left hand supporting my back, right hand looped under my legs. I clung tightly to him in surprise, then hit his shoulder in protest. It was wholly ineffectual. He treaded up the steps without missing a beat.

I mustered my most commanding tone. "Andrus, put me down. Now."

"No. I'll put you down at the top. You're too tired to climb the stairs, so I'm carrying you up."

My dwindling patience finally left completely. "You idiot. You were wounded. From the looks of things you've lost a lot of blood. I just needed a break, not someone to carry me!"

He looked down at me in surprise, navigating a landing before starting up the next set of stairs. "I'm fine. Doctor Moreau healed me, as you saw."

"Yes, but you're obviously exhausted! You already put your life on the line for me once tonight fighting Beasts. I don't need you fainting from blood loss and dying from a broken neck on a flight of stairs."

His chest rumbled and shook under me. I craned my neck to see his face. He still looked drained, but his lips were curved into a smile and his eyes crinkled around the edges. He was laughing at me.

"Typical," I muttered to myself, relieved that he seemed to be steady and in a good humor, but irritated from worry that it was just a show. "Male bravado at its finest. Not a care for his own safety. Can't use that prodigious brain to take a few precautions for his own health. No, he has to sacrifice it for the useless Princess who isn't allowed a rest before tackling stairs after a long night."

My muttering trailed off as I realized that his laughter had as well. He slowed to a stop on a landing just before the top of the stairs.

I looked up to find him staring down at me, eyebrows drawn together. *Back to grim stares and furrowed brows then. It's enough to give you whiplash.*

"My own safety?" came his rumbling enquiry. "I'm fine, Rosebelle. I'm used to dealing with many more Beasts than that in a fight. I was just caught without most of my weapons." His scowl deepened. "I'm tired, yes, but I would never endanger your life if I thought I might pass out. Whatever you might think of me, I would never put you in danger."

He continued walking, and I mulled over his words. We passed a startled looking footman as we entered our corridor, who forgot his servant disguise to the point that he actually saluted when Andrus barked an order to fetch Hazel. Pausing when he reached my chamber door, Andrus maneuvered carefully to unlatch it before shoving it open with his back and striding in. He stalked right into my bedchamber.

A squeak escaped me as he deposited me on my bed. I sprung up before too much dirt and blood rubbed onto my comforter. His eyes followed me as I fiddled with the clasp of his cloak. Handing it to him with nod of thanks, I walked over toward my sitting room, intent on a quick bath before collapsing into bed. The dirt and blood and fear of this evening needed to be washed away before I could think about sleeping, no matter how tired I felt. The hot water would help the chill in my bones.

Andrus put a hand out to stop me as I approached the door. "What are you doing?" he demanded gruffly.

"I am going to go run a bath while I wait for Hazel to come."

He looked at me darkly as I continued. "There's no reason to send for her, you know, she needs her sleep too. She's just going to get here to watch me drift off."

"Exactly. Someone to watch over you. And no bath. You need sleep. Stay."

He whirled toward the door connecting our rooms, hidden behind a tapestry depicting a unicorn, a maiden, and a minstrel. The lock clicked as he opened the door and passed through, returning after a moment with a large flask.

"This will help you sleep and promote healing." He poured a measure into the flask's cap, offering it to me. I made no movement to take it and he stepped closer.

"Take it. You won't care about whether you've had a bath. You'll wake up with your cuts and bruises gone."

"Thank you, Andrus." I gritted my teeth. "But no thank you. And don't expect Hazel to just sit here and watch me sleep. I don't need a nursemaid."

"Apparently you do!" he shot back, anger growing along with the volume of his voice as he shoved the flask and cap onto my night stand. "What exactly were you doing so far down into the city without a guard or even Hazel? It's the middle of the night!"

"I was—I was taking a walk!" Irritation flared even as my brain conceded his point. I was stretched too thin to be reasonable. I wanted a bath, maybe a pastry from my food basket, and then sleep.

I didn't want to yell at Andrus. In fact, I wanted him to go to bed too, so I could drift off, safe in the knowledge that he was nearby. Although I still felt odd about his revelation from earlier tonight, I wasn't scared of him. I knew him too well now to be afraid that this part of him was bad or would hurt me. I was still deeply unsettled, and a part of me wanted to make someone else feel as unsettled as I did.

"You think you can keep me cooped up here all the time, running from one appointment to the next." My voice rose louder. I could see his eyes tightening in response. "Well fine.

It's part of my duty, I know. But sometimes—sometimes I need freedom! Space to just be myself, without anyone watching, or correcting, or stuffing my head full of information or—or—keeping secrets from me!"

Andrus scoffed, folding his arms. "You can hardly blame me for wanting to keep you safe. Look what happened the first time you ventured out by yourself! You wandered outside the castle walls, outside the city walls even! Could you have been any more irresponsible!?"

"Irresponsible?! What about you, chasing people in the dark?" I stepped toward him jabbing my finger to punctuate my words. "You scared me in the cemetery! I thought you were a monster! So if it wasn't for you, I never would have found that passage to the outside and run into the woods. I was just exploring. In fact," I continued jabbing him right in the center of his chest and looking heatedly into his eyes, "if you had just been honest with me to begin with, I would have known what the full moon meant to your people. I never would have gone exploring if I knew there's a heightened chance of stumbling across a Beast!"

The anger in his eyes snuffed out, hurt flashing before cold fury slammed into place. I was confused at the hurt I saw, wondering at it when he hissed his reply, much more quietly than my shouts.

"And is it any wonder that I didn't tell *you*, a Pelerine raised to despise everything we stand for? You never could have reacted with anything other than fear and revulsion."

I flinched back, feeling as if he slapped me. After all the friendship we had been building these last months, this was how he still thought of me. A foreigner. I didn't belong and couldn't belong. I strode into the sitting room, clutching my hand over my aching heart and willing away the tears in my eyes.

The injustice of his accusation stung. After all, I hadn't known it was him when I ran from him in the cemetery. Once he had revealed himself, I had quickly recognized the friend I had come to know over the last month, despite his exterior.

His presence entered the room behind me, followed by a low growl. "You didn't ask for this, I know, but you agreed to be my wife, regardless of the circumstances. You're stuck with it, and you're going to have to find a way to live with it. And the first thing you can do is learn to stay where you belong!"

Anger cut through my sadness, and I strode toward him again, shaking my finger in his face. "If I'm Princess here, then I *was* where I belonged—in my own city, and in my own forest! And if you'd like to discuss what we need to learn, I have something for you to study: your temper! One minute you're hot, the next you're cold. You act like you care, then you're yelling at me!"

I turned to go but he caught my wrist, preventing me from walking away. I pulled on it, my arm extended fully as I tried to walk toward my dressing room, but he yanked firmly, pulling me in a stumbling step toward his side.

"You will stay where you are safe," he growled.

Glaring into his eyes, I was surprised to see a vulnerability next to his tiredness and anger. I hesitated, not knowing what to say, but was interrupted by a cough.

"Belle?" It was Hazel. A flush swept over my face as I looked over at her in surprise.

"I'm sorry to interrupt," she said slowly, looking guardedly at Andrus and hovering at the open door. "The footman said it was urgent that I attend you. Should I... do you want me to call him?" she asked directly to me.

"The footman? No," I replied, confused.

Andrus dropped my wrist and stepped away from me. I felt the lack of his presence—the warmth that continually rolled off of him had been keeping the chill away, along with our heated discussion. He bowed, not making eye contact, then strode to the door, stopping to address Hazel as she edged out of his way.

"Stay with your mistress and see that she doesn't leave her rooms. I will post extra footmen here to fetch anything you need, but you are not to leave her side. She had a harrowing night. My mother will come to check on you later."

Hazel nodded to him warily.

His back to me, he hesitated for the briefest second, but strode out of the room without looking at me again. I burst into tears as Hazel shut the door behind him, bolting it before running to my side.

"Belle. Belle!" she whispered urgently, grabbing my shoulders and looking me over. "What happened? Did he... what are those bruises and... are those cuts?" Anger colored her voice.

"Yes, but they're fine." I tried to mop up my tears and stem the flow of them. "The Doctor healed the worst of them and my hand, so I just need to rest."

"The worst of them?!" Hazel screeched, her grip tightening painfully before releasing me. She led me by the hand toward the fire. "Belle, you must tell me what happened. Now." She guided me to my favorite chair, then sat down across from me, perching on the edge of her seat.

"Did he do this to you?" she asked, her voice low and urgent.

I wrinkled my brow in confusion. She gestured toward my injuries and I jumped out of my chair.

"No! Hazel! No." Agitated, I paced back and forth. "How could you think that? He would never! In fact, he saved me." My voice broke, and I stopped speaking, willing myself to hold it together again. Hazel hurried over, putting her arm around me and leaning her head against my shoulder.

"I'm sorry Belle, I had to ask. He was gripping your arm when I came in and you two were staring daggers at each other. Then there were all these injuries that you didn't have when I left you a few hours ago. What was I supposed to think?"

I crooked a rueful smile, rubbing tears from my eyes and cheeks. "Well, I guess that makes sense." I sighed. "I'm so tired. I just want a bath and to go to bed. Andrus left me medicine that will help me sleep for a long time and heal. Can you help me get cleaned up and into bed? I'm a little stiff. Actually,

Andrus carried me all the way up the stairs because I was so tired."

"Hmmm," Hazel replied, guiding me toward my dressing room.

I told her the whole story, with breaks between changing, showering, and getting ready for bed. She followed me into my room, pulling a chair next to my bed and stretching her feet out toward the fireplace while I spilled the rest of my tale. I earned a sound scolding for having wandered out on my own, and she tensed when I told her about the Beasts. She was quiet as I described how Andrus fought them off, revealing himself to me before helping me back to the castle.

"Are you telling me that the *Prince* changes into a *bear* at the full moon?" Hazel's jaw hung open.

"Um, not exactly," I responded, my brain too foggy to try and detail what I had seen tonight. "He looked sort of reminiscent of a bear. There were enough small changes that I could tell what he would have changed into if he, you know, shifted the entire way. But he also still looked like himself once you looked past the other stuff. This is making my head spin."

"You can say that again. So the Beast Men of Asileboix are real. *Real!* And everyone... oh heavens, don't tell me that everyone here changes into a beast! Wait, no they can't, because we've been with some of them at the Vigil." Hazel gasped. "Is that what the golden light is! A spell that makes them change?!"

I shook my head, trying to follow her thinking even though my body just wanted to sleep. "I don't think so. You said the light is strong around me, too, and I don't change."

My eyes snapped to hers, my brain suddenly on high alert. "Wait, I don't change do I?! Did you notice me looking strange earlier?!"

Hazel gaped at me with wide eyes, then started to chuckle. "No, no. I was making faces at you half the night to keep myself awake, so I would have noticed."

After a minute of silence her voice floated out cautiously.

"Do you think you will start changing?"

I considered it for a moment. "I don't know. Andrus didn't say anything, but we didn't have time to talk much. He said it was something in their blood though, so I don't think so. It sounded more like something they're born with. Intellectually, it's quite fascinating if you think about it."

Hazel gave a soft laugh. "You *would* think that. I bet you already have a list of questions for Mathilde tomorrow." She sobered. "If it's something they're born with, then, you know... will your children have it?"

I stared at the fire. "I don't know, Hazel. We really didn't have time to talk. He said the royal family usually have an affinity with bears, so it seems likely." I shivered, not sure how I felt about that. What would it be like to have a child that acted like a bear every full moon? Would my non-Asilean blood be enough to suppress the changes? *Would that be a good thing?* Andrus had taken down three Beasts with only a knife and his fists. Maybe my bloodline would make our children weaker, less able to protect themselves as Andrus was able to do.

"Well, they'd still be your children," Hazel said, rising from her chair and speaking the command charm to bank the fire. "Kids are bad enough without transforming into bear cubs once a month. You'll have your hands full if nothing else. That is, if you're still going through with it." She looked at me sideways.

"Going through with—oh, you mean having children." A flush swept over me. I hoped the lowered firelight hid it. "Obviously. He's the last of the royal line. If we chose not to have children, there would be no one left. Besides, it can't be that bad. I've seen lots of children around here, and they all seem normal. I feel like we wouldn't have been able to miss any serious destruction caused by shifted children on the last two vigils we attended. The priest's baby was in the Chapel with us, and she was an angel."

I laughed, remembering two of the children that had attended the service. They had been shushed by their parents endlessly through the vigil before falling asleep in their laps. That happened in Pelerine chapel services just as often.

"Okay, well you seem to be taking this all in stride, although maybe that's just shock. I guess nothing has actually changed, we just know more." Her voice turned to a scold. "I can't believe you didn't come get me to explore the passage! That sounds amazing! And although I would have been useless with the Beasts, I know enough woodsmanship that I probably could have found us a safe place to hide."

"Sorry, Hazel. I just wanted a little adventure to myself, you know?" I explained, trying to placate her. Sadness returned as I remembered my fight with Andrus. "I'm glad we finally know their secret. I just wish Andrus had trusted me to tell me before now. He views everything I do as the actions of an outsider. I thought we had become friends over the last two months. I guess I was wrong."

"Belle, you're obviously too tired to think clearly." Hazel shook her head deprecatingly. "And you like to think of yourself as a scholar. Dense, sometimes, is what you are."

I clucked my tongue at her.

She snorted as she collected an extra blanket from a basket near my bed. "I'm not defending how he kept this secret from you, although I can understand if they were planning on easing you into it. But even though your beginning was rough, it seems to me like he's been focused on keeping you safe—and maybe sane—since you got here. If I were him, I'd think you would hate me because I'm a Beast."

I shot up in bed. "He is *not* a Beast!" I said accusingly. "I told you, he has some sort of—I don't know—something in his blood that makes them seem *like* Beasts, but they're not. Sounds like blood magic to me actually," I mumbled the last remark more to myself.

"I know it may seem scary, but he's still Andrus. Even when I didn't know it was him, I could see that he was trying to protect me." I shivered, the memory of how brutally he dealt with the Beasts skittering across my mind before I could stop it. "He was savage, but even in the middle of it, he stopped to make sure I was safe and uninjured. It was..." I trailed off with a small smile, remembering how he had snuffled my hair. Bewildering at the time, but now I realized he was just trying to reassure himself, and maybe me, in the midst of the fight.

"Uh huh." Hazel's dry tone broke through my thoughts. "I don't need convincing. I wasn't trying to say that he is as bad as the enemy. Maybe you should give that speech to him instead of me. No doubt he's loping around the castle, berating himself for the way you found out and the danger you were in, thinking you're disgusted and could never return his love. He definitely seems the type to play the tortured hero."

I opened my mouth to both defend him and question her about the comment on returning his love, but didn't know where to start. She giggled, then gestured toward the flask Andrus had left on my nightstand. "Is that the medicine you're supposed to take?"

"Oh, yes." Leaning over, I downed the cap full of liquid in two sips. It was cloying, tasting of honey and something chalky. I put the cap back and pushed the flask toward the center of my nightstand.

"Off to sleep now, little Belle. Your stalwart Hazel is here to ward off any Beasties overly concerned with your safety!" she teased, pushing an ottoman over toward her chair before searching through a pile of books on another table for something to read.

"My books!" I exclaimed, suddenly remembering them. They still sat in the storage by the chapel.

Hazel looked over at me wryly. "Go to sleep, Belle. They're not going anywhere. Besides, you're the Princess of the castle, you can just order the library to replace them."

I chuckled at the thought, sleep pulling at my eyelids.

CHAPTER SIXTEEN

Andrus

Shutting the door on Rosebelle and Hazel, I strode down the hallway toward the footman-guard. "Were you on duty when she left her room?" I snarled. My temper itched to lash out at someone.

"Yes, Sire." He saluted. I ground to a halt, inches from his face.

"Why, in the Lady's name, did you allow her to go out *alone*?!" Although most of my physical changes had receded, I was still partially shifted and my voice came out almost as a roar. I wanted to toss this soldier into the forest. If he had done his job properly, I wouldn't be in this mess.

It was you she ran from, an accusing voice sounded in my head.

The soldier flinched backward. "Sir! She said she was taking Hazel with her. They were going to the library."

I snarled, my anger only growing. No doubt Rosebelle had spun a likely story, and apparently had the ability to lead my guards around like lambs.

"I've ordered additional guards here for protection. They are not to relieve you. You will finish your shift, and then pull the next shift as well. Maybe by then you'll have enough experience as a *footman* to understand how to guard a *Princess*.

BELLE & BEAST

I knew I was being harsh. Rosebelle's comment about time to herself prickled my conscience. But I stuffed it down and blew past the footman, making my way to the stables.

The attendant on duty had already prepared my horse. Leaping into the saddle, it took every ounce of self-control not to storm down to the Forest Guard headquarters. It wasn't worth alarming any citizens that lived along the roadway. If any more Beasts were nearby, I would have heard by now.

The steady rhythm of my horse's hooves lulled my thoughts toward Rosebelle, but I bullied my brain back to the task at hand. Three Beasts so close to the castle was a blow. My capitol city was located far from the border. They would have traversed leagues of woodland to get here. Not to mention they required exceptional skill to avoid our patrols. That indicated intelligence and direction, something we weren't used to seeing from the Beast hoard. My shoulders tensed at the ramifications.

By the time I reached the Forest Guard, my nerves were stretched taut. The streets in the city were silent, but the Guard Headquarters was a hive of activity.

General Morvan greeted me with a perfunctory salute. "No additional sightings, Your Highness. No word from those on the trail of the three you killed. I've re-deployed a unit along our usual patrol route. Teams have already swept the city and confirmed it's clear."

"Good. I need to be doing something. Do you have any routes left?"

General Morvan eyed me, his thoughts hidden behind a tired but professional mask. "Just the southern road."

I nodded, feeling slightly sour. It was normal policy in a defensive sweep for Beasts to leave it until the end. It was accessible only from Pelerin, so least likely to present a threat. I wanted more of a challenge. But I also wanted to actually help, not just get in the way running off energy, so I nodded.

"Thank you, Sire. The team leaves in ten minutes. They'll be glad of the extra eyes."

I climbed back into my saddle, joining the designated squad minutes before they left. The sweep was uneventful, and we arrived back at headquarters with the rising sun. Reports from every unit had been clear. The trackers reported that the ones I fought had been living in a makeshift camp for at least a few weeks.

My horse pounded the cobblestone streets on our way back to the keep, the exhaustion of a normal shift and patrol intensified by the additional events of the night. After stopping at the stables, I stepped into the kitchens to grab a makeshift meal, then wearily mounted the stairs to my chambers. Three footmen were on duty, snapping to attention as I passed. After a quick shower, I made my way to my bed, eager for rest, only to find that I had left my sleeping draught in Rosebelle's room.

The irritation that had been drowned out by work flamed back to life. I had given that to her to help. *She doesn't have the decency to return it? Or send Hazel if she's too scared herself?* A growl escaped me. My temper teetered on the edge of a knife. My body's attempts to heal itself after the shift would wake me every hour or so for the next six hours, making it impossible to feel truly rested. The healing draught was essential for those of us with significant physical shifts. With a potential threat on our doorstep, I had to be ready to lead a defense. I scowled at the door leading to Rosebelle's room. No doubt it would be locked. *Maybe, in the heat of our fight, she forgot?*

I padded over softly, pausing to listen for movement in the next room. Pulling my door open, I reached across the short space separating our rooms and gently twisted the knob on her door. To my surprise, it wasn't locked, so I pushed it open. No protest sounded. I slid inside, eyes trained on the place I had left my tonic. It was still there, closed and sitting on her bedside table. The room was dark, but sunlight streamed around the edges of her curtains, combining with the embers in the fire to cast just enough light to see.

Picking my way over to the table, I extracted the bottle as

soon as I was in reach, tucking it into a pocket. Against my will, my eyes strayed to the sleeping form next to me.

She lay on her side. Her face was turned toward me, illuminated in the glow of the fire. She looked at peace, no doubt caused by the healing draught.

Something in my heart contracted painfully, and I dropped my hands to my sides. I didn't want her to be in a drug induced peace. I wanted her to *truly* be at peace. And I wanted to be the reason she felt peaceful and safe. But tonight I had played the opposite role.

A monster. She had run from me in the cemetery. Fear of *me* had driven her right towards those who would truly hurt her. Yes, I had been able to protect her life, but she hadn't been without injuries.

I studied her face without reservation, craving evidence that she was well. The small cuts that had dusted her cheeks and temples when I had last seen her were healed, the bruise on her forehead gone too.

My eyes drifted over refined, even features. A long, straight nose. Thin lips curved upwards at the edge in the hint of a smile. Long hair splayed over her shoulders, a mix of brown and gold, gleaming in the fire. It was surprisingly long. I had never seen it down before now.

Her eyes were hidden behind closed lids now, but I didn't need to see them to be able to picture their honey-toned depths. They haunted my dreams and the corners of my thoughts these days. When we were in the same room, my own eyes searched for hers unconsciously. Over the last month, it seemed as though her eyes had started to do the same. That would change after tonight. She wouldn't bear to look at me, no doubt.

Nor did I want to see those eyes flick open and look at me now. I knew the fear and loathing that I would find there, and like a coward, I couldn't face it. Turning, I paced unseeing back toward the door.

"Sire." A whisper floated across the room. My eyes darted

in the direction of the voice, and I saw Hazel perched on a chair in the far corner of the room, a book in her hand. In my exhaustion I had forgotten that I told her not to leave Rosebelle's side. I was glad she had taken my order literally, even as I was a little embarrassed to have had a witness. I stood rooted in place and just looked at her, too tired to try to convince her of my intentions or humanity.

"She's alright." Curiously, Hazel seemed like she was trying to reassure *me*. "She had calmed down by the time she went to sleep, although she was worried about her library books." A soft chuckle accompanied this information.

"Library books?"

"Yes, part of her ruse to get out of her room alone."

I remembered the footman's words and nodded.

"Is she... was she...?" I wanted to know what she had said of me, how badly she despised me, but didn't dare to ask. I changed tack. "She looks well. I assume she took the medicine?"

"Yes," Hazel answered, looking at me expectantly.

I didn't know what she wanted. Too tired to puzzle it out, I turned toward the door to my room instead, muttering, "Good."

"I thought *you* had given her those injuries." Her words like a whip on my skin. I whirled, half in anger over the slight to my honor, half in fear that she still thought it so.

A smirk and a quiet snort met my eyes. "Belle quickly disabused me of that notion, defending your honor and extolling your virtues quite ably." She cocked her head, seeming to study me. "I thought you should know."

I stared at her, puzzling through her meaning and storing up her words for later.

She gave me a deep nod before settling back into her chair, eyes straying back to her book. I rotated toward the door again, allowing my eyes to flick one last time to the peacefully sleeping Rosebelle before walking through to my room, closing both doors behind me. I stood beside them for a few moments,

BELLE & BEAST

waiting for the snick of Hazel locking her door behind me, but it didn't come.

I wondered at it, and at her behavior toward me. Perhaps Rosebelle hadn't told her much of what happened? By the time Hazel had arrived, my physical shift had receded, so she wouldn't have seen it for herself.

Downing my accustomed measure of the healing draught, I laid down in my bed, Rosebelle's sleeping form appearing in my mind as I closed my eyes. I whipped them open again, willing the image to go away. It could have easily been of her lying dead instead. I could have lost her before I had even had a chance to know her fully: to give her the life that she wanted, to build our princedom, to see our children, to make her fall in love with me, as I was dangerously close to doing with her. I wanted it. I wanted all of that. But how could she ever love someone as cursed as me?

Now more than ever I needed to find the cause of our shifts. Once I understood that, I could work on a cure. Once I was cured, maybe she could start to see me as a man, not half of a monster. And maybe our children wouldn't have to live with the same curse. Would she even agree to have children, knowing what they might be like?

My unease began to dissipate as the medicine started to take effect. My limbs were heavy, my mind wandered. Hazel's words came back to me. *Defending your honor and extolling your virtues.* I struggled against it for a moment, but hope took root in my heart as I slid into rest.

* * *

Clattering dishes welcomed me back to consciousness. Lueren's cheerful whistle reached my ears, calling me fully awake, along with an audible rumble from my stomach. I reveled in the feeling of being fully refreshed, except for a slight itch on my side. I absently scratched the area before the memory washed over me. My side was itchy because it had been torn open and healed quickly by Doctor Moreau. It had been torn open in an effort to protect Rosebelle from Beasts at the castle walls. Throwing back my covers, I stormed into the sitting room, squinting at the sudden influx of light before noting that the sun was already inching toward the trees. Late afternoon then. Lueren looked up from where he was laying trays out on my table.

"I assume all reports from General Morvan are clear, otherwise you would not have allowed me to sleep so long," I grumbled at him, striding toward the food.

"Of course. All routes clear," came his reply. "No evidence of other Beasts was found. The trackers weren't able to follow their trail all the way to the border, though. It's obvious they had been hidden nearby for many weeks, using a small cave system to stay out of sight. It won't be a problem again."

I nodded, and mumbled a thank you through a scalding mouthful of eggs. "What of Rosebelle?" I asked once I swallowed. "Is she in her chambers? Is she up yet?"

Lueren handed me a napkin and sat down at table. "Yes, Sire. She woke up an hour ago and took breakfast in her room. Princess Mathilde has already collected her. They're in Mathilde's office right now, with a footman stationed outside of it."

"She'll love that," I muttered, taking a swig of coffee to wash down my food. She was sure to be in an at least partially justified temper today. I made a mental note recall the additional guards. *And probably have them wear their regular uniform and stop pretending to be footmen.* I wolfed down bacon and hash as Lueren reviewed my schedule for the following day. The day after a full moon patrol was kept as free as possible in case the recovery time was long. Since the area around the castle had been cleared last night, there wasn't much I would need to address today. *Other than Rosebelle.* I didn't want to face her, but I also needed to reassure myself with my own eyes that she was well and whole. Actually, if she was in a temper that might be the best signal of all that she was well. *I'd rather face anger than fear and disgust.* Either way, it didn't matter. Better to face her reaction head on and get it out of the way. Then I could see what could be done towards rebuilding her trust someday. I sighed, setting my fork on my plate and glancing over at Lueren.

"Did you say Rosebelle is in my mother's office?" He nodded. "Fine. I'm heading there as well. Don't interrupt me for the rest of the day. I have some work to do."

We both rose from the table. I started towards my dressing room and he pulled the now empty dishes toward the tray. "Good luck, Andrus," he called over his shoulder, his usual lightly mocking tone replaced with a more serious one.

"I'll need it," I muttered back at him.

After preparing for what remained of the day, I walked briskly down to my mother's office, hoping they were still there.

The presence of footmen standing outside her office door confirmed their presence. A rush of relief hit me even as tension continued to build between my shoulders. Rapping on the door, I hesitated a beat after hearing my mother call out to enter. Preparing myself for a tempest, I stepped inside and closed the door behind me.

It was just Rosebelle and my mother, seated in chairs by the opposite wall. Mother called a cheerful "Hello," but my eyes were locked on Rosebelle. She stared back at me, her usual blush creeping across her face.

"Um, yes. Well." My mother cleared her throat and stood up from her chair. "I will just excuse myself for a moment and see if Clement is available to join us, as Rosebelle has questions about the Forest Guard and Castle Guard structure and he could answer them even better than I could..." she trailed off. I could sense her looking between us, but couldn't spare a glance her way. Rosebelle's face was giving nothing away, and I was searching for any indication of her feelings. Mother bustled toward the door. As she passed me I could hear her muttering to herself. "Neither one of them hearing a word I say. They better sort some of it out by the time I find Clement..." The door closed gently, cutting off her quiet monologue.

My feet were rooted in place. The space between us seemed huge even as the office walls felt close. I had been expecting anger and hatred, maybe fear or even revulsion. But other than the flush on her skin, I couldn't read any emotion on her face as her eyes bore into mine. Silence stretched between us. Alarm flared within me while I scrambled for words. After a few minutes, she rose from her seat and made her way toward me, her expression still closed off. All of the little quirks and tells I had discovered over the past few months of our relationship had fled, offering no hint as to what was going on inside her mind. She stopped a pace away and folded her arms, hands clutching her wrists in a gesture she used to use constantly when she first arrived, but I hadn't seen lately.

"Andrus," she began, licking her lips, my eyes tracing the motion. "I know you think me an outsider still, and I suppose with good reason. After all, no matter how hard I try to become Asilean, or feel at home, or love this country and its people, it turns out that my blood will always set me apart. I'll always be lacking something you all have. But please know that I'm trying my best. And I meant my vows. I'll do my best as your Princess and your—" she swallowed heavily, "your wife, as I can. But if that's not going to be enough for you to be open with me, I'd like to know now, instead of constantly thinking I'm earning your trust only to discover that you think of me as a foreigner." She looked at me steadily, but the way she clutched her wrists signaled her discomfort and vulnerability.

Her words surprised me, but after a minute, our argument from last night came back to me. A *Pelerine raised to despise everything we stand for? You never could have reacted with anything other than fear and revulsion.* I had said those words out of anger because I felt rejected and monstrous in her eyes. But the look she was giving me now spoke more of a feeling of lacking on her own part rather than a judgment of me.

She continued before I could formulate a response, her voice sounding stronger. "And I *am* sorry for having left the palace. We need to discuss my security team. I must have time to myself. But I can see now why they're important. I should have returned to the palace immediately upon finding myself outside the walls. That was an error in judgment."

She surprised me again, not only for her apology, but for how quickly she had realized her fault and admitted it to me. I moved toward her involuntarily, then froze, waiting for her to shrink back from me. When she didn't, I offered my arm to her, which she took, and guided her over to stand by some windows overlooking the city. She didn't drop my arm once we stopped moving, so I didn't bother trying to distance myself from her, taking encouragement from our physical connection.

"Rosebelle, I'm sorry too," I said finally. She turned toward me, surprise evident on her face. "I kept this secret from you even when you proved your trustworthiness very soon after our marriage. In fact, I'm surprised at how quickly you've become Asilean." Her face flushed at my praise, and I wondered if it was more to do with my notice of her trustworthiness or in calling her Asilean. "I never imagined you would have adjusted to living here so soon. At best I thought you would start feeling comfortable within a year or two. I expected to have to keep our secret until well after that. With the way you were raised, we all thought that you would have deep prejudices to overcome. And maybe you still do," I laughed. "But you seem to absorb everything with ease." I shook my head. "Beyond that, I'm sorry for how I treated you last night. I never should have yelled like that. You had just had a huge shock. I was tired, and I was anxious to have you safe in your bed, with people watching over you while I confirmed the scope of our situation. You deserved better. Can you forgive me?"

Tears pooled in her eyes. She turned from me and looked out across the city. "I could forgive much worse from someone who put his life on the line to save me from my own mistakes," she murmured with a quiet laugh. "And I know it's just part of your job as my husband, and as the Prince, but your desire to protect me is very, very much appreciated."

"Speaking of protecting you," I said, studying her profile, "I want to start giving you self-defense lessons." She whirled back to me, her brow furrowed. "I'm assuming, of course, that you've never had any. As I recall, you were quite handy with that rock last night."

Her skin took on a green hue and I cursed myself as a fool. She had killed that Beast, and although it had been necessary, there was no way that it wouldn't have affected her. I untucked her arm from my side and pulled her cold hands in mine.

"I'm sorry, Rosebelle. You were very brave last night. Quite collected all things considered, but I'm guessing that's the first time you ever took a life." She nodded, looking down at our clasped hands and squeezing tightly. "It's not easy. Not ever, and not even when you're fighting things like the Beasts. But the world is better for it. You may have saved my life right back by doing that. So thank you."

A small, slow smile curved her mouth upwards. "I didn't think about it that way. I guess I wasn't just a useless lump after all."

I chuckled. "No one said that, certainly!"

"Oh please," she insisted, her smile turning wry, "aside from a timely application of a rock, I ventured out alone, mistook my husband for a Beast, managed to find myself outside the town walls, stumbled into a pack of actual Beasts, sustained several injuries, and then yelled at you once you had us safely back to our rooms. I'm not exactly up for Princess of the year so far."

I bit back a growl. "I'll thank you not to talk so disrespectfully about my wife, Madame." Rosebelle's smile faded slightly. "If she caught you at it, she'd cut you down to size and eat you for lunch."

She burst out laughing, and I grinned down at her, wondering how we were standing here laughing together, when only ten minutes ago I had thought my chances were ruined forever. She continued to surprise me at every turn.

"In all seriousness," I continued, once our laughter had subsided, "self-defense lessons were already included in your training plan, but I'd like to start them now. *Not* because I think you're in immediate danger. But because it would ease my mind to know that you are already learning the basics."

"As you wish," she acquiesced, looking earnestly into my face. "I can't say that I'm excited to learn, and I don't expect I'll be very good at it, but I'm willing to try. Who will teach me?"

"I will, of course." I couldn't help grinning at the look of panic on her face.

"What?! No. Don't you have a country to run?" she pleaded, her hands tightening in mine again.

"No. I have a team of experts to run my country. I'm only needed to make the few decisions that they can't. Oh, and read boring reports—and now, train you."

"Wow." She closed her eyes. "I'm really getting every opportunity to let go of my pride." Her amber eyes flicked open again. "Are you sure there isn't someone else available to watch me humiliate myself? Clement maybe?"

"Absolutely not. I claim that right for myself alone," I assured her, smirking. "It won't be that bad. I'm not going to treat you like a soldier, and we'll take it slow."

She wrinkled her nose at me, provoking another laugh.

The noise of the door opening startled us both and we sprang apart guiltily. Heat crept up my neck. Completely illogical as we weren't doing anything untoward. And even if we had been, we're married so it wouldn't have been improper.

Clement followed my mother into the room. "Ah Clement, Mother," I greeted them, wracking my brain for a distraction from the sudden awkwardness—as well as the list of untoward things I could have been doing with Rosebelle instead of holding her hand—which had suddenly started compiling in my head. *Still too soon. Get a grip on yourself.*

"I've brought Clement, as you can see. In case he can help with any questions Rosebelle may have," she replied, glancing between us with a catlike smile on her lips.

"Actually, I was wondering if you and Clement would give us a self-defense demonstration. We were just discussing starting her lessons immediately instead of waiting."

Mother looked surprised, but Clement voiced his approval.

"Never too early to start. It's a mindset more than anything, although form and strength are important too. Mathilde?"

She nodded her acquiescence then bid us to go to the training room while they changed.

We followed them out of the office, Rosebelle on my arm again. I issued instructions in an undertone to Rosebelle's head guard on to reduce his rotation, and to begin dressing in uniform. Rosebelle quirked an eyebrow but said nothing as we continued on to the training rooms. The need to explain the change in her security pressed on me as we arrived.

"The castle and woodland surrounding us have been cleared, so it should be safe for you to roam the castle on your own. In the city, you'll still need an attendant."

"You don't have guards," she replied pointedly.

"That's because I'm as highly trained as any of them, more so in some cases. But even I usually do when I venture outside the city. I won't be comfortable until you've mastered self-defense training. And please, by the Lady, do not go exploring any secret passages you find without checking with me first." She opened her mouth to speak but I held up my hand and continued on. "I really, truly understand the need to be alone sometimes and to have your own adventures. I won't stop you from doing so, or even spoil the surprise. But I do want to make sure someone knows where you're going and have a chance to confirm that the passage you've found isn't dangerous. Most of them aren't. But a few lead to unprotected places, and several are basically elaborate traps. I need you to promise to check with me first, please?"

She tilted her head as she considered my words, then dipped her head in a nod. "I will. But you promised to show me more of them after that time in the library, and you haven't. I've only found the one in the chapel storage room so far, and that was by accident. I've been looking for them in my free time."

I crooked a smile at her. "Yes, they're difficult to find. You have to have the royal blood to see the insignia, or it has to be revealed to you by someone with the royal blood."

Her brow furrowed. "I found the one from last night on my own. No one showed that to me."

"You have royal blood," I explained, lowering myself onto a bench. "You remember the blood ritual during our wedding ceremony?"

"Yes..." she replied slowly, settling down beside me, her deep purple gown bunching up against my leg and spilling over the sides of the bench.

"The priest explained that the blood we exchanged linked us as one flesh in our marriage union," I reminded her.

"Yes, but that was just a symbol, wasn't it?" she replied, her brow still furrowed.

"Partially, but it was also literal. We now share our blood, and that's why the symbols recognize your right to use them. The blood drops we exchanged provided a link for magic to flow between us, allowing a connection to be established that can be deeper and stronger than a marriage otherwise would be without the blood ceremony if we choose to pursue it."

"So that's why no one else has stumbled on these passageways. I had wondered about that." She mulled everything over for a minute before turning to me suddenly. "Is that why there is a golden glow around me during the vigil?"

"Yes," I replied, eyes widening. "How do you know there is a glow around you?"

"Hazel has seen it both times, at the beginning and end of the Vigil. I've just seen it as a golden haze that sort of settles over my vision. I thought it was just the setting and rising sun the first time. But the moon set early on the second Vigil. I didn't have a chance to ask Mathilde about it after the Vigil ended last night."

"You see a golden haze? And Hazel can see it too?" I asked carefully, not quite able to keep astonishment from threading through my voice.

"Yes... is that wrong?" she asked, perplexed.

"No, not at all! I'm just surprised. My mother never mentioned it, or Father Caplen. And I never expected..." I trailed off, my mind racing.

"Hazel says that everyone there has it to some extent, mostly at the beginning and end of the Vigil. I've never seen it on anyone else because I can't see past my own hazy vision."

"Yes, you wouldn't be able to unless you've had mage training." I tore myself out of my rapid train of thought. "I'm just surprised you see it at all. I never, ever thought that our bond would be strong enough for you to manifest such a large amount of magic. No wonder these past patrols have felt different. I thought I was just better prepared. You're helping more than I could have ever expected."

"Why, because I'm a worthless Pelerine?" she said, her mouth compressed in a line.

"No!" I replied quickly, reaching out to take her hand. "Well, actually, yes, that's exactly why." I changed tack, smirking at her. She made to pull her hand out of mine, scowling, but I tightened my grip. "I'm joking! What I meant was, we never expected you to be able to manifest very much magic during the vigil, since your bloodline is Pelerine. You would be able to manifest some, since we're bound by blood, but the fact that it's strong enough to see is incredible.

"Really? Why?" she asked, curiosity overcoming her wounded dignity.

The doors to the practice room swept open. Mother and Clement strode in wearing practice clothes. Clement was dressed in a Forest Guard uniform of brown leathers. My mother wore loose-fitting black breeches with a grey tunic. They set about stretching and warming up. In an undertone, I started answering Rosebelle's earlier question.

"The reason it's so surprising is that it means you either

have a hidden magical aptitude or you've been working to deepen our blood bond somehow."

She turned to me, interest lighting up her face. "Magical aptitude? Could I really? How can I find out if I do have any magical abilities?"

"Come to my workshop after this demonstration and I can test you. It's quite simple," I invited.

She beamed in excitement. "If I could become a mage, that would be immensely helpful as Princess!" Her expression turned thoughtful again. "How could I be deepening our bond without realizing it? Wouldn't that involve using magic?"

I studied her for a moment. Her face was alive with expression. She had been so reserved when I first knew her. Careful and correct around me, always. Now she seemed open, trusting. Could that be the result of our strengthening bond?

"I'm not entirely sure, actually," I replied. "Usually the connection between partners is very strong before a marriage, so it's more maintaining what was already in place and solidified from the marriage ceremony. My mother used to compare it to gardening—needing to tend and water the plants every day, be vigilant for weeds, etc. I confess I never really saw the application. But I do know that magic talent isn't required for a strong bond. It's something separate."

We turned our heads as Clement walked toward us, blunted practice weapon in their hands. He bowed to Rosebelle as he came to a stop.

"Princess, we will go through a round of basic training forms to show you what you will master in the coming weeks. Afterward, we'll provide a demonstration of those techniques in a live fight scenario." Clement bowed again and rejoined my mother at the center of the mat. Mother set her weapons to one side, and they proceeded to walk through a round of defensive forms, Clement explaining their uses as they went. After that, they went through several slow-motion scenarios, with and without weapons, to demonstrate how the forms could be used together in evolving situations. After a quick water break, they came back together at the center of the mat, practice weapons in hand, and began to fight.

They held back the pace from a full onslaught so that Rosebelle could follow what was going on. Each pulled their punches slightly, but they did that subconsciously whenever they fought each other. It had been one of the first clues that Clement was interested in my mother years ago. He certainly didn't pull punches on anyone else. Mother was a proficient fighter but nowhere near as skilled as Clement. She still practiced regularly, as her stamina proved, but she was completely overmatched by him. Still, she was able to hold her own and used the techniques they had reviewed to keep on her feet.

Next to me, Rosebelle sat ramrod straight on the bench. Her right hand hovered in the air between us, and every time Mother was on the defensive, it skittered toward me, as if to grab my forearm. When mother got the upper hand and put Clement on the defensive, it fluttered back toward her, landing lightly on her throat, before dancing back my way when the tide changed again. I watched with amusement, trying to keep a smile off my face.

My eyes snapped back to the fight as my mother let out a whoop. I turned back in time to see Clement brace himself to keep from falling onto the floor at the last second. He swept the legs from under Mother as she was crowing in victory, sending her flat on her back instead and ending the demonstration. Rosebelle did clutch my arm then, looking anxiously at my mother, who was now pushing herself to her feet and scowling at Clement.

"Is she alright?" Rosebelle asked, the light callouses on her hand rough on my arm.

"Definitely," I reassured her. "She's just a very poor loser at this sort of thing."

I looked back at the practice mat and let out a quiet laugh. My mother slapped Clement's proffered hand away and pushed herself to her feet. Clement bit back his own laugh and jogged over to get some water before walking towards us. Mother did the same, but a bit more slowly. No doubt trying to reign in her temper before facing Rosebelle and myself. She was usually a picture of equanimity but always got worked up when she lost or didn't do well in physical training. It was something Marguerite and I used to tease her over endlessly once we figured it out as children.

After a few minutes of chatter about the match and questions from Rosebelle about the forms, Clement and Mother left to clean up and prepare for dinner. I lead Rosebelle up to our tower. Instead of dropping her at her own chambers, we continued on down to the end of the hall into the set of rooms facing my own.

Lights flickered on, revealing the guest quarters I had converted into a workshop. After my abrupt ascendance to the throne, it had been expected that I take over the Royal Tower. I had been living in the Forest Guard headquarters for almost a year at that point, after leaving my childhood room in my parent's tower to start my training. I couldn't bear to move back there on my own. Instead, I took over the rooms I currently lived in, which had been recently renovated for my sister's wedding. The set of rooms across the hall hadn't been completed in time. Since we weren't hosting any state occasions after my coronation, I didn't see the need to spend money redecorating. Instead, as my interest in studying the curse began to grow, I converted them into a workshop and laboratory. The musty furniture had all been removed to storage and replaced with long work tables, stools, test tubes, magic-fueled detectors, and relevant reference materials. The old bedchamber was converted into a small office with a large desk and rows and rows of shelving, housing my notes and treatises on completed experiments.

Rosebelle looked around with undisguised interest as I quickly lit the fire and activated the protection and regulation charms. I hadn't been here for several days so the temperature was frigid.

Striding toward a work station, I motioned Rosebelle into a nearby stool. She perched on it gingerly, eyes tracing over every object on the table before turning to me.

"Is this alchemy?" she asked, her arms tight around her waist to ward off the chill. Goosebumps covered her exposed wrists. I took my jacket off and offered it to her. She smiled gratefully as she pulled her arms into the sleeves.

"Yes, actually. Although not exactly in the same way they refer to it in Pelerin, as I understand. I'm not studying how to turn things into gold. Alchemy is a branch of magic most akin to natural science, except it's study is the magical world."

Rosebelle pulled my jacket tighter around her as she sorted through my answer. "What is it that you're studying?"

I turned, pulling a clean apron from a peg on the wall and pulling it over my head. "My curse," I replied simply, tying the strings tight.

She stared at me, her jaw hanging open. "What curse?!"

At a loss, I stared back at her. "What do you mean? You saw it last night!"

"Oh, the *shift*. I thought you said no one had cursed you?"

"Well technically, no one has. But that's what I call it. It is a curse, you know. It's difficult to control if you have a strong amount of it—especially as a young adult. It's one reason why we send our children to apprentice at sixteen. For those who are becoming Forest Guards, it's the perfect way for them to work out their aggression. Those who aren't as aggressive are usually inclined towards obsessiveness. It's better for everyone to channel their long attention span into learning a future trade instead of something much less productive. Even now, I find it difficult to control my moods in the week or so before the full moon, as you've no doubt noticed." I looked apologetically at her, and she tipped her head back and laughed.

"That's one way of putting it," she agreed, grinning at me. "But today you seem very calm."

"Yes, after the highest point of our shift at the full moon, our bodies go into a recovery mode. It's actually quite painful, but several generations ago a team of magicians at a college in Spindle created the healing draught we use today. It speeds up the recovery time and makes it almost painless while we sleep. If you don't have access to the draught, it takes a full day for your body to heal from a physical shift. Instead, we're usually back to normal, or sometimes feeling even better, within a normal sleep cycle. Like I said, not everyone shifts. Most just experience emotional or spiritual changes. The emotional changes are what make us difficult to be around. The spiritual ones are what make us able to connect during the Vigil and protect each other as a community during our prayers."

Rosebelle shook her head slightly. "I think it's incredible. Mathilde was describing it to me before you came in today. She said that the connection between those with the shift opens during the full moon, and you're able to use it to send strength and power along the ties you have with loved ones. How does that work?"

"That's the question. It hasn't been studied very much. As far as I know, we're the only country that does it in a corporate setting like this. We don't advertise it to outsiders, not even our allies in Sherwood. We also don't have many Alchemists or Sorcerers in Asileboix, so our capability to study it is low. That's precisely why I started to after my ascension to the throne. I wanted to see if we could use the connection more strongly. But soon I started trying to find the source of the curse itself, to see if we could break it."

"Why?!" Rosebelle demanded.

"Why?" I repeated, taken aback. "It's a burden. Very much so. Imagine," I hesitated, not sure how to bring it up tactfully, "well, just imagine your own children having as strong of a strain as I do. It seems to be getting stronger with every generation. I've been able to isolate it to a marker in our blood, so I know that it's passed down from family to family, and if two people with strong strains have children, they're most likely to have children with even stronger shifts. Our country has been so isolated from the rest of the continent for so long that I believe our people are in danger of being overwhelmed by it." I paused again before plowing on, not wanting to frighten her but knowing I should be honest. "We've had cases where people have basically turned into Beasts. You saw some actual Beasts in the woods. They were all vaguely humanoid, although mostly Beast. I have a theory that all the Beasts were once human—or at least the first ones were—and were turned into what they are now by the same strain of magic that's in our blood. If we're careful, we may be able to, well, sort of breed it out of ourselves over time. But it would be better to find the source and cure ourselves without having to resort to other measures."

Rosebelle's face was grim. *Well, you just basically told her she's part of a breeding program.* I backpedaled quickly.

"When I said breed it out I didn't mean … I meant, well, like horses or dogs, you know you match them according to the characteristics you want and just track their lineage so you know what to expect, and then through several generations you can get the result you want…" I trailed off, cringing.

Rosebelle looked at me sardonically. "I understand what you're trying to say, Andrus. And while I don't enjoy being compared to a breeding animal in any regard, we've been through all this. We both married for ulterior motives, and we've been honest from the start. At least you were thinking of the welfare of your people." She raised her eyebrows at me, and I felt a flush creep up my neck. I was allowing my excitement for my work to take over common politeness.

"So, from what you're saying, our children won't have as strong a strain as you do since I don't have it in my blood?" she asked, returning us to our conversation.

"Ah," I said, pulling out some sterile testing equipment from a drawer and holding my hand out to her. "That's something we can test right now. If you'll let me, I'll take a few drops of blood from you and can analyze whether you have the strain and also how much magic you have inherent in your blood."

"Yes, of course!" She proffered her left hand. I pricked her ring finger, squeezing a few drops of blood into various slides and containers, then wrapping it with a plaster and bandage.

Focusing on my first test tube, I added a solvent, stirring briefly to mix. I placed it in a clamp near the fireplace to force the liquid to evaporate. The volume of the remaining residue would correspond to the magical capability she possessed. It was an ancient and reliable test, and only took a few minutes.

The second test I was performing was one I had developed on my own. I wanted to run it twice, in case there were issues with the results. Pulling the chilled testing solution out of a box cooler, I poured two measures into a beaker and placed it at the fire as well. While I waited for everything to come to the right temperature, I prepared a slide of blood. It clattered slightly as I pushed it under a magnifying lens I had purchased from the last magical engineer visiting from Spindle to update our castle spells. It had been invented within the last decade, allowing for rapid progress in my research of late.

I glanced at Rosebelle, who had wandered away from my desk and was inspecting the equipment spread all over the room. Turning back to my magnifying lens, I opened a logbook and began recording what I saw in Rosebelle's smear.

There were no mage markers. I hadn't expected any as they were only present when a mage had very powerful inborn magic, indicating a fairy or fae lineage. If she had been that powerful, she would have known it by now. Everything else looked normal, except a few markers that usually coincided with the shift strain. I finished my notes, then sat back from the microscope, looking consideringly at Rosebelle. Either those markers were present because of our shared blood bond, or because her family carried the shift strain as well. It was possible since they were the owners of Croiseux, a property that had originally belonged to an Asilean woman who married into a Pelerine family. But that had been hundreds of years ago, so any inherited blood would be very diluted by now. I mentally took myself to task—if I had found a way to take a sample from her before our marriage, I would have been able to confirm the results. *Maybe I could find a way to collect samples from her family members.* I shook my head. It didn't really matter at this point. Turning toward the fire, I noticed that both solutions were boiling. I took the beaker full of the shift strain testing solution and poured most of it into the test tubes holding her blood, setting the rest down. Both test tubes were clear. I held them up to the light. They contained the slightest shade of pink.

"What does that mean?" Rosebelle's voice sounded just over my shoulder. Turning slightly, I caught her peering over my shoulder, her eyes alight with interest. Placing one of the vials down I brought the other up to the light again.

"Essentially, the strength of the color indicates the amount of shift strain in your blood. The darker the color, the more of the strain is present. If you don't have any, it would run completely clear."

She looked at me in surprise. "So I have it?"

"Yes, only a slight amount. Actually, it may be the lightest amount I've ever measured, other than the few that don't have any. They were all from Spindle or Pelerin."

"I suppose it makes sense," Rosebelle replied thoughtfully. "I do have an Asilean ancestor, although she is very far back in my family tree."

I nodded. "It may also be affected by our blood bond. I'd need samples from your family to confirm. I should have taken a sample before our wedding."

She raised her eyebrows. "I'm glad you didn't. I can't imagine what I would have thought." She tapped her lips, thinking for a minute. "I'm sure we can get samples from my family the next time they vist. I'll have to think how without revealing what it's for."

"If you could manage that, I'd be extremely grateful." Placing my test tube down, I flashed a smile at her.

"Hmmm," she considered, smirking. "I'd never turn down a chance to have a Prince's gratitude—it may come in handy one day. Leave it with me. I'll figure something out." I chuckled as she turned back toward the test tube with her blood in it. "If that's the lightest sample you've had, what color are they normally?"

"It varies widely, but most Asileans are between a solid pink to a dark pink. Most of the guards are a dark pink to bright red."

"What color is yours?" she asked curiously. A grim laugh escaped me.

"Would you like to see?" I asked, and she nodded emphatically. "Just don't run screaming from the room," I warned, half serious, half in jest. She looked at me askance, so I grabbed a clean test tube and nicked my own finger, letting a drop of blood fall into it. Pouring the still steaming solution into the test tube revealed a dark red liquid. I head Rosebelle gasp behind me and stiffened.

"Yours is so dark!" she exclaimed and I felt her move closer. She reached around me to pluck one of her own vials from the stand and held it next to mine, comparing them gravely. I wondered what she was thinking. After a moment, she turned to look me in the eyes, sadness lurking there.

"Our children..." she started hesitatingly, and my heart sank. She was right to feel uncertain about having children. I had put her in a place where she was going to have to deal with cursed children, even with her own clearer blood helping.

"How much will my blood weaken them?" she asked, eyebrows contracted in worry.

"Enough, hopefully," I reassured her. "I haven't been studying this long enough to be able to tell you exactly how much your blood will counteract my own. Like any characteristics children inherit from their parents, it is too variable to know exactly how it will end up." I hesitated only a moment before continuing. "But if I'm telling the whole truth, it's likely that they will all still be strong shifters."

"Thank the Creator," Rosebelle breathed, relief showing in her face. My jaw dropped. "Andrus," she scolded when she noticed my surprise, grabbing the test tube I held and putting

307

it—along with her own—back into the stand. She put her hands on her hips and gave me a stern look. "I know you think this is a curse. And you're probably right. After all, your people have lived with this for hundreds of years, and you've been studying it for much of your life. I know that I don't know the half of it. But from what see, it makes you strong. And if our children will be even half as powerful as you were when you fought those Beasts, I'll feel a lot less anxious about them and the roles they will need to play for our country."

I glanced from her back to the test tubes, shocked by her response. I had expected a completely natural fear from her, and once again, she was looking at everything from an angle I hadn't even considered. A sense of pride grew in my chest. I was glad of her strength of character—that she didn't give in to fear of the unknown; grateful that she was my partner.

Looking back at her, I took one of her hands and lifted it up to my lips, pressing a gentle kiss on it.

"Thank you," I said simply, "for your fearlessness. I wouldn't blame you if you were afraid. In terms of strength, I have to confess, I hadn't really looked at it in that light before. We usually assess our warriors based off of how much aggression we have to manage when they're young. Your mind.... I like the way it works."

A deeper blush than I had seen yet swept over her at my last comment, and I thought I saw tears gathering. Belatedly I remembered that Pelerine ladies were discouraged from academic pursuits and realized I had probably insulted her.

Before I could open my mouth to apologize, she leaned forward and placed a gentle kiss on my cheek. "Thank you, Andrus. You don't know what that means to me." There were tears in her eyes, but her smile was wide. I felt bemused by her words and her nearness. Everything she did and thought was a surprise to me, offering a new perspective or shattering misconceptions.

She pulled away and turned her back to me, probably trying to gather herself back together. It seemed like it was important for her to present a calm front to people at all times. *Except when we're fighting*, I thought with a small smile, *then she lets me have it.*

With a start I remembered the test tube by the fire. I quickly made my way back to it, relieved to see it was only just finishing evaporating. Another moment more and all the liquid was gone. I removed it from the clamp with a pair of tongs and brought it closer to the late afternoon sunlight streaming through a window. Rosebelle joined me.

"I don't see anything," she said, squinting.

"Neither do I. If you had any inborn magical aptitude, there would be a substance left behind. It looks like you don't have any." She looked slightly disappointed as I put the test tube down. "Don't worry, if you want to learn magecraft you can. Anyone can learn magic if they want to. It would just have been a lot easier if you had any magic flowing through your blood."

Her expression was thoughtful as I put my equipment away. I took the test tubes and beakers into the washroom and scrubbed them, placing them on a rack to dry before walking back to the laboratory area. I couldn't see Rosebelle, but I could hear her rustling around in my office. Pulling off my apron, I threw it into the laundry bin near the door, then padded across to my office.

She was perusing a report I had completed years ago on the link between certain professions and stronger shift tendencies.

"I hope it's okay that I'm in here," she said, offering me a crooked smile. "I was just poking around and saw these manuscripts. Have you written them all?"

"Yes. Although some of them are reference materials and other boxes just hold raw data."

She turned back to the shelves, closing the book in her hand before sliding it home. Suddenly I noticed that the sun had actually set and the room was only lit by lamps and the fireplace. "We need to dress for dinner!" I announced, standing and striding over to the door. A thought struck me before I opened it, and I turned back to Rosebelle. "Unless—would you like to join me in my rooms for dinner instead? That way we don't have to go all the way to the family dining area."

"Yes," Rosebelle agreed, smiling. "I've never seen your chambers before. After touring your workshop I'm quite curious. Hazel is probably waiting to help me dress. I'll just run over to dismiss her and join you in your rooms. Will you order the food?"

I nodded and held the door open as we left. After issuing orders to the actual footman in attendance at the end of the hall—not the guard, who was now dressed in uniform— Rosebelle rejoined me as I passed her room and we walked together to the door of my chambers. I gave her a quick tour, which she seemed to find anticlimactic as the layout and decorations were a direct mirror to her own set of chambers. She insisted on walking out to my balcony just so she could say that she stood on it, and we watched the bustle in the courtyard below as we discussed questions she had about the vigil, and magic, and self defense lessons. Before long, a knocking on the doors reached our ears, signaling the arrival of our food. We dined over a simple meal of baked chicken, pureed potatoes, and roasted vegetables.

Time passed quickly. After the meal, we sat around the fire trading stories. She was more comfortable and open than I had ever seen her and made me laugh at her witty remarks on her training and the adjustments she's had to make to palace life. I found myself trying to make her laugh just as much, telling stories about funny incidents during patrols and my own training.

"Andrus—it's so late!" Rosebelle exclaimed, and I followed her gaze to the clock on the mantel. It was after midnight. Standing up, I offered my arm.

"Let me escort you to your rooms," I offered. She stood as well, taking my arm slowly.

"Actually, can I just go through our connecting doors? It would be easier," she asked, and I paused in surprise. Surely

310

she had locked them after everything that had happened last night. *Apparently not if she's asking to go through them, idiot.*

Instead of taking her out into the hall, I led her through my bedchamber and opened my connecting door, before turning the knob to her own. It clicked open, and I stepped back to allow her through. She paused on the threshold to bid me good night, gently pulling the door shut again. Her amber eyes, alight with laughter as they had been all evening, stayed in my mind until I fell asleep.

CHAPTER SEVENTEEN

Belle

Three weeks had passed since the full moon. Hazel and I were adjusting to our new understanding of the world quickly. The biggest shock, after the initial life or death events, had been discovering that Mathilde used to be a very strong shifter. I knew she had to have a fair amount of the "Beast Strain," as Andrus called it, since she was Andrus' mother, but I had seen her during the full moon, and she hadn't shifted physically at all. Apparently, shifts become less pronounced and eventually cease as people age, and the only change she experiences anymore happens to her ears, which she covered with an elaborate braided hairstyle to hide them from Hazel and myself.

"Well, what is your affinity?" I had asked, curious.

She laughed as she replied, "Can't you guess?" and pointed to the two aged hunting dogs snoozing at her feet.

I sat back in my chair in shock. "A dog, of course. Is it a particular type?"

She grinned and scratched one of the dogs, behind the ears. "Greyhound."

That had been almost a week ago. Now I was was standing

in the main courtyard by the fountain with Hazel beside me, waiting for the carriage bearing my family, Eddie, and Henri. The final two guests had been a surprise request from Mama when I had written, but I had been happy to approve them. It gave me an opportunity to apologize to Eddie for my treatment of him over the years.

Henri's presence was more difficult. I knew Eddie would be all that was gentlemanly and probably tell me my apology wasn't necessary, etc, etc. Henri certainly wouldn't cause a scene, but I had watched Hazel's agitation grow with each passing day. *I hope seeing him isn't too stressful.*

A clattering of wheels on cobblestone streets reached my ears and I grinned at Hazel before adjusting my posture. I had chosen my gown and hairstyle very carefully today: a regal deep blue velvet, with a small sapphire circlet nestled into the hairstyle Hazel had arranged. I wanted to be welcoming, but also display my status and convey how valued I was here, mostly to reassure my mother and sister, but also for Eddie and Henri's benefit too. If they were convinced of my happiness, they would spread tales of it in Croiseux. I told myself it was protect Andrus and the Asileans' reputation, but in my secret heart, I knew that it was also to prove that I had risen to the station I had always wanted. I felt a little ashamed at that, but tried to push it down and out of mind.

The carriage stopped and a footman stepped up to help the ladies out first. Rochelle rushed over to me, wrapping me in a hug and squeezing tight.

"Belle! I'm so glad to see you!"

Tears gathered in my eyes as I hugged her back. I had been so busy since my marriage that I hadn't had much time to pine for my loved ones, but now that they were here, I could feel an aching empty spot in my heart filling up again.

Rochelle released me to my mother's gentler embrace. She already had a handkerchief out to dab at her own tears through her smiles. Papa came last of all, gravely looking into my face and patting my hand.

"I have to make sure you are really alright, my dear," he whispered into my ear as we hugged. "Say the word and we will find a pretext to bring you to Croiseux and safety."

I hugged him even tighter. "Oh Papa, I couldn't be happier. Everyone here is so kind, and I'm coming to love them already." Heat climbed my neck as one of "them" in particular sprang to mind. I was glad Papa couldn't see my face in our embrace.

After I released him, Eddie and Henri made their bows to me as my family gathered around Hazel as well. I smiled at them, my higher rank necessitating only a nod of my head. Hazel took charge of everyone to show them to their rooms.

We had given them spaces in the guest wing, just a floor below my own chambers. Papa looked worn out from the trip, so I ordered him a tray and made him promise to eat and nap until we came to collect him. The rest of us met in a nearby reception room that held tea and refreshments, and we caught each other up on news. Hazel sat down near Eddie, but I could see her eyes straying toward Henri.

"I'm so glad to have you all here! We will have a family breakfast in the morning, so everyone can get to know my new family better. The coronation will be in the afternoon, followed by a banquet and then a grand ball." I couldn't help but beam at those words. I had been looking forward to the ball since my marriage. It was finally here!

"Eddie and Henri, please allow Hazel to take you on a short castle tour. Mama and Rochelle will come with me. We'll meet again for dinner later."

We filed out, Hazel leading the men toward the start of their tour. I took my mother and sister the opposite direction, up to the Royal Tower to review the work being done there. We chatted happily, looking through design books in what would be my sitting room once renovations were complete. The tower was empty today, the workmen having been given the day off in preparation for the coronation.

During a break in the discussion, Mama shared a look with Rochelle and asked hesitatingly, "Belle, darling. How are you, really?"

I gave her a soft smile, putting down the pattern book I had been flipping through and leading them over to a large window seat that had already been roughed out.

"I know I said it before my marriage, and it meant something different then, but I'm happy. Really, truly happy." They exchanged glances again so I hurried on.

"Before, when I said that, I meant I was satisfied with my decisions." I shifted in my seat, and smoothed out my skirts. "Now I mean that I feel happy, that I feel—I don't know—joy and maybe hope. Mathilde and Clement have become advisers. I've started making friends with some of the other people here. Really everyone has been genuine and friendly."

"And Andrus?" Rochelle inquired.

"Oh, well, Andrus is wonderful too," I said lamely.

"What a convincing testimony, Belle, I can absolutely see how wonderful he is!"

Mama shushed Rochelle but I chuckled.

"I know. It's just, it's difficult to put into words. He is so intelligent! And he sees me—really sees me. We can talk for hours. We've also had fights that would embarrass me to tell you about. But we make each other laugh too. He's kinder than I thought at first. Don't get me wrong, he has a temper, but I understand all about that so it's not a problem. And wouldn't you know it, I suppose I have a bit of a temper myself so... Oh I'm babbling. That happens more than you'd think these days." I put my hands to my cheeks.

Rochelle snickered, lifting her eyebrows with a smirk. "So the Beast Prince isn't so beastly after all?"

I stiffened at her remark, my heart stuttering before coming to my senses. *She's joking.* The urge to defend him, to make them like him, rose up.

"He's not a beast at all. In fact... well actually he saved my life a few weeks ago."

They stared at me in shock. "I didn't put it in my letter because all ended well, and I didn't want to alarm you, but it's true." I hesitated, thinking through my words to make sure I didn't accidentally tell them about the Shift.

"You must swear that you'll tell no one about this, not even Papa. I'll tell him someday, but I want to make sure no one overhears about the secret passage!" They nodded, my mother frowning a bit but my sister's eyes lighting up at the mention of a secret passage. I conveyed an abbreviated outline of events of that night, skipping over the most sensitive parts. Mama and Chelle were aghast by the end of it, and I made them promise again not to tell anyone.

Mama reached for my hand with a gentle smile. "Belle, darling, from what I'm hearing, Andrus sounds like he may have a better character than we had hoped to imagine." She hesitated before continuing, "I have to say, it sounds like you might be, well, falling in love."

A flush ignited across my face. "I think I am, or more accurately, I already have," I answered, my voice quiet.

Rochelle squealed and clapped her hands, but Mama looked more grave than ever. "And does he return your feelings?"

I dropped my hands to my lap, my eyes following them, as I thought. *Did Andrus return them?* He was a very good friend: funny, interesting, and certainly there were sparks between us. *But was he falling in love with me?* I turned that over in my mind. To me, love meant the sweet affection and gentle support that my parents offered each other. Missing each other when they were apart. A deep knowing of each other, a willingness to sacrifice to help the other live a good life.

I felt some of those things with Andrus. The more I understood him, the more I appreciated him, and I know he appreciated some of my qualities even more than I did. I was beginning to miss his presence heavily during busy days, especially when he rode out for missions. When we were together I felt drawn to him, wanting to touch him, if only to link my arm with his, or to draw his attention my way somehow. The desire to be his best support, the one he could turn to for advice and refuge was stronger every day. *I would sacrifice anything for him*, I realized with a shock. To protect our people, to secure his line. Even more to help him realize that he wasn't cursed, but gifted. *Does he think of me that way?*

I recalled our conversations. He certainly thought of me as a friend, sharing the happenings of his day, and asking me about mine. His trust in me was growing—very slowly, but surely. I felt his eyes on me when we were together, and I knew he thought me beautiful. *But does he miss me when we're apart?* I hadn't seen signs of it. *Would he sacrifice for me, for Belle?* He had already put himself between me and danger, as I had just told my mother and sister, but he would certainly have done that for any Asilean. It was part of his job. How much of it was because I was me, precious to him as just Belle? He had seen enough of my own faults in our fights to know the ugly parts of me.

Our fights. I groaned internally. My parents had never treated each other that way! My heart sunk. Before despair could overtake me, I brushed it aside. My friends and family were here to celebrate. Whether Andrus had seen too much of my bad side to be able to fall in love with me didn't matter. I fixed a smile on my face and shot a rueful smile at my mother.

"I'm afraid he's a little too incisive Mama. He's seen my faults rather quickly. I don't think there's much chance of falling *in* love. But he does love me and treats me as a friend. He'll take care of me, and our children. I'm content." My heart cracked at that word, and I felt the need to be stern with myself. *You are content.*

Rochelle's stomach rumbled loudly and we laughed, breaking the seriousness that had settled over the room.

Rochelle pursed her lips, unabashed. "It's been a long day. What time is dinner?"

"Not long now, don't worry." I stood, leading them out of the tower, and chattering again about the renovations.

Hazel, Papa, Henri and Eddie were already in the dining room, Eddie and Hazel gossiping away. Henri stood close to Hazel, not looking at her. I grumbled at him under my breath as I pulled the bell to signal for dinner to be brought in. We didn't use hot plates when guests from nonmagical countries were around, so the servants were bringing the courses in as needed.

It was a lovely time. Papa was lively, re-telling all his funny anecdotes that we've heard a hundred times before. Eddie, of course, was an excellent conversationalist. Whereas before, his easy charm would have irritated me, now I could just enjoy the witty banter and appreciate the way he sought to balance conversation, drawing even LeFeu out into discussion from time to time. I allowed myself to relax and enjoy the feeling of friends and family around me again.

* * *

As dinner ended, my parents were yawning and even Rochelle looked done in. I waited just outside the dining room door as everyone filed out. The sun hadn't yet sunk below the horizon, and I could hear Eddie and LeFeu discussing whether to check on their horses as Hazel led my family away.

"Allow me to walk you down to the stables, gentlemen." With quick kisses to my family, I motioned for Eddie and Henri to follow me.

I visited Lodestone and Ironheart as they checked on their horses, then wandered into the courtyard for some fresh air. Eddie finished first, rolling his eyes as he came out.

"Henri is insisting on checking their shoes."

"Well, he's a blacksmith so that I can understand," I returned with a smile, "but what I don't understand is why you brought your horses along behind the carriage. You hardly need them out here!"

"Yes, now I realize that!" he replied with a laugh. "But I didn't know if there would be a hunt or something, and if so, I wanted my own horse. I convinced LeFeu to bring his favorite from our stables as well, and now I'm paying the price. He met your farrier inside and they struck up a conversation about something or another. They'll be at it for ages, you'll see."

Laughing, I pulled my arms around my waist to block out the April chill.

"Are you all right, Belle?" Eddie asked, and I stiffened slightly. "I mean, Princess Rosebelle," he corrected hastily.

I sighed. "Belle is fine, Eddie. We've known each other too long for anything else. Although at my coronation tomorrow you'll have to stick to titles you know!" I grinned and his eyes crinkled.

"I'm glad we have a moment alone, actually," I said, steeling myself and straightening my spine. "I *am* fine, thank you for asking, but I've been wanting an opportunity to make amends. To apologize. But I didn't think I could do it on paper."

He looked confused so I plowed on, describing my change of heart and asking forgiveness for behavior all those years, and especially for the way I treated him in our last conversation alone.

He was quiet for a few moments. My discomfort grew in the silence, but I said nothing, knowing he didn't owe me comforting words. My pride was screaming to use my new rank and show him that he should be grateful for any acknowledgment, but I shoved it down. I wanted to do this right.

"Thank you, Belle, for saying those things." His eyes were soft. "You must know that it wasn't necessary though. It's been my honor to be your friend for so long and to be bound to you closely."

Tempted to roll my eyes, I focused instead on his earnestness. He brought his hand up to a pocket in his waistcoat, slowly pulling out a small bundle. Looking at it for a long moment, he offered it to me. It was a frayed and faded blue ribbon, hung with a motley collection of mementos.

"What is it?"

He smiled fondly. "My good luck charm."

"How nice," I said politely, bewildered as to why he had shown it to me. I offered it back to him.

"Oh, no, I'm giving it back to you. The ribbon is yours, or it was. I should have given it to you when you broke our engagement, but I didn't think of it at the time. To be honest, I couldn't bear to part with it. You lost this ribbon during a fight we had as children. I've used it ever since as a good luck charm. It saw LeFeu and me through the war. That's where most of the trinkets came from. Mementos of battles we won or friends we lost.

I examined it a little closer. Pieces of carved wood hung from loops around the knotted ribbon: a rearing horse, a piece of foreign currency with a hole punched through the middle, various bits I couldn't identify, and what looked like a long tooth. I didn't look too hard at that one.

I glanced up. He stared at it longingly, a hint of pain in his expression. I took his hand and dropped the charm into it, closing his palm around it.

"It's yours Eddie, not mine. It's been yours much longer than I ever owned it, I'm sure. The rate at which I lost hair ribbons as a child was criminal. Let it be a reminder of our friendship and continue to ward off bad luck for you." I smiled at him, and he couldn't hide the relief in his eyes.

"Belle, thank you. You have no idea what that means to me."

On impulse, I gave him a quick hug, then looped my arm through his, leading him on a walk around the courtyard as Henri still hadn't come out of the stables.

I caught a glimpse of Andrus in his study window, observing us, and waved while Eddie was distracted with the nearby fountain. He waved back, his usual grim look in place. I chuckled internally. He had been catching up paperwork all day, and was probably behaving more like a bear than usual. He hated being cooped up. As Eddie and I headed back to the stables, I glanced around to make sure we couldn't be overheard.

"Eddie," I began, my tone serious, "I need to talk to you

about LeFeu."

"What about him?"

"It's been lovely to see him. I didn't know how much I missed his dark scowls." I couldn't help snickering. "But after today, would you help keep him away from Hazel when she goes back to help her father?" He stopped in his tracks, surprised.

"I'm not trying to meddle, but Eddie, you have to understand. I know I can rely on your discretion, so I'm telling you something in confidence." I hesitated, shifting uncomfortably on my feet. "Hazel has been in love with Henri for years, before you left for the war, even. She waited all that time. But when you came back, she says he's been clearly uninterested. To be frank, she needs time to heal. That's probably half the reason she came with me. I think, if she could just have time to move on, she would be happier."

Eddie's frowned deeply as I spoke, then tilted his head back in a loud laugh. I drew back, confused.

"I'm sorry," he said, smacking his forehead with the palm of his hand. "It's just—incredibly—the thing is, LeFeu has been madly in love with Hazel for just as long. He wouldn't shut up about it while we were deployed. Always asking for news of her when I got a letter. Prompting me to find out information somehow from my mother without tipping her off. He said he had mucked things up and Hazel was too good for him. But when I told him to move on it was like poking a hornet's nest."

I threw up my hands. "What a couple of blockheads." We continued walking, both chuckling and comparing notes on our friend's feelings. Just before we came back to the stables I stopped him.

"Should we tell them about each other?" I asked urgently.

He shrugged his shoulders. "They'll probably never find it out themselves. I say we both find a time to talk to them once all this coronation and ball business is over, and the next time Hazel is in town, she can find a way to see him if she wants to do anything about it."

I nodded. "That's a good idea. Let's do it." My eyes caught his and we shared another laugh before collecting Henri.

CHAPTER EIGHTEEN

Andrus

Light faded fast as I watched Rosebelle lead Monsieurs Marchand and LeFeu back towards the Guest Wing. A few minutes ago I had been evaluating information ahead of the attack we were launching at the border during the next full moon. Needing a break, I had wandered over to my office windows, Rosebelle catching my eye almost immediately. Peace settled over me as I watched her gaze up at the evening sky, the lines of her body broadcasting happiness. She had been anticipating her family and friends' visit for weeks.

A man appeared a minute later, and I recognized Edouard Marchand. *The former betrothed.* My mood turned sour at his presence, but I tried to dismiss it. Rosebelle had made it clear that there had been nothing between them. Still, seeing them chatting so seriously, heads close together, had sent a spike of heat through my chest.

She's mine now. Part of me wanted to turn away. How many times would I end up watching them from afar? Another part of me couldn't, especially after I saw her give him a brief hug, taking his arm to walk around the courtyard.

I scowled. I knew Rosebelle was mine. But I couldn't help but wonder if she would have been happier with Monsieur

Marchand after all. If I hadn't inserted myself into their lives, she would be married to him or marrying him soon. Wealthy, mistress of a fine house. The man was obviously honorable, and from the looks he gave her when she wasn't looking, adored her still.

Instead she was stuck with me, a moody Shifter that quarreled with her when she needed rest and dragged her into a cursed existence. She glanced up to my window, a smile lighting her face as she waved to me. I waved back but couldn't muster an answering smile. How could I when she was on someone else's arm?

Jealous idiot. I looked up into the darkening sky instead, but my eyes were inevitably drawn back to Rosebelle. She and Monsieur Marchand walked slowly arm-in-arm until they rejoined Monsieur LeFeu and all three continued towards their quarters. Jealousy raged even hotter. I wanted to be the one she was walking with. I wanted her to be as easy and natural with me when we walked. I wanted to be the center of her attention. *You want her to love you.* I tried to scoff at the idea, but couldn't.

I *did* want her to love me. I had fallen in love with her hard and fast—I had attempted to ignore it for days now. It worried me, but now was the time to brush worry aside. Facts were facts, and I had fallen in love with my Princess.

I knew she liked me. Her blushes betrayed her attraction as well, as difficult as I found it to believe. Now I needed to pursue her heart and win it. Our tower would be finished soon, and when it was, I wanted us to move into it madly in love, the way the realm's rulers should be.

Looking down, I realized I had snapped the quill in my hand, splattering ink on my skin and tunic. I sighed. Tossing the quill away, I turned the lights and fire down in my study and hurried toward my chambers. I needed to change my shirt before the stain set.

A thought occurred to me and I grinned. *It would be very husbandly of me to check whether Rosebelle wanted company.* Now that I had decided to pursue her fully, I couldn't think of a reason to waste a single moment.

* * *

After scrubbing my hand clean and changing my clothes into sparring gear, I hesitated in my bedroom, considering whether to try knocking on our connecting doors, but something drew me toward the balcony instead. I stepped outside into a slightly chilly night breeze, grinning as Rosebelle turned towards me from her own balcony.

"Andrus!" She made her way towards the balustrade that divided us. "I'm glad you're here. I'm not nearly sleepy enough —too excited for tomorrow."

"Perfect," I said. "Want to spar for a few minutes? We can use the empty chambers across the hall from you."

She looked at me skeptically and I smiled wider. "Ah, I see, my dainty Princess doesn't want to risk a black eye at her coronation ceremony."

She moved immediately back to her room. "I can see straight through you, you know, but I'll bite. Meet me there in five minutes?" She turned, her eyebrows raised in a question.

"I'll be there," I agreed, tamping down my excitement and making my way to our meeting place. Turning on the lights as I entered, I looked around, not bothering to light the fireplace. The room was empty. It smelled a little dusty, but was otherwise perfect for a quick practice match.

The door unlatched behind me and Rosebelle slipped inside dressed in her gray sparring clothes. We both completed a warm-up circuit and started going through our forms. As usual, she was terrible, but showed slight improvement from her first lesson a few weeks ago. She understood the theory behind each stance and movement, but often lacked control in execution. It took a lot not to laugh at her, but she was trying hard and I didn't want to make her feel bad. Besides, I just enjoyed being near her, being able to touch her—even if that touch was so she could practice drills.

As we moved into a practice fight Rosebelle started taking more and more initiative. About ten minutes into our round, I feinted left to give her an opportunity for her to use a new movement she had learned. Instead she shrieked and threw herself backwards. She fell hard, somehow managing to turn it into an awkward roll, only to slam face first into the wall. Shocked, I jogged over to make sure she was okay. She lay there, her hands covering her nose, her eyes squeezed shut. I knelt by her side.

"Rosebelle?" I murmured, brushing her hair aside as I searched for signs of a bloody nose beneath her cupped hands. As I got a good look at her, I realized her shoulders were shaking not in tears, but in laughter. I relaxed and let a chuckle escape as well. Before long we were both howling with laughter as I helped her pick herself up. We sat on the floor next to each other, our backs against the walls, convulsed in laughter.

"That's probably the most ridiculous thing I've ever done," Rosebelle said, wiping tears of laughter from her eyes. "I'm only sorry I had a witness."

I let out another burst of laughter and then grinned at her. "I'll be thinking of it in my next cabinet meeting and burst out laughing when one of my ministers is giving a report—then I'll be the one looking foolish."

She grinned, nudging me with her shoulder. "Well, in an effort to give you more fodder for ruining your serious reputation, let's go through another drill. I can go one more round. Heaven knows I need the practice."

She pushed herself to her feet and I followed suit. "Don't be hard on yourself. Just get the basics down so you're able to defend yourself. Hopefully, you'll never need to."

❋ ❋ ❋

I walked steadily toward the retiring room directly off the entrance to the throne room, carrying case in hand. Rosebelle and my mother were using the tiny room to get ready for the coronation. Later they would use it to get ready for the ball as well. We had all been busy with preparations, but nothing could quite distract me from the nervous, but excited, tension I felt. *Still, as long as we are safe and Belle is happy, it will all be worth it.*

Stopping in front of the retiring room door, I waited until a maid stationed there cracked it open and announced me. She opened the door fully, dipping a short curtsy and grinning as I stepped through, before pushing it shut again behind me. I made my way around a large screen and stopped when I caught sight of Rosebelle.

She was standing in a tight knot with my mother and Hazel and had turned to look at me while I entered. Mother made a shooing motion at me, so I slipped over to a couch placed against one wall and set my case down gently. Rosebelle shot me a smile, saying something to the other ladies before making her way towards me.

I studied her openly as she walked. Her long brown hair was unbound, trailing almost to her waist. She was dressed in a simple white gown, the only decoration a panel of lace, only visible when you were within a few feet of her. Her first visit to the town on her own had been to the lacemaker's along with Clothilda to discuss their work. She had come back full of ideas on how to encourage industry through fashion, especially if we wanted to open up trade beyond our borders. After her coronation she was scheduled to begin working with our trade and industry minister on bartering proposals.

"I have a present for you. I'm not sure if I'll get a private moment before the ball, and I wanted to present it myself, so here I am. I'm sorry these took to the last minute."

She grinned at me. "Your wedding rubies?"

I laughed, "Not mine, yours! I hope you like them." I pulled open the case, raising up the top two layers to expose all three at once.

Rosebelle gasped. A diadem sat in the bottom portion. Rubies the size of robins eggs sat in gold settings, each one surrounded by small diamonds. I watched her eyes trace over the crown before looking toward the raised trays. One held a matching necklace. The other was portioned off to hold a pair of matching earrings and two bracelets. She turned to me. "Andrus, I don't know what to say."

I smiled down at her and closed the case, nodding to Hazel as she came to take it away. "Don't say anything, just enjoy them. Will they match your dress for the ball?" I offered her my arm.

"Yes, they'll be perfect." She beamed as she took my arm.

"Excellent, but that's not the only surprise I have. Are you done with your preparations?" She nodded and I lead her out into the hall, promising my mother I'd have her back in a few minutes. I directed our steps across to the ministry wing, just a few minutes away. I could feel her curious eyes on me, but she didn't ask questions. Almost at the end of the hall, I drew us to a stop, my hand on the latch of an office door.

"Close your eyes."

She raised an eyebrow at me, but obeyed without protest. Pushing open the door, I led her through gently, leaving her to shut the door before coming back to stand behind her, my hands on her shoulders.

"Go ahead and open them," I said, looking down at her profile as she did so. At first, she looked confused, eyes examining a cheerful but mostly empty office.

"Andrus, why are we standing in someone's office? It seems nice but..." she trailed off as her eyes caught sight of an open door leading into another room area, bookshelves lining it's walls.

"Wait, is that the old supply closet?" She took a few steps toward the open door before whirling back to me.

"What's going on?" she demanded.

"This is your office," I replied, grinning at her. "You'll need one once you're crowned, and I thought you could use an attached library, knowing your penchant for reading…"

She laughed, walking straight into my arms and reaching up around my neck to hug me.

"You gave me an office with a secret passage to the library!" As she squeezed tightly, I couldn't help inhaling the scent of her hair and pulling her as close as I dared, adoring the feel of her wrapped in my arms.

"Do you like it?" I asked as she pulled back.

"You know I do! You can keep the jewels, I'll take my own secret passage to a library any day!" She laughed, eyes sparkling.

"Why not take both? You're a Princess of the realm so you can afford to be a little greedy," I suggested, smirking. I followed her into the former storage closet-turned-personal library, and watched as she flitted among the bookshelves, finally checking to make sure she knew where the secret passage to the main library was located. When she turned back, her contented smile warmed me straight to my core.

"Thank you, Andrus."

I held my hand out to her, pulling her in close to me so I could feel her warmth again.

"You're welcome," I said simply, daring to trace the line of her cheek with the tip of my finger. Her smile softened, but she didn't break eye contact. I wished we had time to stay in her new office all afternoon.

"Well, let's get the coronation out of the way so we can get to the good parts," I suggested instead, tucking her arm back under mine. We reached the lobby of the throne room just as the clock on the wall chimed the hour. As we waited to enter, my awareness of her jumped along my muscles where we touched. Rosebelle was a picture of serenity, but I could feel her fidgeting, a betrayal of her nerves.

Manciple motioned for the footmen to open the large double doors, and string music swelled as we took our first steps down the center aisle. Light streamed in from the tall, clear glass windows at the other end of the room, spilling onto the raised dias, illuminating our thrones. I felt my heart lighten as we walked toward them. This coronation marked the turn of our country's fortunes, and the woman beside me was just the right mix of intelligence, steel, and kindness to help me see it through.

The ceremony took almost an hour. Rosebelle was a picture of grace throughout it all, and bore the weight of the tall state coronet with ease. When we finally turned, hand in hand, to walk back down the aisle, the roar of our people echoed loudly. I peeked at Rosebelle. She held her head up high, but glanced over at me, grinning when she caught my eye. We proceeded outside to an open carriage, touring the city as people celebrated in the streets; hope for our future renewed.

Upon arriving back at the castle, we parted briefly to prepare for the ball and banquet. I was already wearing my dark blue ceremonial Forest Guard uniform, so I didn't need to change. Instead I stopped in at my study and was promptly cornered by Lueren.

"Sire, you've received a missive from Sherwood." He proffered a sealed envelope marked urgent.

I tore it open, reading through a message from Robin himself. He gave a detailed description of increased movement at their border, heading in the direction of Asileboix. A warning—war was coming.

"Bring me Clement and find General Morvan. I need them here as soon as possible. We'll need to cut them off at the knees before they attack."

"Should I fetch Princess Rosebelle too?" asked Lueren. Technically, since she had been invested as reigning Princess she should be included in any major planning.

"No," I told him, "I want to give her some time to adjust. She'll join us after this next full moon patrol."

Ten minutes later, both men were in my office. We spent the next hour devising a plan of attack based off of the new information from Robin. We worked steadily until Lueren indicated it was time to leave for the ball. I stretched in my chair, then sprang up.

"I'll meet with you gentlemen again in two days for the attack. If any issues come up in the meantime, let me know. Until then, enjoy the celebrations." I returned their salutes and headed to the ballroom, my grim expression lightening the closer I got to my princess.

CHAPTER NINETEEN

Belle

"Phew!" Hazel huffed as she finished wiring my ruby crown into my elaborate hairstyle.

I grinned at her and gently tilted my head this way and that, testing how secure the tiara was. "Not a bit of movement!" I declared.

Mathilde gave an approving nod. "Nothing worse than worrying your tiara is going to fly off your head during the next spin in a dance!" she said.

I grimaced, then turned to Hazel. "Are you sure I can't convince you to wear one of my circlets during the ball?" I asked again.

"No!" she protested with a laugh. "I would worry about it the whole time, and I don't want the other servants thinking I'm getting above myself. I'm more than happy with a new gown." She looked beautiful in a turquoise gown that brought out the light green in her eyes. Her strawberry blonde hair had been twisted up into a simple knot at the crown of her head, anchored with a series of matching turquoise and white hair ribbons. A few curls trailed down her neck, mingling with the ribbons.

"LeFeu is not going to be able to keep his eyes from you tonight!" I whispered as Mathilde walked away to finish her own preparations.

"We'll see," she said, pressing her lips into a line.

I hesitated, remembering Eddie's request to wait until after the ball, then brushed my qualms aside.

"Hazel, I have something to tell you," I admitted, sitting gingerly on the edge of the settee where she had plopped down a moment before. She raised her brows at me.

"Eddie and I had an interesting conversation yesterday evening when I took him and Henri to the stables."

"Oh boy," she said, rolling her eyes at me. "This ought to be good. I thought you two made up."

"We did! Or at least, I apologized and he was magnanimous. But I meant about you and LeFeu."

She started in her seat and sat straight up.

I cringed. "I asked him to keep LeFeu away from you when you go back to help your father. And somehow, your feelings for LeFeu came up." Hazel's glare made me nervous. "He told me LeFeu has been in love with you for ages, and wouldn't quit pining over you while they were gone!"

She got up, turning away from me, her hands balled into fists.

"Hazel, I'm telling you this because you have a chance tonight. Eddie didn't want to talk to LeFeu until after they went home, but I'm telling you now because looking like this, Henri won't be able to keep from your side. You have a chance to move things forward between you *now*." I stood up, smoothing out my silk skirts, waiting for Hazel to turn and chew me out. Instead, when she did turn back, she looked thoughtful, and sad.

"I'm upset that you told Eddie, Belle. But I can understand that you were trying to help. I just don't know if I want help." She raised her hands and let them fall uselessly. "I love him. I have for years, and I can't imagine falling in love with someone else. But I don't know if I can see a way forward. I may love him, but I love you and Asileboix too. And although this was supposed to just be an adventure for me until you were settled,

I honestly don't think I can go back now. I can't imagine living anywhere but here!"

She looked away, nervously plucking at her sleeves. "Henri would never move here. His roots are in Croiseux—his family, his father's forge. Even if he loved me enough to follow me here, what then? We'd never be able to keep the Shift a secret from him. He hates the Beasts. In his mind, they would be the same." Tears glittered in the corners of her eyes. "I almost hate that you told me he loves me. If I had stayed in Pelerin, maybe we would have come together eventually. But I didn't. And there's no way I'm going back now."

I rushed toward her, enfolding her in a hug as she dabbed at her eyes. "I'm sorry, Hazel. I meddled where I shouldn't have. I've made things worse."

She laughed shakily. "That's enough of that. I've moaned about him enough over the years, you were just trying to make me happy. I'm the one responsible for my own choices, and I don't regret them." She laughed again, sounding a little more steady.

"I think you should at least talk to him about how you feel. Maybe the Beast thing is insurmountable, I don't know. And I certainly couldn't imagine him living in Asileboix. But here's what I do know: you have tonight. Why not enjoy it? Ignore the future. Ignore your feelings that you won't be together. Dance with him as much as you can. Make him laugh. Have fun. Then, if you never see him again, you can at least treasure tonight."

A slow smile started on her face. "Belle, you may be on to something. We're trying to be more Asilean, right? Well, an Asilean woman wouldn't let a man destroy her peace! I just might do that."

"It's time!" Mathilde's voice rang out from across the room, making me and Hazel jump. "I'll go ahead down the interior stairs and through the front of the ballroom. Hazel, please escort Rosebelle to the top of the ballroom stairs for her grand entrance as we discussed, then you can run around to the front entrance as well." She waggled her eyebrows as she said grand

BELLE & BEAST

entrance and I found myself giggling.

My first ball as Princess. Excitement bubbled through my veins like champagne. I turned back to the mirrors to make sure my appearance was perfect.

My silk gown cascaded down in a golden froth of lace. Tight sleeves ended at my elbow with a small ruffle, bordered by tiny gold ribbons. The crown and jewelry that Andrus had presented me with earlier in the day twinkled in the lights. Under the crown, my hair had been braided and looped on top of my head in an intricate design.

As I adjusted the bracelets on each wrist, the ruby of my engagement ring caught my eye, making me smile. I couldn't help twirling around once for the joy of it. I didn't mean to be vain, but I thought I had never looked better, not even on my wedding day.

Andrus' face flashed through my mind, the approving look he gave me earlier before the coronation. My stomach fluttered in anticipation.

"I'm ready," I told my reflection. In a sparkle of gold, I followed Mathilde out of the room.

✿ ✿ ✿

The grand ballroom's huge vaulted ceilings soared up for two stories at least. Whereas the ceilings in the throne room were covered in carved wooden panels, the ceiling of the ballroom was a midnight sky, flashing with constellations. Manciple had told me that although they were quartz gemstones, they had been spelled to twinkle slightly in order to be more visible to the dancers below.

The stained glass windows on almost every wall were some of my favorite in the palace. Their craftsmanship was breathtaking, although they were at their most beautiful when the sun shone through them.

I stood on a small indoor balcony at one end of the room.

It was an observation area mainly used by servants so they could monitor the progress of the ball. Now, the curtains had been drawn, and I was listening to Mathilde and Clement being announced from the main entrance on the ground floor. Hazel stood several paces behind me, next to an enormous column, giving me moral support until it was my turn to be announced. We had practiced the entrance several times a day in the last week, but I was still nervous about the long flight of steps I was about to navigate in heels and a long skirt, not to mention balancing the heavy tiara on my head.

A blast of trumpets was followed by Hazel's squeak. As the curtains drew apart in front of me, I heard my name and titles announced.

The ballroom was a blaze of light below. Candles and lamps had been placed throughout, and ornate chandeliers glowed the color of rich honey. People fairly glittered in their finery. I gazed around in wonder until my eyes locked on Andrus, waiting for me at the bottom of the stairs. He was smiling so broadly I could see it from where I stood. My feet descend the first few steps, drawn down by his warmth. My train dragged on the stairs behind me, threatening to throw me off balance, so I turned my focus to keeping my equilibrium with as much grace as I could muster. I was a bundle of nerves by the time I reached the bottom and placed my hand on Andrus' outstretched arm.

His smile softened as I met his eyes, and I felt my heart swoop out from under my chest. Then he was leading me forward to the center of the ballroom, and he swept me into our first dance as the reigning Prince and Princess of Asileboix.

We danced that first waltz alone, a spectacle for our subjects and visitors. I had a hazy impression of smiles and colorful dresses as we whirled around the open space in the middle of the room, but my eyes were locked on Andrus. His gaze was locked on me and I couldn't help the probably too wide smile on my lips. He executed a complicated turn, using it to pull me closer, and whispered, "You're the most beautiful woman I've ever seen."

My breath caught and I whispered back, "You too." His eyebrows shot up. I realized what I had said and felt a blush sweep across my face. *That didn't take long.*

He chuckled at the look of chagrin on my face and said in a low tone, "If you'll look in the mirror, you'll see that I must be the second most beautiful woman you've ever seen."

I tipped my head back in a laugh. "My tongue ties itself in knots around you," I whispered back accusingly. "I don't have this trouble with anyone else."

"I'll take that as a good sign, then," he murmured, his hand tightening around my waist. "And I like the idea that I'm the only one who can fluster you."

I felt a hum of awareness zip through my body, and my eyes dropped to his lips briefly, wondering what it would be like to be kissed by him. And not just the chaste peck on the lips he had given me at our wedding. A real kiss, with a depth of emotion and promise and passion behind it.

My eyes flicked back up as his wide grin started to fade, and I found him staring at me, his gaze intense. The music began to wind down and we slowed our steps, breaking eye contact and suspending the heat building between us.

I fixed a smile back on my face, which soon relaxed into a grin as I started picking people out of the applauding crowd around us. Madame Manciple was there, holding her youngest child's hand and surrounded by the older ones, all dressed in their finest. Lueren was nearby, speaking earnestly over the noise to a lovely woman on his arm who I didn't recognize.

"Who is that with Lueren?" I asked Andrus quizzically.

"That's Josephine," he answered with a chuckle, glancing over at them. "He's been chasing her for years without success. You'll have to meet her tonight. She's the most scatterbrained person I've ever met. Sometimes I think Lueren is only in love with her because he wants to follow in her wake, tidying up her life like he does my filing. She runs a chain of successful laundry businesses. She's been too busy setting up her shops to pay attention to him. I wonder if she's finally decided to slow down."

I sneaked glances at the two of them out of the corner of my eye, between nods to others in the crowd as Andrus led us to the far end of the ballroom. It was fascinating to see the debonair charm Lueren was oozing in the mystery lady's presence; he was normally so briskly efficient.

We were scheduled to lead several dances before our dinner banquet and would open the dancing again after we ate. As we stood facing each other at the top of the set, and I could see Andrus looking everywhere except for the window beside us, the only clear one in the room.

The story he told me in the woods rushed back to me. He had witnessed his own sister and new brother-in-law's death in this very spot, leading a set of dances. Judging by the serious look on his face, he hadn't forgotten but was trying to celebrate regardless.

What can I do to ease his mind? I don't want to offer meaningless reassurances, but I do want him to relax if he is able.

I glanced around us, ensuring that only Asileans were within any sort of hearing distance and took a step toward him.

"Andrus," I called, garnering his attention while we waited for the rest of the set to organize itself beyond us. "What are the security measures on the windows in this ballroom?"

He glanced at me, startled, then looked over to the window next to us. He took a deep breath, then released it. "They've been *spelled*," he said in an undertone, "so that they cannot be broken except with excessive force."

"What sort of excessive force? Do you know?" I asked, when it became clear he wasn't saying any more.

"I believe it was a cannonball at short range that broke the test window," he said, his eyes turning toward me thoughtfully. "Although, I'm not sure if they tried a cannonball at long range after that. They may have just stopped with the understanding that a cannonball would prove enough. I would have to ask Manciple."

I could see the wheels turning in his mind and waited patiently, noticing out of the corner of my eyes that the set was almost fully organized.

"They put the same, uh, treatment on the rest of the windows too. Although it's apparently not as strong as if you do it during the creation of the windows. But still, each window should be strong enough to stop a bullet one or two times before shattering. No one will be able to come crashing through these anytime soon."

He stopped abruptly, looking directly into my eyes. I offered a sympathetic smile.

"I see. My clever Rosebelle is distracting me," he said, lifting my hand up to his mouth and grazing my fingers with a kiss. "Thank you."

I shivered as his breath fanned across my fingertips, that buzzing hum traveling up my arm again and warming my whole body.

Suddenly the music began and we both startled, then stood up straight and prepared for the initial steps. I focused on calming my heart, which was already beating fast even though we had been standing still for several minutes. I stole glances at Andrus as we danced, relieved to see him more at ease. Soon enough, it was time to break for dinner.

Andrus led me through to the banquet room, and we took our places at the center of the head table. Seated with us were my parents, as well as Mathilde and Clement. Rochelle, Eddie, Henri, and Hazel occupied a table near us, and Rochelle beamed at me from her seat next to Eddie. I tried to catch Hazel's eye, but she was turned away, deep in conversation with Henri.

My coronation banquet had no less than ten courses, many of which were traditional Asilean delicacies, but Chef had also outdone herself in mastering some more of my favorite Pelerine delicacies. Creamy mushroom soup was followed by a forest greens salad and dressing with smoked salmon. Roasted wild boar was accompanied by a plethora of vegetables, including my favorite: steamed, buttered broccoli. I had questioned Chef as to whether it would be out of place in a menu filled with exotic delicacies, but she just chuckled and said "A dish of perfectly steamed buttered broccoli is one of the best vegetables in the world. The question is whether it will outshine my other efforts!" After a small portion tonight, I knew I wouldn't question her judgment again.

Night had fallen through the windows as Andrus and I guided everyone back to the ballroom. We led another waltz to start the dancing again, then broke apart to mingle with our guests. I sought out my family after awhile, finding Mama and Papa sharing a small plate of desserts on the side.

"How can you eat anything else?!" I demanded, sitting down carefully so as not to wrinkle my gown.

"Oh, but darling, these tarts are simply divine!" Mama responded with a grin. Papa nodded around his mouthful of chocolate tart.

"I don't doubt it," I laughed. "The pastry chef found out that pralines are my favorite and sends them up to my rooms at least once a week. One of the perks of being a Princess!" I said with a grin.

A group of children who had been playing nearby wandered up, claiming my attention. The boys wanted to know if I was in charge of school and whether I could make the teachers give them more playtime. The girls wanted to know if they could wear my jewels. I had to disappoint them all with a resounding no, although I did confess that I was in self-defense classes just like them, but was probably even worse than they were. They ran off giggling, quickly organizing a pretend sword fight. All children were taught self-defense as part of their schooling, and those who excelled were screened for Forest Guard training when they were older.

I saw another wave of guests headed my way, so I gave my parents each a kiss, promising to see them at breakfast the next morning before they left, and turned to work my way back through the well-wishers. In between conversations, Rochelle danced in and out of view, clearly having the time of her life and not wanting for partners. I saw Henri and Hazel dancing several times as well and smiled. I didn't accept any other dances, as I had too many guests to greet and listen to, but after some time, a hand caught my elbow as I made to find a seat, my feet aching.

Andrus's baritone sounded in my ear. "May I have another dance?" The orchestra struck up a waltz.

I turned, smiling, to find him much closer than I thought. Off balance, I wobbled, putting my hands on his chest for balance.

"So, was that a yes, or did you just want to paw me in public?" he asked, bending his head to whisper as he grabbed my upper arms to steady me. My blush returned with a vengeance and I glared up at him.

"You can't go around knocking people off balance and then accuse them of pawing you when they're just trying to stand up straight!"

He laughed, sliding his hands down my arms to grasp mine. "Well, if that's what it takes to get you in my arms then your world is going to be a little less stable in the coming days."

I gaped at him, a slow smile spreading across my face. An answering one spread across his own face and he tugged me towards the dance floor.

As we whirled around, I simply enjoyed the moment. The security of being held in his arms, the happy faces I could pick out in the crowd as we turned, twinkling lights overhead, beautiful music and laughter filling my ears. Best of all, the feeling of oneness in our movements as we danced in harmony. I gathered up the memory of every sense and stored them in my heart.

When the music finally slowed, Andrus led me out the side door to the banquet room, somehow managing to slip us out of the ballroom before anyone was the wiser. We rushed through the dark room, into the hallway leading to our chambers.

Other than a few guards on duty, we passed no one, soon making our way up the tower. When we reached my chambers I smiled up at him.

"Meet me on the balcony!" he murmured, continuing down towards his own door, trailing his hand out, still connected to mine.

I yanked on it, stumbling a little, but he came to a stop. "Just come through my room."

He followed me in, and I didn't bother turning the lights on as we through to the balcony.

I walked to the railing and peeked over the edge. Golden light spilled from the windows of the ballroom, and a few groups of people were seated near the fountain, wrapped in cloaks, or walking sedately around the courtyard. The air was chilly, but I was still heated from the dancing.

Andrus appeared behind me, leaning his arms against the railing on either side of me, and peeking over the edge as well. Heat rolled off of him, banishing the night air, and I leaned back against his chest. After a moment, he wrapped his arms around me and I relaxed, completely at ease with the world.

His voice came at my ear, low and gravelly. "I couldn't take my eyes off of you tonight." I shivered, and smiled. "You were without doubt the most beautiful woman there, and you charmed everyone."

I turned slowly until I was facing him and looked up. "I'm glad I charmed everyone. That was, after all, the point of the celebration." I hesitated, not sure if I had the audacity to voice what was on my heart. I thought of Hazel in the ballroom, braving heartbreak for a chance of an evening of memories with LeFeu, and decided to be bold.

"What I want to know is whether I charmed you."

This time, it was Andrus' eyes that dropped to my mouth and my smile widened. Before I could think of anything witty to say, he drew me in and pressed a gentle kiss on my lips. I was shocked for a moment, my mind blank, but as he made to move back I followed him, enjoying the feel of his firm lips on mine and resting my hands on his chest. He deepened the kiss, just a little, before pulling back and resting his forehead on mine.

"Did that answer your question?" his raspy voice broke the silence between us.

I laughed softly. "I'm sure it did. If only I could remember what the question was."

He tipped his head back in laughter and I grinned up at him. Several whistles sounded from the courtyard below, and I looked over the edge of the balcony again in alarm. A few of the soldiers stationed below were looking up at us, whistling, then started to fan themselves, and one pretended to faint. Andrus chuckled and waved them off as I covered my eyes in embarrassment.

Slipping out from under his arm, I made my way over to a couch near my door. Andrus dropped down into the seat next to me, draping his arm over my shoulders.

"Should I put them on an extra rotation tomorrow morning for their impertinence?" he asked, still chuckling.

"Of course not! After all, we were the ones kissing in full view of everyone."

"Maybe we should add that into our schedules. It seems like it's good for moral." He ducked away when I shot him a withering glare.

"Scheduling kisses would take all the fun out of them," I insisted sternly.

"Hmmm, if I knew I had an appointment to kiss my wife at the end of the day, it might make all the other appointments move a little faster," he countered and I couldn't help but chuckle.

We sat in happy silence for a few minutes before I found myself confiding in him. "I told Hazel. You know, about the shift."

He was silent for a minute, and I braced myself for a reprimand. "When?" he asked finally.

"The same night that you saved me. She thought you had hurt me, and it just all ended up spilling out. She was surprisingly open to the idea. She wants to stay here now more than ever."

Andrus turned to look at me, pulling his arm back from around my shoulders, cold air taking its place. "She wants to stay? But I thought she was in love with Monsieur LeFeu."

I let out a long sigh. "Yes, hopelessly, but she doesn't think she could be happy going back to Croiseux. She says he'd never leave, or even if he did, that he wouldn't be very open to the Asileans if he ever found out because of the Beast Wars... wait a minute. How did you know she's in love with him?" I demanded.

He laughed again, picking up my hand and tracing my palm with his index finger. "Anyone with eyes and half a brain knows it. She's a very transparent person. You can tell that his sun rises and sets with her too."

I shrugged my shoulders. "I told her to talk to him about it all." I looked up at Andrus, startled. "Her feelings for him, I mean, not the secret!"

"I know, Rosebelle. I don't mind that you told her. She obviously has a good head on her shoulders. I know we can trust her. I just hope things work out for her, whatever that looks like."

"Yes, she deserves it," I agreed quietly, thinking of her goodness as Andrus threaded our fingers together. Trustworthy, capable, and honest. Words she had spoken to me just a few days while helping me find a book for my clandestine research haunted me. *"You'll have to tell him sometime. You can't sneak around behind his back doing this and expect him to be open and honest with you."*

I squeezed my eyes shut for a second, then squared my shoulders and sat up straight. She was right. I needed to be honest with Andrus, before we became so close that it would hurt him even deeper. I knew he wouldn't be happy, but I had proved myself to be trustworthy. Maybe he wouldn't be as upset as I was thinking. He had taken my revelation about Hazel knowing his secret in stride, after all.

BELLE & BEAST

"Andrus, I need to tell you something else."

He looked over, his brows furrowed, and pulled me close to his side. "What is it?"

I took a deep breath and forged ahead. "You recall in our marriage articles that you forbade my father from pursuing his research on the Lady?" I asked, slowly.

"Yes. You know why that was so important now, don't you?"

"I can see why you did it, of course. And he did stop," I rushed to assure him. "He's completely given it up."

"I know," he replied, his brows furrowed deeper. "If you think that I am suspicious of him, I'm not. Don't worry, my Rose." His hand squeezed mine encouragingly.

My lips crooked a half smile at his endearment, but I continued on before I could lose my nerve. "Good. The thing is, he had an assistant with his work."

Andrus stiffened beside me. "Who?" he demanded. "My spies said nothing about an assistant. He had no office and worked solely from home."

"Me," I announced, not daring to look at his eyes. "I was his assistant. I saved some of his research and have been working on it since shortly after our wedding. I worked with him since I was twelve years old. I know every branch of inquiry he's pursued. I even suggested many of them myself over the years. But it's not something a Lady should be doing in Pelerin so we always kept it a secret."

I felt the loss of his warmth as he stood up from the settee and strode a few paces away. I kept my seat, but followed him with my eyes, anxious to explain myself.

"In the beginning, I was suspicious of you and of your motives for wanting the research to end. And I thought if I dug up whatever you were afraid of, I could use that knowledge to keep myself safe." He put his hands on top of his head, and I pushed on.

"Of course, after awhile, I realized you would never hurt me, or Hazel, or my family, so I sort of let it go. But after you revealed your secret to me, I started again. Some of the things we had been working on seemed to pertain to the shifts, and I wanted to see if I could find something to help your own research. The thing is," I shifted forward, excitement bubbling up as I thought about my work, "I actually do think I'm on to something. I've pulled a lot of information together, but there's a book I left at my parents' house in a secret compartment—I had found it just before everything happened. I'm the only one who knows about it, so I'm sure it's still there if I could just go back and get it!"

A growl interrupted me, and I looked back at Andrus to find him only a few paces away, fury written across his face.

"So, all this time, you've been deceiving me," he spat, his words as frosty as the night air.

"No!" I cried, bolting out of my seat. "Well, yes, I suppose. But it wasn't like that."

He cut me off. "I know exactly what deception is like. Don't bother trying to explain."

I watched him, not knowing what to say or how to restore the easy familiarity we had enjoyed only a few minutes ago. I cursed my timing silently. *Couldn't I have waited for another day?*

He closed his eyes. When he opened them again his face was a mask. "You asked to go home to retrieve your book. Go tomorrow to do that. Don't come back until I send a guard unit to escort you."

I took a few steps forward, stopping when he stepped back from me. "You're sending me away? Why?!"

His grim laugh stopped my words. "It's for your own good. We're launching an offensive at our patrol tomorrow, and you'll be safer in Pelerin. Away from harm, and not able to *inflict* any harm on those necessary to the well-being of this country."

I flinched at his words, then felt my backbone snap into place. "In case you forgot, I was crowned Princess of Asileboix earlier today. My place is here with my peopl and you—especially if you're launching an offensive. Why didn't you tell me that?!" I demanded, frustration coloring my voice.

"For some reason, I wanted to keep you out of the worst of things until after your coronation. I wanted to protect you. A mistake, it seems. I should have protected myself."

I flinched again, tears gathering. Yes, I had been deceiving him about my research, and yes, in the beginning I was planning to use it against him, but now I was sure that I was on the brink of discovering something that would help him. *When was he going to see that I was on his side?*

My heart ached, and I gathered myself together, needing to just get through the inevitable breakdown of this conversation and get myself to bed.

"I'm not going to Croiseux tomorrow. Our people need me. And right now, I need space. Please leave." I snapped my mouth shut to disguise the wobble in my chin.

He took several steps forward, crowding me. "Fine. Stay tomorrow, but as soon as our offensive is completed, you'll go to Croiseux and get the work you've hidden. That's not negotiable."

I conceded by nodding my head, too angry to look him in the eye. He leaned closer to me, his voice low.

"And I'll be happy to leave your presence, but first, you'll be handing over every last piece of work. Now."

I whirled, anger and despair warring in my heart, and led the way to the writing desk in my bedroom. Kneeling in front of it, I opened every secret compartment, jerking out the papers I had hoarded, the few books I had managed to save, as well as everything I had worked on since I had arrived, flinging each piece on the floor as I did so. I sat back heavily when I was done, looking at the pile of drab papers stacked next to my glittering gown.

Andrus crouched down, gathering them into a neat stack before standing up. I could feel his glare, but couldn't bring myself to return it, knowing I had tears in my eyes and not wanting to expose them to him.

"There is nothing else of the research left? Nothing

you're keeping back again?" he asked, his voice layered with displeasure.

"No. Save what was hidden in the Dower House." I couldn't completely hide wobble in my voice, and hoped he hadn't heard it. After a minute of charged silence, he strode over to the doors connecting our rooms, slamming them both behind him.

Pushing myself up, I gathered up my ball gown and trudged over to my dressing room, my heart detached from my chest. Sitting down at my vanity, I pulled at the wires anchoring my crown to my hairstyle. The first one was twisted tightly around a coil of my light brown hair, and I looked in the mirror, trying to find an angle where I could see which way to turn it. Instead, I noticed my pale face, tears trailing down my cheeks. Red rubies glinted on my head, ears, and neck. My gown shone in the lamplight. "His Rose," I repeated to my reflection, heart breaking a little more. "Not exactly."

Abandoning my efforts with the crown, I pressed my eyes into my hands, finally venting the angry tears that had been building inside.

When I had finished crying, I carefully cleaned my face before ringing the bell for one of Clothilda's seamstresses to come assist me. I had given Hazel the night off so she could enjoy the ball and arranged with Clothilda to have one of her attendants assist with my gown. The woman on duty came, and if she noticed that I had been crying, didn't say anything. After she left, I quickly prepared for bed.

Although I was exhausted and my feet hurt, I dawdled, not wanting to go into my room—knowing that Andrus was probably asleep only feet from where my own bed was. When I finally did slide into bed, I tossed and turned, examining our argument from every angle and wishing I had found a different way to present it. I was equal parts angry that he hadn't given me a full chance to explain everything, and miserable that I had ruined such a perfect evening. In the back of my head, I knew I had done the right thing coming clean, but

I worried that the better thing would have been to continuing researching until I found the link that I expected was there, proving the blood magic tie. *It's in your hands, I guess.* I whispered to the Creator, half resentfully, half prayerfully.

* * *

At some point, I must have fallen asleep because suddenly, Hazel was there, shaking my arm to wake me up.

"Quick, Belle! Breakfast with your parents starts in thirty minutes!" she cried, dashing out of my room. "Sorry I'm late! I had to re-pack some things when I woke up this morning and it took longer than I expected," she called from the the other end of my chambers.

I stumbled out of bed, and rushed around with Hazel, getting ready as quickly as I could. Despair settled like a weight on my chest as I remembered last night, and I bit my lip, worrying how Andrus would act at breakfast. I didn't want to alarm my parents, but I wasn't sure I could put on a cheerful face with him nearby.

Hazel asked me several times if I was alright, but seemed to chalk it up to exhaustion from the day before. The third time she asked I remembered Andrus' warning from the night before. "Hazel, Andrus told me something last night! When you get to you parent's house, warn your father that we're doing a bigger patrol tonight than usual. They've probably already let him know, but just in case they didn't think it was necessary, I think he should be told. I wouldn't want him to be out camping or something and get caught up in it. And he'd know if there are any Pelerines in the wood that need to be warned off."

She looked at me in the mirror from where she was pinning my hair up, eyes wide. "Of course! No wonder you seem out of it, you must be worried sick for Andrus." She hugged me from behind, then went on pinning up my hair. "Don't worry too much, Andrus will be fine. And I'll make sure Da knows as soon as I'm home, even if he's out in the field."

I gave her a tired smile in the mirror, and we rushed through the rest of my preparations as quickly as we could. We were the last ones down to breakfast, except Andrus. Mathilde's voice cut in while I looked around for him.

"Oh he sends his regrets, my dear, but needed to attend to something first thing this morning. He won't be able to join us unfortunately."

I nodded, relieved, and put a smile on my face while I turned to greet my family.

Breakfast was delicious, of course, but we were all a little subdued, tired from the day before and my family's departure hanging over us. Time passed in a whirlwind and before I knew it, I was waving everyone into the carriage, telling them I would come for a visit soon giving kisses to my parents, Rochelle, and Hazel, and shaking hands with Eddie and Henri. They swept out of the gate and I looked after them for a moment before turning to where Mathilde stood on the steps behind me.

She opened her arms to me, and I walked into her hug. "Don't worry, dear, if you want to visit them soon, I'm sure we can manage it." She linked her arm in mine as we walked back into the castle.

"Do you know where Andrus is?" I asked her, resigned. "I wanted to speak with him one more time before he leaves for the patrol."

"He's already gone, Rosebelle," she replied, looking at me with concern in her eyes. I swallowed, pasting on another smile and thanking her before heading toward my rooms again. I had the day off to recover from my coronation and spent it in my room, reading and trying to keep keep the memory of our argument at bay.

When the time finally came for me to meet Mathilde and proceed to the Vigil, I was a bit of a mess. It was to be my first in the throne room along with the other castle members, and I was expected to lead it since I had been crowned the day before. The closer I got the the throne room, the more anxious I felt. The privacy of the Chapel called to me. A sudden desire to run toward it instead of the throne room overtook me.

Mathilde joined me just as I was truly considering it, and I steeled my resolve. I was these people's Princess and it was my duty to lead them. I pushed back my shoulders and entered, leading the way to the thrones on the dias.

My nerves vanished the moment I caught sight of everyone's tight faces. They must know that this patrol was going to be more dangerous. There was no way to hide troop movements from any who lived in town, and those who lived inside the palace were all essential in helping prepare. *Other than me, apparently*, I thought resentfully, before banishing it.

You're better than that, Belle. I took a deep breath in and started the opening prayer. The now familiar golden haze took over my vision for a moment and I breathed out. *It's begun.*

The Vigil went off without a mistake—although I felt a heaviness that hadn't been there in previous sessions. *Probably nerves.* During a quiet time in the middle of the liturgy, I found myself asking the Creator to reveal the secret of what happened to the Lady, and surprised myself by realizing that I didn't think of her as a mythical figure anymore. There was so much information on her in the archives across Asileboix and Pelerin, there just had to be a real person at the root of it all. *I'm sure the Shift is connected to her, Creator, please show me how!* I pleaded. *And keep him safe. Please, please keep him safe.*

CHAPTER TWENTY

Eddie

"She's in love with you, you complete and utter idiot."
LeFeu and I were devouring a late night snack in the Croiseux kitchen. "I'm telling you, Belle and I discussed it while you became best friends with the Asilean farrier. She actually asked me to keep you away from Hazel because she didn't think you loved her back."

LeFeu was silent as he contemplated the apple tart on his plate. His face was expressionless, but I could still read him like a book. His jaw was set more than usual, which meant he was considering his words and what he should do with my information.

"Go tomorrow while she's home. Talk to her," I suggested, taking a bite of my own food. "You two were wrapped up in each other for the entire ball last night. This is the time to strike! Besides, Belle was going to tell her about you after the ball, so she probably already knows." He turned his glare in my direction. "I didn't realize she was coming home with us yesterday!" I said defensively. He shook his head and contemplated his food again.

"That farrier is a good'un," he said finally. "Knows his stuff and taught me a thing or two as well."

I stared at him, my jaw hanging slightly open. *I've just given him confirmation that the love of his life feels the same way, and his response was to talk about the farrier?!*

"LeFeu—" I started, but he held up his hand.

"I'll talk to her." He took a bite of his tart, chewing morosely. "I have to, I suppose, but I don't expect it will do anything."

I spluttered, but he continued on implacably. "You saw her there, Marchand. She was more beautiful than ever last night in that fancy gown, surrounded by all her friends. She loves it there. She'll never want to come back to Croiseux. And as for me... Would she ask me to move there? I never pictured living anywhere but here." He stared down at his plate, and finished chewing before looking over at me again.

"I reckon she'd have mentioned something about it before now if she wanted it. She's always been a little bold—but she hasn't said a word. She might love me, but I think she's moving on from me now. Still," he said with a sigh, lifting another bite of food to his mouth, "I owe it to both of us to talk to her. At least she can put me in my place if that's what it is."

I shook my head at him. Henri was never exactly a cheerful person, but he was as blind as a bat when it came to Hazel.

"She'll be crying tears of joy, Henri, mark my words," I predicted, turning to my own plate.

A knock sounded at the kitchen door. Popping the last of my food into my mouth I wound my way around the kitchen table to look out the window.

Hazel's father stood there, rubbing his hands together briskly in the night air. Unlocking the door, I stood back so he could pass inside. He doffed his hat.

"I have a message for your Da, Master Eddie, is he still awake?"

"Of course! He's in the downstairs study, working. Do you want me to take you there?"

"No, no, I'll find my own way, don't bestir yourself." He nodded at LeFeu as he made his way out of the kitchen.

I waggled my eyebrows once Monsieur Veneur was out of the room, but he just shook his head at me. After cleaning up after ourselves, we trudged up toward our rooms. Da called us in as we passed his study. Monsieur Veneur stood in front of him, hat in hands.

"Boys. Do you have anyone on patrol tonight?"

I nodded. "In town. Henri and I usually ride but didn't tonight since we just came from Asileboix. Why?"

My father looked grim. "Monsieur Veneur just brought a warning from Belle. Apparently the Asileans are running a large patrol tonight to combat some recent beast activity. She wanted to make sure no Pelerines were in the woods, just in case." He shook his head. "They do this every now and again, but usually they give Veneur a tip beforehand. I'm worried something happened."

I gave LeFeu a look and he nodded, heading out of the office to prepare our horses without needing to be told. I turned back to the others. "Don't worry, Da. Henri and I will escort Monsieur Veneur back and ride the wood line behind the Dower House. They said nothing while we were there. Not even Belle mentioned it!"

"Maybe she didn't like to in front of the Asileans," Da replied slowly, and I stiffened.

"She seemed quite happy, and we were able to have a private conversation while I was there," I said thoughtfully. "But maybe she didn't know about it until the last minute. She didn't seem herself this morning, now that I think about it. I assumed she was just tired like the rest of us. And her husband wasn't at breakfast. He had been called away suddenly." I shared a look with my father.

"Let's go, Veneur," I called, leading the way out of the room. He fell in step beside me as we left the house.

"Can you ride behind LeFeu?" I asked as we approached the stables.

"Aye, son," he replied. "I can't think why they didn't send me a message. They always have done, so far as I know. It's just luck we don't have anyone out tonight."

"Well, here's hoping it was because the situation isn't as dire

BELLE & BEAST

as Belle thinks," I said as we reached the stable yard, LeFeu already mounted on one horse. I assisted the gamekeeper up behind LeFeu, then mounted my own. We turned toward the gamekeeper's cottage and sped away.

* * *

After seeing Monsieur Veneur back to his cottage, we rode around to the Dower House. After confirming it was secure, we followed the wood line around toward the Dower Hamlet, then on towards the Lady's Shrine beyond.

The moon was high by the time we made it to the shrine. After a brief discussion, we turned our mounts back toward the forest, steering them carefully along a game trail until we came to a larger path that twisted its way back to the gamekeeper's cottage. It wound far up into the wood, almost to Asileboix. The trees were gloomy, but a full moon shed just enough light to see. We walked our mounts carefully, keeping alert for any sign of Asilean soldiers—or worse, Beasts.

There had been nothing unusual until we followed a curve in the path that wound only a few feet from the border. It afforded a view of another trail which led into Asileboix. Just before it curved off to the right, maybe fifty yards ahead, we could see trampled undergrowth. I signaled to LeFeu, and we back tracked until we came to a small meadow by a stream.

Tying our horses up within reach of the water, we started back toward the disturbed area on foot. The moon was beginning to dip below the tree line, making it harder to see, but I hoped that meant it was harder to see us too.

We crept forward over the Asilean border as quietly as we could, without resistance. Slowly, we came within sight of the disturbed area and froze at the same moment.

There was a small clearing, but it wasn't a pleasant meadow like the one we just left. Perhaps ten square yards, it was simply devoid of life. The trees on the edge looked sickly, their bark peeling. What looked like a large den, sat in the middle of the clearing, having been torn open to expose a nestlike interior. A Beast's den.

Examining the area, we could see the bodies of at least ten Beasts, clearly dead. Blood had been splattered indiscriminately, the muddy ground churned up during a fight. After taking in everything that the clearing could tell us, I signaled again to LeFeu and he nodded. We crept forward, following signs that soldiers had exited the clearing after the fight. It seemed that whatever unit had dealt with the Beasts had suffered casualties. Drag marks from at least two litters stood out starkly on the path. A set of deep set footprints showed that someone was being carried.

Creeping alongside the path as the sky continued to lighten, noises drifted toward us. Someone was moaning, and a set of voices rumbled back and forth. It reminded me of a triage tent after a battle.

We crept as close as we dared, finding shelter among some pine trees.

As my eyes adjusted, I could pick out the backs of several warriors, crouched over their compatriots. One of them was out cold, possibly dead. Another was staring up into the sky as someone bandaged his leg. The third one was moaning through gritted teeth as someone knelt over his side, two soldiers holding his legs and shoulders down.

Light flared in the hands of the one kneeling at his side, and I barely managed to keep from making noise. Magic was being cast.

We all knew that the Asileans didn't have anti-magic laws like we did, but I had never seen evidence of it the two times I visited the capitol city. LeFeu stiffen at my side a minute later and I glanced at him, questioning. He nodded his head toward the soldier being worked on, and I looked again. The man was growling in pain, thrashing back and forth. I caught a glimpse of his features and stiffened as well.

Andrus, the Prince of Asileboix.

He had sustained heavy injuries, blood gushing from his side, a mangled leg and arm. His thrashing stilled, and his head dropped back. He had obviously passed out from pain or blood loss. My mouth dropped open as I took in his face, the golden glow of magic revealing it clearly in the meadow.

He was a Beast.

His jaw had changed. Sharp canines protruded where his mouth had fallen open slightly. His eyes seemed closer together, dark brown hair had grown in on his arms and at his throat. He looked somewhere between human and almost bear-like.

Another face came into the circle of hazy light as the soldier that had been holding his legs down reached for a bandage begin re-wrapping his leg. The Prince had bled through the bandages already in place.

The attendant's face was humanoid too, but had also changed subtly to be reminiscent of a badger, black hair striped with white tapering onto his face, and the jaw slightly elongated. We were frozen in horror, watching the soldiers work on their Prince with both magic and conventional medicine.

As daylight blossomed in earnest, I worried over our position. *Could they see us?* Especially if these beast men had heightened senses, the longer we stayed, the more danger we would be in. But if we moved, they may hear us and come after us.

Instead of anxiety, calmness blanketed me. I felt as if I was back in the war, scouting enemy territory to compile a report on Beast movements. It felt right. I was more myself than I had been in the months since returned. My thoughts sharpened. My body felt alive, alert.

Part of me drew back from those feelings, worried that my excitement at danger wasn't right, but I stuffed it down. I needed the skills I had honed in the war now more than ever —especially if Belle and Hazel were in the clutches of these people.

Hazel! I knew she was planning to head back to Asileboix today after helping her father and brother bring the snares they had set yesterday afternoon. My mother was hosting a celebration dinner for the birth of Clair's first child, requiring a substantial amount of meat.

I caught LeFeu's eye, communicating an order to settle in for the time being and he nodded. We quietly found comfortable positions, stretching our aching legs periodically as soldiers bustled around the wounded.

The morning was burning away when another group of Asileans came into view, bringing mounts and a small cart. They loaded up the injured, climbed onto their horses, and were gone in a few minutes.

I took a deep breath but otherwise remained still. We sat still in our hiding place for another thirty minutes at least, making sure no one had doubled back.

After confirming we were alone, we crept back toward the path, working our way to our horses. The sun was past it's zenith when we finally reached them, and we sped back to the border, passing into Pelerin and heading toward the gamekeeper's cottage.

Hazel was already gone.

LeFeu stormed out of the cottage, angry at having missed our chance to ensure her safety. I related a quick version of events to Monsieur Veneur, leaving out our discovery that the Asileans were some sort of Beasts, and confirmed that we'd be in touch soon.

On our way back home, LeFeu and I strategized ways to get a hold of Belle and Hazel and get them back to safety. Although I was horrified at their vulnerability, and desperate to get them back home, part of me hummed in approval. With everything we had seen, there was no other way forward than war. Why was I happy about that?

PART III – THE WAR

CHAPTER TWENTY-ONE

Andrus

Pounding hooves echoed on cobblestone streets as I urged my horse away from the castle keep. Soldiers followed, pressing their own mounts to match my pace. Most of the warriors in the eastern patrol unit, including the sergeant, had fallen ill. Their places would need to be filled by less hardened recruits. General Morvan had sent notice, and since I had been unable to sleep, I decided to join him to help reorganize units. There's nothing for me here anyway.

My conscience prickled. Rosebelle had been hiding tears when I left, which was unlike the woman I thought I had come to know over these last months. She would never cry, or if she did, she would use it as a weapon to gain her own ends. It was something I deeply respected about her—the ability to take control of events and use them for her own purposes.

But earlier this evening, she had just seemed withdrawn. I had almost locked my door to her room, expecting her to come sweeping in, demanding that I hear her out as to why what she had done had made sense and was in my best interests, but she never came. The anticipation, mingled with anger, had been too much. Sleep had eluded me. Now I was riding away from her, angry and relieved that I didn't have to face her before attending to the patrol.

You should apologize. Hear her out.

I sneered at my own thought. No, I needed to focus, to prepare my soldiers for combat.

After a lengthy meeting with Morvan, I was able to sleep for a few hours in the officer's bunkhouse, wolfing down a meal and checking back in with my officers before final formation.

"So with Yves' unit supplementing the forces at Montblanc, Nanne's unit shouldn't have to deal with much on the eastern front. Hopefully nothing, as long as the Beasts haven't slipped across our border," General Morvan finished outlining before glancing at me. We were gathered around a table-sized map of the princedom, along with our officers.

"Agreed. And instead of taking the direct road back from Montblanc, my squad will swing around and meet up with Nanne at the old mill. Any hostiles should be flushed out as we head back toward the castle." I looked approvingly at our battlefield map, dusting the chalk we used to mark assignments off of my hands. "Even better than we discussed earlier, General Morvan. Good work."

Morvan dismissed the officers and we filed out behind them. My platoon was already mounted and waiting, so I swung up into my saddle. There was no fanfare as we passed through the Forest Guard gate. I had given a speech almost two days ago during formation as Morvan issued the original assignments. These soldiers were professionals and prepared to do their duty. Most were already deployed, waiting until sundown and the Shift before starting our push into the Wasteland.

I would be visiting four outposts along our northern border, providing support as teams made strategic sorties into the wasteland. One of our biggest pushes would be from Montblanc. It sat right in the corner of our boundary with the wasteland and Pelerin. The soldiers there would be striking deeper into wasteland territory than any of the others in an effort to keep any Beasts from spilling into Pelerin territory.

My shift began as night fell, just before we reached the town of Callay. It was a spur of land jutting out into the wasteland and saw continual action even during slow years. The people there were hardy and pragmatic. I didn't expect them to need much assistance.

We slowed to a stop just outside of town to allow everyone to shift. The process could be distracting at times. Better to allow yourself to focus—if you were able. We were trained to shift while completing other tasks in an emergency. Although it wasn't impossible, it could lead to mistakes.

Once everyone finished, we walked our horses into town, heading directly toward the guard headquarters. As expected, the Callayans had everything under control. Their first squad was already clearing a large den, not far into the wasteland. After greeting the Mayor and civilians at their Vigil, we left, following a road that roughly traced the border. The other two border outposts were much like Callay, and we found ourselves ahead of schedule as we came into sight of our final destination.

Montblanc was hidden from sight of the path. As we came around the final turn, billowing smoke met our eyes, pouring from the tower yard. I signaled an advance to my unit and we sped down the trail as quickly as we could.

Shouts and feral growls reached our ears us on our approach. From our elevated position on the road I could see several pockets of fighting, visible in the light cast by burning houses.

Outside the castle walls, groups of warriors fought desperately, sword and dagger pitted against tooth and claw. Inside the curtain wall, a platoon of soldiers was defending the inner keep, even as Beasts trickled through the outer defenses.

Like clockwork, decades of training and experience kicked in. I shouted a few targeted commands to my platoon. Two squads streaked away, arching behind the curtain wall to support the eastern side of the castle, and flank the invading hoard at the same time. I plunged into the skirmish closest to us, my remaining two squads following suit. Although my platoon was relatively small, our numbers combined with the Montblanc warriors to easily overwhelmthe Beasts still outside the walls. As the last one was dispatched by one of my sergeants, the leader of the Montblanc company saluted me, gasping for breath as he attempted to update me on the situation. I motioned for water from one of my nearby guards, and she handed the Captain a flask, his breathing slowing as he gulped down water.

"Sire, it's good to see you."

"Report, soldier, and quick."

"They attacked at sundown. The extra platoon you sent earlier helped stem the tide, but they were cut down defending the castle gates." Anguish flitted across his face as he handed back the water flask. "The Beasts made it through over an hour ago, but not before we evacuated our citizens. We're only barely holding the line. Haven't heard from any of the teams we sent across the wall. The only reason we've been able to hold so long is because two of the squads scheduled to go into the Wasteland had been delayed, enabling them to help in the town's defense."

The soldier's hurried communication swept over me like a wave of cold water, shock replaced quickly by grim determination.

Yves' unit was gone. Presumably, the teams already inside the wasteland were killed in action or in the fight of their lives. Our border was barely holding, and from the looks of things, enemies may have been able to slip through already.

I turned to the soldier next to me, one of the fastest riders in my unit, and spat out terse orders. He turned his horse and sped off in the direction of the next way station. He would return with reinforcements, as long as we could hold the line.

"Is Major Brieuc still in command?" I swung around to ask the Captain.

"Yes, Sire, as far as I know. She was leading a platoon inside the castle to prevent the Beasts from taking the keep. She sent us to protect the flank of the evacuated citizens."

"Understood. Keep to her orders. I'll take my teams to assist the Major in securing the castle. May the Lady be with you." I urged my horse into motion as I spoke, my warriors only a beat behind me.

We thundered into the castle courtyard by the rear gate, clearing a wide swath of Beasts as we did so. I almost lost my mount as we entered, but someone on the ground clubbed the attacking Beast on the head and I surged forward into the melee.

Major Brieuc had already made significant progress, judging by the carcasses littering the courtyard. My soldiers cleared the rest with ruthless efficiency. After a quick exchange with the Major—a hardened, middle-aged woman whose shift was reminiscent of a lynx—we sallied out of the castle and worked hard for the next hour to clear the battlefield and reinforce the border wall. It was well past midnight before we were satisfied that it was completely secure.

"I'll have to send units into the wasteland to retrieve our teams," Major Brieuc said, taking a sip from a flagon of water before using the rest to clean blood and dirt from her hands.

"You should be receiving support within the next half hour, unless my messenger met with problems. Wait until you've been relieved, or better yet, send one of the fresh units after them."

Brieuc barked a laugh. "No offense to them, but I'd rather send a tired border squadron into the wasteland than fresh-faced foresters. You know what the magic can do to you there. I heard it gave you a glowing crown over your head the last time you led a patrol in." She cackled as I nodded my head ruefully.

"Point taken," I replied. "Unless you've been through the magic before, it can be a little distracting. It's up to you. I'll leave you two of my squads in case anything happens before you get back up, but I'm overdue to rendezvous with the eastern guard. Dispatch an update to Asileboix castle at dawn."

BELLE & BEAST

I returned her salute and stepped out of her headquarters at the wall. Relaying my commands to my sergeants, the two squads riding with me found fresh mounts. We formed up at the edge of the forest. Although I could read weariness on the faces of everyone around me, the warriors by my side were highly trained. We were more than capable of taking down any hostile we might stumble across.

Fatigue swept across my body as we started down the road, the rhythmic pounding of hooves a lullaby for my tired muscles. The forest was quiet as we galloped toward our meeting place, an old mill not far from the Pelerine border.

Nanne's unit was waiting for us when we arrived and she reported an uneventful patrol. I relayed the events at Montblanc and our need for haste before leading our column down the path back to Asileboix Castle together. We hadn't made it far before Nanne's shrill whistle broke out calling for a stop. I reigned in my horse and sought her out, finding her a few paces behind me, sniffing the air. She was a canine shifter, vaguely reminiscent of a bloodhound with deep-set, slanted eyes that became more pronounced when she shifted. Her sense of smell was affected the most.

"Beasts ahead. A lot of 'em," she said in a low growl, then sniffed again, pointing off the trail to the left. "Smells like a full den. Over there."

I nodded, swiftly signaling instructions to surround the den. After a restless pause to allow time for everyone to get into place, I whistled a bird call to signal our advance and crashed forward.

Plunging into an unexpected clearing, I barely had time to notice the deadened wildlife before something ripped into my side, knocking me from my horse and shooting pain into my abdomen.

I had stumbled almost on top of a vaguely rodent-like beast. Snarls issued from its pointed snout as it gathered itself to attack once again. A few swipes from my knives dispatched it permanently, and I moved forward, not bothering to check my side. My horse was already out of sight and my guards were locked in fights all around me. We would need to clear the den before attending to wounds. The bear in me growled to see the threat to its territory.

Fury coursed through my veins as I engaged two more beasts. One of them clapped its mouth around my leg, right over a minor wound I sustained at Montblanc. A growl of pain escaped me, but I whirled around to continue fighting as soon as it breathed its last. A few minutes of hard work cleared the area around myself and Sergeant Nanne.

She and I stopped to survey the rest of the scene. A soldier was smashing in a part of the den, while another came out a separate entrance. "Nothing left inside, Sergeant," he called over to Nanne.

"Good." She nodded in satisfaction, sniffing the air distastefully. *Why are they speaking so quietly? They sound far away.* I frowned at Nanne as she issued additional instructions.

"Destroy as much of the den as you are able, then we move out. Sire?!"

She practically shouted my title at me, which was annoying and rang in my ears. Suddenly I was on the ground, soldiers talking over me, blood pounding in my ears. I realized they were lifting me onto a makeshift stretcher a moment before the pain in my thigh and side caught fire. I groaned, and one of the ones carrying me looked down.

"There's a clearing ahead with a clean water source. Nanne's unit has a healer."

Everything went black and I couldn't bring myself to listen, even though something niggled at me in the back of my mind.

I'm glad she wasn't in Croiseux with all this going on. At least she's safe at home.

❇ ❇ ❇

I surfaced to consciousness just as a healing mage poured magic into the wound at my side. I moaned through gritted teeth, the clenching of my jaw becoming an anchor for my brain to the physical world. Tingling spread across my limbs, a thousand pins pricking me at once. I felt the bear part of me wanting to swipe a claw at the very ones trying heal my broken body.

The healer worked on a rough fix for my side, connecting only the most vital tissues and organs, as was standard protocol for field healers. Even so, he had almost exhausted himself before he was satisfied.

"I don't think I got all of the blood vessels patched, but it will hold for now, Sire." His voice betrayed his weariness as he finished tying up a bandage over his work.

"Well done, soldier. Thank you," I replied weakly. He nodded, then made his way toward another patient a few feet away.

A medic from my platoon wrapped the less life-threatening wound on my leg with a spelled bandage as I took a report from Nanne, who had a bandaged forehead. She had lost one of her soldiers on the attack, and we had several seriously injured, although her healer was doing his best.

With most of our horses either dead or scattered, we decided to wait for backup. Time passed in a haze of moonlight and cries from the wounded. Darkness lightened incrementally, although the usual pre-dawn chorus of forest birds was absent, no doubt in response to our recent combat.

"I got a pulse back through the moonstone, Sire," Nanne reported sometime after dawn had broken and our shifts had all faded. "They're on their way."

I nodded in relief, and she helped me sit up, my back against a fallen tree. We were mostly surrounded by pines here, but there were a few oaks and maples as well, particularly around the freshwater spring on one side of the meadow. Accepting a flask from the sergeant, I gulped down the cold, crisp water.

I was exhausted from lack of sleep and blood loss, but I felt better than I had only hours before. By the time the rescue unit had arrived, I asked for a horse to ride but acquiesced when the healer instructed me to climb into the cart with the other wounded.

Our journey back was slow, but we made it eventually. After passing in through the Forest Guard gate I hopped down from the cart, waving off offers of help from my soldiers, and strode toward General Morvan, viciously tamping down the tiredness pulling at my limbs. He was standing with the head healer looking through a list as I walked up.

"Sire!" He threw up a salute, before clapping me on the shoulder. "It's good to see you. I'm just reviewing the casualty list. We took presumed heavy losses at Montblanc, although she's still waiting for information on several units. Callay held well, with no losses and few injured."

I looked over the lists, the amount of dead sickening me. We had expected to engage heavily with our enemy, but we hadn't expected so many to die.

"Status?" I asked, my head beginning to spin again.

"Border is secure, we're still waiting on the final tally of cleared dens, but it will be high. A company has been deployed to Montblanc, as well as Valery. They had trouble with an incursion as well. The southern, western, and eastern borders were quiet."

I nodded, turning my head to where the healers had set up a triage station. They seemed to be almost overwhelmed. I brushed aside the warning my healer had given me earlier about his hasty work. I could wait until I made it back to the castle and see Doctor Moreau rather than take resources away from soldiers here. I turned back toward Morvan. "Any attacks on the Castle?"

"None, Sire. Commander Poirier sustained injuries while on patrol outside the curtain. His squad cleared a sole den of beasts west of where we had that trouble earlier in the week."

My eyebrows furrowed in concern. "Where is he?" Clement

Poirier was one of the toughest soldiers I knew and had taught me some of my most vital lessons as I grew up. If he was hurt enough to be worth mentioning, it was serious. My mother was probably beside herself with worry.

"In the castle infirmary now, with one other of his unit. May I suggest you head there?" General Morvan replied, looking pointedly at my bloody bandages. I nodded grimly, instructing him to send me an update as soon as the northern casualties had been confirmed.

I reached the castle in good time. As I was handing the reins of my horse to the stable master, I heard Rosebelle's voice.

"Andrus!"

I turned. Relief flooded my body as I caught sight of her, looking tired but unharmed—and as beautiful as ever. She hurried toward me from the direction of the infirmary.

"Rose," I whispered, inhaling deeply as I swept her into a bear hug. She smelled like linen and parchment and something faintly floral. The scent of her made me dizzy, so I pulled away from our hug. Her smile slid into concern before she twisted her head to shout behind her. She slipped an arm under my shoulder.

I'm going to faint. Amusement swept over me. *She thinks she can hold me up if I faint.* I don't know if she was able to or not because at that moment, the world went black again.

CHAPTER TWENTY-TWO

Belle

I propped Andrus up as best as I could while a stable attendant rushed over. Another came up a moment later, and between the two of them, they were able to lift him into the air, carrying him toward the infirmary. I ran ahead, opening the door and calling into the ward for Doctor Moreau. She soon had him settled on a bed and I dithered as she pulled partitions around it. I didn't want to get in the way, but I couldn't bear to go far.

He had been so pale. I heard the murmur of voices behind his screen and strained to hear what the Doctor and nurse were saying. Of course, I heard nothing. There was a privacy spell around each bed, making conversations muted to any outside the immediate vicinity of the bed.

I sank into a nearby chair, noticing as I did so that the side of my pale yellow gown was streaked with blood. I shivered. *Andrus' blood.*

Moments later, the privacy screen around Andrus' bed pulled back, and the nurse ran out, carrying a bundle of blood-soaked clothes. Doctor Moreau motioned me over, closing the screen around us as I stepped inside. My eyes were riveted to

Andrus, bloody and fragile, most of his clothes cut away.

"His abdomen has sustained a massive injury," the doctor said, her tone succinct and businesslike. "It looks like someone tried to patch it up, but it's been torn open again. He's lost a substantial amount of blood. It's not good."

"But you can do something, right? Surely there's a spell that can help!"

She looked at me gravely, her usual calm demeanor betraying anxiety as she held a compress to Andrus' side. "I cast an examination spell twice to be sure. There's only one option left with such massive injuries, but it's not something we use frequently." The doctor pressed her lips together briefly before continuing. "I would need your participation."

I gaped at her. "I have no mage training!" I protested, my voice sounding shrill to my ears. "I'll do anything you ask, but I don't have any skill. What if I make it worse?"

She gave me a half-smile. "You don't need to do anything, just allow me to place a spell around the two of you."

"Do it. Do whatever it takes," I ordered, staring down at an unresponsive Andrus.

"Please sit while I describe the spellwork. I'm waiting for my nurse to bring back another healing mage—hopefully Madame Manciple—and then we'll begin."

I subsided into the chair next to Andrus, clutching his hand with one of mine and smoothing his hair with the other. "Tell me."

"The spell is an ancient form of blood magic." My eyes flew to hers and my hand stilled. "It requires someone with a close blood bond, either a blood relative, like a parent or sibling, or a spouse who has undergone the blood ritual during the wedding ceremony. The spouse is the preferable candidate for the injured partner, since a marriage bond is formed around a mutual choice. It seems to strengthen the magic somehow. We're not sure why." The doctor shrugged before continuing.

"Basically we will open a channel between the two of you, allowing magic to flow along it. It's dangerous, especially for you. The magic will draw on your strength to repair his body. You may become dizzy or even lose consciousness after the spell begins to work. We will keep you in a bed next to him, as physical contact seems to help."

I nodded once, the details of what she was telling me becoming jumbled in my head save for the main point: I could help Andrus survive. "There's no question. Just do it," I ordered again, eyes still on Andrus.

"Princess Rosebelle," Doctor Moreau said gently, drawing my eyes to her. "If his injuries are as bad as I suspect, it may take all of your strength to heal him. You could be drained to the point that you don't have anything left to give. I don't know if we would be able to detect your level of danger. If not... you would die."

I stilled at her words, my gaze unfocused. "Would he live?" I asked, my voice thick.

"Hopefully. I can't guarantee it, but it's probable that he would get enough strength from you to survive on his own."

I took a breath, steadying myself. "Then I accept the risk. Let's proceed."

Two others bustled in through the partition, the other mage and nurse, I assumed. I didn't break my concentration from my desperate internal prayers for Andrus while they hurried around me, preparing instruments and consulting a large book.

Someone put a hand on my shoulder, and I looked up, startled. It was Madame Manciple. "We're ready to begin, dear," she murmured softly, tension and sympathy warring on her face.

"Fine. Do you need anything from me? Do I need to say or do anything?" I asked, worried about my lack of ability.

"Just a drop of blood, Princess. You'll need to maintain physical contact while we invoke the spell. Holding his hand will be fine."

I placed my free hand in hers, feeling a prick and then a squeeze. She quickly wrapped a plaster on my finger and then turned to face Doctor Moreau, standing on the other side of Andrus. The academic in me flickered with interest to be witnessing blood magic. This very subject brought my father here in the first place, ultimately bringing me and Andrus together, but I was too distressed to focus on it. I brought both my hands to Andrus' and bowed my head in desperate prayer again.

I wondered briefly if I was going to die. It didn't seem likely, even though Doctor Moreau had taken pains to impress it on me. I was young. I had decades to live. How could I die now?

He would blame himself if you did. Your family would blame him too.

Would Pelerin use it as an excuse to start a war? *If they did, they wouldn't get very far against our warriors. But my family would suffer.*

None of that mattered. I wasn't going to die, and neither was Andrus. This was going to work.

My eyes traced Andrus' pale face, usually bronzed and warm. As they drifted downward, I realized suddenly that I had never seen him with so little clothes. His muscular torso was a mangled mess along one side. I couldn't bear to examine it closely. The other side looked fine, and I noted with detached surprise that he had a very large black tattoo, stretching from his ribs down almost to his hip. The pattern was a series of complicated whorls and what I assumed were runes.

A gypsy tattoo? I had read of them somewhere... but where was it? My eyes became heavy as I methodically went through the research I had helped Papa with through the years.

Not supposed to think about research, Belle. That's off-limits. I looked back at Andrus' face. He looked like he was sleeping.

Sleep sounds nice. I laid my head down on his shoulder, still trying to remember the book I'd read about gypsies when darkness overtook me.

* * *

Madame Manciple gently shook my shoulder. I blinked at her, wondering what she was doing in my chambers instead of Hazel, before remembering that I was in the infirmary. Searching wildly, I found Andrus sleeping in a cot directly next to me, our hands still clasped together.

"How is he? Will he be okay?"

She held her hand up. "You're both doing much better than we hoped. He's healing rapidly, all things considered. The fact that you're waking up already is an *excellent* sign. It's still a delicate time, but as long as you both take it easy, you should be out of danger of relapse within a day or two."

My head flopped back as I breathed a sigh of relief. Madame Manciple arranged a tray on my bedside table, then helped me sit up a little so I could eat.

"No need to maintain contact with him if you're well enough to wake up," s encouraged when I hesitated to let go of his hand. I gave a surreptitious squeeze, then let it go, pulling myself fully upright as Madame Manciple slipped a few pillows behind me. "Mathilde stopped in to sit with you both some time ago, as well as Hazel. I sent them both to bed since it's late."

"What time is it?" I asked between mouthfuls of a delicious chicken stew.

"Just past midnight," she answered, settling into a nearby chair.

"We've been asleep an entire day?!"

"Honestly, I expected you would sleep until morning at least. I only brought the dinner because I figured I could eat it if you didn't wake up." I winced as I finished my bite. "I'd offer you some, but if I'm honest, I'm too ravenous to share right now."

She laughed. "Don't worry, my dear, I'll get my own food when I take the dishes back."

As I continued eating, she gave me an update on Andrus' injuries, as well as news from the battle. No other activity had been reported from the Beasts, so General Morvan was satisfied with our current situation.

"My husband has been run off his feet, as you can imagine. He went to bed an hour ago. If the children woke up when he came in, he'll get no rest there either." She chuckled again.

I finished my stew, gulping a cup of water along with it, then sat back. My belly full, a heavy sleepiness settled over me again.

Madame Manciple took the tray. "Go to sleep, Princess, if that's what you wish. It's the best thing for both of you. If you continue healing at this rate, you'll be feeling better by morning." She padded away, closing the partition behind her, and I settled back into my pillows, grabbing Andrus' hand again before sinking to sleep.

✻ ✻ ✻

I awoke in the morning, feeling refreshed. Sun streamed in from over the top of the partition. Hazel sat in the chair Madame Manciple had occupied last night, sewing while singing quietly to herself. Andrus's cot was still directly next to mine, although our hands were no longer linked. I must have made a noise because Hazel looked over at me and gasped, setting her sewing on the bed table and jumping to her feet. I gave her a weak smile, and she helped me sit up, then hugged me gingerly. I hugged her back more fiercely.

"I'm so glad to see , I whispered as she pulled back from our embrace.

"I'm more glad to see you awake and getting up! Doctor Moreau said you could have died…" she trailed off, looking over at Andrus, tears pooling in her eyes. "I'm just glad you're both okay," she finished, giving me another squeeze.

After a quick breakfast, she helped me find the infirmary washroom and change my clothes.

"They don't want you far from him over the next few days.

He needs to be monitored here apparently. If you're ready, they can move you both to one of the private rooms they were able to clear out."

I nodded, and we started the process of moving. After insisting that Doctor Moreau show me how I could help care for Andrus, and I settled into a routine of nursing over the next few days. It was hard work, although there were charms to help with some of it.

Mathilde stopped in often, and we worked together to make decisions in Andrus' place. I was acutely grateful that she was able to shoulder some of the burdens of ruling right now since I wasn't able to be physically far from Andrus, nor did I have nearly enough experience in running a country yet. The strain cast shadows on her face, although she carried out her duties with her usual combination of cheerfulness and competency.

Since I no longer required long periods of sleep, I plunged into the reports that Andrus usually reviewed. The first day was slow going, but by the third day I was getting the hang of it. On the fourth day, Andrus woke up.

I was talking to myself about a particularly dense report when I heard his rumbling chuckle. At first, I thought I had imagined it since I had done so before several times, but when it was followed by a wheezy cough, I whipped my head towards him, jumping out of my chair and barely preventing the reports from scattering across the floor.

Before I knew what I was doing, I was over at the side of his bed, calling for the nurse on duty and setting off a whirlwind of activity. The nurse ran right back out to retrieve Doctor Moreau, who examined Andrus carefully, declaring him well on the way to perfect recovery. The nurse came back with a tray of food, which Andrus managed to eat on his own in between reminders from me not to wolf it down. I updated him as succinctly as possible on the princedom's state of affairs before Mathilde came in.

She spent most of her visit crying. He bore with it patiently, thanking her for how much she was doing, which only made

BELLE & BEAST

her cry more. After Mathilde left to prepare for a meeting with the Mayor, Doctor Moreau decreed that we could move back to our chambers in the morning. To Andrus' increasingly thunderous looks, she explained the magic we had used to save his life, as well as impressing on both of us the need to keep the healing binding open for another week or so at least.

"Distance at this point doesn't matter as much. You could probably stand to travel up to, say a hundred miles from each other without damaging the spell. So if Rosebelle needs to attend any functions somewhere else in the country over the next week, that should be fine. But of course, the closer you stay to each other, the better. Once you've completely healed, either myself or Madame Manciple can remove the spell for you."

I nodded in understanding and saw Andrus give a terse nod.

"You shouldn't have endangered yourself to save me," he accused in a low, frustrated voice after the doctor had left.

"Yes, I should have. It's done, so there's no use arguing over it. No one forced me, you know."

"I know. I wouldn't be surprised if you had somehow thought of it yourself." He glared in my direction, settling back into his pillows and holding his hand out to me. I came to sit next to his bed and put my hand in his, the touch an anchor for my fragile emotions.

"I didn't think of it myself, actually," I replied, grinning at his scowl. "Doctor Moreau explained it all to me. It was the only thing…" I swallowed heavily, my throat constricted, "the only way to save you."

He squeezed my hand and I cleared my throat, wanting to change the subject and landing on the first thing that popped into my mind.

"Is your tattoo a Gypsy design?"

He nodded. "I got it during the invasion at my sister's wedding. We had to fight our way up the stairs as we were retreating to the Old Keep, and one of the Beasts leapt on me, resulting in a fall down the stairs. Not a scratch on me but apparently there was internal damage. One of the Romany Queen's attendants healed it for me. Their treatments leave tattoos." He smiled at me sheepishly and I blushed, thinking of the muscled body that sported the tattoo. His smiled faded.

"Well, here I am, owing my life to you, when the last time I saw you I treated you horribly. I know you gained a lot of things you wanted to through this marriage, but right now you must be wondering if any of it was worth it to be married to such a Beast."

I cleared my throat again and sat up straight. "Well, it may be true that you're a bit of a Beast, but you're my very own Beast, so it makes a difference I suppose," I said, raising my eyebrows and giving him a cheeky smile.

He burst out laughing and I shushed him, not wanting the nurse to come back and give us a stern talking to about his recovery.

I switched tactics by going over the most recent dispatches and my worry over the news of our losses reaching Pelerin. Sleep overtook him almost immediately after dinner, so I tackled the ever-growing mountain of reports, buoyed up by his returning strenth.

✳ ✳ ✳

A view of the Dower House rewarded me as I peered out of the carriage window. I smiled, glancing over at Hazel who was looking out her own window towards the forest. Andrus was almost completely well, and I had argued with him after receiving reports of rumors in Pelerin about our deaths.

"Besides the fact that my family would be reassured by seeing me, I'll parade through the town so that everyone can see how well I am. If I know anything, the Croiseux gossips would love to get one over on everyone in the capitol. Rumors of my grandstanding will circulate faster than you can blink. It's well within the distance limit Doctor Moreau placed on us."

He had grumbled under his breath for an inordinate amount of time but finally agreed and sent me off with a light kiss this morning, Hazel by my side.

Mama came out of the front door as our carriage pulled up, hugging me tightly as soon as I stepped down. I hugged her back earnestly, then staggered as Rochelle cannoned into both of us. Hazel laughed as she climbed down behind me, and Mama broke away wrapping her in a hug as well.

"Papa is waiting inside," Rochelle said, tugging on my arm. I followed her in, finding him in the foyer. He gave me a kiss, and we all tumbled into the sitting room, Holly rattling in with a tea tray as we took our seats, along with Mrs. Comfry. Hazel and Holly exchanged hugs and whispered conversation as I greeted Mrs. Comfry. She handed me a cup of tea and biscuits, all the while wiping tears off her face and detailing how she had set the cook at Croiseux in her place for telling lies about my death only two days ago.

Holly caught my eye and grinned. "Welcome back to the land of the living, miss."

I couldn't help but chuckle as Hazel rolled her eyes and finished serving everyone before pushing Holly out of the room in front of her, Mrs. Comfry trailing behind.

"I'm fine, of course, as you can see," I said, deciding to address everyone's worries directly. "There was an attack at our border. But our soldiers held the wall and all is secure. Andrus was injured, but he's fine now. I'm in perfect health too, now that Andrus is better." It was a slight stretch on the truth of what happened, but it wasn't a lie either.

Papa took my hand while Mama dabbed her eyes with a handkerchief.

"Well, we were deeply worried. But obviously you're as right as rain so I suppose that was a waste of effort on our part," Rochelle chirped, sending me a sly smile and breaking up the tension in the room. Mother threw her handkerchief at her and we dissolved into laughter.

Sipping tea, we traded news and compared notes about my

coronation and ball.

"You looked beautiful that night in your blue brocade Rochelle," I complimented, setting my cup down.

"Yes, it's a shame more of the Marchand family wasn't invited, eh, Chelle?" Papa teased.

I looked over at my sister to find her trying to hide a smile behind her cup of tea, while Mama rolled her eyes.

"So, Thomas..."

"Don't start, Belle! Leave it alone," Rochelle enjoined, frowning at me.

"What?! I was just going to ask how Thomas Marchand has been recently." I grinned at her, trying to reassure her that I wasn't disapproving, but she still looked suspicious. I was certainly surprised that she still had her sights set on Thomas, but maybe she was truly in love with him. I hadn't heard that they were officially courting, but it was possible that she wouldn't tell me because she thought I would be hard on her. That hurt a little, but was probably fair. A determination to get her alone later to get it out of her formed. I started contemplating the best way to do it as conversation flowed around us.

When Hazel and Holly reappeared to clear up the tea things, I slipped out under a quick excuse. Hazel catching my eye. On the carriage ride over, she had agreed to distract everyone while I retrieved my book.

Treading softly over to the wall panel that housed the illicit tome, I searched the molding with my fingers to find the catch. It took me three tries to get it to open, and just as I was pulling the book out of its recess I heard the sitting room door open. Hazel's voice drifted out of the door, a hint of anxiety in it, "Oh Lord Montanarte, please don't let me scare you away with talk of dresses!"

My father's voice sounded loud as I saw his back edging over the threshold. "Oh no, Hazel, you carry on. I'm going to see if I can catch Belle and show her the new research I've been working on."

I pushed the book back in an attempt to hide it again, but it had wedged into the opening at an awkward angle. I glanced back at Papa just in time to watch him close the door and halt, staring at me. I stared back for a moment, then sighed and returned to my attempts to remove my prize. I carefully maneuvered the book around, pulled it out, and shut the panel. I looked back over at my father to gauge his reaction. He was rooted in place, dumbfounded.

I walked toward him briskly, shifting my book to the crook of one arm, and linking my other with his. "Papa, you wanted to show me your new research?" I prompted as I guided him toward his study. He nodded, remaining quiet until we were safely tucked behind closed doors. His study looked much more cheerful than the last time I had seen it, having received a thorough cleaning as well as reupholstered chairs and walls. The bookshelves were still largely devoid of tomes, in stark contrast to the packed mess they had been all of my life. Instead, the central portion was filled with a mixture of old and new volumes, while the shelves on either side held display cases filled with preserved insects and examples of what looked like local flora. I recognized my mother's decorative touch, but from the displays and stacks of notes here and there, it was easy to discern Papa's new interest. I mustered a feeble attempt to distract him.

"So, botany and entomology?"

His face folded into a frown. "Rosebelle, I recognize that book. Why, oh why, hasn't it been burned? Everything hinges on not continuing the research! Your safety, our family's security, the Marchands, every tenant in the manor and half of the town as well! If the Prince finds out..." he trailed off, turning anguished eyes away from the book in my arm.

"Papa, it's alright," I said, putting the book down on a side table and rubbing his arm soothingly. He looked as if he had aged since my wedding. A desire to reassure him rose up in me.

"Andrus already knows about it. He wasn't happy, to say the least," I snorted a humorless chuckle, "but he knows. And actually, the marriage articles didn't mention anything about *me* giving up the research, so legally speaking, we never agreed to any such action. And I have continued with it!"

Papa pressed his lips into a thin line, anger glinting in his eyes. I rushed to justify myself.

"Everything you were researching was true. There *is* a link to the Lady of the Woods in their lineage, and I now believe that she was a real person."

He turned away from me, a dull look replacing the fire I had seen, but I prattled on, excitement over my newfound knowledge making me voluble.

"The Asileans suffer from something that I'm convinced has a connection to the Lady. Andrus calls it a curse, but I don't see it that way. At the full moon, they all go through a shift. Most of it seems to be an internal process, but some of them, especially the royals and their soldiers, have a physical manifestation too. They take on qualities of certain animals. It varies by person."

Papa turned his face back to me in horror, and I realized how much I had inadvertently revealed. I framed my face with my hands in anxiety, remembering my own suspicion when I first learned of the Shift.

"Not like the Beasts! They're all good people. They've been protecting Pelerin for generations, actually, with no gratitude. The fighting we had recently was an attempt to cull the Beast hoard in the wasteland because it's become more active since the end of the Pelerine War. They use their strength for *good*." I had moved directly in front of him as I talked, wringing my hands and searching my mind for a way to prove the Asilean's integrity.

"You remember when I told you how Andrus saved me from an attack last month?" I asked desperately. He nodded, so I related the whole story. I tried to impart how much I loved Andrus and felt cared for by him without actually saying those words aloud.

"Three beasts. On his own?" Papa said finally, his voice

BELLE & BEAST

wavering.

I smiled. "Well technically, I dispatched one of them with the rock, but yes. He was magnificent."

Papa looked impressed. I let him think in silence for awhile, staring out the window. Finally, his voice floated into the air, breaking through my own thoughts.

"Only at the full moon, you say?"

"Yes. It begins at sundown. It seems to run in families, which is the reason Andrus was seeking a bride outside Asileboix."

He nodded, his eyes lighting up again. "Well, I'm glad he's seen the need for looking into things a bit more. It sounds to me like you may be on to something with the blood magic connection. Shame he burned my research before you got him to see reason."

I winced, as he obviously thought that the Prince was approving of my continued research.

"Well, we may not get anywhere really, so don't get your hopes up. And please don't continue your research. If anyone took an interest in it—"

Papa interrupted me. "I gave my word, child. You know I don't break my word." He looked a bit thunderous at the implication that he would go back on what he said, but his face eased back into a smile as I held my hands up in surrender. "In a way, it's quite soothing to think of you continuing on my life's work. But now, I must tell you about my new research. It was your mother's suggestion. I've taken to it like a duck in water. Come and look at these specimens I've collected, right here by the Dower House!"

He chattered on, describing the classification system he was developing, as well as some of the more interesting insect breeds he had found nearby. We were in discussion about an ant colony when Mama, Rochelle, and Hazel interrupted us.

"It's time to go," Hazel announced, and I furtively handed her the spell book in exchange for my cloak. She ducked back out of the room while I said my goodbyes.

"Could I come in to town with you?" Rochelle asked as I gave her a hug.

"Of course," I replied after looking at Mama for approval. She ran off to get her cloak and shopping basket.

"She's made friends with the baker's daughter—not the one angling after LeFeu, but the younger sister. And she's probably hoping Thomas will escort her home!" Mama stage whispered after Rochelle left, a twinkle in her eye.

"Are they courting?" I asked, smiling back.

"Not yet, he's waiting until her birthday I think, but she's getting a bit impatient. Marie Marchand says she's pushing him to just ask your father, but he's sticking to the birthday rule. I think it's because he's convinced she will change her mind now that our circumstances are better, but she won't."

"Well, a bit more time won't hurt anything," I replied, making my way out of the door, my mother and father trailing behind.

"Indeed. I don't think I could stand to lose both of my daughters in one year," Papa interjected, slipping Mama's arm in his.

"Well, if she marries Thomas, it's likely you'll gain a son here at the Dower House than lose a daughter." I stopped for a moment, sending him a grin. "I could see them bumping along nicely in a cottage in the Hamlet actually."

"If you're talking about Thomas and me, you can forget it. We'll be residing in their townhouse of course, although I'll keep my room here so I can escape to some piece and quiet when he starts droning on about trade mergers too long." Chelle's voice rang out from the stairs, followed by her appearance a moment later.

"Rochelle Marie Estelle Montanarte!" Mama spluttered. "If anyone hears you talking like that, they're going to think you're—well, *fast*," she hissed.

Rochelle only laughed. "Oh Mama, I only said that to give you heart palpitations! I'm not ready to get married just yet, so don't worry about losing me, dear Papa." She gave him a quick

BELLE & BEAST

kiss, then flounced out the door, grinning at Mama's sour look. I donned my cape before following her out.

The ride to town was short. Rochelle filled most of the conversation after I asked her to explain Mama's cryptic reference to the baker's daughter.

"Oh she means Louise!" Rochelle replied with a laugh. "Surely you know who Louise is, she's closer to your age than mine. She's been angling after Henri LeFeu since he came back from the war. Ada—that's my friend—says she's been trying all sorts of ways to get his attention and got in trouble from their Ma for taking him pastries." Rochelle let loose a storm of laughter.

"Anyway, no one can tell if Louise is making any progress because Henri is like a brick wall. He could be madly in love or irritated beyond belief and no one would know."

I shot a glance at Hazel as she shifted in her seat. Her mouth was set in a grim line. *Will she speak to LeFeu today?*

"But of course Louise's friend, Lena, is even worse."

I turned my head back to Rochelle. "What do you mean? Is she going after Henri as well?" I asked, shocked.

Rochelle laughed again. "No no, nothing as interesting as that. She's pursuing Eddie, but anyone who knows him at all can see he's not interested one bit. Thomas even mentioned that Eddie invites Henri over to Croiseux more often instead of meeting in town because the girls are always after them."

"You mean Lena Mullin? The miller's daughter? She has experience helping her mother with the tea shoppe, which could give her a foundation in running Croiseux. She would be a good match for Eddie. He'll need someone comfortable being married into a trade network once he takes over from his father. But Rochelle, you've become a dreadful gossip in the months since I left!" I admonished mockingly.

She wrinkled her nose. "I suppose you're right. But it's all so interesting, seeing what people do with their lives! And Lena's terrible. She'd never make Eddie happy. Besides, he has Thomas to help him with things, so he doesn't need to marry

385

someone just for that. I think he still carries a torch for you, *Princess Belle*, but once you start having children he'll probably move on quickly."

"Rochelle!"

"What?!" she replied defensively. "It's only what I think. He certainly never loved you like Andrus obviously does. The Prince could hardly take his eyes from you the whole evening at the ball." She wiggled her fingers at me. "Once you have children, Eddie's idea of the fair maiden Belle won't exist anymore, so he'll have to move on." She shrugged her shoulders and I shook my head. She was probably right, but she had certainly become a little more wild since I left.

Our carriage dropped us at the top of the village square. We stopped in at the Marchand's offices to say hello, and Thomas promised to join us for tea in an hour. We visited the seamstress to check on a dress for Rochelle, then meandered down the line of shops facing the square, buying sundries from each. I spent the most time inside the bookshop, catching up with the bookseller's daughter who practically ran it by now. She was a few years older than me, but had always been kind. I ordered a few books on insects as a gift for my father, as well as a series of novels I knew my sister would like. Rochelle went into the basket shop to discuss an order while Hazel and I waited outside. Unsurprisingly, we drifted toward the nearby forge.

LeFeu's father hailed us, so we went up to say hello. Henri and Eddie appeared just as we were walking back. We had no choice but to wait for them or risk appearing rude.

"Belle! Princess Rosebelle, I mean," Eddie greeted us as they approached. "What a chance. Would you walk with us for a moment? We were just discussing you and wondering—" He cut off as Rochelle appeared around the side of the basket shop and called to us.

"We're about to have tea with Rochelle and Thomas," I replied. "Will you join us?"

They looked at each other and nodded, Henri turning to tell

his father something before heading with us up toward the tea shop. Thomas was already inside, having ordered the tea, and Eddie dragged a table to join his.

It was a slightly uncomfortable affair. Thomas and Rochelle were perfectly happy, chattering away like birds. Lena served us, shooting me pointed looks when she fawned over Eddie. Henri was more stoic than usual. Hazel, having been seated directly next to him, was just as silent. Even Eddie looked strained, and I couldn't blame him. Finally, after we drank all the tea and ate a surprisingly delicious meal, we parted ways.

Predictably, Thomas offered to walk Rochelle home, which she accepted eagerly, taking his arm and steering him back the way we had come. I turned toward Eddie and Henri as they walked us to the stables. "If you're going back to the Manor House, Eddie, we could offer you a ride in the carriage."

He looked at LeFeu. "That would be wonderful, actually. Would you mind if LeFeu joined us?"

"Of course!" I agreed, turning to smile at Henri, who managed a grimace.

As we waited in the stable yard for my carriage, Eddie pulled me into a conversation about horses. I noticed Hazel and Henri having what looked like a whispered argument a few feet away. Finally, the carriage was ready and we climbed in. We had scarcely left town before Eddie captured our attention.

"I'm so relieved that you're here. We have to tell you something that you'll probably find difficult to believe, but it's all true. But now that you're here, we can get you to safety."

My heart thrummed. *Get us to safety? Could he know somehow? Of course not, how could he? He's talking about the rumors of my death of course.* I took a calming breath and interrupted him.

"Eddie, there's no need to be concerned. As you can see we're perfectly safe. We weren't part of the military action that took place in Asileboix. Andrus would never allow me to be put in such danger." I gave him a serene smile, and nudged Hazel to chime in.

She stayed silent however, not looking at either of them. Henri watched her gravely.

"Really, we're safer there than here in Pelerin, no matter what you may think." I settled back in my seat, lifting my nose slightly. *Perhaps a little regal condescension will settle them.*

"Belle. We saw something."

My breath stopped. I stared out the window, careful to keep my disdainful expression on my face. The carriage jostled over some uneven ground in the road and Eddie reached across to help steady me before I tumbled off the seat. I blew out an exasperated breath.

"What do you mean?"

"In the woods, on our last patrol. It was the night the Asileans mounted their attack." Eddie hesitated and glanced at Henri. He was studying Hazel, who was studying the carpet. I sighed internally.

"We came across signs of a scuffle, right at the border, so we followed the trail. What we found..." he shook his head. "It was a unit of Asileans. But Belle... they were half Beasts themselves!" he exclaimed, a look of horror passing over his face. "I know it sounds unbelievable, but it's true. And that's not the worst of it." I steeled myself. He drew in a deep breath.

"Prince Andrus was there."

My eyes snapped to his, the tension and fear I had been feeling igniting in my chest as anger. *Despite all our precautions, how is that Eddie, of all people, uncovered our secret?* He had continued speaking while I tried to marshal my emotions.

"Andrus was the most Beastly of all. He looked almost like... like a bear! His face was terrible. We saw soldiers using *magic* to heal him. It was nightmarish; you can't imagine. LeFeu saw it too."

I drew myself up, clutching Hazel's arm to wake her out of her withdrawn stupor. "I don't know what you think you saw, but here's what I do know. My husband is honorable. A decorated warrior and a beloved Prince. He has protected me with his life, and I love him with my whole heart. If you have a problem with any of that, so be it. But do not *dare* have the audacity to sit across from me and speak ill of him to my face." I rapped on the carriage ceiling, and the driver began to slow the horses. "You can walk the remainder of the way to Croiseux."

Henri's rusty voice broke out, the first time I had heard it that afternoon. "Hazel. We're not lying. Why would we? We've fought the Beasts, we know them. Just... please. Come back with me. Marry me, and I promise I'll keep you safe."

I stared at him in shock, then followed his gaze toward Hazel. She shook her head, tears falling.

"No Henri. I want to stay in Asileboix, as I told you in the stables. I wish you would come to me there. I *would* marry you! But you could never be comfortable with the Asileans, and love won't be enough to change your mind. You had better go."

She was almost sobbing now so I pulled her to me, glaring at LeFeu. *This is exactly why I wanted him kept away from her. He's only breaking her heart more.* The carriage rolled to a stop and one of the attendants opened the door, blinking at the scene in front of him.

"These gentleman prefer to continue on foot," I told him. "Please untie their horse. We will make directly for Asileboix Castle."

He nodded, stepping back so they could descend. Eddie looked at me pleadingly.

"Go," I said in my most authoritative tone. "Don't say another word."

After a helpless look, he left. LeFeu followed, stopping to slip something into the reticule hanging at Hazel's waist. I glared at him, then sighed as the door shut. The carriage rumbled back into motion as Hazel sobbed into my shoulder.

✻ ✻ ✻

I strode down the hall, careful to hold the flowerpot in my

hands away from my cream colored day dress. *Not the right color to be carrying a pot full of dirt around in.*

I had breakfasted with Andrus, Mathilde, and Clement this morning, discussing the situation with Eddie. Andrus hadn't been overly concerned.

"If he reports anything, he'll be dismissed as a madman. If the Pelerine government asks questions, we can send a representative that doesn't physically shift during the full moon to disprove his claims. They would never outright demand that I present myself for inspection. We could always take offense and break off all communication again, like we've done for most of our history."

My anxiety had decreased after that conversation, although it wasn't completely dissipated. I didn't think Eddie would be taken for a madman. Still, what else could we do beyond stilling his tongue with magic? That would only make the situation worse.

Andrus was starting his first full day of duties again since the battle. My heart glowed to see him sitting at his desk again as I entered his study.

"I brought you something. It's from the Dower House. I had to take it to the gardeners to get them to work some magic on it, but it should be fine as long as you water it. Isn't it beautiful?"

He smiled at me, then looked at the miniature rosebush in my hand and raised his eyes. I walked around his desk and plopped it in front of him, leaning against the desk to face him.

He eyed the tiny buds. "It is beautiful, I admit, although not as beautiful as my own Rose."

My heart flipped as he circled his arms around my waist and pulled me down into his lap.

"Hmm, that's pretty good," I responded in mock seriousness. "It shows you have good taste. But unlike the plant, your own Rose has thorns. I won't hesitate to prick you if you don't allow me to help."

"Help with paperwork? I would be ecstatic!" he said,

pushing me off his lap. "Here, you take these, I'll take these, and we'll be done in no time."

I grabbed the papers he held out. After setting my plant on the windowsill and sticking my tongue out at the old one, I settled in near the fire. We worked steadily, finishing about an hour before lunchtime. Andrus thanked me as I handed over my last pages.

"Now that I'm crowned, I'm ready to begin sharing more duties, you know. I enjoy reading through reports," I replied, shrugging my shoulders as he looked at me with surprise. "But that's not exactly what I meant when I said to let me help." I sat up straight in my chair and organized my thoughts.

"First of all, I want to apologize for continuing the research behind your back. It was wrong to deceive you."

He looked at me steadily so I continued. "When I came here, I felt powerless. I wanted some leverage, as I've told you. Assisting my father with his work was the one thing that made me feel comfortable in my own skin growing up. I just wasn't ready to give that part of me up when we got married. It felt like I would be ripping out something essential. So I justified it to myself because you hadn't stipulated that *I* couldn't continue, just my father." I sighed.

"That being said, I really do think I'm on to something. I retrieved the book I told you about when I was at the Dower House yesterday, and I read it on the way back." He frowned but I ignored it. "It's rather a disgusting book, although there are useful spells as well. One of them near the back of the book is a record of an ancient blood curse. It describes a way that blood magic can be used to affect descendants of a specific person through multiple generations. Apparently, the person that is cursed needs to have a strong amount of magic in their blood, and the spell will fade over the generations after the person with the original curse laid on them has died. There was also has a long rambling tale of someone called the Queen of Hearts twisting her magic for evil among humans, and seeking to destroy the keepers of the world. That part I didn't understand, but there's usually some kernel of truth in myths, so maybe it's referring to the sorceress that started the Shift? Obviously your ancestors found a way to work around it, because you all perform your duty whether you've shifted or not, but it's a link! If you could trust me to continue looking into this, it may help you with your experiments. You've already confirmed that there is a marker in a person's blood that correlates to the Shift. This spell may be what put the markers in your blood to begin with! If we could reconstruct the spell, maybe we could understand the Shift more."

I fell quiet, watching Andrus as he frowned at his folded hands. He was quiet for a long time, and I forced myself to resist fidgeting.

"Leave the book with me," he said finally, and my heart sank. I almost picked it up and walked out. There was no need for his stubbornness to ruin his chance of unlocking the mystery! Instead, I took a breath and stood up. *It's his choice.*

"Okay." I decided to give him space. Keeping my tread measured as I left, I allowed myself once last glance back before I shut the door. He was looking at the roses I gave him, his face carved in granite. The door clicked shut.

CHAPTER TWENTY-THREE

Eddie

I lunged for my horse's reins as the carriage rolled forward. Staring until it was out of sight, I turned to LeFeu in confusion.

"Henri… what just happened?"

He shook his head, but didn't say anything. I pinched the bridge of my nose.

"Okay look, we're about halfway to my house. Do you want to stay the night?"

Henri gave a strangled laugh. "I'm going home. I'll see you for dinner tomorrow." He turned back toward town, but I put a hand on his shoulder.

"They must be bewitched. You saw the Asileans using magic in the woods. They're under a spell. There's no other way she would have turned you down."

He looked at me for a moment, then shrugged off my arm. "Could be," was his only reply, and he started back toward town. He obviously wanted to be alone after having his proposal rejected. I would too.

I wondered over Hazel and Belle's words as I rode home. *She loves him.* The thought echoed in my mind, but I mentally shrugged at it. I had known it ever since her coronation ball. They were obviously infatuated. Even if they weren't, she was married. She would never be mine. But I still felt a duty to protect her. I loved her still. How could I not? She was the epitome of what a woman should be.

He probably put her under a love spell to make life easier, I thought bitterly. And Hazel *must* be under some spell or coercion. Henri had poured out his heart to her. Now that I thought about it, she hadn't really rejected his love, she just said it couldn't be. *Was she trapped somehow?* There was something more going on, and I wouldn't put anything past those Beast Men.

I spent the next day trudging through estate business with my father. I didn't mind some of it, but it was becoming onerous. The only bright spot was a visit to Stone Farm to visit with Trinette and her children.

Henri arrived when I came down for dinner after our return. Thankfully, no one noticed his gloom as Clair and her baby joined us as well. She and her husband were leaving for their own house in the morning.

"One last cuddle before we go up," Clair said, as I took my proffered nephew gingerly. "You won't get the chance for a long time!"

I grinned down at the grumpy face in my arms and chuckled.

"I don't think he's very enthused about his uncle at this point," I joked to Clair as I tickled his little fingers. After a few minutes he started fussing, so I handed him back. Everyone trooped upstairs after the baby except for me, Da, and LeFeu. We poured drinks and settled back down, getting right to business.

"I met with Lord Montanarte today like I said I would," Da said, rubbing his chin. "He didn't believe a word of your story. But then he started rambling about the Prince, and Belle, and the coronation, and Eddie's engagement with Belle, and a host of other things." Da sighed. "I think your suspicion was right,

Eddie. He may be under a spell too. He was as sharp as a tack discussing his bugs right up until I unfolded your story. Then he dithered and confused himself as he spoke. It was strange." He looked between the two of us. "Since he's our parliamentary representative, we won't be getting much help that way. I could help as the district magistrate but it would require leveling charges against Maurice and I won't hear of it at this point. He may be losing his grip on reality but I won't see him in jail. What's next?"

I nodded. "I'll write to some of my contacts in the military. General Des Condcordes will take it seriously, I know. There are several others who are suspicious of Asileboix. Between the so-called attack in Asileboix, the knowledge we have now, and the spells being put on Pelerine citizens, we need reinforcements."

Da grunted, his ubiquitous jovial expression gone. "Agreed. If they send a unit, we can shelter the men in the fallow fields near the upper stream. We're too vulnerable not to act." His voice lowered to a gravelly pitch. "Who would have guessed this six months ago?"

I grabbed some writing materials and wrote a quick series of letters to the General and my other contacts, reading them aloud to Henri and my father before signing and sealing them. "You're sure you up for delivering them?" I asked LeFeu.

"Aye. If they're all in the Capitol it will only take a day or two. My Da doesn't have any projects that can't be left for my brother."

"Good man," I said, shaking his hand as he tucked the letters into his pocket with the other. We turned in soon after, LeFeu to get an early start on the road, and the rest of us to mull over our thoughts and prepare as best we could in the meantime. Croiseux may not hold much joy for me anymore, but I would lay my life down defending it and it's people. *We just need to get Belle and Hazel to safety.*

CHAPTER TWENTY-FOUR

Andrus

I stretched in the fading sunlight. A gentle breeze stirred blossoms and leaves before reaching where I sat in the rooftop gardens. Mother and Clement sat together on a bench not far away, and Rosebelle stood in front of them, talking animatedly. The evenings were getting longer, and we were enjoying the late spring blooms in our private gardens after dinner. I felt better than I had in years, and I wondered if our healing connection was the reason.

Am I taking energy that Rosebelle could be using? We needed to get Doctor Moreau and Madame Manciple to remove it soon, but I had been dragging my feet to suggest it. I liked the idea of an extra layer of connection between myself and Rosebelle, and she seemed as energetic as ever. *Still, it would be disastrous if I had an accident.* I made a mental note to track the doctor down before our full moon patrol next week.

The door to the gardens creaked open, and a servant appeared, making his way over to me. He handed me a note as he reached my side.

"Message for you, Sire."

Taking the paper, I nodded at him and broke Robin's

BELLE & BEAST

personal seal. It was short. After a brief personal update came the information I wanted.

We'll send support for your next patrol, of that you can be sure. Our own resurgence of activity has been repelled for now. Red and her unit will go, but how many teams beyond hers I can't predict yet. I'm sorry I can't promise more. I folded the note back up, slipping it in my breast pocket.

"What is it?" Mother called, Clement and Rosebelle looking on curiously. I walked over to them, pulling Rosebelle's hand into my own and taking comfort in the warmth of her touch.

"Confirmation from Robin that they'll be sending Red's unit for the next patrol. They've had their own issues which may tie up more help." I shrugged. "Red's unit alone will turn the tide of any military action. Now if we could just receive confirmation that Spindle will ride with us, we can deal a major blow into the Wasteland."

"Do you expect any trouble from Pelerin?" Rosebelle asked with a furrowed brow.

"I honestly don't know." I glanced at Clement.

"They'll try something if they can. Maybe not yet, but it's probably inevitable," he mused thoughtfully. "They think the Beasts won't trouble them, so they're turning their gaze back to their neighbors. If Spindle rides to our aid they wouldn't dare cast lots against us, so it hinges on Spindle's response."

I nodded in agreement. We'd all been over this in the last cabinet meeting—Rosebelle's first as Princess consort—but our situation was balanced on the edge of a knife. If one thing went wrong, disaster would strike.

"Well, I, for one, have had enough fresh air." Mother said, standing. "Rosebelle, shall we run through your self-defense forms one more time this evening?"

Rosebelle squeezed my hand and then let go. "Of course!" she replied to Mathilde as the two of them went downstairs. My mother had taken over training Rosebelle during my recovery. Now that I was better I wanted that particular duty back again, but it seemed like they enjoyed sparring together so I hadn't forced the issue. I looked over at Clement.

"We've been abandoned. Should we follow suit?"

He chuckled, stretching his knee in the swiftly cooling air. "I suppose it's time. I have orders to review before I turn in."

I nodded and followed in his wake as he walked stiffly down the stairs, his wounded leg obviously still giving him trouble. He bid me goodnight as we entered the castle again, and I looked around, considering what I should do. I was tired, but my mind was still abuzz. The best medicine for that combination was a stint in my lab.

* * *

I tinkered in my laboratory for some time, not getting much done, before my eyes lit on the box of research. Monsieur Webster had reviewed most of the treatises at my request, just to see if there was anything worth storing in our archive. His conclusion had been resoundingly positive, and I was curious to go through it myself.

"May as well look through it," I said aloud, pulling papers out and sitting down in a comfortable chair.

It took me two hours to read everything through, including the parts of the blood magic spellbook she had marked. I leaned back in my chair when I was done, closing my eyes. I was finally tired and ready for bed. Even so, my mind was clearer than it had been in days.

She was right to continue it. You were wrong. Placing the papers back into the box carefully with the spell book on top, I rubbed my hands over my face. Her research was not only interesting, but I could see where it might link to my own. I would have to find time to admit as much to her, and ask to coordinate on our work. There was no question as to whether she should continue with it. She was obviously talented. Together we would make more progress than I had done on my own. I curled my hands into fists, dropping them to my lap.

I had almost let my own fear destroy the very research that could save us. Slamming my fist down on my leg, I berated myself.

Creator, forgive me of my pride. You brought me a woman I didn't deserve, and I dismissed what she was trying to do.

From now on, we would be as one. No more hiding things, no more heavy rules. She had more than proven her bravery and intelligence, an equal partner in our crown. And if I could reign in my pride, she just might find the connection that breaks our curse.

CHAPTER TWENTY-FIVE

Belle

I pushed the heavy double doors of the throne room shut a little faster than expected, resulting in an echoing thud. Wincing, I peered over my shoulder, then breathed a sigh of relief. No one was around to witness the Princess of Asileboix slamming doors. I had been placing extra candles inside, enough for everyone, so we could light them while we prayed for our warriors. I wanted everyone to feel as one tonight, confident in our shared future. The golden glow I saw at the beginning and end of each Vigil had inspired me to choose candles as a focal point for all of our energy. Their light was reminiscent of the glow of the magic we prayed was protecting them. Hopefully it would help instill quiet confidence in us all tonight. I was still easing into my role as Princess, but I was becoming a little more comfortable with the Vigil every time we had one.

We had received word that the regiment from Sherwood had been spotted, so I anticipated extra guests at dinner tonight, but there was still ample time to prepare. Walking out into the sunlight, I wandered over to the large decorative fountain in the main courtyard. The mild May air felt delicious

BELLE & BEAST

and full of hope, and I wanted to soak it up for a few minutes. I found a dry spot on the edge of the fountain and arranged my skirts.

I was wearing a new style of dress—one that Clothilda and Hazel had badgered me into trying since it was common in Asileboix. It was a dark green all-in-one gown, as opposed to the separate skirts and bodices and overdresses I was used to wearing. The hem was shorter, and I could feel a breeze around my ankles as I kicked my feet, then stilled them, remembering I was supposed to be a Princess, not a carefree youth. I snorted quietly. *I don't think you've ever been described as carefree.*

I glanced up toward Andrus' study to see if I could catch a glimpse of him, without any luck, then leaned in to watch the gushing fountain splash and sparkle in the sun's rays. The courtyard bustled as residents rushed back to work after the noon meal. I watched them idly.

A porter rode in on horseback followed by a Pelerine man, his nationality obvious by the formality of his clothes compared with the trousers and tunics favored by most Asileans during the working day. I watched the two with interest until they passed into the stables. Standing, I brushed off my dress and started toward Andrus' office. The Pelerine rider either brought a rare communique from the Pelerine royal family, or was connected to Andrus' informant network and could have news about Eddie's movements. Either way, I wanted to be there when he conveyed his message. Crossing the courtyard with a quick step, I had almost reached the entrance to the Ministry Wing when I heard my name being called.

The two men I had just seen were jogging across the courtyard toward me.

"Princess Rosebelle," the porter said, bowing slightly when they reached me. The Pelerine man followed suit, with a much deeper bow.

"Yes, were you looking for me?"

"This man has a message for you, Madame. He says it's

urgent, and for your eyes only." He gestured toward the Pelerine man, and I looked at him, recognition flashing through me.

"Stephan!" I said, smiling at him. He was one of the grooms at Croiseux Manor. He bowed again, then offered me the letter, twisting his hat in his hands after I took it.

"I'm to wait for a response, Your Royal Highness, and to escort you back. Your mother said you must come."

I paused from opening my parents' seal and glanced at him. He looked extremely nervous, which I had originally put down to simply being in Asileboix. Turning back to my letter, I unfolded it and scanned the short note.

Belle, you must come home immediately upon receiving this. Do not waste a moment even to pack your things, or you will be too late. Your father is deathly ill and is begging to see you. You must come. You must bring Hazel. We are sending Stephan to escort you. We're depending on you, darling.

The world spun around me, and I sat down on a stone bench a few paces away. *Papa is dying. This beautiful day full of life and hope and Papa is dying.*

I gasped, my chest burning, and the two men came into my line of sight, fluttering over me with worry. I read through the letter one more time, trying to still the trembling in my hands. *There's still time to see him.* I needed to pull myself together, and get moving. Turning toward the porter, I began issuing commands.

"Go back to the stables and tell the stable master to prepare Lodestone for me immediately. Then run to the kitchens and gather light provisions for myself and Stephen, and bring them to the horses. Go."

The porter bobbed his head and ran off. I whirled on Stephan. "I'll be ready to leave in twenty minutes. Stay in this courtyard. I'll be back in a few moments." He started to splutter a response, but I didn't stay to listen. Striding toward the front gate, I stopped in at the office next to it. The guard on duty saluted me.

BELLE & BEAST

"I need a guard detail to be ready in the next ten minutes. They'll escort me to my parent's house in Pelerin. I'll meet them at the East Gate." He saluted and stepped into the rear office, where he would dispatch a messenger to alert the guards on duty. I turned on my heel, almost jogging across the courtyard toward my rooms, batting Stephan away irritably as he pestered me with questions. Ordering him to stay in the courtyard, I slipped in the main entrance and rushed down the hall.

As I mounted the steps, I felt a rush of gratitude toward Clothilda and Hazel for badgering me into trying this shorter and lighter dress. It would be easy enough to ride in so I wouldn't have to bother changing, but it wouldn't cause a scandal in Pelerin like some of the other Asilean styles.

I was out of breath by the time I reached my room, waving off my footmen. Running straight into my dressing room, I almost crashed into Hazel, who was setting out my dinner clothes.

"You nearly scared me to death!" she scolded, but I interrupted her, throwing the note onto my vanity.

"Oh Hazel, there's been some bad news," I said, stopping to catch my breath and hold in the tears threatening to overwhelm me.

"What is it? Is the unit from Sherwood not coming to help after all?"

"No, no nothing like that. It's from home. Papa is dying," I choked, then rushed over to my wardrobe, eager to be doing something so I wouldn't dwell on my note. "They said you should come too. Will you?"

"But… we just saw him. He was fine!" she exclaimed.

"I know, I know! Help me get my jewelry off." I sat at my vanity, pushing the crumpled note to one side. I took off everything but my wedding rings as Hazel gently removed the emerald brooch clips I was wearing in my hair in place of a diadem. As soon as she was done, I stood up, fastening my cloak and pulling on my gloves as Hazel rushed to my

403

wardrobe, grabbing a small bag and stuffing several articles into it.

"Here. A nightgown and some underclothes. And here's a scarf for the road." She helped me pull the heavy wool scarf around my shoulders, then crossed over my front, pushing my cloak aside to tie it at my waist in the back. "Are you taking the carriage?"

I shook my head. "Horseback—it will be much much faster."

"I thought as much. I'll stay here. You know I'm no great rider. I'll only slow you down. I can follow in the carriage with medical supplies if you like. Maybe we could bring him back here for Doctor Moreau if he can be moved?"

A gasp escaped me with a painful thrill of hope. "I should have thought of that! Yes, do it. And please find Andrus as soon as you can. I haven't even sent someone to find him yet. I don't think he has his moonstone brooch so you might have to track him down on foot."

I pointed toward my vanity table. "The note is there if he wants to read it. And tell Mathilde that she'll need to fill in for me at the Vigil tonight because—," my voice broke and I squeezed my eyes shut for a moment, "because I won't make it back in time. Wait to hear from me tomorrow before leaving. If things aren't as bad as Mama says, come in a carriage big enough to bring back my family. If not, then... I'll send word about it."

We shared a look of despair before I rushed out of my room and back to the stables. Lodestone was ready by the time I arrived, and Stephan was already mounted. I mounted as well, turning my horse toward the doors.

"But we're supposed to bring Hazel too—uh, Your Royal Highness," Stephan added hastily, urging his horse forward after me.

"She's following in a carriage," I tossed back over my shoulder.

Instead of racing through the streets, I kept us to a trot as we headed to the East Gate, not wanting to alarm any citizens and knowing I would need to wait for my guards in any event.

We waited fifteen excruciating minutes for the Forest Guards to arrive. Stephan tried to argue that we didn't need a guard since he was there, but I ignored him. I had given my promise to Andrus that I would take my security as Princess of Asileboix seriously, so there was no way I would go rushing off into the forest without a detachment of guards. I dismounted, ignoring Stephan's sullen look, and started walking Lodestone, more out of a need to be doing something than for the horse's sake. Finally my guards arrived.

"Captain Riviere, at your service, Madame." The soldier in charge came alongside my horse and saluted.

"Thank you, Captain. Do you know the most direct route toward my former home, by any chance?"

"I do. I've been assigned to patrol the Dower Woods at least three times since your marriage. I know the paths well enough."

"Good," I replied briskly. "Time is of the essence.

Lead on." He spurred his horse forward, and I followed suit. I could feel Lodestone's eagerness to stretch his legs, and I was glad to give him the chance to do it.

❊ ❊ ❊

We pushed the horses as fast as we could, arriving at my parents' house just as the sun was starting to edge behind the trees. I climbed down off of Lodestone, handing the reigns to the closest guard. As I ran toward the back door, the guard captain on my heels, my sister yelled out to me from the stable.

"Go into the study, Belle!" she cried out.

"Is he still alive?" I gasped between breaths, wondering in the back of my mind why she was in the stable if Papa was dying.

"Yes, yes, but go quickly," she ordered, motioning us inside and looking around. She grabbed the arm of one of the other guardsman who was still mounted, but I ran into the house. I went straight to the study, not bothering to take off my cape, and stopped only when I reached the study door. I took a moment to try and slow my breathing as Captain Riviere came up behind me.

"Let me enter first, Your Highness. I need to assess the threat level to you."

I glared at him. "If you think I'll be kept from my father's deathbed just because I might be infected, you need to think again."

A stern look settled over his face. As he opened his mouth to reply, the door in front of us swept open. My father stood in the doorway, fully dressed and looking as healthy as I had last seen him.

"There you are, Belle, come in immediately. You too, sir." He opened the door wider, motioning us in. "Is Hazel with you?"

I drifted into the study in shock, towing the Captain in my wake. "Papa? What's going on?"

"I'm sorry for the deception child but we thought it necessary." My mother's voice, full of tension, came from over near the windows. I looked at her in confusion as Rochelle burst through the doors behind us.

"They came by the back way. They got Stephan in time but she didn't bring Hazel," Rochelle gasped, breathing heavily.

"You didn't bring Hazel?!" Papa rounded on me, fear in his voice.

"No. She… she… I was to send word tomorrow on whether you could be moved. She was going to follow in a carriage so we could bring you back to the castle for the healers." I took a deep breath, trying to pull my swirling thoughts into order.

Captain Riviere seemed to be slightly ahead of me in that department. "Someone needs to explain exactly what is going on. Right now."

"Yes. Yes, of course." Papa turned to Rochelle. "You say they prevented Stephan from going to Croiseux?" She nodded and he looked relieved.

"You must send your guards back to the castle as soon as possible. A regiment arrived early this morning. It's encamped near Croiseux Manor. They intend to attack Asileboix, and soon. Eddie must have convinced his superiors of the threat because they're mustering as we speak."

"How do you know this?" Captain Riviere interrupted.

"As Earl of Croiseux, I'm still the regional parliamentary representative. They're obligated to inform me, although they were hesitant to do so. Our servant girl, Holly, saw the soldiers on her way in this morning, so I had advance notice and was able to think everything through." He took a breath and continued on. "I begged them to let me send one of my servants to get Belle and Hazel out of the castle before they attacked, using an illness as a ruse. They agreed but demanded that I use one of their grooms and to be allowed to read my letter. I couldn't write you the truth, and of course I couldn't trust poor Stephan, so I resorted to trickery, hoping that you would bring your own guards with you. Rochelle stayed in the stable watching in hopes that we could prevent Stephan from sounding the alarm. You must send your guard back to alert the castle, Belle. You'll be safe here with us. Poor Hazel!"

I tore my gaze from his anguished look and glanced at Captain Riviere. "We must return immediately. I doubt there are fresh mounts in the stable. Will our horses last?"

"We have Firefly in the stable. I saddled him while I was waiting for you but he's the only one," Rochelle cut in.

"Send a rider ahead on Firefly to warn the castle, and the others can follow more slowly. You must stay here, you'll be safer here," Papa urged.

"You know I can't stay. My place is there," I replied angrily. "I appreciate the warning, but I have a duty."

Captain Riviere held up his hands. "Your Highness, I disagree. We should send a rider back ahead, but you can't risk being caught by the Pelerines on a tired horse, and I can't let you ride ahead on your own. We should make our way north. We may be able to get to Montblanc in the morning if we make good time tonight."

"Oh my stars!" Rochelle was looking out one of the study windows. "It's Thomas. He was stopping by for a visit on his way home this evening and I forgot. What should I do?!"

I shook my head, attempting to shake my scattered thoughts into order, then walked out of the study towards the front door. Captain Riviere stalked behind me, my family shadowing him.

"Let's send one of your men out now on Firefly to warn the castle. We need to secure the perimeter and I need a moment to think about what we'll do."

"Yes ma'am. My men will have already started clearing the perimeter, standard procedure during a security detail." He held out his hand to stop me as we reached the front door. "Let me go in front, Your Highness—in case there are hostiles."

I looked at him in shock, but nodded slowly to show I agreed. He peered through the window and stiffened.

"Who is that?" he demanded, and my sister peeked over his shoulder.

"Oh that's Monsieur Veneur, the gamekeeper. He's our neighbor."

I nudged her aside to look for myself. Monsieur Veneur stood in the middle of our lawn, speaking animatedly with one of my guards. Captain Riviere pulled open the door and I followed him outside.

"Let him pass. He's a friend," I yelled, and the guard stepped back as we approached.

"Lady Belle." Monsieur Veneur dipped a bow to me and looked back and forth between me and my father, panting. "Whatever reason yer here, I'm glad. The Beasts. They're comin'. They're almost in the Dower Woods—hundreds of 'em. We saw them when we were stalking a stag up in the north end. Send a rider to Asileboix before it's too late. They'll be here soon." We all stared at him in horror for a moment before exploding into action.

Captain Riviere barked orders at one of his men, telling him take Firefly and ride to the castle as fast as he could. I turned towards my family.

"Rochelle, go round up the servants. Tell them to gather as much food as they can and be ready to run to the Shrine in ten minutes. I'll tell Thomas what's going on when he gets here. Mama, go and gather as many blankets as you can find. Papa, grab your sword, guns, powder, and any other weapons we have in the house. Let's meet in the stable. We need to make it to the Shrine before they get here. It's much more defensible than the house."

They each turned to fulfill my orders and I looked around, trying to think and make sure we hadn't missed anything.

"I have to go, Lady Belle," Monsieur Veneur said, still heaving breaths in between each word. "Rowan was with me in the woods. He went to warn the Dower Hamlet. I told 'im to send everyone to the Shrine too. The walls may keep 'em safe, like you said. He'll run down to the Town as well. I told 'im to hole up there before they close the gates. I've got to get my Missus and bring her to the Manor House. Reckon it's safer there. Will you take my Holly with you to the Shrine?"

"Of course," I said, calling an earnest "Good Luck!" as he sprinted away. I motioned to Captain Riviere to let him to pass, adding instructions in an undertone as the Captain walked beside me.

"The Lady's Shrine is not far from here, on the edge of the Dower Hamlet. It's just an ancient tower built around a spring. It's enclosed by thick stone walls that are still in relatively good condition. If we ride it will only take a few minutes to get there. Monsieur Veneur's son is warning the villagers, so we may have additional citizens to protect."

Captain Riviere nodded. "We won't have many soldiers to defend it with, but it's better than a house."

Thomas rounded the corner of the house, slowing to a stop on his horse and his jaw dropped.

"Thomas!" I called, grimly, "You had better get over here. We need your help."

CHAPTER TWENTY-SIX

Eddie

"Surely they're home by now." I said to LeFeu, as I paced nervously. "Where is Stephan?"

Looking over at the stables for the hundredth time, I folded my arms across my chest. Tents were visible in the distance, erected for the soldiers in one of our fields. My father and I had met with General Des Concordes and his staff yesterday to discuss what I had seen and the other evidence we had, indicating that the the Asileans were truer "Beast Men" than we ever thought.

General Des Concordes had been full of righteous anger. "We must deal with them before they come to deal with us. Imagine creatures like that, with human intelligence and the appetites of beasts. The King has been suspicious of the Prince ever since he came looking for a Pelerine bride. Now his suspicions are confirmed, and he wants Asileboix under his thumb. We'll dispatch those who show signs of beastliness. Those who don't will live under Pelerine rule."

I was given charge of leading my unofficial unit of Croiseux soldiers as part of the defense of Croiseux. Most of them were down in the staff dining room right now, eating an early

BELLE & BEAST

supper before the action we anticipated during the full moon tonight. We were hosting many of them, as well as the officers, at the house. Despite Lazard's best efforts, everything was in an uproar. It wasn't helping my nerves. I wanted to be sure that Belle and Hazel were safe.

"I'm running up there," I said to LeFeu finally. "Stay here and get the men into formation once their meal is over. I'll be back by then." He grunted at me in response and I strode out of the room.

Jogging over to the stables, I inquired with the stable master to see if Stephan had returned. He hadn't. Settling into a brisk walk, I directed my steps toward the Dower House, pulling my collar up against the slight chill in the spring air. I was just entering the kitchen gardens when I saw Monsieur and Madame Veneur jogging toward me, carrying two large bundles. I stared at them as they approached. Madame Veneur was breathing loudly, obviously not accustomed to running. Monsieur Veneur's voice rang out in fits and spurts.

"Master Eddie. Beast hoard comin', down from the border. Be here soon. I warned the Dower House, they're headed to the Shrine. We need to get to the Manor House."

"A what?" I asked, shocked.

"Saw 'em at the border of the Dower Woods an hour ago by now, creepin' steadily forward. They'll be here soon, unless they're waiting for darkness. Even so, that's only a few hours away. We need to get to safety."

"Go to the house and sound the alarm. I've got to see Belle and Hazel. Why didn't you bring them here?" Veneur looked at me, confused.

"Hazel weren't there. It's Holly that works there now. Belle just happened to be visitin'. She's ordered everyone to go to the Shrine on account of its walls." He started back into a jog, nudging his wife forward too. "My son's warned the hamlet and town. You'd best come home, Master Eddie."

Instead of heeding his advice, I turned and sprinted toward the Dower House, crashing through the gate of the kitchen garden, blossoms fluttering down around me as I pushed past their branches. When I came out from under them, I could see a flurry of activity going on near the house. There in the middle of it was Belle, arguing with her father. She must have heard my feet pounding on the ground because she turned in my direction, shading her eyes.

"Belle! Where is Hazel?!" I called, looking from her to Lord Montanarte. A shadow stepped out from the shade of the stable, directly in front of me, sword raised. I skidded to a stop, loosening my own sword from my hip.

"State your business," the shadow said, obviously an Asilean guard from his uniform. *She brought guards. Stephan should have come back immediately to tell us that!*

"Where is Stephan?" I asked, immediately suspicious.

"We sent him off to the Shrine already," Belle replied from around her guard. "What do you want?"

"I... there's a beast hoard on its way, I've come to take you to safety. And Hazel too."

"Hazel isn't here. She's back in Asileboix. We're going to the Shrine. Go back to the Manor, and when you do, I'd appreciate it if you refrained from invading my country today. We won't take kindly to that, I assure you." Belle's words became acidic as she yelled, her hands on her hips. "I'm confident my husband and our soldiers can defeat your regiment and the Beast hoard at the same time if needed. So do yourselves a favor, and prepare to fight the Beasts. Don't try to use this situation as an excuse to gain a foothold in Asileboix."

I shook my head, careful to keep out of striking reach of her guard. "Belle, you're obviously under some sort of a spell. I suspected the last time I saw you. You, Hazel, and your father too. These Asileans are not all they seem. What I told you in the carriage is true. I saw them transformed with my own eyes!" I eyed her soldiers. "Your guard may be some of them. Quick, come with me to the Manor House and I'll protect you. You won't be forced back to that monster," I pleaded with her, turmoil roiling inside my chest as everything I thought I knew

BELLE & BEAST

was being turned upside down.

Annoyance marked her brow while I spoke. She dismissed me for the moment to turn toward Lord Montanarte. "Papa, mount up with the remaining guard and catch up to Mama and Rochelle. Right now. If the guard tells you to leave those books here, you had better do it or I'll toss them out myself. There's no time to argue. We need to get to safety."

She swiveled back to me. "You're right."

My heart soared at her words. *She must have suspected she's been under a spell and is finally putting it all together.* I took up a better defensive stance, keeping an eye on her while I sized up her guard a little better.

"You are absolutely right," she repeated. "Captain Riviere does transform. His affinity is with a mountain ibex, I believe. Am I correct Captain?" The soldier nodded but didn't take his eyes off of me. "I thought so. It's quite distinctive. And of course I know about my husband—I'm his wife, after all. It seems you've forgotten that I'm the Princess of the Asileans. If you're calling them monsters, you're calling me one too." She eyed me speculatively. "I can see you're not quite convinced. Fine. Even if I am under a spell, I'll be safe in the Shrine if I can make it there before the Beasts come." She turned her head briefly as her father rode off behind another Asilean soldier, heading in the direction of the ancient shrine. "We're out of horses, so Captain Riviere and I must walk. The longer you keep me here chatting, the more danger you're putting me in. Run along back to the Manor House, secure your family, and for the love of the Lady, convince your soldiers to fight the real Beasts, not my valiant soldiers. Don't be stupid, Eddie." She turned on her heel, starting to jog in the same direction her father had gone. Her guardsman backed away as well, not taking his eyes off me.

I watched her go, torn. She was obviously completely taken in. *The beasts are crafty, you know that. Mix it with human intelligence, and their magicians have probably devised any number of evil spells.*

413

She was right though. I breathed in deeply, focusing on what I could control right now. She would be safe in the Shrine. Surely her guards wouldn't turn on her since she was their Princess.

I needed to get back to my men. Once we cleaned up this mess, I could retrieve her and we'd find a way to break the spell. I backed away, keeping my eye on her guard until he was out of sight, then turned and started running back to the Manor House.

CHAPTER TWENTY-SEVEN

Andrus

"The Lady was a protector, first and foremost!" I practically shouted, although with a smile. This was an argument Red and I debated more often than not when we were together. "She was tasked with shepherding the animals and always protected women and children. Our very castle is built around her sanctuary in the ancient days! You're practically sitting on top of evidence of her protective nature. You cannot deny that."

Red let out a deep chuckle. "I am not denying that! But she's a warrior as well—and a huntress. She may have shepherded the animals, but she didn't coddle them."

Lueren and I had been out in the city, meeting with the Mayor ahead of the patrol. We had just finished when we came across Red and her officers making their way up to the castle. Since we were all in need of a late lunch, we took them to an inn that had good ale and pies and were now ensconced in a private parlor, having spent the last few hours eating most of their provisions.

"Ah Red," I said, stretching in my seat. "I can't tell you how good it is to lay eyes on you. And I can't wait for you to meet my wife. She's too good for me in every way. Why don't we head up to the castle now so I can introduce you?"

"Suits me," Red replied, pushing back from the table. "Let me get to know this paragon. That's what she must be if she agreed to take you on, Cousin. Lead on."

I shouted my plans over to Lueren, who nodded, then turned back to his conversation with one of Red's best fighters, Eileen O'Dale.

The streets were busy, but not enough to prevent conversation as we made our way through. I directed Ironheart close enough to be heard.

"How is your mother? I haven't heard from her in some time."

"Much the same," she replied, watching a street vendor selling colorful wares on the side of the road as he sang a popular folk song.

"She stays at the Lodge all the time and keeps to herself. She's focused on her garden right now." Red shrugged her shoulders. "I don't see her as much as a daughter should." Silence grew between us for a few beats before she continued. "Robin and Marian go down to visit her at least once a month. She has a dutiful stepson." She grinned suddenly. "I went with them to visit just before coming here. Do you know she told Marian that she hoped the baby was a girl because she'd always wanted a daughter? Right in front of me!" She chuckled, hoarsely, then seemed to notice my grim look.

"Oh, come on, Bear. You have to laugh at these things. Sometimes I think she almost means them, if only as a way to acknowledge my existence."

I looked at her sympathetically but she only rolled her eyes.

"Forget I said anything. Tell me more about Rosebelle. She sounds too good to be true, and I'm expecting she'll hate me for how rough I am."

I laughed. "Hate the Red Rider? Perish the thought! She'll love you for my sake, if for nothing else. I warn you, though, she's perceptive. She'll see right through you in about two minutes and know what makes you tick. But she's good. Good for me, good for Asileboix." I smiled over at Red, unable to contain my happiness.

"How intriguing. I don't even know what makes me tick. If she could tell me, I'm sure it will be useful."

I snorted and she cracked a grin. As we passed through the main gates of the castle, someone shouted my name.

"Prince Andrus—sire!"

I turned in the direction of the voice to find Hazel waving from the other side of Red. I motioned her toward the stable and continued on, dismounting and handing my reins to an attendant before Hazel made it across the courtyard on foot.

"Sire, I just sent messengers out to find you. Belle was called away. Her father is sick and may be on his deathbed. She took a unit of guards and left not long after lunch. She'll send word in the morning, and if he's well enough to be moved I'm to go to her with a carriage so she can bring him here. If not—well, she'll send word about that too."

I stared at Hazel in shock. She had tears in her eyes, and was obviously trying not to cry. I put my hands on my hips, trying to gather my thoughts.

"I'll write a note to send with you tomorrow. Come with me to the infirmary and I'll use Doctor Moreau's paper." I motioned to Red. "Hazel, this is my cousin, Red. Red, this is Hazel, Rosebelle's friend and lady's maid."

Hazel dipped a curtsy and Red nodded at her, then looked over at me.

"I'm sorry to hear the news. I'll let you go. I need to run up to my apartments to drop off a few things, but I won't be able to stay after we ride tonight. My orders are to complete your offensive and meet my support team as quickly as possible on our side of the border. I'm expecting orders to deal with that lost patrol mess from the winter." Her tattooed face was forbidding, so I didn't ask her for details, squeezing her shoulder in solidarity instead.

"I'll see you at formation in an hour, then. Hazel, come with me."

We went our separate directions, and I slowed down a bit after realizing that Hazel was having to jog to keep up with me. She was almost a foot shorter than I was and I forgot that her stride matched her height.

"Has he been unwell?" I asked her. "He seemed hearty enough at the coronation."

She shook her head. "No, he seemed better than ever when we visited the other day. I can't understand it. But maybe it was a flu or ague. They don't usually come so late in Pelerin, but he *is* getting older..." she trailed off, obviously distressed.

So long as he can be moved, Doctor Moreau could probably help him. I mulled over our options as we walked into the infirmary, straight to an area I knew held writing paper, quills, and sealing wax. I dashed off a note to my wife, folding and sealing it with my signet ring. Hazel watched my movements with nervous tension, accepting my note as I handed it to her.

"Please give this to Rosebelle when you see her tomorrow. Also, if she sends word that he still lives but is too ill to be moved, I want Doctor Moreau to go with you. So long as she's discreet she may be able to stabilize him enough so that we can move him back here for better treatment."

Hazel's eyes lit up with hope at my words, giving me a small curtsy before dashing out of the infirmary. After a quick consultation with Doctor Moreau about my father-in-law, I jogged up to my chambers, changing into my uniform and armor, and mentally preparing myself for the patrol ahead.

* * *

I ran across Red again as I walked toward the Ministry Wing.

"I was just going to see my mother before leaving for headquarters. Want to say hello?"

She nodded and fell into step beside me. Weaving our way

BELLE & BEAST

past workers heading home, we arrived at our destination quickly. I knocked lightly then went in, Red on my heels.

Mother looked up and smiled, then pulled a frown. "Darling, have you heard about Rosebelle's father?" she asked, before her eyes lit on my cousin. "Red! How good of you to come see me before your patrol."

She got up from her desk and came around to give Red a hug. She was the only person I knew that dared to hug her. Even Robin and Marian only ever gave her a kiss on the cheek, but Mother had always treated her as a second daughter—and Red had always allowed it.

"You know I love to see you anytime I can, Aunt Mathilde. You look well. Have you and Commander Poirier set a wedding date?" Red inquired with her characteristic bluntness.

Mother blushed faintly. "Not quite yet, my dear, although we are thinking in December. Perhaps a Yuletide wedding?"

Red nodded. "That would be cheerful. I'll look forward to it."

"Bless you child. I'll threaten Robin to not *dare* send you on assignment over the holiday. I insist you attend. It will probably be here at the castle, but we'd prefer something quiet, just the family. We'll let you know what we come up with."

"Why not use Barnsdale Lodge? Mother would enjoy the company."

"Red, that's a wonderful idea!" Mother exclaimed. "I'll write to her today. It's been far too long since I've seen her, and a wedding at the lodge might be just the thing. I'll just talk to Clement first."

I raised my eyebrows at Red and she shrugged. Her mother *would* probably love such a thing—as long as she wasn't having one of her turns. A knock sounded at the door, followed swiftly by a sweaty soldier.

"Sire! News from Princess Rosebelle. One of her guards just came in range of the moonstones. There's a Pelerine regiment camped at Croiseux. They're planning to attack us tonight. And that's not all." We all glanced at each other, dumbfounded, as he took a quick breath. "A Beast hoard was spotted in the

419

Dower Woods, heading south and numbering in the hundreds. It could be there any minute. The Princess is taking her family to a Lady's Shrine near their house. It's supposed to be defensible."

My consternation at his news lasted only a moment before my brain caught up. "Go next door and send Commander Poirier to me immediately," I barked out. "Then have someone communicate this to General Morvan with my full approval to adjust his plans as he sees fit." I looked at Red briefly, and she nodded. "Tell him that the Red Rider's unit will be leaving to head off the hoard immediately, with the understanding that our reinforcements will follow. Dismissed."

The soldier saluted and then fled from the room.

"Well, I'd better get going if I want to catch a few Beasties before dinner," Red announced with a mocking smile, slamming a fist to her chest in salute before striding out the door. Mother looked as though she might run after her for a moment but refrained. Red never liked proper goodbyes—especially before a battle.

Clement came storming in only a moment later. "I heard the report. I'll be pulling my units for a tighter defense around the castle."

I nodded and looked at my mother. "We need to get the Vigil started immediately. And send word to the infirmaries here and in town to expect casualties."

"I'll handle all that. But Andrus, did you have the healing spell removed between you and Rosebelle?"

An icy knife of fear stabbed through my chest. I had neglected to remove it, and now, if I was injured at all during the coming fight, I would be draining my Rose's life away—possibly killing her. I started laughing suddenly. *My Rose.* The Gypsy Queen's words rung out loudly in my ears.

Prince of Beastmen, Prince in Darkness; true love's kiss unravels the curse. Look for the sign of the rose and flee Asileboix in its darkest hour.

"It *is* her," I said more to myself than to Clement and

Mother. "Rosebelle—she's the Rose from the Romany Queen's foretelling."

My fate was before me—the destiny I had abhorred and steeled myself against all these years.

"My choice is either to drain her life away as I fight,or to abandon my princedom in order to save her life." I laughed again, the sound too loud and a little wild to my ears. *And I'll be free of my curse because I'm going to die in this battle. And with me dies the Asilean line. Maybe that's what it takes to unravel our curse.*

I looked back and forth between Clement and my mother as they stared at each other. "I can't let her die, giving her strength to me in a healing spell. But I won't hide myself away from the fight like a coward."

Mother snapped her eyes over to me. "She's hiding at the ancient shrine there, near Croiseux, isn't that what the messenger said?"

I stared at her dumbly as Clement nodded.

"It has an altar at a spring there. You could use it to break the bond without a healer. It will probably be painful, but it will do it. Just mingle your blood together at the altar, and speak the breaking words. You have enough magecraft to do it," she said, coming around to take my face in hers.

"Go to her. I'll take charge of the civilians. Clement will see to the castle and city security. You've already ordered General Morvan to take full control of the patrol, and Red is on her way to head off the Beasts. Take your unit and go after her. You're not abandoning your people, you're saving their Princess."

Hope blossomed in my chest. I could save her. I *had* to save her. I knew I was going to do it as soon as I realized she was still connected to me, I just hadn't been able to see how.

"Yes. I'll leave immediately. Once I've broken the spell and seen her safe, I'll lead my platoon in a flanking maneuver, see if we can harry the Beasts from both sides. This may actually work!" I declared, surging to my feet with a wave of energy.

"Mother, Clement, you know what to do."

They both bowed their heads to me, and I pulled my mother into a quick hug before dashing out of the room.

Bells were tolling the alarm all over the city as I reached the stables. My platoon was already waiting with their horses, having responded to the call I placed over my moonstone brooch when the messenger had first come. I explained our mission as quickly as possible. Within minutes we were mounted and charging out of the castle gates toward glory—and possibly our deaths.

I smiled grimly. I wasn't afraid to die. I wasn't even afraid of my fate anymore. First I was going to free my Rose. Then I was going to free our people from our curse, taking down as many Beasts with me as I could.

CHAPTER TWENTY-EIGHT

Eddie

My steps slowed as I reached the Manor House, sucking in gulps of air to quiet the growing agitation inside of me. People scurried back and forth, steeped in controlled panic. The regiment's field accommodation was a hive of activity in the distance as soldiers prepared to deploy. My own company was formed up just outside the entrance of the back gardens. I dodged around the chaos of the stables to reach it.

After a quick conversation with LeFeu, I issued orders. Two platoons were to stay at the Manor House to protect its people. The other two platoons would follow me and LeFeu into the woods to meet the Beast hoard before it arrived. I snagged LeFeu's sleeve as our men fell out to prepare for their assignments.

"I saw Belle. Hazel isn't there. She stayed at the castle." LeFeu looked stricken, and I hated to continue, knowing our worst fears were being realized. "They have to be under the influence of a sorcerer. Belle said they know all about the Beast Men and already did when we talked to them in the carriage." I resisted the urge to punch something in frustration, flexing my hand instead. "We need to deal with the situation in front of us, but afterward, we have *got* to find a way to break the enchantment on Rosebelle before she goes back to the castle. Once she's lucid again, she can help us figure out a way to rescue Hazel."

LeFeu shook his head slowly, his brow furrowed, not meeting my eyes. "I don't think there's any spell, Eddie. I think Hazel was trying to tell me that in her own way last time we saw her. She wouldn't allow herself to get in a situation like that, and Belle's the one who's generally in charge of everything and everyone. I couldn't see some control spell working on her for any length of time."

I closed my eyes and put my hands on my head, squeezing my skull in frustration, not believing what I was hearing. "LeFeu. Think of all the completely nonsensical things we saw magic do in the Beast War. I'm sure there's a sorcerer somewhere that could manage to deceive a couple of young women. Those Asileans are evil—magic users and half Beasts! Our ladies need rescuing. Are you with me or not?" I was practically shouting by now, and drawing a few stares.

LeFeu looked at me steadily. "I *am* with you, Eddie. Always."

"Good," I replied, smoothing my hair and turning to lead him toward the stables. Slinging orders out as quickly as possible, I managed to procure mounts for every man leaving with us. We swung into our saddles.

"Let's get moving. If we let these Beasts and Beast Men go unchallenged, they'll wreak havoc on all we hold dear. Take courage, men! Follow me!"

We skirted the edge of Croiseux Manor's grounds, avoiding the other units still forming up and the rush of civilians seeking shelter in the house. Soon we approached the edge of the forest and slowed to weave through the trees, hitting a cart path after a few minutes. *The horses will be a liability in the woods if we come across any Beasts while mounted. We need to make it as close as we can to the approaching hoard before dismounting.*

One of the Army regiments assigned to patrol the forest

came into view on our left. We each slowed as our units hit the path at the same time, and I conferred with their commander about changes in their orders, our heads bowed over a map while I noted the best positions for defense. Communication complete, his unit joined ours and we fanned out along the path, heading north at a bruising gallop.

The gamekeeper's cottage appeared in view through the trees to our right, and we passed it swiftly. About ten minutes later, I judged that we were north of the Dower House as well. The path took a sharp turn and I motioned for those behind me to reduce speed as we navigated it. I knew from our weekly rides that it turned into a crossroads just around the corner. I didn't want to walk directly into an ambush. As our own hoof beats subsided, my ears picked up new ones, sounding directly ahead of us. I gave another signal, then urged my horse around the bend to see what was coming.

The trees thinned toward the actual crossroads and I could see riders in Asilean colors streaking along the road heading east. My eyes lit on one in particular as they passed: Prince Andrus. The sight of him brought my blood to a boil instantly.

Belle must have warned him, and now he's trying to save his own skin by fleeing his castle. Coward. I roared orders to my unit. A thought flashed across my mind. *He could be after Belle. He'll drag her back to the castle and out of safety.* I placed my hand over the pocket containing my lucky ribbon as determination surged through my veins. *Not if I have anything to say about it.*

Darkness fell as we turned to follow them, a full moon edging over the horizon. Its glow offered enough light to see, but I wished we could have faced them during daylight hours. The Asileans had a sizeable lead and didn't notice us behind them until we broke from the trees. Their rear guard looked back, but didn't make any motions to defend themselves. We were too far way to do anything but follow. I let out a shout of rage as I saw them enter the Shrine's courtyard up ahead.

A mist was rolling down from the north, creeping out from the woods and into the low spots. The moon was still unobscured, but it didn't bode well for our fight. One last push of the horses and we spilled into the courtyard of the Shrine as well, through a tumbled-down gap in the thick walls.

I looked wildly for Belle, catching sight of her at the other end of the courtyard, gesturing in my direction while the Beast Prince attempted to pull her toward the tower.

And this is how he treats his Princess. Rage overwhelmed me and I surged towards them. Everything went oddly quiet for for a moment and her words drifted over to me. "...any of your mages can fix the wall then it will be fine. Just do it, and we'll discuss the spell afterward."

Shouts rang out behind me as I converged on them, and they turned, the Beast Prince pushing Belle so she stumbled backward while he reached for his weapon. He was too late. I glanced a blow on his arm with my blade as I rode by, and quickly turned my horse.

"You idiot!" the Prince growled at me, examining his arm, and looking back at Belle where she sat on the ground. He looked up at me as I turned to face him, and I was startled to see that his face was changing right before my eyes. "If you hurt me, you're going to hurt her! And don't you know there are Beasts headed this way? We need to secure the area, not fight each other."

"The only Beasts I see are the ones right in front of my eyes," I spat at him, fury focusing my energy on the Prince in front of me. I spurred my horse forward again. Andrus parried my sword thrust, but didn't try to re-attack, seemingly distracted by the changes he was undergoing.

My leg stung as I came upon him a second time, trying to trample him with my horse. He had gotten a slice in on my calf, but a glancing one. I was gradually forcing him away from Belle, not wanting to risk injury to her while I finished him off. He met my sword strikes defensively and I pressed my advantage, trying desperately to hit him again. The clang of swords meeting reached my ears as our soldiers fell into battle. Belle cried out, but I couldn't discern what she was saying.

Frustrated, I wished she would just get to the tower and safety.

Andrus' body stiffened for a fraction of a second, then he counterattacked ferociously, pushing my sword away with his own and bodily slamming into my horse before spinning and leaping towards Belle. He was fully transformed, still human but with enormous canines on full display as he roared. Muscles bunched, ears changed in shape and tilted forward, covered in brown fur. I couldn't take my eyes off of the horror of his mutated form as I fumbled to get my horse back under control.

My heart cracked in despair. He leaped onto Belle, pushing her back toward the ground, his mouth near her throat. His Beast nature had overtaken him and I was too late to save her. After all of our planning, every effort, all of my pleading with Belle, I was watching her die in front of me, at the hands of her beloved Beast Prince.

A weight slammed into me, knocking me from my horse. I managed to hold onto my sword and scramble to my feet, almost falling again as I put weight on my left leg.

A huge human-sized version of some sort of dog leaped at me again, twisted beyond recognition, its body covered in scars and oozing in places. *A Beast.* They had arrived.

I pressed forward, managing to push it backwards a few steps, snarling as it retreated, when something else slammed into me, my head hitting the ground forcefully. I had the vague impression of an enormous lizard sinking it's jaws into my shoulder as fire radiated out from the bite. My head dropped down, my strength draining rapidly. Between the various legs dashing to and fro in my dimming field of vision, I glimpsed Prince Andrus, still crouched over Belle's motionless body, roaring forcefully enough that anyone who came near him and his prey skittered backwards.

Too late, I thought, and my world went black.

CHAPTER TWENTY-NINE

Andrus

My deafening roar was enough to convince the few Beasts that made it far enough into the courtyard towards us that they had made a mistake. Rosebelle held herself as still as possible beneath me as I maintained a perimeter around us. I lost sight of Marchand when he was taken down by a lizard Beast. He was going to have to take care of himself. My priority was Rosebelle. One of my guards made it over to me, and together we beat back the other Beasts long enough to bundle Rosebelle inside the Tower. "Lock the door until we're finished out here," I growled and she nodded as she pulled it shut.

Turning, I jumped back into the fray, fighting my way to where Captain Riviere was attempting to close the gates. I rammed one fully closed and held it there with my shoulder. Some sort of rodent Beast tore at the muscles pressed against the bars. Captain Riviere and one of his men pushed the other into place, sliding a rusty bar lock across before casting a reinforcement spell into it. We stepped back and watched for a moment to confirm it would hold.

"Next priority is to seal the gap in the wall," I barked at

Riviere, pausing to examine my shoulder. "I have a mage-level alchemist with me. Join your power to his and we'll cover you while you fix the gap."

Riviere nodded and rushed to the opening. I turned just in time to thrust my sword into a Beast that was leaping at us, killing it instantly. The Beast's forward momentum knocked me back several steps but I kept my balance.

Pulling my sword free, I steadied myself, surveying the scene before me. With the gate closed, the only other entry point was the tumbled-down section of the wall. Several of my men had engaged the remaining Beasts inside the courtyard with what looked like competent assistance from some of Marchand's men. I still didn't see Marchand, but I hoped the seriousness of the attack had dampened his desire to kill me. I had bigger fish to fry.

Joining the fray at the wall, I took turns assisting the soldiers protecting the gap and lending magic to the mages slowly building and cementing closed the gap. Luckily there were enough stones laying around that they didn't have to try and locate any—or worse, try to make some out of pebbles and raw magic. It still took fifteen long minutes. By the time they had built a solid foundation in the gap, half of my soldiers had jumped through the opening in a sortie to hunt down the last of the hoard we had faced.

Those that stayed by me warily eyed the Pelerine men. We had ended up fighting together against the Beasts, but we had started our acquaintance by trading blows. I still didn't see Marchand, but my eyes lit on LeFeu, gathering some of his men together to attend to the wounded.

I signaled to Riviere as he finished with the wall, and he fell into step behind me, obviously tired from the magic use.

"LeFeu!" I called, my voice ringing out in the courtyard. "We are not enemies, though you fear us. We have a common threat in front of us. Will you work with us to defeat them, or do I need to deal with you now, before you become a liability?" I couldn't keep the snarl from my face and voice as I stopped in front of him.

He stared at me in the eye for a moment, considering. The bear in me didn't like the direct eye contact and chafed to put him in his place, but I pushed it aside. A flash of despair passed over LeFeu's face, replaced with bullish determination. To my surprise he threw a salute.

"Haven't been able to find my superior officer, so I'm in charge of these men. Allow me to organize my wounded and I'll be glad to take counsel with you on our next move. Hazel speaks of you as honorable. I'll trust her judgment. You fight with valor, though I can't say I'm comfortable with all of the..." he gestured toward my contorted features lamely. "But I'll vouch that we'll suspend our prejudice for the moment, Sire."

I nodded to him, impressed and relieved. "Good man. Get your wounded lined up in order of urgency. My healer will attend to them shortly." Ordering Captain Riviere to look to our own men, I turned toward the castle door, striking my fist against it and yelling for Rosebelle.

*　*　*

She pushed the door open and I crushed her into my arms. She clung to me just as tightly. I shoved forward, pulling the door closed behind me and half dragging her down a set of stairs to where the ancient altar and spring would be located. At the bottom of the steps, thick oak doors sat under an eroded but still intricately decorated stone lintel. Muscling them open, I hauled her into the chapel behind me.

"We need to break this healing bond between us. Now," I demanded as the doors swung shut.

"Oh no," she protested, "you need it now more than ever. You're going back out into battle aren't you?"

"You don't understand!" I shouted in frustration, pressing my hand against a wound on my thigh as blood seeped through my trousers.

Mulishness and concern mingled with the look of exasperation she shot me as she caught sight of it. She reached down to tear a piece of her petticoat. Motioning for me to take off my left arm bracer, she pressed it to a wound I hadn't even known was there.

I continued on, my eyes boring into her, willing her to understand and agree. "The bond was set up to draw power from you to me. It will continue to pull from you to heal my tiredness, my wounds, all of it. You may even feel some of the things I experience, depending on how strong the connection is. The magic will drain *all* of your strength to heal me. It will drain you until you die, and if I haven't healed by then, I will die too. I *will not* allow it."

She had dipped her head to examine some of my other cuts and I glared at the top of it, waiting for her to acquiesce. Her shoulders heaved as she took a deep breath and released. She looked up, fear and vulnerability displayed in her eyes.

"It's not your choice, Andrus." Her voice was quiet. "I don't have much. I am not a skilled fighter, as you are intimately aware, or used to bearing much physical pain. I'm not trained as the Forest Guard to fight or give my life's blood for our country. But if keeping this spell in place is what I can do to help you, then I will do it. If giving you every ounce of what little I have within me keeps you alive, then I will do it. Probably not with much grace or fortitude, but with all my heart, and sincerely."

I scoffed. "Rosebelle, you must be losing your mind if you think I am going to allow this. I should have severed the connection weeks ago, but it was my own selfishness that wanted to keep it to keep you close. We're ending it now. I won't take your life from you."

Pain flared in her eyes, but was replaced by a strange earnest light that didn't dim. "You may not want me, but you're going to get me. I'd rather die today, giving you everything I have, than live without you. And if one of us is to leave this life, I would rather it be me."

I scowled at her, furious at her words. "I left my castle, my country, *our people*, to come and find you! To break the connection and put you somewhere safe until this is over!" I switched tactics, attempting to help her see reason. "If I die today, you won't be destitute. You will have a dower portion large enough to establish yourself in Asileboix, Pelerin, Spindle... anywhere you like! You can live in comfort and happiness for the rest of your life without the pressures of ruling. Think about this logically, Rose."

Her eyes blazed into a golden fury. "You must be the stupidest person alive if you think I'll take even a portion of that money after you're gone. If you sever our connection and you end up dying, I'll rally as many Forest Guards as are still alive and I will march right into that Wasteland. I'll fight as many Beasts as I can before I'm killed, which we both know won't be many. So, in an effort to use what little resources I have most effectively, you can just shut your mouth, get moving, and plan on not dying today!"

Her hand tightened around my wrist where she was still holding a cloth over my wound and I hissed quietly. I wrenched my arm away from her, grabbing her shoulders.

"Why would you say such a thing?!" I wanted to crush her to my chest almost as much as I wanted to shake some sense into her. Tears filled her eyes, spilling down her cheeks as she stood there, hands down by her side. Her voice was shaky as she replied.

"Because I'd rather take my revenge on as many Beasts as I can and join you in death than live an entire life without you."

My heart felt like it leapt off a cliff, diving halfway down before finding wings and soaring up, higher than I'd ever been before. Our connection throbbed and I could see a golden haze enveloping us. Roughly, I pushed her backward, my right hand sliding up her neck to the base of her skull, cushioning her head before I pressed her up against the rugged stone wall behind her.

I crushed my lips down, tasting salt from her tears mixed with the tang of blood from a cut on her lip. She gasped, then slid her arms around my back, pressing her lips to mine forcefully. I staggered back a step, my leg slipping on the crumbling edge of the channel leading out of the chancel and plunging into the stream bed. The shock of the cold water forced me to break the kiss before we both tipped into the fountain.

Gingerly, I shook water droplets off my boot with a husky laugh, gently nudged Rosebelle back a few steps so I could climb out of the stream. She gazed at me silently, tears still pooling in her eyes. I cradled her face with my hands, rubbing the tear tracks dry with my thumbs.

"Why tears?" I asked tenderly.

She said nothing, only putting her hands on my own face, with the gentleness of a feather, and pulling my face down to hers.

Her kiss was soft and warm, her lips smooth. She deepened it and I tasted the strength of her then. She was right; she wasn't a strong fighter, nor a soldier. But she was strong like steel inside. Implacable. Incisive. An anchor, unmoving in storm-tossed seas, tethering those she loved to the only stable land around. I wanted to take that from her, make her lose the need for strength, and just be free.

Just be Rose, my Rose. The one I had been fearing for years, resenting the idea that I would overthrow everything for her sake. Now I was happy to do it. Happy to lose myself—lose my life—if it meant that she would have room to blossom and grow.

Someone burst through the door behind us and I whirled, breaking the kiss and dropping into a defensive position with Rosebelle behind me, her hands fluttering against my shoulders. I relaxed after realizing it was one of my guards. I couldn't help a growl of frustration at being interrupted.

"Sire, excuse me. Message received through the stones. The castle horns have sounded a rout."

"Go," I ordered, my voice rasping. "I'll be there in a minute." He left, pulling the door shut behind him. I whirled on Rosebelle. My heart felt bruised as I took in the sight of her. Her hair mussed, gown torn. Tear tracks glistened on her cheeks, blood smeared across her lips. This wasn't how I wanted my last picture of her to be.

She spoke first. The steel I knew to be inside giving more strength to her words than I had at the moment.

"Go, Andrus. Don't worry about me, I'll be safe here now that you've helped us secure the wall. But do *not* ask me to undo what has been done."

Desperation boiled up in my chest. I couldn't be the cause of suffering for her. The only reason she wasn't suffering now was because of our proximity and the quick healing that occurred during my shift. I could already feel the wound in my leg closing.

"Rosebelle, don't make me the reason you die!"

"Don't make me the reason you don't survive," she replied, tracing the line of my jaw with her index finger.

Inspiration struck me like a bolt of lightning. I grabbed her hand with a grim smile.

"Rose! I won't make you undo the spell, but I can modify it if you'll let me. I have just enough magecraft to do it, especially during a shift."

She stared at me with furrowed brow, uncomprehending.

"You remember the blood magic book you brought back from your parent's house?" She nodded skeptically. "Well, after you left your research with me, I read through it. One of the rituals it discussed reminded me of an old Romany custom I've heard about, an ancient rite used in marriage ceremonies. I doubt it's done anymore. But our archive has a description, a commentary by a respectable scholar who witnessed it and studied its effects. Portions of the spell are similar to the healing channel the Doctor opened between us... anyway, what I'm trying to say is, I'm sure I can modify it. Will you let me try?"

BELLE & BEAST

"Andrus," she said in a patient tone, taking my other hand in her own as well. "You haven't told me what the spell does."

I blinked at her. "Yes, that might be helpful."

She laughed softly, nodding.

"It's a soul link. I can use the channel already opened between us to link our spirits together, instead of just our bodies. It's supposed to make us both stronger since we will be mingling our spirits, and it would supersede the healing spell, so theoretically one of us should be able to break off the bond if the other dies."

Her eyes were alive with curiosity. "Can you really do that?"

"I'm sure I can. The spell work isn't difficult, it's just not something that's done anymore. It's a serious commitment, and a serious bond, but if we somehow survive, we can deal with any issues later... if you're willing."

She nodded and I tugged her toward the altar, maneuvering so we faced each other across it.

"You'll have to repeat some of the words after me at the end. I'll squeeze your hand to let you know when." I closed my eyes, recalling the pages of the book I had read long ago and making sure I could remember. The spell was simple enough, but required a lot of power and an existing connection, usually a bond of truly deep love. In our case, we also had the healing spell that connected us. I pricked the small scars on our fingers from our wedding ceremony and started the incantation.

A glow emanated from our joined hands, coalescing into twinkling orbs. They multiplied faster than I could track, swirling and hovering in the air until we were enshrouded in them. When I came to the unity vow, I squeezed Rosebelle's hand and she repeated after me. As we spoke the final words of power, the lights blazed forth all at once, blinding us.

They contracted into a single golden orb, then split into two. One floated toward my chest, the other toward Rosebelle's. We watched, transfixed, as they touched the surface of our skin just over our hearts and sunk into our chests. My heart flared with warmth, like the heat of a fire on a cold wet day, and with it, an awareness.

It was Rosebelle. An awareness of her that I had never had before. I felt excited and full of wonder, then realized that those weren't my feelings. Her hand tightened on mine and I looked up, meeting her eyes. She smiled broadly, her face lit up with the emotions I had sensed.

"You felt concerned, didn't you?" she asked, awe tinging her voice. "I felt it! I swear it was you I felt."

"I know. I felt you too. Wonder and curiosity, and just something that was *you*." I replied, moving around the altar and tugging her close. "The books I read described successful couples as being able to sense each other's emotions over large distances, and even fragments of thoughts sometimes. It's supposed to be easier if we're physically connected."

She stepped up to me, dropping a light kiss on my lips. I leaned my forehead down against hers and just basked in the glow I could feel coming from her heart. I gave myself a moment, then broke away.

"Normally this requires a horrible sounding ceremony to break the bond, and we would need additional mages to do it. But bonded couples should be able to break it in a moment of self-sacrifice for the other. If I'm dying, I will do everything I can to break the connection. I don't know if you'll be able to feel it or not. I hope not," I explained, my voice breaking.

"I understand," she said, smoothing my brow with her thumbs. "My only solution to our problems is this: don't die. Go out, win the day, drive the Beasts back, and do what you must. But come back to me. Come back and live a long life with me. Please."

I let out a breath, dangerously close to breaking. Her amber eyes glowed. A desire to abandon everything happening outside and lose myself in her increased rapidly. Instead, I put my hands on either side of her face and kissed her gently, trying to imbue it with the depth of my feeling for her. I pulled away and left, not looking back.

BELLE & BEAST

* * *

Outside, my men were ready to go. A sizeable number of LeFeu's men were mounted and waiting beside them. I mentally shook myself and stalked over.

LeFeu addressed me as I approached. "Sire, I'm requesting that you allow us to ride with you to the castle. I'm leaving a portion of my men here to guard the Shrine and the wounded, but the rest of us are willing to fight alongside you."

"You have proved yourselves as warriors. If you can keep up, we'll be happy to have you. If you betray us, you'll die," I said simply.

He swallowed heavily, and I could see some of his men glance at each other, but he saluted me in acknowledgment.

I conferred with Captain Riviere, who would be staying behind in charge of the Princess' safety, then led the way out of the gates.

With the addition of LeFeu's men, we had almost a full company as we headed back into the forest, rushing toward the rout as fast as we could. *At least I got to see my Rose, safe, one last time.* My connection to her glowed in my chest like a banked fire, giving me strength. Not far into the woods, we came upon a squad of Pelerine soldiers locked in battle with pack of Beasts. We fell upon the Beasts without mercy, dispatching them all in the space of a few minutes, to the shock of the Pelerine soldiers.

LeFeu had an argument with their commanding officer while we regrouped, but he seemed to talk some sense into them. The officer approached me, a pace behind LeFeu, and offered his support. I accepted it, giving him the same terms I gave LeFeu. We started forward, my troops in the lead, followed by LeFeu's and our newest allies.

We pushed our horses faster than ever, using magic to speed our way, but every minute felt excruciating. Finally the towers and walls came into sight, and my heart skipped a beat. The massive curtain wall had been breached. Beasts were everywhere in the fields between it and the city wall, trampling crops and tearing apart every building they came across. I jumped from my exhausted horse, slapping it on the rump to send it away, and rushed forward on foot, my men doing the same. We poured through East Gate, surprising the Beasts just inside.

I roared a challenge, pushing a thread of magic into my voice so that it echoed across the plain. Heads swiveled everywhere I looked, and my men fanned out, preparing for the onslaught as Beasts sensed an easier challenge than the inner walls. I hoped we would tie them up long enough for General Morvan's soldiers to muster.

We fought, the Pelerines at our backs, hour by hour. Many of my soldiers fell, succumbing to wounds faster than our two healers could attend to them. The Pelerines fought more valiantly than I expected, protecting our backs from the slow trickle of Beasts still coming in from the forest.

I had never seen such a coordinated effort from our enemy before and in the back of my mind it worried me. I fought mechanically, pressing forward from one Beast to the next, retreating when several came at me at once. We were slowly being pushed back against the remains of the curtain wall, having been maneuvered away from the East Gate inch by inch. A large number of the Pelerines had been separated from us on our right flank, and we were suddenly fighting in a small knot, another wave of the enemy heading toward us.

We're about to be overwhelmed, I thought, my feelings detached. Just as the first of the new wave of Beasts reached us, a deep horn sounded, shaking the air. A call rang out behind us.

"For Spindle! For The White Queen!"

Relief rippled through my soldiers, almost tangibly. We pressed forward, a last surge of energy enabling us to put down our attackers as soldiers from Spindle poured through the gates, cutting through the ranks of Beasts like a knife. I rallied my guards, exhaustion dragging at the edges of my vision, and we made our way up to the castle, fighting stray Beasts as we went. By the time we reached the city gates, my vision was dark, and I made it only a few steps before falling down, gratitude for our victory warring with concern for Rosebelle as I drifted out of consciousness.

CHAPTER THIRTY

Belle

Dawn broke over the horizon. I watched alone, standing on a small lookout area on the top of the tower. Exhaustion tugged at every fiber of my being, the chill of what remained of the night seeping into my bones. I wrapped my shawl closer to ward it off.

As the sky lightened, smoke trails became visible, drifting up from the woods to the west, the only indicator of the battle Andrus had rushed into.

I felt nothing from our new connection. I couldn't stem a steadily rising tide of anxiety. He had said something about distance playing a part in its sensitivity. I worried he had found a way to sever it as he died, that I had been too far away to know it. I covered my heart with ice-cold hands.

The door behind me creaked and I turned to find Mrs. Comfry carrying a steaming mug, the scent of tea proceeding her. She set it on one of the stones in the crenelation beside me, fishing out a container of biscuits from her apron pocket. I smiled weakly at her in gratitude and she clucked her tongue. "That's a tale as old as time, dear."

I cocked my head, confused. "What is?"

"True love, of course," she replied, a smile creasing her face. "It means your heart doesn't beat only to keep you alive anymore. It beats to see the one you love again. And when you're parted, every nerve is tingling until you can reassure yourself that he's well. Even to the point of ignoring the miracle of my best biscuits and tea in the middle of a ruined ancient shrine!"

I laughed and reached for the mug, sipping some of her bracing brew. "Am I that transparent?"

Mrs. Comfry chuckled and patted my hand before heading back downstairs.

Let me see him again, please. I just want to see him one more time. I looked out over the swaying trees, willing them to reveal their secrets. A moment later, a band of horsemen galloped tiredly out from the wood line and my heart leaped in my chest.

Rushing down the stairs, I made it into the courtyard as the soldiers stopped outside the wall. A tough-looking woman with tattoos on her right cheek and a sword strapped to her side was speaking with Captain Riviere. She looked up as I ran towards the gate.

Although she was visibly exhausted, she looked fierce as she turned her eyes on me. I suddenly felt the weight of my incompetence as a fighter. This was the type of woman that would make a perfect leader of Asileboix. Tough, competent, fearless, and commanding.

"Is this Princess Rosebelle?" the woman asked Captain Riviere, her voice hoarse. The captain nodded as I closed the distance between us, shoving my sudden feelings of inadequacy down.

"I'm Red, cousin to your husband. I'm honored to meet you," she said, not bothering to bow or even nod her head.

"Princess Mathilde has sent for you. The battle is won. My mission is to clear these woods up to the border. I'm unable to escort you at the moment, unless you can wait another day."

I shook my head dumbly and she gave me a terse nod.

"Then go with the Lady." She made to turn her horse and I heard my voice ring out before I even decided to speak.

441

"Wait! What of Andrus? Is he alive? Is he injured?" I asked, desperation coloring voice.

Red frowned and shook her head slightly. "I don't know. I hope so, but I didn't have time to check."

A sudden smile lit up her face, and I was struck by her brutal beauty. "The last I saw, he was leading a charge that turned the tide against the assault on the city. It was a wonderous sight. We'll sing songs of it for generations." Her smile dimmed as she continued. "His company was overwhelmed, but the distraction worked. I'm sorry."

She dipped her head in a small bow and turned, leading her soldiers off once more. I watched her go, turning back to Captain Riviere when he cleared his throat.

"Excuse me, Your Highness. There are enough Pelerine soldiers here to leave with your family until they feel safe enough to return home. We can escort you back to the castle immediately."

"Yes, let's go. I'll just say goodbye to my parents and then we can leave."

Rushing back into the tower, I went up to the first landing, entering the room where my parents, Rochelle, Thomas, Holly, and Mr. and Mrs. Comfry had slept. Everyone was up and talking in low voices except Mr. Comfry, who was snoring off to one side, and Holly, who was curled up next to where Rochelle and Thomas sat hand in hand.

"I... I have to leave," I announced lamely, butterflies multiplying in my chest as my fear for Andrus grew. "The battle was won and I'm needed back at the castle. I'll send word tomorrow to let you know how things go. Be safe." I walked around to each, giving kisses and quick hugs. To Thomas I gave my hand.

"Take care of my sister. And don't wait until her birthday." His eyes widened in surprise. With one last hug to Rochelle, I swept out of the tower.

CHAPTER THIRTY-ONE

Andrus

Seeing her was a balm to my unsettled soul. Safe. The warmth of that word traveled down to my toes. Rosebelle bent over my hand, pressing a kiss to it.

I love you. The phrase echoed in my mind and I couldn't tell if I was thinking it or she was saying it. Slowly I separated my thoughts from her words.

"I love you. You're stronger than this. Come back to me." Her whispers brushed against my skin. I felt a tear drop onto my hand.

A smile grew on my face. *She loves me.* Although my body was drained, my soul soared.

She must have felt the change in me because she whipped her head up, gaping in shock before scowling.

"Beast! You're sitting here letting me go on and on without saying anything?!" Her hand tightened on mine and I laughed, cutting off quickly when I noticed her exhaustion.

"How are you feeling?" she asked tentatively, making to pull her hand away. I tightened my grip, not letting her escape.

"My body has never felt worse," I replied hoarsely, "but my heart has never felt better hearing the the love of my life say she loves me too."

A sob escaped her and she started crying again. I tugged her closer, gingerly. She dried her tears and gave me a quick kiss on the lips before resting her forehead on mine.

"I thought I would never see you again," I admitted, suddenly serious as she pulled away.

"I told you to come back to me," she accused, smoothing my covers. I followed her movements with my eyes, peace soaking into my heart.

"Do you remember when I told you about the Gypsies being present for my sister's wedding?" I prompted Belle, changing topics. She nodded, her eyes curious.

"The Gypsy Queen offered to tell my fate after my coronation. It's not something you refuse, so I agreed. She told me that true love's kiss would unravel the curse. I would be free when I left my kingdom in its hour of need: for the sake of a beautiful rose. I thought you were the rose. And I thought I would be free because I would die after saving you."

Rosebelle blanched and gripped my hand again.

I smiled at her. "Maybe instead of my death, freedom means living openly with our true nature. Not trying to hide it from the world. Using it as a tool, like you've suggested."

She pressed a kiss to my palm. "That may be so. And our kiss in the shrine was certainly the stuff of legend," she quipped with a grin, sitting up a little straighter. "But maybe we can aim a little higher than just living with it. If we work together, perhaps we can discover the source of the Shift and why it's tied to the full moon. Even if we don't find it, I don't mind having a tame Beast to order around when I like."

A laugh escaped me. "I would be a fool to refuse to work with you now. If anyone can figure this out, it will be you."

She blushed at the compliment and I enjoyed watching her squirm for a minute before reality hit me.

"I assume everything is under control since we're sitting here mooning over each other, but how is Mother? And Clement? I lost track of Eddie and LeFeu during the fighting.

BELLE & BEAST

What about Pelerin and Spindle?" I started to push myself up, but Rosebelle put her hand on me, guiding me back down to the pillows.

"Mathilde and Clement are both fine, we have everything well in hand. You've been unconscious, healing for about a day, and I've been either here or assisting in the city with clean up and aid. LeFeu is here in the infirmary as well. We haven't seen any sign of Eddie." She sighed. "Thank you for trying not to hurt him when he fought you."

I offered a sad smile. "He was a skilled warrior. I just wish he had focused on the Beasts instead of me."

A meditative silence stretched between us.

After a moment, I grunted. "If representatives of Spindle, Sherwood, and Pelerin are all here, we need to take advantage of the opportunity to create some balance between us."

An artful smile grew on Rose's face. "I was thinking the same thing. In fact, I've arranged for a meeting with everyone before they leave. Red helped me badger the other two into it. Now that you're awake, let's plan. But oh, let me run and get you a tray first!"

She stood up and raced to the door, turning to smile at me before leaving. I put my head back on my pillow and smiled too.

* * *

A touch of steel filtered through my connection with Rosebelle, and I couldn't help sitting up a little straighter. She was in her element with this meeting, and her anticipation was infectious. I glanced at Red, sitting beside one of her healers. She was the official representative for Sherwood, but tended to let others speak for her. Her forbidding presence was about as diplomatic as she got.

"I don't see how the bonds of trust can be repaired between our two nations," the Pelerine representative, Monsieur

Beauchamp, was saying. They had sent a diplomat directly from their royal court to attend the meeting, and from the sour look on General Des Concordes face as he sat next to him, they disagreed on something. My sources told me that the General was virulently anti-Asilean, so I imagined the Pelerine court was going to fold to many of our suggestions if his discontent was any indicator.

"Indeed," Rosebelle's voice drifted across the table, soft and concerned, but with a touch of asperity to it. "The Asilean people have been guarding Pelerin quietly and without complaint for hundreds of years. As someone who grew up in Pelerin myself, I know the dishonor we do them firsthand. It will take a great leap of faith for the Asilean people to be able to trust those who scorn their honorable self-sacrifice. But since they are willing and already extending the hand of peace, don't you agree that we must all do the same?"

Neatly done, I thought as the delegates all nodded—except for the General.

"And again, we want to thank the people of Spindle for their help in our hour of need. It's so comforting to know we can rely on our long friendship with your country." She exchanged regal nods with the representatives from Spindle, and I saw the Pelerines stiffen out of the corner of my eye.

"And last, but certainly not least, our sisters and brothers from Sherwood, whom we count as family. Your contribution in pushing back the Beast hoard cannot be overstated." She sent a soft smile toward Red, who put a fist over her heart in salute. The two of them had started a tentative friendship over the last few days and I was curious to see how it unfolded.

"The reports we've received from you have indicated increased activity along the Wasteland. Is this true?" a Spindalian representative asked Rosebelle.

She turned to me. "I will have to defer to my husband to answer any questions of that nature. But before I do, please allow me to express my gratitude again for the way you *all* came to our aid. Of course, I am so happy to have a chance to see my birth country coming into an alliance with my new country. It signals great things for the future of our continent." She gave me an angelic smile, and I could feel her self-satisfied amusement as she settled back into her chair.

I returned her smile, then focused back on the delegates in front of me.

"Indeed we have seen increased activity—Sherwood has as well. We've both experienced attacks that seemed coordinated, just within the last few months. As you all know, they're a fearsome opponent, but one reason we've been able to keep them at bay is because they are driven by their animal instincts. They usually have very little capability for working together. If that is starting to change, we'll all be in trouble."

Red's counterpart chimed in, detailing some of the behavior observed in Sherwood. When she finished, I decided to press hard on the Pelerine delegation for answers as to their regiment's presence and to report Marchand's attack on me and my men prior to the Beasts' arrival. After Rosebelle's sunny beginning, they appeared unsettled at my sudden anger.

"Edouard Marchand was not acting under any orders from the Pelerine government, I can assure you. We would never authorize such an attack on the reigning monarch of a neighboring country. Our King would never countenance undermining another ruling family: such a precedent would surely be dangerous. It's unthinkable!" Monsieur Beauchamp squeaked, hands twitching in the air. "I understand Captain Marchand is missing at the moment. If he is found, we will, of course, pursue justice in this matter. I can assure you that we will treat it with the gravity it deserves."

Ah, so they mean to make him the martyr for their eagerness to invade. Not altogether surprising. I nodded solemnly, pretending that their pronouncements satisfied me.

We ended the meeting soon afterward, Rosebelle escorting the Pelerine delegation to the stables where their carriage was waiting, no doubt seasoning her conversation with ideas they would think were their own later on. I chuckled to myself as

I watched her go, then turned back to Red and the Spindalian representatives.

"I'm glad I have a moment with you both alone." They shot me curious looks and I folded my arms in front of my chest. "You both know of my research. Rosebelle has been conducting some of her own, and we may have an interesting development in understanding the cause of our Shifts, although we're still putting the pieces together. We need copies of any books or documents outlining the Red Queen's connection to the Asilean Royal Family. We believe it may have something to do with blood magic that is targeted to certain families. Any information would help, no matter how obscure. The better we understand our own Shift, the more we may come to understand the Beasts as well."

After a brisk discussion about our research, we all parted ways. Red gave me a tight hug and promised to see me for my Mother's wedding, if not before, then left to report back to Robin in Sherwood. The exhaustion I had been feeling all morning swept over me like a wave, and admitting defeat, I made my way up to my chambers to rest.

CHAPTER THIRTY-TWO

Belle

After waving off the Pelerine and Spindalian delegations, followed by a brief goodbye with Red, I made my way to the infirmary. Many of the patients had already been released, but some required more complex healing regimes. I visited with each to boost morale.

The last patient was in the back corner of the large room. I came around the partition just in time to see LeFeu lift Hazel's hand to his lips, bringing forth a flush that matched her strawberry blonde hair. I couldn't help feeling a little satisfaction at seeing someone else blush for a change.

Clearing my throat to announce my arrival, I dragged an additional chair over to LeFeu's bed and sat down.

"How are you today, Henri?" I inquired innocently, shooting Hazel a sly glance to let her know I had seen all.

"Better than I ever could have hoped," LeFeu replied, moving his feet back and forth restlessly under the covers. "Thought I was done for. When I realized the Doc had saved my life, I thought it was a given that I would lose my legs. Now here I am, able to move them already. She says I can try walking tomorrow." His face lit up as he glanced at Hazel. She gazed back at him, teary eyed and beaming.

"Wonderful! As you can see, there are many benefits to magic use that are never discussed in Pelerin!" I said cheekily. "But really, I'm glad you're healing so well."

He looked over at me soberly. "Hazel and I were just talking. I'd like to petition the Prince to allow me to move here—if you think he would allow it. My case is weak, I know, since we attacked him at the Shrine. But Hazel thinks he would consider it. Would he?"

"I can give you permission to move here just as much as he can. I would love to have you here, if you've really changed your mind about the Asileans. But Andrus was impressed with your conduct in the battle. He'll be happy to gain you as a citizen."

LeFeu cracked a smile, a rare occurrence. I almost fell out of my chair in shock.

"That would be the making of me," he rumbled quietly.

Hazel burst out, joy threading through her voice. "You ought to be the first to know, Belle. Henri just asked me to be his wife. I agreed, of course!"

I jumped out of my chair, squealing in excitement, throwing my arms around Hazel and giving LeFeu a kiss on the cheek. I settled back down into my seat, vowing not to disturb the other patients with further displays of giddiness.

"Congratulations! When will you have the wedding? And where? We could have it in the chapel here and invite your families to stay at the castle! Now that our secret is out in the open, we can have more visitors without fear of being discovered."

Hazel laughed and held up her hands. "Rosebelle, we've been engaged for maybe five minutes. First we need to get Henri well again, then we can figure out the details."

I grinned sheepishly, jumping as Mathilde's voice rang out behind me. "There you are Rosebelle! I came in here to lift morale among the patients, only to find you had already done so. You've had a long few days as well, my dear, you need to rest."

"I'll admit that I'm a little tired. Perhaps I'll go rest if you don't need anything?"

She shook her head.

"Oh, Belle, I completely forgot!" Hazel exclaimed as I turned to leave. She fished a note out of her pocket. "Andrus asked me to give this to you when I came with the carriage, you know, to fetch your father when we thought he was ill. It's probably old news, but just in case."

I grabbed the letter, then waved goodbye to everyone, making my way slowly up to my chambers. Nodding to the guardsman on duty at the end of the hall, I entered my rooms, kicking off my shoes in the dressing room and removing my jewelry before settling in front of my fire. I pulled open Andrus' note.

My Rose - Hazel told me about your father. I'm preparing the infirmary to receive him if he's well enough to be moved. Our healers will be ready. I pray he's well enough to come here. If he isn't, so long as he lives, I'll send Doctor Moreau along with Hazel to see if there's anything she can do discreetly at the Dower House. Do not give up hope. Come home as soon as you are able. - With Love, Your Very Own Beast.

I smiled at his thoughtfulness, and especially at the use of my nickname for him at the end.

He loves me, I thought, suddenly giddy again. I folded the note back up and set it on my coffee table. Sighing over our tentative new relationship wasn't going to help me rest, so my eyes searched for something to settle my mind, lighting on a pile of papers I had been working on earlier. Pulling them toward me, I found the place I had left off and started reviewing the last few lines. A rustling sounded from my bedroom, followed by Andrus' voice.

"Rose? Is that you?"

"In here!" I called and turned my head to watch him limp through my bedroom door.

"I suddenly felt giddy and wondered if that was you since I

was laying down with a heat plaster on my leg; not something to be giddy about, really." He limped over to sit on the settee next to me.

I moved a stack of books just before he flattened them and beamed. "Hazel and Henri are engaged!"

"Ah, I take it back, now I do have something to be giddy about," he replied dryly. I smacked him with a book.

"He wants to ask you for permission to live here. I told him he'll be approved, but I think he feels he owes you. You will approve him, won't you?"

"Of course. We'll always have a place for warriors like him."

Andrus ruminated thoughtfully, settling back against the couch. "He's a blacksmith, isn't he? Can't have too many of those. I wonder if he has any magical talent."

"LeFeu?! Don't hold your breath," I retorted skeptically. "Oh, and Hazel gave me your letter. Thank you." I pressed a kiss to his cheek. He slipped his arm around my shoulders, pulling me against his side.

"For what? What letter?" he asked, bewildered.

I nudged him. "The one you wrote when we thought my father was ill. Thank you for going to all that trouble."

"Of course. I'm glad he wasn't actually ill, although I could have done without the regiment of soldiers and the Beast hoard. Your father doesn't do anything by halves, does he?"

I rolled my eyes and he chuckled, settling deeper into the couch and propping his leg up on the table in front of us. I started back on my research and we sat in silence for some time.

"You know," his voice yanked me out of an interesting paragraph, and I turned to him, eyebrow lifted in annoyance. "The Royal Tower should be completed tomorrow. We could move into it next week if you like."

I stilled, suddenly nervous. "Is that what you would like?"

"By the Lady, yes! But what about you?"

"Obviously! I've been wanting to for ages!" I declared, heat rising on my face.

He grinned, pressing a gentle kiss to my lips, which I deepened quickly, leaning into him. He hissed, and I pulled back.

"What is it?"

"You leaned into my bad shoulder," he said, wincing.

"I forgot! I'm sorry." I settled back into my seat. "I'll behave, you go back to resting." Butterflies tangled in my stomach as I tried to find my place again and he chuckled, leaning his head back.

"Hopefully LeFeu will adjust quickly. From your stories of their camaraderie, he must be missing Marchand. I know he feels responsible for not looking for him right after the battle at the Shrine. Working through that grief and living in a new country won't be easy."

I paused in my reading again, a wave of sadness mellowing my former joy. "Yes, I've been wondering what happened Eddie. They didn't find his body. I wonder if he's injured somewhere, not able to send word."

"I hope he's okay too, but just to be clear, I will *not* be giving him permission to emigrate to Asileboix," Andrus growled.

"Well, I should think not!" I replied indignantly. "I doubt he'd want to live here, but still. I won't be forgiving him for attacking you anytime soon. His best hope is that he gets a slap on the wrist and stays at his beloved Croiseux. He'll be happy there, which I won't begrudge him. But if I had to see him regularly, I'd lose my temper."

Andrus laughed again, pulling up a blanket and leaning comfortably against me. I went back to my reading.

"Of course the matriarch of our beloved Asilean royal family, the Red Queen—sometimes referred to as the Red Lady, or the Lady of the Woods—has gifted her descendants with her own magical powers, much diluted due to their mortal nature. It is this power which first enabled the Queen of Hearts to teach Shifting to humankind before her downfall. It remains to a certain extent in those of purer bloodlines."

I shot straight up, startling Andrus. "This is it! I think

I've found the key!" I said, shoving the book in front of him and distracting him with a kiss. "This is the start of how we unravel your curse!"

EPILOGUE

Knowledge of pain entered my mind. Not pain itself, but the understanding that pain was occurring. My entire body was lit up. Everywhere the light touched, fire ignited. A strange dream to have. Definitely not normal. *The war is over. I should be dreaming of blue skies and peace.* I tried to bully my mind toward a picture of home. A fresh wave of white hot light swept over me instead, radiating from a wound in my shoulder.

A wound in my shoulder. My eyes snapped open and it took every ounce of self-control I possessed to strangle the cry rising up in my throat. Pinpricks of agony were everywhere. I felt hot, feverish. Turning my head towards the shoulder that hurt the worst, I could see rivulets of blood gushing from it, the skin torn and mangled. One of my hands felt fuzzy and indistinct. My eyes searched and found my left arm trailing behind me at an odd angle. That's when I realized I was being dragged.

Craning my neck the other way, I was treated to a view of my knees. Beyond my knees, an enormous scaly neck and shoulders, over which my legs disappeared. I was being hauled, upside down, by a lizard-like Beast almost as large as I was.

I had seen lizard Beasts before but never up close. They didn't seem to be as common as the canine or feline varieties. Its skin was greenish gray, leathery in patches, and had long stretches of scales in others. Its ears were at an odd angle and very small, but looked almost human. *In fact*, I squinted, *yes those are earrings.* The ear closest to me had three hoops in it of varying sizes.

The back of my head bounced against a log on the ground and brought a moment of clarity to my thinking. I needed to escape. *What are my options?* I closed my eyes against my dizzying surroundings and tried to take stock of my situation. I couldn't feel my left arm. I was losing blood, and fast—every part of me hurt.

There had only been one Beast in sight, the one dragging me, but I was clearly far away from the Shrine and other Pelerines. After a moment, I realized all of my limbs felt fuzzy, and then remembered something I had heard about these lizard Beasts—they had poison. *That explains the fire in my veins.* I thought grimly. My head tilted back involuntarily. The burning in my veins began to lessen and left in its place cotton wool. *May as well sleep.* Darkness crept around the edges of my vision.

I snapped back to focus after a minute of drifting. *Fight it! It's the poison!* I tried desperately to move my right arm, but it only flopped slightly. I wasn't sure if it was because I had tried to move it, or if it was because the Beast that carried me had sidestepped a large rock in its way.

Suddenly, I hit the ground, my lower back landing on a stone and one of my legs folding under the other awkwardly. I moved my eyes around, expecting to find the Beast looming over me. Instead, I saw it stagger sideways, two arrows protruding from its gut. An angry hiss escaped its mouth and it slashed forward with a huge claw.

I watched, detached and hurting, as another arrow lodged in it's neck and a man entered my view, his sword following where the arrow had led. After a moment, the lizard Beast joined me on the ground, its glassy eyes staring up into the sky.

I turned my own eyes toward the man that had felled it, and watched him jog over to me. A rumpled mass of curly black hair sat atop a deeply tanned face. Shadows hid his expression from me, covering part of his brow, extending down his neck and peaking out the short-sleeved tunic he wore to wrap around his arms. *Not shadows. Tattoos. Romany.*

I dragged my eyes back to his face, but it was turned away from me and he was gesturing urgently. A middle-aged woman appeared over his shoulder. Her dark brown hair was gathered in thick dreadlocks and tied back from her face. She was putting a bow into a sling on her back and listening as the man said something to her. I couldn't understand what they were saying. It sounded like I was listening with my ears underwater. The woman pulled out a knife and took up a defensive position nearby. The man turned back to me, his light green eyes glowing with a light that seemed to twist along the edges of his dark tattoos, winding around his skin before pooling into his cupped hands.

Not killed by a Beast after all. Killed by a magic user. Resignation and despondency set in as the man brought his hands over my shoulder and poured light over it. Pain flared like hot coals and I lost consciousness.

*　*　*

Sometime later I awoke in the dark. I tensed, disoriented, and groaned in agony as my shoulder stabbed and an hundred aches and bruises made themselves known. Sweat beaded across my skin. My mind raced, remembering the magic user —the Romany who had captured me after felling the Beast. My body still felt lethargic and my thoughts were jumbled, pieces of the last day coming together after a moment.

Belle! I remembered wildly. She had been attacked by Andrus, the Beast Prince. I hadn't been fast enough to save her.

Anguish flooded my heart, mingled with anger and bitterness. A few tears gathered in my eyes and spilled over silently, cool against my feverish skin. *Failure.* She was dead now. Dead from her own folly and pride. Dead because she hadn't trusted me. Dead because my skill in battle wasn't enough to make a difference when I needed it most. I groaned again, loudly, not caring if the magic users heard me. Whatever torture they had in store for me was well-earned.

Shivers wracked my body, the pain of which made me long for oblivion again. Everything ached. Suddenly a face appeared above me—the middle-aged archer from before. Brow furrowed, she looked into my eyes and said something garbled, then called out to someone behind me. Dizziness swept me as I started rocking side to side suddenly. I realized I was strung up in a hammock inside a darkened, enclosed wagon that was slowing to a stop. The hammock cocooned me, and claustrophobia set in. I tried to move my arms so I could pull myself out, but I was sluggish, and the fabric seemed to close in tightly. Disoriented, I stopped moving and focused on calming the panic rising in my chest.

A man's face appeared over me. The same one that had killed the Beast. His features seemed blurred, the tattoos on his face smearing into the shadow of the dark caravan.

His tone was questioning, but I couldn't understand the guttural language he was speaking. He tried again, in a different language that sounded smoother and almost like singing. The noises still sounded slurred together, as if he were speaking in another room. I stared at the darkness shifting around my vision. He disappeared again for a moment, then brought a small vial to my lips. I tried to pull away, but after a minute of struggle, I was exhausted. A sweet liquid slid down my throat and horrible stories I had heard as a child about the Romany flashed across my mind. The murky shadows of the caravan merged with the shadows in my mind and I drifted.

✳ ✳ ✳

My eyes snapped opened. I was still in the caravan. Sunlight streamed through a window, revealing the shadowy man. My muscles tensed. *Am I strong enough to fight yet?* I could feel all my limbs, move my fingers and toes, but I still felt groggy. I couldn't find my equilibrium, swinging in the hammock.

Another face appeared—a grizzled looking soldier, at least ten years older than me. The part of my brain that was still working sized him up. Bald head, long beard, muscular: a jagged scar ran the length of his face, a dark tattoo like sun rays along its edge. He wore black leathers over a military uniform. The two men spoke in garbled noises, then motioned to me. I didn't understand what they wanted so I just stared at them.

Slowly, they pulled the side of the hammock down and helped me out, lifting me gingerly to a nearby bench. A young woman sat down next to me, smiling gently. Stacks of bracelets slid down her wrists as she brushed back long, wavy brown hair. Another Romany, probably. She looked kind.

The woman took my hands and started speaking slowly, her words unintelligible, then nodded at the two men standing on either side of me. Before I could react, the soldier snaked his arm around my neck in a headlock. I writhed as the Romany man clutched my injured shoulder. The young woman gripped my hands firmly, her strength belied by her slight frame.

She and the Romany man started speaking in tandem. Light flared between them and I felt a wave of heat pass over me, the worst of it searing my shoulder. The man moved his hands up to my face, the tips of his fingers behind each ear.

Noise broke over me in a snap. The words they chanted were still foreign, but crisp. I could hear my own gasps for breath, the scrape of the chair as the woman sat back in her seat, insects buzzing outside the open door. *My hearing must have been damaged. The Romany man healed it.*

He sat back heavily, propping himself against a table nearby, his face ashen. He looked almost as tired as I felt. The soldier loosened his choke hold on me, although he didn't move far. My eyes caught my injured shoulder and I froze. Instead of torn muscle and tendon, it was whole and unbroken. A moon-shaped ridge of scar tissue was the only evidence of the previously rendered flesh. On top of the scar sat an enormous black tattoo, centered around the ball of my shoulder. The curve of my scar had been worked into the center of the pattern as the spine of a lizard. Tiny geometric shapes layered in concentric circles radiated out from the lizard to form the larger medallion. I stared at it in wonder and horror.

The bald soldier spoke to the two Romany in that same guttural language, then took a step towards me.

"Come with me, I'll take you to the infirmary until my Captain arrives back," he ordered in perfect Common Tongue.

Shock was making my thoughts swirl, I couldn't even manage a response. He shot an amused glance at the Romany man, then bent over and slung an arm under my right shoulder. As he helped me stand, I started to come out of my exhausted stupor.

"Where are we?"

"Sherwood Forest."

So far from home. Very little trade or information was exchanged between Pelerin and Sherwood. I had no idea how they would treat me here. *Will they guarantee safe passage home?* I doubted they would spare enough soldiers to escort me through the Wasteland to the north. I certainly wouldn't be welcome in Asileboix. If I could make it far enough south, I could probably find the short border below Asileboix that separated our two countries. I was desperate get back to my family and move them to safety, assuming the army had somehow managed to hold back both the Beast hoard and the Asileans in battle. I shoved the alternative out of my mind.

"The Romany brought you to our outpost on the border of the Wasteland," the soldier continued, maneuvering me so he could step out of the back door of the caravan and down the steps. A small mirror hung on the curved wall. As I turned sideways to follow him down, my reflection flashed before me.

I looked haggard. Someone had obviously tried to wipe my face clean, but grime and what looked like flecks of blood dotted my messy brown hair. A bruise ringed one of my eyes.

My injuries barely rated my attention. My eyes were drawn instead to a pair of stark black lines snaking out from behind

BELLE & BEAST

my ears, spilling down my neck in a complicated pattern. I stumbled as the soldier continued down the steps. Leaning against him more heavily, I managed to prevent a fall, but my mind drifted back to what I had seen in the mirror. Pelerine society would never accept me now. No one would dare speak with a man with visible Romany tattoos. *Are they even legal?*

Another thought hit me—my father's trading partners would forsake him just for his connection to me if I showed my face in public. The empire he had spent his entire life building would be ruined. I could hardly concentrate on putting one foot in front of the other as the soldier led me to a cot in a nearby tent.

"Lay down," he ordered, helping me sit. "The medic will come to see you in a minute. I'll go and get you some food."

He snorted a laugh. "You look like you're going to faint— don't run off." The last bit sounded like a joke but I heard an edge beneath it.

Peering around as I lay down, I counted one other occupied bed and a soldier on duty at the entrance. I relaxed slightly. This was obviously an organized and competent military unit. The black leather uniforms of the men I had seen were unfamiliar, but I had never met anyone from Sherwood before, let alone a soldier. The structure of an army unit was comfortable to me. It wouldn't do to let down my guard, especially as I was still weak, but military units worked on similar principles no matter the country. If I played my cards right, I may be able to talk my way out of here.

The soldier helping me came back with a flagon of water and bowl of stew, turning to speak with the soldier at the entrance while I wolfed it down.

When he came to collect my empty dishes, I gathered the energy to begin establishing a rapport with with him.

"What's your name, soldier?" my voice was raspy but steady.

"Call me Reynold, stranger," he replied with a smile. "What do I call you?"

461

"My name is Eddie." I handed my bowl over to him. "What happened to me? Why am I here?"

"You tell me, Eddie," Reynold countered. "The Romany Prince said he found you in the Wasteland just north of Pelerin, captured by a Beastie. You were full of lizard poison, but he healed you enough to get you here. Between him and the Romany healer that's been helping our unit, they patched up your shoulder, drew out the rest of the poison, and fixed your ears." He clapped me on my newly healed shoulder with his free hand. "You'd be dead if it weren't for them."

"So it seems," I said slowly. "But why didn't they take me back to Pelerin? What am I doing here?"

"They're not going back to Pelerin. They have business elsewhere. Are you some sort of Lord or Prince that merits special treatment?" he asked teasingly, just a hint of scorn in his tone.

"No, not at all. Just a lowly Captain. Can you tell me how to find my way back to my country? I'd like to head back as soon as I am able. There was a skirmish near our border with Asileboix and I need to find how it ended."

The soldier's laughing demeanor closed up at the mention of the fight. "Aye, I know about the skirmish, as you call it. A major Beast incursion, more like. Most of our unit went there in answer to the Asilean's call. As for your future, well, you'll have to wait for the Captain to discover that."

He pointed out the privy in the corner of the tent, then left me to my own devices. I had barely enough energy to wash my face at a communal washbasin before I collapsed on my cot. As sleep overcame me, so did a fresh wave of despair. My hands went involuntarily to my vest pocket, and to my surprise, my lucky ribbon was still there. I pulled it out just enough to rub the frayed silk with my thumb.

I thought of Belle; her beauty and strength gone now. Hazel and LeFeu were probably dead as well. Instead of laying my life down alongside them, I had been cursed to live by a Romany. I was in an unfamiliar land, injured, my fate in the hands

BELLE & BEAST

of a Captain allied with the Asilean Beast Prince. Exhaustion overcame me as I stuffed my ribbon back into my pocket, my eyes closing out the trouble ahead—at least for the moment.

Eddie's story continues in Book II of the Istoire Awakens series, where he clashes with the infamous Red Rider. Will he ever find a way out of Sherwood alive?

AFTERWORD

Thank you for reading *Belle & Beast*, I hope you enjoyed immersing yourself in a new world. The next book in the Istoire Awakens series is available now! Search my author page on Amazon to buy a copy of The Red Rider today.

If you want to read more of my work, sign up for my newsletter and receive Forget-Me-Not, a free novelette set in Istoire as well. You'll meet a few characters that will appear in future books.

My newsletter is released quarterly and contains updates on current and upcoming projects, freebies, and other exclusive content. Thank you for your support!

ACKNOWLEDGEMENTS

I have a *lot* of people to thank, and while I couldn't name everyone specifically, I have to name a few here.

First and foremost: my sister, Rachel, and my sister-in-law, Beth. I wouldn't be publishing without your support. You showed up for me, read my (terrible) third draft, and encouraged me wholeheartedly. I can't thank you enough.

To the Foehn Wind Writers (Makayla, Paige, and April) —you ladies pushed me to be a better writer from the minute we got to work. Your feedback has been invaluable, direct, uncompromising, and seasoned with grace and encouragement.

To the Hope*Writer community, this book wouldn't exist without you. I joined to become a better nonfiction writer, and discovered along the way that I needed to give these stories a chance. Your kind words, helpful feedback, and shared experience has been a treasure.

Ginna and Maggie, thank you for beta reading my second to last draft! You helped me get this over the finish line.

To Steve and the kids, thank you for making space for my writing, and agonizing, and drafting, and dramatics. Your love and support is the reason I'm doing this at all. Your antics are what inspire me!

To Mom and my brothers, Mike and Dave, thank you for being in my corner, and believing in me. Everyone needs people to have their back while they do something crazy!

All my friends and family that reached out to support me— you have no idea how much it meant to me, every time you did so.

Last of all, it's been humbling mimicking the Creator by creating. I pray my words are not only fun, but give a different perspective and little hope.

ABOUT THE AUTHOR

Rebecca Fittery is a fantasy romance author who writes clean, immersive fairytale romance. Her characters grow through relationship while adventure unfolds. Everyone who deserves a happy ending gets one, and even those who don't deserve one have a chance. Whether they take it or not is up to them!

She lives in rural Pennsylvania with her husband, their two children, and a friendly dragon disguised as an orange tiger cat.

Discover more at:

www.rebeccafittery.com

www.facebook.com/Rebecca-Fittery-Author

www.instagram.com/rebecca_fittery_author

www.pinterest.com/rebeccafittery

BOOKS IN THIS SERIES

Istoire Awakens

Belle & Beast

A war hero. A prince with a secret. A distressed damsel intent on beating the odds. They're not the fairytale characters you're used to.

BELLE: My family lost everything at the start of the Beast War. I've been waiting on my hero fiancé to come home so I can gain back what's mine. Just as the war is ending, a mysterious Prince threatens ruin not just for me, but my fiancé and our whole town too. Everything I've worked for has been destroyed, but I may know a way to bargain with this monster...

ANDRUS: I've dealt with the threat Lord Montanarte presented neatly. Now his daughter is here, complicating things with a deal I can't refuse. What began as a problem may end up strengthening my crown ... but the way her eyes haunt my dreams could be my undoing.

EDDIE: It's been a bitter struggle to drive the Beasts from our northern border. Victory secured, I'm heading home to my fiancé. But home doesn't feel like the same place I left five years ago, and the person I thought I knew best is turning out to be a stranger. Have I left a war only to enter the fight of my life?

Belle & Beast is a clean, fantasy-romance retelling of the French fairytale, Beauty & the Beast. It is the first book in the Istoire Awakens series, but can be enjoyed as a standalone.

The Red Rider

The day Red walked through the woods to meet her grandmother was the day her childhood ended. But she's not a little girl anymore.

RED: I not only survived the revolution, I thrived. I'm now sister to the Duke and Duchess of Sherwood, Captain of an elite border unit, and revered by the people as The Red Rider - the one who turned the tide from the dark days of civil war. But even though I've conquered the monsters of my past, shadows have started creeping into my present. It's getting harder to tell whether my worst enemy is the Beasts we fight in the Wasteland, or the horrors still in my head. When I'm tasked with guarding a tight-laced Pelerine soldier, his contempt for me and my country makes me want to shove his ignorance in his face. But as we start to become friends, I find myself relying on him more and more.

EDDIE: I woke up to a brutal reality after the Battle of Asileboix. Alone and wounded in a potentially hostile territory, I'm at the mercy of the intriguing and dangerous Captain Hood. She's everything I should hate, but I can't deny that I'm drawn to her. We're bound together for now, and sparks are flying as we force each other to confront our demons. It's hard for me to admit, but I'm hoping one of those sparks catches and ignites something powerful.

When Red is called upon to right the wrong of her only failure, Eddie turns out to be the one person who can stand by her side through it.... if they can trust each other first.

The Red Rider is a clean fantasy-romance retelling of the French fairytale, Little Red Riding Hood. It is the second book in the Istoire Awakens series, and although it can be read as a standalone, is better enjoyed when read as part of the series.

Glass Slipper

Growing up in the midst of tragedy and triumph, Ella knows better than anyone that what's inside a person counts more than their appearance. Even so, a pretty dress and a pair of oddly beautiful glass slippers change her life more than she ever imagined.

ELLA: Ever since my father died, I've been so busy running my ancestral estate and caring for my family that I haven't had time for romance. But a chance meeting during a visit to my stepsister has me re-thinking whether I have room in my future for love. Every time I'm with Luca, I'm convinced we can take on any challenge life throws our way. And it's getting hard to ignore the way he makes my heart beat faster.

LUCA: I've always believed that love at first sight is real. What else would explain why the strange girl I met before my coronation ball has never left my (or heart) over the last decade? I've finally found her again, and she's even more beautiful than I remember - inside and out. I'm convinced she's the one I need by my side, and I know I can make her happy too. The only problem? She doesn't know I'm the crown prince, and she's not exactly the person my parents have in mind as our next queen.

A pair of glass dancing slippers seal Ella's fate with her true love, but the very magic that tests their hearts and binds them together drives a wedge between them; and reveals a talent Ella never wanted.

When events in Charmagne reach a tipping point, will Ella and her Prince find a way to lead their country, and each other, into the future together? Or will their splintered relationship fracture the kingdom and continent beyond repair? Glass Slipper is a clean fantasy-romance retelling of the classicfairytale, Cinderella. It is the third book in the Istoire Awakensseries, and although it can be read as a standalone, is better enjoyed whenread as part of the series.

Snow White

In a warlike country where magic is outlawed and mages are put to death, the Snow White princess has no power to aid those suffering. An evil embedded deep within the court has grown strong enough to resist even the most powerful players of the shifting Snowdonian court. But there may be one thing it's overlooked – kindness can be a weapon too.

NIEVE: Even though I'm a princess, I've lived a quiet life. My biggest royal role is singing the Snow White song at court for Winter Solstice. All I want is to support my loved ones, and feel their love in return. That dream was shattered the day I discovered I have forbidden magic, and the depths my stepmother would reach to get rid of it. My unlikely savior is the best friend I rejected years ago. Somehow, after all this time, he's willing to risk his life to get me to safety. Does the future I thought was gone still has a chance at coming true?

ALARIC: I've been living a dangerous double life as a Snowdonian warrior-huntsmen for the last ten years, but I've abandoned it all in order to get Princess Nieve to safety. Now it turns out that the refuge I brought her to may be just as dangerous as her murderous stepmother. I'll sacrifice almost anything to keep her safe, but I don't know if I'm ready to make the most dangerous sacrifice of all – my heart.

When the illusion of safety for Nieve and Alaric is suddenly shattered, will it destroy the second chance of love between them? And will Nieve find the courage to stand up for her oppressed people, even if her only weapon is the strength of her heart?

Snow White is a clean fantasy-romance retelling of the classic fairytale, Little Snow White. It is the fourth book in the Istoire Awakens series, and although it can be read as a standalone, is better enjoyed when read as part of the series.

Briar Rose

Deerbold Academy was founded to bring the ruling families of Istoire together. After years of hard work, its purpose is finally being achieved—but with a threat gathering in the Wasteland to the north, it may be too late.

Briar Rose: The Headmistresses of Deerbold Academy took me in when I was a baby: giving me a family, a home, and opportunities I never would have had otherwise. As graduation approaches I seem to be losing control. My migraines are getting stronger, my magic is getting weaker, and the future I thought I was building at the Academy feels like it's slipping away. I'm supposed to be an adult now, but instead of knowing what to do, I think I'm losing my mind. The only constant is my best friend, Prince Raleigh. He says he's in love with me, but I'm not exactly princess material and I never envisioned leaving my home in the ancient forest.

Raleigh: As sixth in line to the throne of Spindle the weight of ruling won't ever fall on my shoulders, but it doesn't mean I don't have royal duties. One of those duties sent me to Deerbold Academy to ensure it's success. I've spent the last four years and more happily fulfilling that task. As graduation approaches, I've started to realize my devotion over the years wasn't dedication to the mission, it was dedication to someone-my best friend, Briar Rose. What I feel for her isn't just friendship, it's steadfast, wholehearted love. But there are mysteries swirling at the Academy, and the more I dig, the more it seems like Briar Rose is at the center of them.

On the night of her twenty-first birthday, Briar Rose's questions are answered, and her world shattered. She's left with a clear plan that could save the continent, but the only person who believes her is Raleigh. Can they find a way to fulfill Briar Rose's vision despite the prophecy foretold at her birth? And will the feelings growing between them make them stronger, or ruin their friendship forever?

Briar Rose is a clean fantasy-romance retelling of the classic fairytale, Sleeping Beauty. It is the fifth book in the Istoire Awakens series, and although it can be read as a standalone, is better enjoyed when read as part of the series.

Rapunzel

Princess Persinette, code name Rapunzel, has been trapped in a tower deep in the Wasteland for two years. Her last companion left in a desperate bid for help. Injured and alone, she's finally succumbing to the madness of her surroundings.

Persinette: As fifth in line to the throne of Spindle, I don't have the weight of the crown on my shoulders, but I do have a responsibility to my family—and my country—that always comes first. I've dedicated my life so far to studying the biggest threat to both—the arcane and twisted magic of the Wasteland. After my last mission ended in disaster, I'm stuck in a tower with no hope of rescue. The magic here is pulling me under, and as I inevitably give in, I can't help sinking into memories of a simpler time, when my heart briefly ruled my head. But when the object of my dreams shows up for a rescue, we discover that my wounded pride isn't the only thing that was keeping us apart.

Petro: The day that Persinette rejected me—and our bond— was the day my heart died. As the infamous Gypsy Prince, I've traveled the continent my whole life, running from a fate that I know will eventually catch up. In the last year however, I've been focused on one thing—finding Persinette by any means necessary. When a young seer from Spindle sets me on the path to my true love, I leap at the chance. Finding her turns out to be the easy part. Getting both of us back home alive is proving almost impossible—but rekindling the fire that once burned between us may end up killing me.

As Petro and Persinette seek a way home, they discover that Persinette wasn't trapped in the Wasteland by chance, and the person who wants her blood and soul isn't going to give up easily.

Rapunzel is a clean fantasy-romance retelling of the classic fairytale by the same name. It is the sixth book in the Istoire Awakens series, and although it can be read as a standalone, in order to have a full understanding of the larger story of the series it is best enjoyed when read in order.

Made in the USA
Middletown, DE
02 May 2024